A PROMISE OF PLEASURE

Her eyes met his without flinching. "My lord, you swore to seduce the queen's most virtuous lady. I am offering you the opportunity to win your wager."

"Why me—of all men living?" he asked.

"Despite your shortcomings, you have shown yourself to be a man of honor." She inclined her head, gracious as a queen.

Nay, that he was not. The Raven gritted his teeth. "Many maids would seek more in a lover."

"Well, one must grant that your hygiene is satisfactory. I cannot deny that is a point in your favor." Her lashes dropped. "Also, Lord Raven, you are not . . . unattractive."

Her whisper ignited him. Since the night he first saw her, passion for Alienore of Lyonstone had possessed him like a demon. He burned to claim her, to strip away that cool composure and fire the ardor of the woman beneath.

He sought her gaze. She met him like a knight on the tourney field, all courage and resolve—and a feverish exhilaration that made her eyes glow.

A bolt of guilt shafted through him. She was too good for this, too honorable and brave and fair; she did not deserve this betrayal. Still, whatever her misguided purpose, he'd be a fool to waste this shining opportunity fate tossed in his lap.

A lightning charge of anticipation sizzled through him. "Intriguing plan, lady. But I've a condition of my own."

"Why, what more can you desire   innocent, her eyes lifted.

"Pleasure, Alienore. Let's grasp
tonight."

D1713146

Laura Navarre

The Devil's Temptress

Dorchester
Publishing

This one's for my extraordinary agent JD DeWitt, who let me pitch her in the pasta line and never stopped believing. And also for Steven, my own alpha hero. Darling, they're all for you.

DORCHESTER PUBLISHING

February 2011

Published by

Dorchester Publishing Co., Inc.
200 Madison Avenue
New York, NY 10016

ISBN 13: 978-1-4285-1131-6
E-ISBN: 978-1-4285-0963-4

The "DP" logo is the property of Dorchester Publishing Co., Inc.

Printed in the United States of America.

Visit us online at www.dorchesterpub.com.

The Devil's Temptress

Chapter One

Poitiers, France—1174 AD.

The stolen armor fitted her poorly—a minor annoyance if she was lucky, a fatal encumbrance if not. The chain-mail hauberk weighed Alienore down, like the doubts she dared not acknowledge. As for the helm, seated perilously low, she could barely see through the eye slit.

But at least the faceplate disguised her identity—and that must be her paramount consideration.

"Milady, will ye mount?" Luke squared himself to boost her into the saddle.

"Quietly!" she whispered. "I am no lady this day."

God's mercy, let the lad misspeak when we enter the lists, and I am certain disgraced.

Whether the squire guarded his tongue or nay, she would be fortunate indeed to emerge unscathed from this debacle: stolen armor, a squire bribed to secrecy, and a half-wild charger borrowed from a friend.

But she would not lose her courage now. A lady's honor stood at stake.

Outside the stable, the clear blast of trumpets split the air. Tightening her jaw, Lady Alienore of Lyonstone gripped the pommel and sprang up.

Mounted behind the familiar shield, command settled over her like a garment. When the trumpets blared again, she spurred Charlemagne into the milky light of day.

Beneath slate-colored skies, jewel-bright pennants snapped

and fluttered in a cruel wind. Patches of dirty snow dotted the tilting yard of Poitiers. The battlements soared overhead, looming like a calamity over the crowd near the tourney field.

Dismay swept through her to behold the unruly rabble. Her breath exploded white as Alienore reined in.

"Jesus wept!" The oath slipped from her. *Dear God, let no man challenge me over the armor.*

Cold sweat broke out on her brow. She prayed her hazardous dead-of-night incursion to the armory went undetected. She had taken nothing she would not return. But her fate must be as God willed it.

Squaring her shoulders against the knife-sharp cold, she reached for the lance. Luke swung it into her hand with a reassuring slap. With an ease honed by training, she swept up the wicked point and couched the spear against her saddle.

Swallowing her reservations, she spurred her warhorse onto the field.

Before her towered the royal box, dominating its surroundings. The Plantagenet standard billowed scarlet, blazoned with a golden lion. Beneath the canopy glittered a dazzle of gold and crimson: Eleanor of Aquitaine, Queen of England, her splendor undimmed by the disgrace of captivity.

Despite her fear of discovery, Alienore's heart swelled with love. The queen would understand what compelled her to act, but she could never condone a public scandal. Nay, if Alienore were unmasked, she would lose her place for certain.

For she was no mere lady, but the queen's privy chancellor—the only woman in the council of ministers. How they would all rejoice to see her unseated!

A wave of heads turned as Alienore cantered along the barricade. Snatches of conversation drifted to her ears.

". . . rides without a standard and hides his face. Who can say what man he is?"

"Heard of such a one . . . itinerant knight, too modest to reveal his name. He champions distressed damsels—the ones no other knight will defend."

A woman's malicious laughter floated on the wind. "*Depardieu*, the lady Rohese must be wearing out her knees in gratitude!"

"That was how they came upon her, aye?" A man guffawed. "On her knees! And the man half-naked, I heard."

When she reached the royal box, Alienore stared straight ahead—not at the sea of spiteful faces, but only at her queen's blinding blaze. Exerting her unwomanly strength, Alienore hoisted her lance toward heaven in salute. A sudden commotion drew her like a lodestone, nerves already screaming with tension. A lady was floundering onto the field, fiery curls spilling against an ermine pelisse.

Ah, the lady of the hour, for whose honor I find myself in this dangerous dilemma.

"God lend you grace, monsieur!" Rohese de Rievaulx cried. The stallion shied violently, and Alienore fought to hold him. With a shaft of alarm she missed her own steed, but that horse was too well-known on this field.

She stared down from her towering height at the victim. Her cousin, her own dead mother's very image—Marguerite de Rievaulx come again, and it twisted her heart to see it.

Rohese gazed up. "Will you not bear my favor into battle? You have earned it by your courage, for no other would ride against *him*."

Alienore dared not speak, for Rohese would know her, and glimpse the truth—

Behind her the rumble of hooves built like an avalanche, a measured cadence that shuddered the ground. Flushing, Rohese hastened behind the barricade.

Alienore pivoted for her first glimpse of the opponent. He had made his entrée at court while she was away, about the queen's secret business in Bordeaux. When she returned last night, chilled and sagging with weariness, Rohese had way-laid her with the sordid tale.

This nameless cur had assaulted Rohese, bent upon steal-ing her virtue. When they were discovered, the rogue dared to claim the lady encouraged him. And such was his sinister repute that no knight would challenge him, nor champion the lady.

So honor demanded that Alienore resume the perilous disguise she had left behind when she fled English soil—no matter the terrible risk.

The villain swept into sight. The breath froze in her lungs.

He was an apparition straight from the abyss—a black warhorse with red-rimmed eyes, plumes of vapor shooting from its nostrils, bearing a rider whose pointed helm threw sparks against the vault of heaven. Pale breath leaked around the knight's lowered faceplate.

Overhead, a raven cawed and circled. As the charger thundered toward her, his three-beat gait sounded the knell of doom.

All is lost, all is lost, all is lost . . .

Superstitious fear swept down her spine. Saint Swithun save her, he could be Beelzebub or the devil himself, come to claim a damned soul. He did not even carry a Christian name to Aquitaine, only a letter of commendation singing fulsome praise of the black knight called le Corbeau—the Raven.

At the last instant, the black stallion juddered to a halt. Up and up he reared, screaming with rage as her mount tore the ground. With razor-sharp precision, the Raven uncouched his lance to salute the queen. A tomblike chill seeped from him with each chuffing breath.

Dispassionate, Eleanor of Aquitaine surveyed them from her high-backed chair. Her clarion voice rang out.

"This contest is highly irregular—between two knights who claim no name. We are not accustomed to abide hidden purpose at our court in these uncertain times. Lord Raven, we overlook your origins from gratitude, for the service you rendered our son. Your challenger, however, bears no such mark of favor."

Alienore nerved herself for the risk of speech, and pitched her voice low.

"May it please Your Grace, I beg your indulgence. A lady's honor is at stake."

Armor chimed as the black knight shifted, pushing out a harsh breath. The queen's stern eyes passed over him and fixed Rohese de Rievaulx. The damsel drew her hood close, concealing her heightened color. In silence, Eleanor of Aquitaine studied the mismatched knights—ebony and argent—before her.

Alienore lifted her gaze to her sovereign's face. Reddened with cold, worn by care and the birth of ten children, still her queen shone pure and fair—a beacon of honor gleaming in a wrongful world. In silence, Alienore implored her for support.

"A lady's honor," the queen mused. "And a good English knight, by your speech. I'll allow three passes with the lance and one course with the sword. To first blood, nothing more."

Alienore released her breath with shuddering relief.

"And you, Lord Raven." The Queen of England surveyed the black knight coolly. "You are a stranger to this court, but your reputation precedes you from Outremer. I will have no stouthearted English lad meet his death by your blade today. Do you comprehend me?"

In silence the Raven bowed, a courtesy of surprising

grace. Then he wheeled his black and galloped across the field. The ground trembled beneath his passage.

All is lost . . .

Heart pounding, Alienore pivoted Charlemagne and cantered to her place. She knotted the reins around her pommel, swung her lance forward to point at the black knight's heart. Above, the raven still circled, sending a chill cascading down her spine. An expectant hush descended.

The trumpets blasted the cry to combat.

Before Alienore could instruct him, her charger surged forward, building speed like a battering ram as he thundered down the field. She guided the horse by seat and legs as she crouched behind her shield—protected yet vulnerable. An unlucky blow could pierce her and drive the steel links of her mail into flesh, with death by the green rot the certain result.

Swelling to fill her vision, the black knight loomed like a disaster before her. Then the deadly length of his lance was arrowing toward her. She braced for impact.

At the last moment, she twisted aside. The two horses hammered past without consequence. The first course, and both spears had missed their mark.

She wheeled her charger for the next pass. Jittery, Charlemagne fought her, tossing his head and whinnying. She had barely settled him when the trumpets screamed. Without waiting for her signal, the angry stallion plunged forward.

As they charged down the field, Alienore struggled to hold a level course. Her arm and shoulder burned beneath the lance's weight. Grimly she fixed the black knight with her point.

Too quickly, he was upon her, dark spear whistling as it split the air. He would skewer her dead between the eyes—

She ducked behind the shield, barely deflecting his blow. The shock of impact slammed through her. He had grazed her, but her lance caught him squarely. As the black stallion swept past, his rider swayed in the saddle.

Her breath exploded from her lungs as relief coursed through her. With God's grace, this dangerous contest would end now, with her disguise still secure. Yet when she wheeled her mount, she saw with sinking disappointment that the Raven retained his seat. Calm as a man at prayer, he sat in his saddle and watched her.

Her chest tightened with dread. By her faith, he should have fallen. Was it uncanny skill that kept him upright, or the devil looking out for his own?

She struggled to couch her lance as Charlemagne reared beneath her. She longed for the reins, but had no hand to spare for them. When the trumpets blared, the horse lashed out with his rear legs, almost unseating her, before plunging into the fray.

Her sword arm ached from the lance's weight. Her shield arm tingled from his blow. The unfamiliar stallion weaved and veered, forcing her to hold him with tensed thighs and determination.

Squinting through the eye slit, she riveted her lance on the looming knight and braced for impact. Her blow glanced off his shield—

Then the hammer of God whelmed her square in the chest, lighting her breastbone on fire as he struck. Her desperate grip on the saddle dislodged. The world tilted and fell away beneath her. The lance was slipping from her fingers . . . her shield flying wide . . . the ground rushing up to meet her . . . then the sickening slam of impact as she landed on her back. Her head thudded against the earth.

Long seconds passed as she lay dazed, gasping for air. Gradually her vision cleared, reduced to a skewed slice of daylight. Blind, she groped to reseat her helm. When she could drag breath into her lungs, she levered herself up on one elbow.

Across the field, the Raven sat on his charger and watched her. A stable lad was running to catch her horse. And there was Luke, trotting toward her with the sword.

Alienore groaned. Every bone in her body throbbed. But that was nothing, she knew, to the sustained distress she would endure later. *The honor of Rievaulx—my mother's honor—is at stake.*

Somewhere in the stands, Rohese was depending upon her. All hope was not lost. She could still defeat him at the sword, by far her strongest weapon. Doggedly she struggled to her knees, the world reeling around her.

The Raven sprang down and tossed his reins to a swarthy Saracen in a blood-colored turban. The squire presented his master's blade—a deadly crescent of Damascus steel. Fire smoldered in the hilt from a slitted topaz, like a dragon's eye.

Alienore unsheathed her broadsword and raised her shield, thanking Luke with a nod as he melted away. The black knight stalked toward her.

God's mercy, he was unnaturally tall. She towered over most men, but this one made her feel small, even fragile. In his coal black armor, he moved with sinuous grace, like the panther in the queen's menagerie.

Just beyond the range of combat, he halted. Through the pointed helm, she sensed his eyes upon her. She knew she looked winded, muddied and battered from her fall. She straightened her shoulders and saluted him with her blade. Not that his honor required it, but she would adhere to the rules of combat before the queen.

Negligently, he tossed his shield aside—a silent declaration that he would not need it.

Breath hissed through her teeth at the insult. A rumble of disapproval rose from the viewing stand. So they favored her now, all these fickle folk. This Raven must be disliked as much as he was feared.

Holding herself erect, she cast her own shield aside. A sprinkle of applause acknowledged her gallant gesture. She braced for assault, but he seemed content to wait.

So be it.

She lunged forward, thrusting. His crescent sword swept around in defense. Steel clashed as his blade whined along hers, deflecting the blow. She danced back and parried toward his flank. Again he pivoted to repel, his notched blade whirling through the air.

His style and equipage were unfamiliar—Eastern blade and a Saracen squire. Was he one of those so-called Old Settlers, descendant of a knight from the First Crusade, dwelling in Jerusalem for generations? Did he worship God with the heathens, keep a harem of veiled women and call that a holy life?

Whatever he was, he possessed uncanny skill at arms. Quick as she attacked, he was quicker to defend, a fraction of his strength deflecting her. His sword tumbled in whistling arcs to parry her. He made himself the axis she pivoted around; he became the quiet planet around which her blazing sun revolved. Already she was overheated under the armor's dragging weight. Her breastbone throbbed where his lance had struck, dull waves of pain rolling through her. Slick wetness trickled between her breasts—sweat or blood, she knew not which.

She burned, but he was ice, undaunted by her flurry of blows. Yet her anger was mounting at his casual defense. The buzzing in her ears was growing . . . her heart laboring . . . her sword arm burning as she swung her blade.

She gathered all her strength for a final gambit. His scimitar carved the air as it swept up to defend. Summoning every shred of agility, she crouched and swept around, broadsword dropping with disarming swiftness.

One blow, first blood—

A blinding flash of silver pierced her vision. Somehow his blade intervened, moaning as it slid along hers. With a twist, his point dislodged her sword and found the seam between her gauntlet and sleeve. A tendril of fire licked along her forearm.

As her sword tumbled from her fingers, his long leg hooked hers. A gentle nudge sent her flailing backward, a cry bursting from her lips. Unable to regain her balance, she landed flat on her back—for the second time that morn. In a heartbeat, his blade rested against her throat.

"Yield," the black knight rasped.

A dark fog crept around the edge of her vision. Through a tunnel of blackness, she discerned him, silhouetted against the leaden sky. Lady Alienore of Lyonstone sprawled on her back in the dirt before Eleanor of Aquitaine and the entire royal court.

Yield? In her mind she saw not Rohese but Marguerite de Rievaulx as her mother lay on her deathbed, weakly protesting her innocence to the daughter who longed to believe her. No knight had defended Marguerite from the scandal that killed her.

"Never!" She blazed with defiance. "Varlet, do your worst. I do not fear you."

Laughter scraped behind the black faceplate. "Then, boy, you're a fool."

The Raven dropped to one knee. Alarm knifed through her. He gripped her hauberk in a careless fist, hauling her head and shoulders from the ground. She dangled from his grip like wounded prey.

Through the eye slit, she glared straight into his shadowed helm. Uncanny golden eyes glittered as they fixed her, feral as any beast's.

"Who are you?" She fought for breath.

If he intends to slit my throat here in the dirt, then at least I will know his name. I will meet my fate without flinching . . . this time.

"Why, boy, did no one warn you?" He uttered a jarring laugh. "I'm the devil."

Overhead, a bird cawed. Suddenly the Raven's tawny eyes narrowed. As Alienore stared into that sinister gaze, an unnerving notion bloomed. Somehow, through no device but the devil's own knowledge, could he sense it was a woman who defied him?

Without warning, he dropped her, then rose to tower over her like an avenging angel. Pivoting toward the queen, he pulled off his helm. From her vantage, Alienore could see only a gleaming rope of sin black hair swinging down his back. Her pulse raced as she waited to be unmasked, or worse.

He addressed the court in Norman French, voice rasping. "It's small pleasure to trounce a half-grown boy, swimming in his father's armor. Let the lady send a new champion, or two—or a hundred. I care not."

He stalked from the field, breath billowing around him like smoke from the netherworld.

Alienore's face burned as she struggled to her feet, a trickle of blood dripping from her arm. Her disguise was intact— but deep within, a slow wrath kindled. With all the resolve of a knight and an earl's daughter, she stoked it like a forge fire. Her family's honor stood twice insulted—her own precious honor, her most prized possession. Grimly, before God and Saint Swithun, she swore she would have justice.

Alienore vaulted the stairs two at a time, skirts gripped in an agitated hand. Beneath her sleeve, her bandaged arm throbbed with every step. After that debacle on the tourney field, she was late to answer the royal summons.

Before the double doors, she masked her anxiety and bent to soothe the four-legged friend who trotted at her heels. The doors swung wide, revealing the beating heart of the civilized world.

The Maubergeonne Tower seethed with restless courtiers bundled against the bitter cold. The odor of corruption assailed her: the stench of unwashed bodies and stale perfume, spiced by the pungent stink of a hidden garderobe. A tide of

spiteful murmurs rolled over her, gossip and intrigue, punc-
tuated by the nervous riff of a woman's laughter.

Indeed, they did well to be fearful. The entire court was
tainted by its sovereign's disgrace. Their queen had betrayed
her husband—Henry, King of England, master of Aquitaine
and all the vast lands between.

Hers was a gilded cage, but Eleanor of Aquitaine was
closely guarded. And the man who warded her while the
king battled rebels abroad was the very man Alienore herself must avoid.

To her dismay, he was watching the door—Sir Guy Aigret,
the queen's jailer, a florid-faced Englishman whose eyes bulged
when he sighted her. Thrusting upright, he bulled through
the crowd toward her. Quick as running water, she shifted
course and made for the queen's throne.

Idly her sovereign turned the gilded leaves of a volume in
her lap. But her keen eyes lingered on Sir Guy, parting the
sea of bodies like a thick-prowed ship as he plowed after
Alienore. Such was the queen's skill at subterfuge that Alienore knew herself warned to avoid the man.

A slender gallant, resplendent in azure brocade, blocked
her path.

"Sweet lady, I have been searching for you everywhere."

The need for haste hummed in her nerves. "Sieur de
Beaumont, give you good day. I beg your indulgence, for the
queen—"

"Alienore, for mercy!" Thierry de Beaumont squeezed her
fingers. "I must know the truth. Whatever besotted fool
defended your cousin, he made an appalling poor showing.
Soon or late, someone must learn the horse was mine. I
cannot hide the beast forever."

Her certain knowledge of Sir Guy coming up like a thun-
dercloud behind clenched her teeth over a stiff reply. The
queen sat so still she barely seemed to breathe, watching
Alienore weave and dodge like the fox before the hound.

Gripping Thierry's arm, she turned him toward the queen. Golden-haired, clear-eyed, with a glorious record on the tourney field, Thierry de Beaumont had won many hearts. But he was her declared admirer.

"Have I a rival for your affections?" he pressed.

She sighed. He was fair and brave, the only knight who vowed to win back her lands from her misguided brother, who held them. Why must Thierry annoy her when he spoke? He had not seen fit to champion her, yet he would criticize her performance?

But she had not been raised to quarrel like a fishwife in public. Instead, she lifted a shoulder in frosty indifference. "My affections are unengaged. As for the identity of my cousin's champion, I cannot divulge it."

Thwarting her progress, he dug in his heels. "Do I not have the right to know?"

She slanted a glance at Sir Guy—detained by, God love him, Geoffrey of Brittany, the queen's ill-favored son. Though Alienore disliked the prince, she felt grateful to him now.

Cold as winter seas, she turned back to Thierry. Not for nothing was she the queen's privy chancellor. "Monsieur, you have no right over my person at all. The queen—"

"No right?" His face reddened. "Why must you be so cold? Does my love count for nothing?"

"Oh, hush!" Now she was both angry and desperate. She darted for the throne, but he clung, stubborn as a hunting mastiff with a buck. Abandoning discretion, she struggled in his grip.

A growl of warning rose from the floor—and Thierry de Beaumont froze. From his place at her heels, the albino wolf bared his fangs.

With ill-concealed dread, the gallant crossed himself. Thierry held her beast in superstitious terror, while Remus barely tolerated the man.

"We shall speak later, I pray." Gently she dislodged his grip.

"As you will." Thierry ducked her a sullen bow. Red eyes gleaming, the wolf dogged her heels as she eased toward the throne.

"There ye are, by God!" Sir Guy thrust past a running page, with a clout that sent the lad spinning out of his way. "Lady Alienore, I'll have a word with ye—"

The queen's clarion tones rose above the clamor. "God grant you welcome, privy chancellor. Come here to me at once, I pray you, for I am eager to learn how fare my estates and good subjects at Bordeaux."

A tide of relief surging through her, Alienore sank into a curtsy.

"Madam, by yer leave." Sir Guy bowed shortly. "I've business with Lady Alienore—"

"*Depardieu*, my privy chancellor and I have a great deal to discuss. Certainly, you will forgive her if she comes first to me."

Sir Guy beetled his brow. Stubborn he was, and graceless, but the man did not lack courage. "I'm no less forgiving than the king your husband."

"That is well," the queen murmured, "for why should forgiveness be only a woman's art? Alienore, my dear—to me."

Gratefully Alienore mounted the dais. Awe and humility swelled within her, mingled with soaring love. Although the legendary beauty of her youth had faded, the queen retained many admirers, even in these uncertain times. Nor were they driven by ambition alone.

Now, with her easy charm, Eleanor smiled and stood, raising her up with both hands. The two were of a height, both taller than the dainty court beauties.

"Come take the air with me, my dear." The queen drew her toward the courtyard. When the sea of attendants shifted to follow, Eleanor lifted an imperious hand to stay them. Thwarted, Sir Guy scowled.

With Remus trotting at their heels, the two women glided

into a high-walled privy courtyard. The cold struck Alienore like thrown knives, and she shivered as they strolled arm in arm. Remus bounded off to explore last year's withered roses.

"So, Alienore, what news from Ombrière?"

Alienore's skin prickled as she glanced toward the guards. She would never grow accustomed to these dangerous intrigues. Indeed, she had not wanted this delicate position in which the queen had thrust her. But she must be grateful for any place at all, after her haphazard flight from the wretch who would wed her.

Following the queen's lead, she shifted to Latin—a language her watchdogs would not comprehend. "All was arranged at your bidding. I contrived to meet your uncle while hunting in the wood."

"So . . . my eldest son? Is he well?"

"Madam, he is in Paris—the honored guest of French Louis. Your husband did not capture him after all."

Tension ran like water from the queen's stately figure. Yet her sovereign strolled as though they discussed nothing more than whether to plant white roses or red next season.

"*Avoi!*" The queen sighed. "Then there is still hope for our cause."

Uneasy, Alienore lowered her eyes. She had never intended to act against her king—especially now, while she appealed to him to restore her inheritance.

Who could have predicted the Queen of England would turn against her husband to advance her sons, snatching their inheritance before their father was even dead? Alienore hardly knew where her duty lay, but strove to be faithful to both sides.

"Madam, surely the king will advance his sons' welfare of his own accord. You need not force his hand."

"My dear Alienore." The queen smiled. "How can you retain such touching faith in the honor of men? Your own ungrateful brother would see you wedded to an aging lecher, merely to prop up his own prestige."

Alienore defended her younger brother from habit. "When my father fell fighting the Saracens, Benedict knew not his wishes—"

The queen arched her reddish eyebrows. "He wishes to deprive you of land Theobold clearly meant for you."

"My brother returned from crusading but a year ago, grieving and weary of war. He has hardly been in his right mind for sorrow! I have appealed to King Henry—"

"Who will refuse you, for he must secure your brother's loyalty as Lyonstone's new earl. Henry cannot afford another rebellious lord on the unsettled Scottish border. And what of the Duc d'Ormonde?"

Alienore braced against the tide of shame. *Aye, my would-be husband. I fled his coming like a thief in the night—abandoned my duty after one look at his sour old face.*

"Let us not speak of him, madam."

"Never fear, child. When my son is king, he will send the duke packing."

Alienore clasped her hands to still their tremor. She was Theobold's daughter, loyal unto death to her king. The old earl would be spinning in his grave to hear these words. But she could not abandon Queen Eleanor, her godmother and benefactress. She must steer some middle way between dangers, veering neither toward one nor the other.

"I belong at home, Your Grace, tending to the welfare of my people. I am not meant for a life of plotting and intrigue."

"'Tis your very candor that I value." The queen angled their course toward the hall and the enemies within. "You may return to your beloved manor in the fullness of time. For the present, your queen requires your service."

Alienore bowed her head, knowing she had no choice. If she would win back her stolen lands, she must rely upon royal will to uphold her. Nothing else mattered but to regain the manor and restore her sullied honor. *But do I deserve as much?*

"As you are just returned to court, perhaps you have not heard." Before the door, the queen paused. "We shall be amused this night by a lavish masque in honor of Richard's knighting. Of course you will attend."

"Nay, madam, you know I do not care for masques and revels. I am utterly buried with work—"

"Oh, Alienore, sometimes I think you are far too serious. Richard will be gravely disappointed if you forgo the affair. For you know how well he loves you."

Alienore slanted her sovereign a guarded glance. Prince Richard loved no woman or man so well as himself. "Madam, you have accrued an alarming backlog of correspondence—"

"Let duty wait for one night, my dear. I will entertain no further protest."

"As Your Grace commands." Alienore dipped into an ironic curtsy. "If you would have one more masked fool wasting time at a banquet, who am I to protest?"

"In truth, I have a deeper motive for desiring your presence. I want to know more about the black knight who impugned your cousin's honor."

Alienore had always been an abysmal failure at subterfuge. Whistling for Remus, she turned from the queen's discerning eye as the wolf bounded toward her, and buried cold hands in his shaggy ruff. "Why?"

"He arrived at court with glowing credentials. Yet he begs nothing more than a place in my barracks, giving instruction at swordplay to earn his bread. He was a scandal in Outremer and Castile, leading a notorious band who sold their swords to the highest bidder. They call him the Devil of Damascus, for he was at that horrible siege there years ago."

"A mercenary." Fresh shame stung Alienore's cheeks. *Trounced on the field of combat by a common rogue!* "It sounds as though you already know quite a bit about the man. You hardly need me."

The queen hesitated. "My dear, these are uncertain times. My royal husband does not stint at peopling this court with his spies."

Alienore pushed away Remus's muzzle and glanced up. "You believe the king has dispatched this knight to spy upon you?"

"The possibility cannot be ruled out. In truth, I would value your impression."

"Madam, I am poorly skilled at reading the minds of men. What would I know of this Raven?"

"He displays a marked interest in the fairer sex. In the main, his ardor is reciprocated with enthusiasm by my ladies. Or at least, let us say, Lady Rohese is the first to protest him. You underestimate your own appeal, my dear, if you believe the Raven will show no interest in you."

Alarmed, Alienore rose. "I am a virtuous woman—"

"And you believe that will deter him?" The queen laughed. "My dear child, that will only spur his ardor. There are many who find you an irresistible challenge."

Uncomfortably, Alienore thought of Richard. "Madam, I pray you, reconsider! I have no time to idle about in games of courtly love. I cannot conceive of approaching the Raven."

"You approach him—by good Saint Thibault, nay!" The queen laughed again. "My sheltered innocent, you need only appear tonight looking aloof and stately and beautiful as always. Do nothing more than that, and our Raven will fly to you."

Chapter Two

Alienore of Lyonstone was his last and only chance. But he would ensure she never knew it—until it was too late. Lounging in the great hall, the Raven frowned at the chessboard. As in the game, he would move indirectly, using guile and deceit. He dared not reveal his desperation.

"Aha!" Richard of Aquitaine's cobalt eyes flashed with triumph. "I have perplexed you, monsieur! Admit it."

"I'm perplexed." The Raven's mouth twisted in a humorless smile. His gaze raked from the prince—too much like his mother, that one—to stalk the chamber for his quarry.

This pleasure palace was nothing like the sea-raked Norman stronghold where he'd grown to manhood. Still less did it resemble the sun-blasted sands of Outremer, where he'd forgotten everything of softness and courtly grace.

Poitiers seethed with determined revelry, for the queen would have her masque, no matter what doom hung over her. Mythical heroes and leering monsters swirled past, but he smelled fear beneath their frantic gaiety.

This entire court teetered on the razor's edge of treachery— and yet they frolicked.

His lip curled as the Raven scanned the hall, a corner of his mind plotting escape routes by habit. Not finding his quarry, he lowered his ruined voice and adopted a confiding manner.

"A lady perplexes me."

"What, another lady?" Richard slapped a brawny hand on the table. "*Mon Dieu!* I wager we have not heard the last from your latest conquest."

"Aye, the fair Rohese now curses my name." He forced a shrug. "Pity."

And why should the damned affair offend him? He'd thought himself well past minding his blackened reputation.

Ah, but his life now took a different turn. He'd sworn it on his mother's soul. Slave and concubine though she was, at least Yasmin of Acre had possessed a soul—as he did not.

"No doubt the Rievaulx girl is dismayed by your triumph, but that cannot distress you much." Something ugly surfaced in the prince's eyes. "'Tis Rohese's cousin, the demoiselle Alienore, who should concern you."

At her name, the Raven's pulse quickened. He let his hair slither forward to shield his scarred features—an old concealment, to hide his thoughts. "Aye?"

"She cannot be pleased with the way you trounced this champion of hers, whoever he was." Richard nudged his bishop along the board. "Alienore is proud as any princess. She will not suffer this insult you have dealt her family. Indeed, the lady can be somewhat tedious where matters of honor are concerned."

The Raven arranged his expression in lines of ennui and advanced his rook. Here was his moment to do what he did so well—listen and learn, betraying nothing in return.

"I don't know the lady," he rasped. "Yet she's much spoken of. Heard a curious rumor—that she's the queen's chancellor. Took it for naught but gossip."

Reaching for his goblet, Richard smiled sourly. "Monsieur, that is no idle gossip. She is my mother's privy chancellor, a title the queen created for her when Alienore came to court. She handles my mother's personal correspondence and intimate matters, but leaves affairs of state to Sieur de la Haie, the queen's chancellor proper."

Aye, that was the tale they gave out. Henry suspected it for a ruse, behind which his treacherous wife smuggled messages to his enemies, seeding a fresh rebellion to spring forth from

Aquitaine's war-torn soil. Despite his preoccupation over the war with France and his own rebellious nobles, Henry saw to it Sieur de la Haie was closely watched. But Henry could hardly guard each of Eleanor's sixty ladies-in-waiting.

The Raven's orders were to nip the dangerous shoot of treason in the bud before it could bear its deadly harvest. Henry didn't concern himself with the Raven's personal motives—so long as he deprived Eleanor of her privy chancellor in a manner that could not be attributed to Henry.

Like any man married overlong, even a king must fear his lady's sharp tongue.

The Raven frowned to find his goblet empty. Though wine was forbidden to a Muslim, the hearth smoke stung his damaged throat, and only wine would ease it. He beckoned to a serving girl. "The lady's fair, they say?"

"Fair?" The prince's eyes clouded. "That maid garbed as Venus yonder, she is fair. Your coy little Rievaulx is fair. Even this wench here is fetching, eh?"

Subtly, the prince's voice deepened. "Alienore of Lyonstone is like the Holy Grail. She is the vision you see in a dream and spend the rest of your life searching for. She is nothing at all like these easy-come lasses."

The Raven's blood froze to ice. So Richard wanted the Lyonstone girl, but the lady eluded him. The prince might say what he liked, but the Raven knew otherwise. Alienore of Lyonstone was no saint or holy relic. The chit was reckless at best, spoiled and willful at worst, a menace to herself and all those dependent on her. She'd fled the marriage bed like a rabbit before the hounds—like a giddy, undisciplined girl. But Ormonde would have her back.

"Do you know what they call her?" The prince brooded. "'The queen's most virtuous lady.' She is convent reared, an ice maiden, aloof and untouchable. They say no man can win her heart. But I know the lady's price, and I intend to meet it."

So Ormonde had a rival for the lady's affections. Worse, a royal suitor, wealthy and blazing with the glory of a new-made knight. Precisely the man to turn any maid's heart.

Hooding his eyes, the Raven advanced his knight. "Checkmate."

Richard roared with honest laughter, his bonhomie restored. "Ah, you're a wily fellow! You distracted me a-purpose with this talk of women."

Across the hall, a flash of white and gold snared his eye. A solitary woman had appeared before the doors, blazing like a beacon over night black seas.

By her attire, the lady was Athena, goddess of wisdom and war. Silver damask draped her form to sheathe high breasts and supple hips in a manner any man would notice. She held an argent spear easily as a knight and wore a shining breastplate as though born to it. Beneath her helm, a river of gold and silver hair rippled to her waist. At her feet a white wolf bristled, watchful beneath her hand.

By the wolf, he knew her—the wolf they all spoke of. Inevitably, Richard confirmed it. "Behold, monsieur, the very lady. 'Tis Alienore herself."

Alienore of Lyonstone, the shape of his salvation—the single straw that waved above the morass of death and destruction he'd made of his life.

A prickle of recognition raced across his skin. From head to foot he tingled as if struck by lightning. He'd been waiting for her all night—nay, all his life. Allah be merciful, what was this madness? Lyonstone's daughter was all that stood between him and damnation.

The lady swept into the room, one hand draped over her escort's sleeve. What in hell was this—another rival? A pretty-faced gallant squired the lady with an elegance the Raven had lost, burned away by fourteen years of hell on crusade.

An unpleasant frisson clenched his belly. In another

man, he would have called it envy. He swallowed it down and cleared his damaged throat. "The lady has an admirer."

"That yapping puppy? He is nothing—the Comte de Beaumont's landless son, come to court to find a wealthy wife."

"Does she favor his suit?"

"Alienore wants nothing to do with marriage, believe me." Richard snorted. "But Beaumont is a clever lad. He has sworn to her cause, vowed to win back her stolen lands. So she tolerates his affection. I assure you, monsieur, he means nothing to her."

So the lady wanted her lands back. Well, she could not want them very badly. For she need only become the Duchesse d'Ormonde—no lowly position—to claim them.

Draining his wine, the Raven swirled its tart sweetness around his tongue. There were times on crusade he would have killed for so fine a vintage . . . or perhaps not. He'd done enough killing to last any man a lifetime.

He cloaked his intent, mouth twisting in a scoundrel's smile.

"There's no diversion so amusing as virtue. Introduce me?"

"Ah, so you too thirst for the Holy Grail." Richard tilted back his chair, powerful limbs sprawling as he eyed him. "Do you fancy a wager?"

"A wager." The Raven studied his cup. Empty again, and he had best ensure the wine did not dull his wits. "What do we wager on?"

"Why, the demoiselle's favor! I shall make you known to Lady Virtue—for she would never speak to you otherwise, would she? The first to bed her wins . . . what?"

The Raven's lip curled. The man was a prince of England, yet he stooped to this. A boy's game, a dirty trick to play on a highborn lady—and what a lady. Brash and reckless though she might be, he possessed no desire to disgrace her.

Yet he could not afford to earn the prince's enmity. Without

Richard's intervention, the lady would cut him dead as soon as look at him, after that blasted business with her cousin.

So he lied—which was what he did best, the Raven thought bitterly, save for killing.

"Wealth doesn't interest me. Say you win. Then I owe you a favor of your choosing. If I win, you owe me the same."

"*Avoi*, the favor of a king's son is no trifling thing."

"For trifling stakes, the game will bore us." The Raven shrugged. "You're a prisoner in your own castle, and I a free man. Time may come you need a favor from a man like me."

The prince drummed his fingers on the table, then flung back his lion's mane of hair and laughed. "Very well, monsieur! But I must warn you I am unlikely to lose. The demoiselle favors me, as you shall see. Come, you, and meet her."

She had managed to elude the queen's jailer all day, but Alienore feared her luck was about to turn. When the queen insisted she attend this frivolous revel, Eleanor had thrown her to the wolves.

Resigned, she stationed herself in an alcove to await Sir Guy. Then the shifting crowd parted like the Red Sea before Moses. Slowly she lifted her gaze, and saw *him*.

By his height she knew him, a colossus casting his blade-straight shadow across the flagstones. By his sinuous grace she recalled him, stalking toward her across the tourney field.

Not for him the courtiers' costumed frippery—unless he came as descending Night. He drew her gaze over his forbidding frame, starkly clad in a black surcoat. A belt of hammered bronze, knotted at his hips, divided the darkness. But his face made her tingle, head to foot, with the lightning charge of wariness.

Swarthy as a Saracen, with aquiline features, sharp planed and cruel, he was beautiful as her father's sword: lethal and humming with contained violence. Amber eyes burned beneath drooping lids; bitter disappointment had carved lines around his mouth. The jagged seam of an old scar sliced from his ear to his shaven jaw. His mane of ink black hair poured over powerful shoulders to slither around his hips. Dismayed, she stared into his exotic countenance as a feverish shiver raced through her. She had been waiting for him all her life—but that was utter nonsense. She mistrusted this dangerous excess of emotion. Leaning into Remus's shaggy bulk, she anchored herself against the black knight's pull.

How does she manage it? The Raven groped after his scattered wits. She did nothing to command attention, but stood before a hundred eyes with dignity and the queen's own poise. Now a frisson of response sizzled through him as the blade of her gaze pierced him.

He stared into her wide gray eyes, darkening with storm clouds of anger and alarm. *I know those eyes,* he realized, incredulous. They belonged to the masked knight—the knight he'd left sprawled in the mud that morning. The knight he'd thought for a fleeting second was a woman, before he dismissed the instinct.

Allah save him, he was a fool! Who else would defend the Rievaulx girl, with her dubious reputation?

Richard of Aquitaine strode forward to stake his claim. Clenching his fists, the Raven fought an impulse to haul Alienore of Lyonstone bodily away from her lusting prince, haul her into his own arms. He wanted to demand what in hell she thought she was about, masquerading as a knight on the tourney field. He could have killed her before he knew her!

Grimly he mastered his jostling emotions and girded himself with an armor of calm. He would not reveal that he knew her secret. Why should he? For all he lacked a courtier's charm, women seemed to find him appealing enough. Let her swoon into his arms as her damned cousin had done, and the battle would be halfway won.

Alienore swam up from her curtsy before Richard of Aquitaine—the queen's heir. Costumed as the Sun, he blazed in crimson, tongues of flame leaping from the crown over his ruddy hair. Larger than life, he eclipsed lesser mortals, yet somehow she had overlooked him until his jocular voice boomed out. Near her feet, the wolf rumbled a warning only she could hear.

"My demoiselle, you are the evening star, throwing radiance over the mortal world." Richard kissed her cold fingers.

"Your Grace, I am Athena. Surely that is evident."

She battled a familiar rush of impatience for the court's empty compliments, while the outcast knight hovered on the edge of vision, marking her every word and gesture.

To the prince she said, "I am given to understand you are newly knighted. 'Tis a very great honor."

Even at barely sixteen, three years her junior, Richard of Aquitaine possessed his mother's subtlety. His piercing gaze saw past platitudes, and he barked out a laugh.

"Poor Alienore! Already chafing to return to your duties? Tonight you're mine, to do with as I will."

She flushed beneath the words, darting a look toward the Raven's sleepy gaze. Would the black knight recognize the champion who'd defied him? Unlike others at court, she had never been crafty at concealment.

"Ah." Richard scowled. "You recall me to my duty. I promised an introduction for monsieur. Sieur le Corbeau is our new master-at-arms . . . for a time."

She itched to give this Raven the cut direct, but churlishness ill became an earl's daughter. After a palpable delay, she offered an unwilling hand. "I am the queen's privy chancellor. In her name, I must bid you well come."

She would bid him well come in the queen's name, but never her own—this wretch who'd left her lying in the mud!

"You're Alienore of Lyonstone." The Raven's sword-toughened fingers closed around her hand.

From the minstrels' corner, the clash of tambours underscored his rasping voice, hinting at old injury to his throat. Somehow, she found it not unpleasant. An exotic aroma curled in her nostrils: musk and sandalwood. A shiver rippled up her spine as he bent over her, night black hair spilling forward to tickle her hand.

No doubt Rohese found him pleasant at first. She herself held the advantage of knowing him for the unprincipled rogue he was. She would not be taken in.

But he had captured her sword hand, a danger she must deflect. Let her sleeve slip an inch, and he would glimpse the linen bandage. She tried to withdraw, but he tightened his grip.

"My lady," he rasped with his ruined voice. "I've waited long for this."

"Indeed?" She spoke in her chancellor's voice. "Have you business with the queen? I should warn you. Unlike others, I am hers before I am any man's."

"Oh, I don't think so." His topaz eyes mocked her. "Surely you serve your king?"

Of course I serve my king—can you doubt it? Yet somehow the words tangled on her tongue. "'Tis the same service."

"Be at ease, lady. I'm no grasping courtier, come to plead your support with Eleanor."

He raised her hand to his lips. A shocking heat arced through her.

"In that case, monsieur, what is your business here?"

"Why, lady," he whispered. "My business is you."

Villain! Does the man think to amuse himself with me, now he has disgraced my cousin? Outrage flashed through her, mingled with a faint disappointment she could not comprehend. She jerked her hand away.

"In that case, monsieur, we have no business at all."

Prince Richard laughed and claimed her arm, eyes flashing with curious triumph as he met the Raven's gaze. Something was afoot between these two, but she could not fathom what.

Growling at the prince's nearness, Remus curled back his muzzle and bared wicked teeth. She swung her spear aside and bent to ruffle his fur, thus freeing herself from the prince. When the wolf licked her jaw, her disquiet dissolved as she inhaled his familiar doggish smell. He had remained strangely placid before the black knight, but Richard's closeness roused all the wolf's protective instincts.

The prince scowled at the unfriendly animal, but kept his distance. "Dangerous beast. You should keep him chained up."

Protective, her arms tightened around the wolf. Remus would never harm anyone without her express command. She had trained him from a pup with her own hand, slept curled against his shaggy bulk at night. He adored her as no other living creature had ever done.

"By my faith, Your Grace," she said, "I could say that of half the men in this court."

Irritation sparked in the prince's gaze. "*Mon Dieu,* if any other spoke to me so . . . but I can deny you nothing." Turning to the black knight, he adopted a jovial air. "You see, monsieur, you must have a care with this one!"

Before the Raven's watchful presence, she couched her spear against the flagstones and rose to her full height. Still, the outcast knight topped her by well over a head.

The Raven arched his eyebrows. "You manage that spear with surprising ease."

I would like nothing better than to thrust it through your black heart. But caution prickled her skin, and she held her tongue. She had known it was risky to choose such attire, bringing her secret too close to the surface. But how she tired of cowardice and deception. Sometimes she longed to shout her truths into the court's astounded ears.

She clenched her spear, and her moonstone ring flashed like a star as it caught the light. Richard's eyes narrowed as the stone snared his gaze.

"Bah, do you still wear that paltry jewel? I can't believe your devoted Sieur de Beaumont is so ungenerous. Does his father hold his purse strings too tight?"

"'Tis no suitor's gift, but my mother's ring." Her throat swelled. "I wear it with pride."

The fog of memory clouded her vision: Marguerite's fragile features as she lay on her deathbed after the tragic accident that had broken her body and shattered the trust between husband and wife.

Richard broke the painful spell. "Proud or humble, lady, only royal favor will return your precious lands and restore your precious honor."

She observed the flush beneath his tanned skin and wondered how much he had been drinking. Jesus wept! He was going to be difficult tonight, in front of this rogue knight.

"As it please Your Grace, I seek only justice, by the king's law—to confirm my rightful inheritance."

"The king!" Richard sneered. "Soon my father will have no authority to confirm anything. You had best place your wager with me."

"You speak treason!" Hastily, she glanced left and right. Where was Sir Guy? And why did Richard not take greater care before this Raven? "Guard your tongue, I pray you, else we be all undone."

The Raven's uncanny eyes burned into her as if they stood alone.

"If you'd gain your inheritance, you should remain on your lands, aye?" She found herself noting his clipped cadence, and wondering if his damaged voice pained him. "Surely absence weakens your claim."

Beleaguered, she tightened her jaw. "Monsieur, the matter is not so simple."

Richard pressed a cup of wine upon her. Bowing her head, she accepted it without drinking. There was enough drunkenness about the court this night.

The prince flourished a brawny arm. "The demoiselle's holdings are occupied by a rival claimant—her fiancé, the Duc d'Ormonde. Isn't that so, *ma chère?*"

A deathly stillness settled over the Raven. Suddenly he seemed a stalking beast, crouched to spring on his quarry. Though her betrothal was common knowledge, little though she liked it, she felt reluctant to air the tawdry business before him. "Your Grace—"

"Our Raven is a well-traveled man. Surely he has heard of your duke, even in Outremer?" Spiteful pleasure lurked in Richard's gaze. "Ponce d'Ormonde was once the most dissolute libertine in the realm, including my brothers. No small achievement, eh?"

"Your Grace—"

"Nay, why should I not tell him?" Richard brandished his cup, wine slopping over the rim to spatter the floor. "They say Ormonde squandered a king's fortune, so now the old man must marry money. Worse, he's grown repentant in his old age, become a pious fool mumbling prayers, complete with hair shirt!"

Prodded by guilt, Alienore stirred. "'Tis not well done to mock a man for piety. Well for him if he has repented—"

"He's a doddering travesty." Richard scowled. "Your beauty would be utterly wasted upon him. But your idiot brother won't cede you the manor otherwise . . . and you desire that manor, don't you, *ma chère?*"

"I am an earl's daughter! I would never shame Lyonstone by marrying a baseborn man."

"Baseborn?" The Raven raised skeptical eyebrows. "The man's Duke of Ormonde."

Wrath swelled within and scalded her cheeks. "Ponce d'Ormonde's sire was a panderer who won his title by warming the king's bed with whores he liked!"

"Few are privileged to share your pedigree." A muscle flexed in the Raven's jaw. "Do we all lack honor?"

Nineteen years of breeding rose to the forefront and banished the vermin of self-doubt that had nibbled away at her since the night she fled Lyonstone. "I cannot speak for most men. But my father always said it. In the end, blood will tell."

"You're a fool to think so." The knight's voice scraped out. "There be lecherous lords and noble knaves in this world."

"What would you know of honor?" She should not have spoken so plainly as to give offense, but she had not taken this outcast for a man jealous of his honor.

"Why, nothing at all." His face twisted with bitterness. "What can the devil know of honor?"

"Brother, I crave a word." A scowling nobleman pushed into their alcove—Geoffrey of Brittany, the queen's younger son. Richard pulled him aside with a muttered excuse.

Disconcerted by the ugly words that had flown from her lips, she turned away from the Raven's piercing gaze. While the princes huddled in conference, she and the Raven stood alone, though in full view of the court.

Courtesy and guilt compelled her words. "I should not have spoken thus."

It was the closest to contrition she could bring herself, for her cousin's ravisher. When he said nothing, she steeled herself to meet his gaze.

"My lady's proud." Something stirred beneath the Raven's bronze-skinned features. "Too proud to marry a panderer's son."

"'Tis not pride, but honor." With exquisite pain, she remembered her mother. "I have sworn to forgo all that I own before I make this marriage."

"Pretty sentiment," he mocked, oddly intent. "Does honor always echo your heart's desire? If you'd say aye, you be luckier than the rest of us, or less honest."

Outrage knifed through her. How dare this dog—the Devil of Damascus—presume to lesson her upon honor and integrity? "We do not all choose to wallow in the muck of our baser natures, Lord Raven. If you cannot comprehend that, I pity you for it."

"I comprehend you right well." He leaned close, tugging at her senses. She waited for Remus to growl, but the wolf merely panted up at him. "I thought you fled your marriage with a maid's fears, and no father living to curb you. Now I see the truth. You fled from some naive sense of honor."

"You forget yourself, monsieur." She blazed at him. "No man on earth speaks to me in this fashion."

"Except Richard of Aquitaine, who sullies you with every word. But nay, I've forgotten. He's noble born, can do no insult."

"I never said—"

"Nay, I understand you. You paint the world black and white, like the perfect world you dreamed in your convent. But virtue and honor are complex matters in infinite shades of gray."

"Do not believe I have spent my entire life within the cloister. You know nothing about me, no matter what you may hear at this court."

Unexpected humor tugged at his lips. "Grant you this, lady—you fear not to speak your mind. Bravery's a fine quality . . . for those who can afford it."

"Here, now, what's this?" Richard shouldered into the alcove. "Why, demoiselle, your color is quite fetchingly high.

Can it be our Raven has managed to provoke a display of passion from Lady Virtue?"

Over his shoulder, she caught sight of Sir Guy, features stamped with determination as he marched toward her. A resolve to match his stiffened her spine.

I am weary of fleeing this man. If he wishes to tilt with me, so be it.

Catching her expression, Richard followed her gaze. They watched as fox-faced Geoffrey darted into view and slid up to Sir Guy—blocking his path, as he had done that morn—almost as if someone planned it.

"Come along." Richard caught her elbow in a proprietary grip. "I've taken a fancy to dance, and I will be denied nothing tonight."

She managed to check the protest before it tumbled from her lips. She trod a careful path with the prince and strove always to temper her distance with courtesy. When she glanced at the Raven, he was tracking Geoffrey of Brittany, who marched off with the angry Sir Guy in tow. Over his shoulder, the Englishman flung her a grim look—unwilling to yield, but bound no less than she to dance to the royal tune.

"As you can see," she told the Raven dryly, "our prince has spoken. Bid you good night, monsieur."

The Raven's eyes never wavered as they stalked Geoffrey through the hall.

No doubt I have bored him with my wholesome convent-bred ways. She spun away, skirts swirling around her knees. She should be thankful he'd treated her no worse. Only consider what had happened to Rohese—

Unexpectedly, the Raven spoke. "My lady."

She couched her spear and turned, eyebrows lifting to belie her pounding heart.

With careless grace, the black knight bowed, that sinful mane slithering down. His infernal eyes flickered with fire.

"We'll speak again." Those topaz eyes dared her to fling defiance in his face—and how she itched to do it. But nay, that would be unlordly.

Instead, she elevated her chin. "If I were you, I would not wager anything I value upon that."

Chapter Three

A band of pain tightened around Alienore's temples. With a grimace, she glanced up from her writing table.

Before her, tidy piles of parchment contained a fortnight's worth of correspondence, marked with her neat notations. She had labored since daybreak and accomplished much.

But not enough, her conscience whispered. And now she would pay for it.

Saint Swithun grant mercy, I cannot afford a megrim now. She pressed cramped fingers against her eyelids to ease the stabbing pain. If she could only shut out the inferno of daylight—

Beneath her writing table, the wolf growled. Her eyes opened to find Sir Guy Aigret filling the doorway to her oratory. Recognizing the steely gleam in his gaze, she sighed and braced for battle.

He addressed her in their common English. "I've run ye to ground, milady—though it's taken three days to do it."

"By my faith, have we an appointment?" Coolly, her eyebrows lifted. "If so, I do not recall it."

"Ye'll not slip the net this day. Need I remind ye I represent yer king?"

Her jaw tightened with stubbornness. She descended from the earls of Lyonstone, by God. She refused to allow this bull terrier with a minor title to intimidate her.

"Need I remind *you,* sir, that I am the queen's privy chancellor? My schedule is not mine to command."

Clearly prepared to wait her out, Sir Guy braced his stout legs and straddled the doorway. When Remus uncurled, a growl rumbling from his chest, she whistled the wolf to her side. Vexing though she found the man, it would not do for Remus to spring at his throat. "Are you here upon the king's business? In that event, I am at your disposal."

"Aye." He watched Remus warily. "I'd like to hear how ye found matters at Bordeaux."

"Unsettled, sir. I did what I could to convince Aquitaine's noble seigneurs these rumors of rebellion are much exaggerated. 'Twould come better from the queen herself."

"Don't hold yer breath waiting for that. The king knows better than to set that virago loose. They've always been her men, and Henry knows it!"

"The queen is loyal to her husband. Once he returns, he too will see it."

"Unlikely." He snorted. "What news from the queen's uncle, hey?"

Her meeting with Raoul de Faye was supposed to remain secret, a private matter between the queen and her uncle. With every bone in her body Alienore abhorred lying, even by royal command. Worse, she knew she was abysmal at it. Always, always, her face gave her away.

She unsheathed her long-knife to sharpen her quill. "I am unclear of your meaning."

He showed no better patience for evasion than she. "I know ye went sneaking off to meet Sieur de Faye, and so will the king. So I'll ask ye again—in the king's name—what did he say?"

With steady fingers, she honed her quill. She drew strength from the blade, a long-knife no other lady would carry. A blazing lion clawed around its hilt toward a fire red ruby—a gift from her father.

But she dared not resist outright. She was loyal to Henry no less than to Eleanor, and she did not believe one must negate the other. "Sieur de Faye conveyed messages of love and concern from the queen's son in Paris. 'Twas a family matter."

"Oh, come, lass! Ye can't expect me to believe that doggerel. It's my duty to see the queen causes no more mischief while Henry has his hands full with the Norman rising. Did that snake give ye a message?"

"Aye!" She was no woman to be intimidated by a man's raised voice. "I conveyed the sealed parchment directly to the queen's hands, so I can say no more."

When he strode forward, her belly clenched.

"Lady Alienore, I knew yer father all my life. Perhaps ye didn't know it, but we fought together in the Holy Land. I mourned his passing, lass."

The ache of loss swelled in her throat. Her love had not been enough to keep Theobold at home. He had abandoned a grieving girl and taken his cherished son away with him to war.

Benedict was a comfort to our father, as I was not. My father saw naught in me but his wife's betrayal.

She swallowed the lump in her throat. "Say on, sir."

Often her directness disconcerted the subtle courtiers of Aquitaine, but Guy Aigret was an Englishman to the marrow of his bones. He looked at her without condemnation, as though he understood the many facets of her grief.

"Theobold was an honorable man," he said gruffly. "I can't believe any daughter of his would practice betrayal. For yer father's sake, I'll warn ye. The king suspects ye. 'Tis treason, milady—and the consequences of that are dire. Be warned."

She stared up at him, pulse beating hard and fast at her throat. Aye, who did not know the penalty for treason: death by hanging, to be cut down from the noose still living, then disemboweled, the traitor's entrails burned before his eyes. Then to be drawn and quartered, as a grim warning to others whose loyalty would stray.

Jesus wept, this could not be real. How could she, Alienore of Lyonstone, be suspected of such deadly offense? She was no traitor!

Allowing herself a single moment of weakness, she wrapped her arms around the wolf's warm body. Remus whined in sympathy and licked her jaw. For a time she said nothing, until she regained command of her voice.

"Sir Guy, I am . . . grateful for your concern. I swear to you, I am loyal to England."

"I trust that's so. But ye cannot serve two masters, lass."

"The queen regrets this estrangement! Perhaps she has been . . . overzealous . . . but I am certain she has learned from her mistake. My duty to the king lies in serving his lady and ensuring she does not stray further."

"Fairly spoken, like a true counselor." His whiskers lifted in something like a smile. "I hope ye'll not find yer faith misplaced. She'd use yer innocent love sure as any other tool—easy as she used her husband's trust, by God."

"Nay, sir, I will not hear her so abused. She is a good and virtuous lady, and loves me truly, as she loved my mother."

"Pray that's so, milady, that ye might exert some influence. Be wary she don't exploit yer trust to her own advantage."

To that she could find no response. She bowed her head, and hoped he would take that for acquiescence.

When he had gone, she ground her fists to her aching brow. She had forgone the modesty of a veil within her sanctum, yet now she wished she had worn one. She gave too much away with her bearing.

Indeed, Sir Guy's warning had done naught to alleviate her headache. This megrim showed every sign of degenerating into one of the hideous episodes that sent her to bed, weak and nauseated, with a cloth soaked in lavender over her eyes. Groaning, she kneaded her scalp.

Remus bounded up with a happy yip—his greeting to those he considered friends. Her eyes flashed open, whirring thoughts spinning to a halt.

A sinister figure commanded her doorway, black surcoat

swirling around him, his silken hair plunging to his waist. At his belt, the curved Saracen sword with its topaz eye gleamed in wicked promise.

She stared into those deep-set eyes, burning like embers beneath his eyebrows. He watched her as though he knew her, knew all her secrets. Yet he concealed his own behind his hard face.

Alienore stood to confront the black knight. Softly she said, "You."

He'd been angry since he learned her name, irritated and impatient when the antics of a headstrong girl sent him galloping across two kingdoms to claim her, when so many needs clamored for his attention. When he'd stared into those stormy eyes at the masque, one thought had pounded through his brain.

Allah, be merciful. This is worse than I feared.

Was the lady so undisciplined, so heedless, that she disguised herself and took the field for a lark? But then, who'd taught her the lance and the sword? Even encumbered by ill-fitting armor and that half-wild charger, she would have unseated a lesser man.

That she possessed the fortitude to withstand a man's training, and the discretion to do it in secret, told him Alienore of Lyonstone was more than he'd taken her for—more than a stubborn spinster fearful of the marriage bed.

Lurking outside her door, he had overheard the exchange with Sir Guy, and that alone was enough to freeze his blood. How could the lady fly so far down the road to treason and the hangman's noose in a few short months? Surely she couldn't be so pure a fool she didn't know it. But this business would take time to unravel—time he did not have, damn the girl.

He could not merely assert his authority over the unruly

minx, toss her over his shoulder and sail cheerfully for England. He would have to woo her, worm his way into her
confidence. Who could say how long that would take?

Annoyance and perplexity gnawed at him like rats. *A
beauty, she is—Allah's heart, there's no denying it.* Grimly resisting her pull, he resolved to shatter this shining illusion.

The lady stood bathed in winter sun and blazed like a
torch. Surely there were dozens of beauties more comely,
with the same pale fire of gold and silver hair?

There must be others with skin like ivory silk, proud cheekbones and Norman nose, the cleft of a determined chin
beneath lips whose generous curve made a man dream of
kissing. Surely there were other eyes like hers, flashing lightning silver and storm gray at will.

She was the tallest lady at court, and that could be naught
to recommend her. She dressed sober as an abbess, and where
was the allure in that? A great cat snarled from her hilt—a
man's knife, a fighting knife no proper maid would carry. Yet
something about her called to him, an incandescent spirit
that blazed in her, like the fires that raged in his own soul.

He leaned a hip against the doorframe. "So this is where
you've been hiding."

A furrow of annoyance appeared between her ash-blonde
eyebrows. She spoke with a deep-throated contralto, a husky
voice to make any man think of bedding—until he looked
into her wintry gaze.

"I do not hide from any man living. I attend Mass and
Vespers with the queen each day . . . though I have noted
you do not."

Well, that was encouraging. At least she thought to look
for him. "Your God and I are not on speaking terms."

Surprise and curiosity glimmered in her gray eyes. She
clasped her hands like a nun— and why in hell should that
beguile him?

"I take the noon meal at the queen's table, monsieur. I have not seen you there."

"I'm no man of leisure." Had it frustrated her that their paths failed to cross, the way it frustrated him? "I'm master-at-arms. I've duties in the lists."

"Yet you are not there now."

A flicker of appreciation tugged at his lips, but he contained it. It would never do for this proud and stately lady to believe he was having sport at her expense.

He bent and whistled to the wolf. With a yip, the beast bounded across the floor to him, braced large paws on his shoulders and slathered on affection with a pink tongue. Mindful of the wicked teeth, the Raven scrubbed the shaggy ruff with a sense of wonder that the wolf allowed him these familiarities.

He glanced up into Alienore's surprised countenance. "This fellow and I've made friends, when he's not with you."

"That is odd." She frowned at the wolf. "He is accustomed to match his likes and dislikes to mine."

Wryly, he smiled. "My lady's not subtle."

Color bloomed beneath her skin as she busied herself with her parchments. "I know well that I have not the clever quips and subtleties of a proper courtier. I had not the benefit of being raised at court."

"Who calls that a benefit?" He recalled his own unsettled youth.

He must put her at ease, but charm was no longer an art he claimed. Fourteen years of hell in the Holy Land had scraped away all his court polish. Besides, he suspected Alienore of Lyonstone would scorn any conventional wooing.

Skirting the wolf, he prowled toward her. She stood her ground, pale yet composed.

"May I inquire why you are here, monsieur? If you have not seen me, 'tis because I have no time to waste in idle pursuits. The queen receives correspondence from petitioners throughout the realm and from foreign courts. Many of these find their way to me."

Across the writing table, he stared at her. Neither his physical presence nor his ominous repute seemed to daunt her, and he had to admire her for it. Whatever her shortcomings might be, she did not lack courage.

And she inspired surpassing loyalty in her creatures. Take that squire from the tourney. The lad hadn't betrayed her, even when offered good silver to reveal her identity. Of course, Beaumont had loaned her the warhorse—the young pup who was sick with love for her, Lancelot to her Guinevere. The thought annoyed him for reasons he didn't care to explore.

The Raven did not smile, knowing his scarred features were ill suited for it. But he allowed his mouth a rueful twist.

"We began badly three nights ago. I come to make amends."

"Marry, I do not see how you may." She dipped her quill in the inkpot. "You have dishonored my cousin and my mother's name. You humiliated my . . . champion . . . on the tourney field. By your own words, you value honor and virtue not at all, and those principles are the beating heart of me."

He gritted his teeth at this recital of his alleged sins. He could refute every one of them, damn it, but she wouldn't believe him and then they'd be fighting again.

"I'd have your regard, Lady Alienore."

His tongue lingered over her name. *Ah-lee-anor*, like the clarion call of a silver trumpet unfurling on the wind.

The lady busied herself and did not meet his gaze. "I fail to grasp why my regard should matter, unless you have some hidden purpose."

"What purpose could that be?" By the Prophet, what did she suspect?

Color rose beneath her ivory skin. "You are said to be highly fond of the company of women. I am called the queen's most virtuous lady. If the challenge of capturing my affections is appealing, you would not be the first to think so."

Allah be praised, she suspects nothing. But Richard would seduce her for no better reason, besmirch all her shining fairness with his sordid touch only to win a wager.

"Dishonor is not my purpose," he rasped.

"Then what is your purpose?" She lowered her quill to fix him with her gaze.

"The queen goes to hunt, under escort. She invites you to join the sport."

She eyed him narrowly, as though she suspected a trap. "So this is the queen's game rather than yours . . . this 'invitation.'"

The Raven held his breath. He was no fool. It could be no coincidence that from the dozens milling in the courtyard, the queen had singled him out to bear this message. Clearly Eleanor of Aquitaine had her own purpose for throwing the two of them together. Did the queen suspect him? Did she know who he was?

Alienore puffed out an impatient breath. "Nesta!"

The door to her inner chamber swung open, revealing a plump wren of a serving girl wearing red cheeks and a brown woolen kirtle. The girl's eyes rounded to see the Devil of Damascus with his Saracen sword towering over her mistress. Yet she bobbed a curtsy.

"Aye, milady?"

"Take Remus into my chamber." Alienore gathered the parchments into her strongbox and locked it. "It seems the court goes a-hunting, and they are not accustomed to a wolf in their midst."

"If ye say so, milady." The serving girl cocked a wary glance at the wolf. "H-here then, ye great beastie."

Remus eyed her scornfully. Alienore swept an authoritative hand toward the girl. "Remus, go with Nesta."

The wolf whined his disappointment but trotted into the

inner chamber. Alienore switched to Norman French, though the Raven had followed her English.

"So then, Lord Raven, you may inform Her Grace that I come anon. If you wish to earn my charity, pray instruct my groom to saddle my stallion."

So easy she dismissed him like any court lackey. The Raven swept back his heavy surcoat and bowed with an irony he knew would not escape her.

But he had her now, his elusive prey, and he wouldn't squander his chance. He would stay closer than her own shadow—with Eleanor of Aquitaine's connivance.

The party was feasting on candied fruits and sugared almonds when the huntsman brought Eleanor the spoor. A king stag, and noble prey. Sharing an ironic glance with Richard, the queen laughed and commenced the hunt. With good-natured shouts and jostling, the royal party thundered off, hemmed in by the king's crimson guards. Still, they could pretend they were free.

The hunt streamed through the snowy wood, a river of bay and chestnut under bright-clad riders. The hunting horn's *taroo* unfurled like a banner overhead. The baying of hounds split the air as Alienore clung to her stallion's dappled withers.

Split skirts allowed her to ride astride, Galahad's flaxen mane lashing her face, cold wind burning her cheeks. Fresh air and exertion had dissipated her headache. Now euphoria swelled, making her laugh aloud.

Only one man could spoil her pleasure in the day. The Raven clung to Galahad's silver-painted hooves, tenacious as a burr despite the bursts of speed she employed to lose him.

He wished to win her regard, did he? Well, there could be only two reasons for that. Either he pursued her for diversion. Or he was the king's spy, dispatched to nose out any whiff of disloyalty. Either way, Alienore meant to unmask the scoundrel. It would serve him well if the queen tossed him out of Poitiers.

She ducked to avoid a low branch and slanted a glance over her shoulder. Mounted on his fire-eyed black, he filled the path behind her like oncoming night, mantle billowing in his wake.

Her jaw tightened with determination. Had she not made it plain she did not desire his company? Well, she would make it plainer.

She rode these woods freely—often alone, with only Remus for company. Ahead the path forked, a little-known lane that meandered through the bracken.

Jostled on all sides, with the hounds tangling underfoot, she edged Galahad toward the fringes of the dangerous melee. Gamely he swerved at her bidding—no lady's palfrey, but a Norman destrier standing eighteen hands tall, a prize any knight would treasure.

The lead riders surged ahead, the queen bareheaded and laughing like a girl, a stray spear of sunlight flashing on her auburn hair. Prince Richard thundered at his mother's heels, blind and deaf to all save his own pleasure. The press of galloping bodies carried them safely past the fork. Then the dark gap in the foliage opened before Alienore.

Judging her moment, she reined hard to the left. Satisfaction surged through her when Galahad responded, veering onto the fork. They vaulted a fallen trunk and crashed through the undergrowth into the shadowy stillness of the forest.

Now the blue-white silence of the wood enclosed her. Behind them the thunder of the hunt faded, blurring with distance. Ahead, the trees parted before a frozen stream.

With heart-stopping suddenness, Galahad staggered and almost flung her off. Hastily, she reined in and dismounted, rubbing his sweat-streaked shoulder. When she looked down, her heart sank to her boots.

Her faithful steed stood on three legs, favoring a foreleg.

"Poor Galahad." Unhappily, she thought about the leagues of forest between them and the castle.

"I suppose we shall now be walking back." She fought the uneasy impulse to whisper and kept talking, to hearten them. "We have not my sword, but we're naught to be trifled with, are we? And we've a good hour of daylight left."

Still, night fell swift on the forest in winter.

She leaned against Galahad until he shifted his weight, letting her examine the damaged hoof. She braced his knee under her arm—an undignified placement, but who could see?—and spotted the stone wedged into the soft frog.

"By my faith, lad! 'Tis a wicked sharp stone, but never fear. We'll have it out—"

Without warning, the stallion flung back his head and neighed. Her heart froze as her hand flew to her long-knife. The three-beat tattoo of hooves thudded on the trail behind.

All is lost . . .

Chapter Four

The black stallion erupted into view, snow spraying beneath his hooves.

All her senses sharpened as the outcast knight thundered toward her like a nightmare against the gray-white forest. The world paled with dismay at his passage. Even the small woodland sounds—the rustle of branches, the yip of a hunting fox—receded as the stallion halted before her in a scramble of hooves.

Then a raucous scream split the air as a dark bird raked across the sky. Her heart froze as razor-sharp talons sliced toward the knight's unprotected face. But he stared straight ahead as the raven arrowed toward him—and landed, delicate as a lady, on his shoulder. Wicked claws flexed gently as the bird settled. Suspended breath escaped her lungs in a rush.

"Dear God, sir, what are you?" she whispered.

In her turmoil, she'd spoken English—a tongue rare in Aquitaine—and he did not reply. Unperturbed by the corvine preening on his shoulder, the knight studied her through eyes like flickering flames. Her skin prickled with foreboding, and an ungodly thrill.

So she had not given him the slip after all. Why must the infernal man always find her at a disadvantage?

"Have you not the good grace," she said in Norman French, "to know when a lady wishes to quit your company?"

His lean face hardened, cruel as any Saracen's. Topaz eyes glinted as they raked the forest. "Expecting someone?"

Sweet mercy, does he think I am trysting with rebels? If he is Henry's man, this will be my undoing.

She swallowed down her fear, defiance sparking. "I expected no more than a private hour. But it appears I am to be denied even that much."

When he swung a leg forward over the pommel to dismount, the raven flew from his shoulder to perch in a tree. Paying the uncanny creature no heed—as though accustomed to the devil's creatures—the knight sprang from the saddle. Light-footed as a cat, he landed in a swirl of stark wool.

Her senses stretched to tingling alert as he stalked toward her. Alone they were in the forest, but she did not fear him. Was she a lion or a mouse?

"Were you thrown?" He looked askance at the wounded Galahad.

"Hardly," she said proudly. "My destrier picked up a stone."

He gestured her aside. Sparing with words, but at least he could not be accused of idle chatter! A twinge of curiosity plucked her nerves as she wondered again whether that shredded voice troubled him when he used it.

Aware of the bird's beady gaze, she circled away, keeping her distance from the wicked crescent of Damascus steel at the knight's side. He frowned over the injured hoof, and she suffered a stab of guilt. Aye, she should not have been galloping down this ill-kept trail. She was fortunate to fare no worse, though finding herself marooned with the Devil of Damascus—a known ravisher of women—was bad enough.

The knight slid a curved dagger from his boot. Alarm spurted through her as her hand flew to her long-knife.

But he only swept that banner of night black hair behind his shoulder. Then he pried at the embedded stone with the dagger's notched tip. Embarrassment warmed her cheeks as she dropped her hand and brushed needlessly at her mantle.

While he worked, she studied him. Even preoccupied with the delicate procedure, bitterness lingered around his eyes and mouth. Perhaps he was merely weary, features lined with years of privation and war. The jagged scar raking from ear to jaw contributed to his disreputable air.

Yet his hands were gentle as he handled her injured horse without aggravating the inflamed hoof.

When the stone dropped, she peered at the hoof. "'Tis only bruised, thank Heaven."

An exotic aroma wafted from his clothing—the spice of incense, heavy with musk and sandalwood. Then he released the hoof and straightened. Like a startled deer, she shied away.

"That sprint was foolish on this terrain, lady. Could have broken his neck—or yours."

He echoed her own thoughts, yet it vexed her to hear him say it.

"I know what I am about, monsieur. This path is familiar to me."

"No doubt." His eyes narrowed. "But reckless all the same, and you know it."

Did he speak of more than her ill-conceived flight? Had he discerned her identity, that day on the tourney field?

"I am bold, perhaps." She tucked ribbons of hair beneath her hood. "But rarely reckless. There is a difference."

His own hair slithered forward, decadent and unconstrained, as he slid a practiced hand along the stallion's leg. "You're no empty-headed sparrow, a woman of your station."

A dangerous thought, if he is Henry's man.

Briskly, she gathered her reins. "Pray do not concern yourself on my account. You need not forgo your hunt. I shall return to the castle on foot so my horse sustains no greater damage."

When he did not spring to obey, she added, "I know the way, so you need not linger."

Abruptly he straightened, shaking back that profligate hair. The bird startled into flight, a flurry of black wings and beak as it raked away. When the knight claimed her reins, apprehension spiked through her. She stared at his hand: sun bronzed, long fingered, rough with use—a fighting man's hand beyond question, deadly yet graceful, like the man himself.

"You bid me come and go like a stripling page," he said with dangerous softness. "Best not become accustomed to it."

Prickling with unease, she pondered her situation. Stranded in the wood with only a lame horse and this rogue for company, and darkness coming on. And his presence was no coincidence, she knew it. An intensity lurked beneath his brusqueness that sharpened all her instincts to tingling alert.

She edged her tone with the frosty courtesy of an earl's daughter. "I am no common maid, so witless as to lose myself in the forest a mere league from home. I *can* return without assistance, I assure you."

"I don't make the mistake of thinking you common."

"Well, then—"

"You can't make the castle on foot before dark. When you don't, the alarm will be raised. They'll call me to find you anyway, aye?"

Her practical mind acknowledged his logic, but his lack of enthusiasm made her speak tartly.

"God save me from a chivalrous man."

"Don't delude yourself." His voice turned harsh. "I'm the devil—or have you forgotten?"

She could not like his abrasive tone. But verily, she had no desire to wander these woods after dark without her sword or Remus to ward her. Grudgingly, she yielded.

"If you insist upon it, I suppose you may walk with me."

"Show more wit than that," he muttered. "My horse can carry two."

Misgiving bloomed as she eyed the black stallion, who sidled and rolled his eyes as the knight tethered her dappled gray behind. *'Tis that horse who is the devil, if you ask me.* As if he heard her thoughts, the beast bared his square teeth at her.

She eyed the high saddle—not that she feared the horse, though she held the beast in healthy respect. But the thought of sharing a saddle with his rider!

Reading her expression, the Raven hoisted mocking eyebrows. "Never say you're frightened."

"There is no horse living that frightens me, even this ugly brute. What is he called?"

"Lucifer." The Raven captured her in his arms.

How had she ever thought him cold? The heat of a stoked fire burned in him beneath his layers of fur and wool. The musky sweetness of incense surrounded her as he swung her effortlessly through the air—and she no slip of a girl like the court beauties—and settled her in the saddle.

She swung a leg across to ride astride. Slitted skirts parted to reveal her knees, sheathed in woolen hose above her boots, before she tugged her skirts into place. Diligently she avoided looking down at him.

"Fie, monsieur! I do believe you encourage these dark rumors that swirl around you."

"Fear can be useful." He swung up behind her.

She strained forward to allow him room, but could not avoid sliding back against him. Sinuous legs, clad in leather chausses, closed around Lucifer's flanks. His arms wrapped around her to catch the reins.

Breathless, she found her back pressed against his disconcerting chest—while her derriere snugged against the apex of his thighs. Desperate to terminate that scandalous contact, she gripped the pommel and hauled herself forward.

"Careful." His warm breath brushed her temple. "You wouldn't fancy a spill. The horse would be . . . discomfited to find you under his hooves."

"No less than I." Her voice came out husky, which she hoped he would not notice.

She could almost hear his mighty heart beating—a steady rhythm, unfaltering as the march of time. He possessed an impressive physique, there was no denying that. Whatever else he was, the man was no weakling. His nearness sparked a frenzy of emotion she'd learned to wall away: panic, desperation, an odd euphoria.

"Stop struggling," he said hoarsely into her fallen hair. "You'll upset the animal."

Which one? Striving to collect her wits, she said the first thing that came into her head.

"What happened to your voice?"

For a heartbeat he stilled. The entire forest held its breath.

"Does it bother you to speak of it?" She fumbled. "You may forgo the question. I—I should not have asked."

"Nay." He kneed his stallion onto the frozen stream, with Galahad crunching along behind. "But I'm rarely asked. Happened long ago, near Antioch. I fought for Henry in those days . . . saving the Holy Land from the infidel." Mockery twisted his words. "Heard of Greek fire?"

"Who has not?" She shivered, and he tossed the heavy sweep of his cloak around her as Lucifer heaved and pitched onto the far bank.

They passed from slanting sunlight into shadow. Between the skeletal trees, the winter sky reddened toward sunset.

"Greek fire." She cleared her throat. " 'Tis a blend of quicklime and the black water that flows beneath the ground in Outremer. I have heard men speak of it."

"Aye—and sulfur." He shifted, leather creaking. "Dissolves into acid when it burns, and the fumes are poison to breathe. The Saracens used Greek fire at Antioch."

A chill struck inward, knotting her belly. *Jesus wept, the thought of him burning . . .*

"Were you—?"

"Trapped in a burning alley with my—men. Like a lack-wit I delayed, trying to save them all. I was a chivalrous fool in those days."

Loathing hardened his voice, a contempt directed inward. Compassion plucked at her heart. He had not always been an outcast, had he? Perhaps he'd even claimed some semblance of honor once. He must have sworn a knight's vows, to uphold God's will, to defend the innocent and shelter the weak.

"Did you save them?" she whispered. "Your men?"

"The flames spread too swiftly. Thank your God on bended knee you've not seen the horrors of crusade. Captives staked out under the burning sun for torments no living thing should endure. Tongues torn out for calling Allah by the wrong name. Living men consumed by flames no water can quench, that cling to a man's skin and burn till death is a mercy."

"How did you escape?"

Was that how Theobold had died? Benedict had never told her, and would not speak of it when she asked. So it must be some horror—

"I turned coward." His arms hardened to bands of steel around her. "Scurried like a rat through the flames, wrapped in a wet blanket. Noble image, aye? But I couldn't avoid breathing the fumes."

"God's mercy!" Appalled, she swallowed down the compassionate phrases that gathered on her tongue, knowing he would rebuff them. "You were fortunate to survive."

"Oh, aye—*fortunate*." His jaw clenched, muscle flexing beneath golden skin. In that moment she glimpsed his iron discipline, the fierce restraint that held his demons at bay. "I survived when my—when others did not. Didn't seem so fortunate then."

Not knowing how to respond, she turned away. That

glimpse of inner strength sat poorly with what she knew of the lecher who'd dishonored her cousin.

She gathered her nerve. "May I ask another question?"

"Ask—on one condition."

"What condition is that?"

"For every question I answer, you'll answer one of mine."

Her skin tingled. There were some questions she would not wish to answer, but retreat would be cowardly. He was the one with secrets she must unearth, by the queen's command, to get at the truth of him—if she could.

"That is fair, if you will answer honestly," she said.

"Want honesty, do you? So certain you're prepared to hear it?"

"I have naught to fear. Do you?" She turned to watch his face. "Truly now—what happened between you and Rohese?"

"I'm no saint." Black humor threaded his voice. "Wasn't Augustine the one prayed for chastity . . . later in life, but not yet?"

Curiously, she felt disappointed. Though why she'd expected more from this rogue she could not imagine.

"So you did accost her, just as she claimed. 'Tis a pity God did not see fit to unseat you at the tourney and prove your perfidy."

"Lady Rohese is a hot piece." He fired the words like crossbow bolts, as if to wound her—or himself.

"Monsieur, you are despicable." Bitterly, she stared ahead into gathering twilight.

"I'd no notion who she was. The lady was veiled—another damned masque—but she made her desires clear."

"No true knight would say such words." She blinked back the sting of tears. Lies . . . he was lying to her. What else had she expected?

"By the Prophet, that's the truth." More angry than amused, his laughter scraped against her ear. "When we were found, the fine lady cried rape. With my reputation, what use denying it?"

"Do you say my cousin, a good and virtuous lady, encouraged your attentions? I thought we had sworn to honesty—but I should have known better than to accept your word."

"Accept it or nay." His mouth twisted. "No other would defend her."

"They were all afraid of you!" she cried.

"Save one." His eyes scorched her. "You're a trusting innocent, lady, where those you love are concerned."

An image of Marguerite seared across her brain: twisted and broken, repudiated by the husband she adored. Weeping as she pleaded innocence to her horrified daughter.

Alienore had sworn that she believed her—and she had believed, she had—but Theobold had not. Marguerite had taken months to die. Then her father took the cross and thundered off with Benedict . . . leaving his daughter alone.

And a year later Theobold was dead, lying in an unmarked grave somewhere in the burning sands before he ever reached Jerusalem. And her own brother had not seen fit to tell her. Until the day she died, Alienore would wonder if her father had warned Benedict not to trust her. *Like mother, like daughter?*

"Your turn to be honest," the Raven said. "What knight rode against me?"

Caught flat-footed, she floundered to gather her wits. Her first shameful impulse was to lie, and hide her secret. *The queen will dismiss me from the council in disgrace. I have nowhere else to go . . .*

If she lied, she would be no better than he. So she turned and met his gaze.

"Do you not already know?"

"Allah's heart, it *was* you. Couldn't bring myself to believe it."

Gripping the pommel, she braced to withstand whatever

he flung at her—raucous laughter, threats, blackmail? No other man save one knew her secret, and now she revealed it to *him*?

"Little fool! I could have killed you." He pushed out a breath. "Why?"

"Why what?" She turned away. "Why did I take the field? Honor required it. There was no one else."

"The girl's honor? She has none."

"My mother's honor!" Heat flamed in her cheeks. "Rohese is her sister's child."

"Why take on a knight's training? And who dared teach you? Can't credit your Lancelot with that."

She flushed at his scornful reference to Thierry. "I believe 'tis my turn for a question."

Over the path, the shadows were deepening, violet against pale blue snow. In the distance, a lynx's angry scream tore through the fabric of twilight. She shivered, grateful she was not relegated to a solitary walk home after all.

Firmly, she recalled herself to duty. Eleanor had thrown them together to discern the knight's motives. "Why did you come to Poitiers?"

"The queen's fugitive son thought she could use a man with my . . . talents."

Aye, he is hiding something.

"But you are no English vassal," she countered. "You are a mercenary who sells his sword to the highest bidder. Why did *you* come to Poitiers?"

"Why do you think? Henry sent me. Wanted another set of eyes and ears to spy on his treasonous wife. Can you blame him?"

Saint Swithun grant mercy, the queen is right to be wary.

She had expected him to dodge the matter, even to lie outright. She'd never expected honesty, no matter what he'd sworn. Why entrust her, of all women, with such a dangerous truth? Unless he was lying still.

"What did you do to gain the prince's trust?" she asked.

"My turn for a question."

"Very well then," she said, eager to get past his query to her own. "Ask."

Through her loosened hair, his breath licked her ear, tendrils of sensation unfurling all through her. The odor of sandalwood made her head swim.

"Your inheritance lies before Henry, aye?" He paused for her assent. "So does your brother's counterclaim. Yet he's not suspected of treason. What'll you do if Henry takes his part and bids you marry Ormonde?"

Hugging herself, she stared over Lucifer's head into the gathering dark. "Marriage to such a man would mean the ultimate disgrace. I could not enter into such a travesty and remain my father's daughter."

"But if your king commands it? Or your queen?"

Visions of disaster multiplied in her brain. Her father had thought her unworthy and left her behind to mourn her unworthy mother. But she would prove herself worthy of Wishing Stone Manor—prove she was not Marguerite. Surely, even beyond the grave, her father would know it.

"Neither king nor queen could command me to dishonor. I would fight rather than flee—this time."

"Some would say you speak treason," he whispered. Such a dangerous word, even borne on a breath in the wild.

"Then let them kill me," she whispered. "What would I have to live for?"

His hands clenched the reins as if to hold her back from that fatal course. He turned his face into her hair. "Alienore—"

As they rounded a bend in the path, a horse's startled neigh rang out. At once the Raven released her. Steel hissed as he unsheathed his scimitar, battle ready in an instant.

She gripped her long-knife. Ahead, something large crashed through the undergrowth. *That lynx we heard—but this creature is larger.* Through the trees she glimpsed a mounted figure, sunlight glinting on silver hair—oddly familiar. Then the forest swallowed him up. The rapid tattoo of hoofbeats receded.

Before them, another man waited, broadsword gleaming as he crouched in his saddle. Then he swept back his hood: Geoffrey of Brittany, Richard's unpleasant brother.

He's been meeting someone in secret. But whom? In the tumult of the hunt, one of Eleanor's eagles had flown the nest.

Though caught by surprise, the swarthy prince threw back his head and brayed with laughter.

"*Par Dieu,* what have we here? The mysterious Raven, blackguard and despoiler of women, keeping company with Lady Virtue? My brother will be devastated when I tell him."

"Your Grace," she said stiffly. "'Tis nothing of the sort. My horse was lamed in the hunt. Lord Raven is doing no more than his duty to see me returned."

"Are you so dutiful, monsieur?" Beneath his thick eyebrows, Geoffrey flashed a mocking glance. "You disguise it well."

The Raven bowed from his saddle. Yet she sensed no lessening in the battle-keen tension that gripped him. "Why are you here? So far from the hunt . . . and Sir Guy?"

The prince's eyes narrowed. "Why, like the lady, I returned with an injured mount. Can't you see the beast is limping?"

"Must be so," the Raven rasped, "if Your Grace speaks it."

She strove to defuse the tension crackling in the air. "Let us all return together, before we are missed. 'Twill be full dark soon."

"Aye, won't that set them all wondering, to see the three of us keeping company?" Geoffrey uttered a jarring laugh.

He wheeled his mount and spurred before them, the horse unhindered—so far as she could tell—by any injury. Ahead, the wood fell away to reveal the castle heights, where hidden eyes marked their return.

Chapter Five

Sleep was a cunning adversary these days. Tonight it slipped before Alienore like a mocking rival, evading every attempt at capture.

That disturbing encounter with Geoffrey of Brittany, lurking where he had no business, lingered in her mind. But the disgraced knight was a greater distraction. What had he meant, telling her outright he was spying for the king! Why should he reveal such a thing—unless to test her loyalties?

For she no longer believed the interests of the royal couple coincided. In the end, she would be forced to choose.

So, as the courtiers lingered below, roistering into the small hours, Alienore turned to her work and held it like a shield between her and her demons.

Her candle burned down to a puddle of wax; her quill scratched over parchment. Her lids were listing when the wolf lifted his head and growled.

A thundering knock rattled her door.

Startled, she sprang up, clutching her pelisse over the night rail beneath. "Who goes?"

Wood groaning like a tortured soul, the door swung inward. When she recognized Richard of Aquitaine's broad-shouldered frame, alarm tightened her chest.

At her feet, Remus rose and rumbled a warning. Just in time, she caught him by the ruff.

Richard studied the candlelit island of her writing table, floating in a sea of darkness. "What, still hard at your labors? Do you never sleep, nor romp?"

"Romping is for children, Your Grace." She wished for a

veil to cover her hair, a heathen tangle of beaten gold. But who would expect to receive a man at this hour?

The prince chuckled. "Surely even lords may romp a little, don't you think?"

He strode forward, filling the oratory with his larger-than-life presence. His surcoat billowed behind, garnets winking in russet brocade as they caught the light.

Highly improper—even scandalous—for him to visit her privy chamber alone at midnight.

"Why are you here, Your Grace? 'Tis not my habit to receive guests at this hour."

Deliberately, Richard circled the table. Remus rolled back his muzzle to bare sharp fangs. Sensing the wolf's coiled tension, she gripped his ruff harder, and the prince's eyes turned wary. Beyond range of the bared teeth, he halted.

"You refuse to appear for meals, my demoiselle. When you are enticed into company, you diligently avoid my presence. *Mon Dieu*, you slipped away from the hunt like a villain!"

"Your Grace, I never intended—"

"With any other lady, I would say you did it to beguile me." His cobalt eyes sparked. "But nay. Not Alienore of Lyonstone, the queen's most virtuous lady."

She measured his temper, the threat of his presence, the fruity bite of wine on his breath.

He was a prince of royal blood. She needed his goodwill. If his elder brother died without issue, Richard would be her king some day.

Clearing her throat, she called, "Nesta!"

After a worrisome delay, the inner door flew open to reveal the girl's sleep-fuddled features. Hastily Nesta bobbed a curtsy.

"Will ye be wantin' yer bath, milady? I—oh! Beggin' yer pardon, milord—"

"Never mind, Nesta. Pray stir the fire, and bring ale for His Grace."

As the girl bustled about, Richard eyed Alienore with dry appreciation. Perching a hip on her table, he smiled blandly and swung a booted foot.

With a sigh, Alienore locked the queen's correspondence in her strongbox.

Nesta thumped down two brimming cups of ale. "Will ye be wantin' me to take that wolf out, milady?"

"Nay, leave him. You may draw my bath, for I intend to retire shortly."

Richard waited until Nesta retreated, then leaned over Alienore with an intimate smile.

"Why not let the girl seek her bed? I'll wager you've never had a prince attend your bath."

A flood of humiliation scalded her face.

"Pray do not say such things, even in jest! 'Tis bad enough—"

"Have I shocked your convent-bred sensibilities? Surely, *ma chère*, my presence is not a complete surprise. Even you can't be quite so innocent."

"Perhaps you would be good enough to say why you have come." Grasping after her composure, she crossed to the brazier. "The hour is late, and I am weary."

"So quick to business?" His heated gaze burned her back. "Very well. Let's speak about your new champion, Lord Raven."

Now she felt grateful that he could not see her face.

"Your Grace, the Raven is no lady's champion. I suppose my lord of Brittany has mentioned our encounter."

"Aye, Geoffrey mentioned it." Her scalp crawled at the undercurrents beneath his negligent tone. "The Raven's the most notorious man at court. Innocent damsels, comely widows, young wives who've tired of the marriage bed—even the serving wenches aren't safe from him. *Mon Dieu*, have you forgotten your own cousin!"

"I have not forgotten." Rigid, she twisted her fallen hair

into a knot. But lacking any pin to hold it, the heavy mass spilled down her back again.

Aye, she knew what the Raven was—none knew better. So why should her heart sink?

"Pray do not be concerned on my account, Your Grace. No woman at court is more immune to that rogue's advances."

"Has he offered you any?" Casually, he strolled toward her.

"Of course not!" She voiced an unconvincing laugh. "If you would warn me, of all women, against falling prey to the Raven, you are wasting your breath."

"Am I?" His features shifted, became crafty. "The fellow has acquired the habit of confiding to me his conquests. Unfortunately your virtue . . . your chastity . . . has piqued his interest."

"'Tis not my virtue that interests him." Distracted, she'd allowed Richard to trap her before the brazier. Now she tried to edge around him. Hooking an idle hand in his sword belt, he shifted to prevent it.

She raised her chin and met his gaze. "Surely your lady mother has confided her suspicions? The Raven is the king's man, no more than another spy sent to watch her. Indeed, he admits as much. I—I plan to inform the queen tomorrow."

Aye, tomorrow. Surely it could wait until then, though she could not fathom her reluctance. Surely the Raven had known she meant to do it.

"Is it so?" His eyes narrowed. "*Avoi*, two can play at this game."

"What game is that?"

"Alienore, my sheltered innocent! He's told me outright—the man has no shame. He intends to add you to his list of conquests. And when I scorned him for thinking you'd submit to his tawdry advances, he offered me a wager."

"A wager?" A seed of coldness sprouted within her.

"He wagered he'd have you in his bed. Of course I declined to wager against a lady's good name. Yet nothing I said could dissuade him."

That cold seed broke open and flowered into fury—and a maddening sense of disappointment.

"I—I see," she said faintly.

She'd been a fool to think the Raven's interest was almost honorable, if the king himself commanded it. To hear instead all her worst suspicions confirmed, she seethed with righteous wrath. How she burned to hunt down that villain in whatever den of depravity he wallowed and vent her outrage upon his head!

"I should never have told you, *ma chère*, but I feared the knave was worming his way into your affections. Forgive me?"

"Of course." She fixed him with unwavering eyes. "I am grateful to you for telling me."

He captured her hands in his sword-hardened grip. Though he was a tall man, he needed barely to look down to meet her gaze.

"You know what they call you, Alienore—all those spurned suitors? The snow maiden, the ice queen. Idiots, every man of them."

"I have no spurned suitors, Your Grace." Seeking freedom, her hands stirred in his. "What would I bring to any marriage, with my inheritance in dispute?"

"Ever the diplomat," he chided. "You may lower your shield of words for me. I'll protect you."

"You are kind." Uncomfortable, she lowered her gaze to their locked hands, her pale fingers trapped in his sunburned paws.

She'd guarded against such intimacies all her life, from the day she'd seen the ruin a woman's passions had caused Marguerite and all those who loved her. The day her mother died, a victim of her own carnality, Alienore had sworn she would never give way to those treacherous passions herself.

"I would be more than kind, Alienore."

A man's passion, God save me—precisely the situation I prayed to avoid.

"Your Grace," she whispered. "Pray do not do this."

"I can no longer keep silent!" Agitation spiked as he slid a muscled arm around her waist and drew her against his hard body. "Don't you know I'm mad with love for you?"

Love? She all but snorted. Perhaps he desired her— Richard of Aquitaine desired everything in skirts, for an hour at least. For a dangerous moment she almost said it out loud. Instead, she fumbled for tact.

"This is an . . . honor . . . I had not looked for. I—You are betrothed to the princess of France—"

"Alys of France is a child. She is a crude vessel of beaten bronze, while you are the Holy Grail, holding the very waters of life! And I am a desert wanderer who longs to immerse himself in you—"

"Jesus wept, Richard!" Her temper slipped. She was an earl's daughter, not some wine girl to be wooed with silly love talk. "Are you mad, or merely drunk?"

"I am drunk with love."

Straining against his hot grip, she pushed against his chest—to no avail. "I protest being handled so intimately. Release me!"

"That chilly facade is cracking, *chérie*." His wine-scented breath washed over her. "I may be your king one day. What harm can there be in a kiss?"

Behind him Remus barked, almost drowning out the brisk rap on her door. Relief and panic warred as she struggled to push the prince away.

"Richard, there is someone—"

"Ignore it," he breathed, eyes clouded with lust. "Your future king commands it."

Remus launched toward the door. Desperate to escape this absurd dilemma, she called, "Enter!"

Majestically the door sailed open to admit Eleanor of Aquitaine, resplendent in crimson velvet over cloth of gold. To Alienore's profound gratitude, her sovereign was unescorted. The fewer eyes to witness this ridiculous tableau, the fewer tongues would wag later.

"Madam, you are most welcome." Pushing free of Richard's startled arms, Alienore sank to a curtsy, her spine rigid.

"It seems so." Gliding inside, the queen swept the door closed. She stroked Remus as the wolf sniffed her skirts, and lifted her eyebrows toward Richard. "*Carissime*, I must say I had not anticipated finding you here."

"Would you believe we were discussing our alliance with the Count of Flanders?" With a grin, Richard bowed over his mother's hand.

"If indeed you were, with a woman of Alienore's beauty, you must have ice water running through your veins in place of hot young blood." The queen's cat green eyes glinted. "Alienore, my dear, be at ease. Your secret amour is safe with me."

Alienore cast an aggrieved look at Richard, who grinned back amiably.

"Madam, allow me to arrange—"

"Stay, my dear." The queen lifted a slender hand. "I have not descended upon you at this hour for pleasure. I am sorely troubled by a matter of grave importance."

"Indeed?" A prickle of premonition crawled down her nape.

"Privy chancellor, I require your aid."

"Of course," Alienore said, her stomach sinking. Already she walked a tightrope between king and queen. On either side, the threat of treason yawned. A misstep would cost her inheritance, or her life. But she was Eleanor's sworn servant, not a fair-weather friend.

"I am yours to command as ever, Your Grace."

Smiling, the queen caressed her cheek. "You are a beacon of constancy on these troubled seas."

Lounging on the table, Richard quaffed his ale. "Mother, what troubles you?"

Evidently, no matter how imperative the need for secrecy, Eleanor did not consider the matter unsuited for Richard's ears. Of the ten children she'd borne two kings over her remarkable lifetime, this second son was her undoubted favorite. Richard would inherit Aquitaine—the land of her birth, her greatest love.

"Your Grace." Alienore reached for her quill. "How may I serve you?"

Standing before the brazier, the queen warmed her hands. "I must send an urgent message to the King of Castile."

"To King Alfonso? What matter could require—? Wait . . ." Alienore's thoughts raced. "Does this concern the marriage negotiations underway between England and Castile?"

"By good Saint Thibault, you are a blessing to me, for I need not spell out my intentions in child's words. My petite Aenor has seen her twelfth birthday and is quite prepared to make this match. Yet it seems that my husband intends to refuse Alfonso."

"Refuse him?" Alienore stared. "When you have been planning this for years?"

Bitterly the queen smiled. "Henry will insult the King of Castile for no better reason than that I support the match. He would see another hostile kingdom bristling on Aquitaine's doorstep."

"But if King Henry opposes the match—"

"I merely wish to assure Castile, in secret, that this is a negotiating gambit, and so preserve the alliance until my husband alters his course."

Alienore studied her sovereign's lined features. Outside, the castle had fallen silent, as if the entire world had sunk into an enchanted sleep. Darkness pressed against her ice-rimed window. Richard was scowling into his cup, no doubt disconsolate to have his wooing interrupted.

Why should her nape prickle with this sense of looming menace? She studied her queen, those green eyes gleaming with secrets.

"My dear," the queen murmured, "you are the only friend I dare trust with this delicate matter. You must travel to Alfonso with all haste and arrive before Henry's messenger. *Depardieu*, we dare not lose a single day! You must ride at once."

Alienore's sense of danger deepened. She had performed a dozen such missions—though never to a land as distant and dangerous as war-torn Castile. Every bovate of soil from Barcelona to Gibraltar was well watered with crusader blood.

Of course she would have her sword, her escort and Remus to see her safe. Still, her instincts whispered, *Be wary.*

"Your Grace, 'tis a matter of state. Perhaps Sieur de la Haie or, indeed, your ambassador to the court of Castile might—"

"Nay, for they are watched." The queen sighed. "I lied to you when I said Henry acted from spite. In fact, he has embarked upon a systematic effort to strip Aquitaine of its allies. He intends to divorce me and see me locked behind convent walls."

"Oh, Your Grace!" Dismay for her sovereign swamped Alienore's qualms. "You are the most powerful queen in Christendom—and he has always held you in abiding affection. He would never divorce you."

"He loved me once, when I was young and beautiful." Eleanor smiled, her expression bittersweet. "But Henry is eleven years younger than I—a man in the very prime of life. Now he has his English mistress, the fair Rosamund, for love. I must deal in fact rather than fiction, no matter how . . . unpalatable those facts may be."

Alienore floundered in an ugly tide of memory. Marguerite had feared Theobold would divorce her, merely on suspicion of infidelity. But in the end he had only ignored her as she languished, until she died of heartbreak.

"Madam, I will . . . undertake the matter, if no other counselor will suit. Whom shall I trust for escort?"

"Aquitaine's best fighting men shall protect you. I have asked Lord Raven to attend to the matter personally."

Alienore's head snapped up. Richard leaped up, cursing.

"Nay, Mother, not him! Send some other knight. Send her so-called champion, Thierry de Beaumont—"

"The Raven is the most formidable knight in Poitiers," the queen said coolly. "While Thierry de Beaumont is a child with a pretty sword—I am sorry, Alienore, but that is the truth. A monarch cannot allow personal feelings to interfere with sound judgment, Richard."

"*Mon Dieu*, don't you know the Raven is a spy for my father!"

"I have known that since the day he arrived." Eleanor of Aquitaine stared him down. "It relieves me that you have finally discovered it as well. Ridding Poitiers of his watchful eye will further serve our purpose. The Raven will know nothing of where she goes, or why, until it is far too late to warn Henry."

Alienore cleared her throat, and drew two pairs of angry eyes.

"Madam, I am your servant, but . . . I would prefer some other escort. The Raven is no man of yours, and I fear his intentions may not be—honorable."

"Aye!" Richard cried. "He'll rape her in her bed. Look what befell her cousin!"

"Enough," the queen said. "I have made my decision and need not justify it to anyone. The Raven will lead this party, and I have instructed him to that effect. Alienore will meet him near the postern gate at Matins with a sealed missive for Castile's eyes alone."

For the first time, Alienore felt a surge of anger toward the queen who had sheltered her. Still, though this missive came perilously near treason, she could never deny Eleanor in her hour of need.

Besides, 'tis a family matter, not truly an affair of state.

Yet this decision to entrust the Raven with her safety, despite his reputation, infuriated her. She struggled to swallow down her wrath.

"Your Grace, it shall be as you say."

"There's my good and faithful girl." Ignoring Richard, the queen clasped Alienore's cold hands. "I shall not forget your loyalty, my dear. When my time comes, I shall personally sign the writ of seisin that confirms your inheritance. This I swear by good Saint Thibault. Trust in me."

"I trust in you as I trust in God." Unfortunately, she had little choice. Eleanor had become her only port in the tempest that swirled around her.

By placing her under the Raven's uncertain protection on this mission some men would call treason, she hoped the queen had not thrown her to the wolves . . . or the Plantagenet lions.

Chapter Six

The scene was like a hellish inferno, a page torn from the volume of memory the Raven would have closed forever—if he could. Bloody torchlight flared on the curtain wall and flung a ragged cloak of shadows over the bailey. Fog roiled against ice-rimmed flagstones, making the footing treacherous, as he led Lucifer toward the postern gate.

Poitiers, not Damascus, damn it. He forced clenched muscles to relax.

A secret mission of the utmost urgency, the queen's message said. By the Prophet, this business was utter madness. The postern guard, the stable lads, any early-risen lover stealing from his lady's boudoir, could glimpse them. A single careless word would alert the queen's enemies and loose Henry's bloodhounds on their heels.

Still, he couldn't turn down this double opportunity: to woo Alienore and serve his king.

A flurry of panic erupted among the horses as a streak of white fur loped across the bailey. Behind the wolf, a tall woman strode through the billowing fog, steel flashing at her belt. Briefly he glimpsed a pale oval face crowned by wheat gold hair, before she raised her hood.

Even without the wolf, he would have known her anywhere. *Alienore.*

When Lucifer's restless hooves struck sparks against the flagstones, her head swiveled toward them.

"My lady." The Raven sketched a bow. "Another chance to serve you."

Within the hood, her steel gray eyes speared through

him. What the devil? He'd done her a good turn yesterday. Now she all but froze his balls with this scornful look.

"How fortunate for you," she said coldly, sweeping past with her head high. *Dismissing me again like a bloody page.* Grimly he stalked after her.

Ignoring him, she strode toward the squire who held the mare the Raven had chosen. "Where is my Galahad?"

"Too lame to be hard ridden, milady." The squire ducked his shaggy head. "He'll be right as rain in a day or two."

"Of course. I had forgotten." She managed a reassuring smile for the anxious lad. "I am grateful for your good care, Luke."

The boy reddened with pleasure—clearly besotted with her, like every other man at court.

The Raven felt irritated, for no reason he cared to explore. "We should make haste. Where's your tiring girl?"

"Terrified of horses," she said dryly. "I travel without servants upon the queen's business."

"I'm told we ride south but not why." He tossed his reins to the squire and braced to help her mount. "Enlighten me."

"In due time." Ignoring his extended hand, she sprang into the saddle with a knight's assurance. He caught a searing glimpse of her long legs, encased in boots and woolen hose, before she swept her skirts into place.

Left standing empty-handed like a lackwit, he peered sharply into her averted features. Then Lucifer sidled and rolled his eyes at the strange squire, which commanded his attention. Swishing her tail, the lady's palfrey stood placid.

"Could you not have found me a proper rouncy?" she demanded. "This pretty-mannered mare will be eating your Lucifer's dust all the way to Castile."

Castile! Has the queen run mad?

"This mare's sound winded and steady." He kept his tone level.

Alienore responded with a skeptical snort. An unexpected grin tugged at his lips, though this was surely no time for levity. He cast an eye over her confident seat, then sprang into Lucifer's saddle. With a practiced sweep, he freed his scimitar from his cloak.

"You'd do well to divulge our mission, lady. Else we charge blind into peril."

"You were not my choice of escort, but the queen's." She prodded her drowsy palfrey. "If she did not see fit to trust you, I cannot see how I may."

He frowned at her obvious suspicion. Were he another man, he would have said it wounded him. But he never allowed himself an emotional response to any woman, beyond the brief sparking passion of a night's release. He was not fool enough to break his rule for her sake.

"'Tis your safety, not Eleanor's, at risk," he pointed out. "Reconsider."

"I shall think upon it." Noncommittal, she urged her palfrey toward the gate.

His niggling unease sharpened. Something was sore amiss—had set her on guard against him. Scowling, he raked the battlements with a keen eye.

Nearby waited the man-at-arms he'd chosen to accompany them: a sturdy bearded soldier of middle years named Owain, with a steady hand and eye. Now the man bent from his saddle to instruct the porter, the queen's silver gleaming as it changed hands.

The gate swung open, revealing the black tunnel that burrowed through the wall and a glimpse of snowy forest. Eagerly the wolf bounded into that dark maw.

Hoofbeats rang on the flagstones. A stern voice ordered, "Hold!"

Alienore pivoted the palfrey, long-knife flashing free in her fist. Alarm spurting through him, the Raven wheeled his destrier and unsheathed his scimitar with a hiss.

Behind them, a mounted figure filled the bailey, armor glinting under a surcoat rich with malachite and copper thread. Allah's heart, he knew that horse—the half-trained beast that nearly unseated Alienore at the tourney.

"Thierry?" she said in disbelief.

On the bare edge of attack, the Raven reined in with a muttered curse.

"By my faith, monsieur!" the lady exclaimed. "What are you about?"

"Prince Richard honored me with his trust," the boy said proudly. "As your champion, my lady, I claim the right to join your defenders on this mission."

Damn it to hell—this was all they needed. The Raven sheathed his sword, steel rasping against leather. "It's a foray through hostile terrain, boy, not some game of chivalry. Go back to bed."

"Monsieur, I will not!" Thierry's nostrils flared with outrage. "I intend to join this party with your consent or without it. I am son to the Comte de Beaumont. I do not come or go by any man's leave."

"Ah," the Raven growled. "That's the problem, aye? Queen gave me command of this party. I'll suffer no man in it who can't follow orders."

While he wasted precious time bantering with this boy-knight, the Raven's gaze swept the heights. Etched against the starry heavens, a sentry paced. The castle's darkened windows peered out like lidless eyes, watching them. Every instinct he possessed shrilled the need for haste.

Beaumont said with heat, "I am here at His Grace's own behest—"

Impatient, Alienore flung back her hood.

Now she'll send the boy packing.

"I forbid the two of you to waste any more time upon this foolish quarrel," she said. "'Tis my desire that Sieur de Beaumont join our party."

The Raven stiffened, feeling an absurd sense of betrayal. And it would be bloody inconvenient to his own designs if the lady's besotted puppy trailed after them all the way to Castile.

Grimly, the Raven turned toward her. "Decision's not yours to make."

She straightened in the saddle, every inch an earl's proud daughter. "I am the queen's privy chancellor, about the queen's own business. That gives me all the authority I require—"

"Not so much noise and racket, if ye please," Owain urged from the shadows. "We're in a bad place just here. If ye must argue, ye can do it as we ride."

Clearly recognizing the wisdom of this advice, she subsided. The Raven eyed Thierry's defiant features. The lad was not entirely feckless with his blade. Maybe he would be of some use if they met trouble on the road.

"Very well, puppy," he growled. "You join this party on one condition—you'll obey me on the road. I'll have your oath on it."

He paused as the younger man bristled. "Find that not to your liking, Beaumont, I'll settle this another way—and leave you trussed like a Yule goose for the guard. Choose quickly."

Striving to stare him down, Beaumont's gaze locked with his. The Raven all but rolled his eyes at this absurd display, but held the look with his own burning gaze.

The lad's eyes flickered and slid away. "For my lady's sake, I swear it."

"Good. Be sure you don't forget."

Wheeling Lucifer, he spurred his stallion through the tunnel. Capably, Alienore pivoted her mount and loped after him. Behind them, Beaumont cursed and struggled with his half-trained charger. But his hooves soon clattered in pursuit.

* * *

A misty sunrise found them south of Poitiers, winding through a thicket of trees. Despite their stealthy departure, Alienore could not dismiss the disquiet that gnawed at her, nor dispel the prickling at her nape.

Remus appeared and vanished in the fog with unnerving suddenness, inspiring fits of panic from her timid palfrey. Still, it comforted her to think of the wolf's keen senses warding her. Remus would warn them if anyone followed.

Locked in tight-jawed silence, they picked their way along trails the Raven had chosen. Thierry, still petulant after his earlier setdown, trailed behind. Despite his sulks, she was grateful for his presence—one more safeguard between her and the Raven.

Their path zagged across a clearing. Barely visible against the snow, the wolf bounded after a flash of russet fur, but the fox dove into its burrow. As the Raven rode beside her across the open ground, she thought he too felt uneasy, exposed to hostile eyes. Beneath a roof of steel gray clouds, the black speck of a bird drifted.

"The wolf appears well trained," he murmured. "Is he biddable when danger threatens?"

"Usually." She managed an indifferent tone. "I must approve your vigilance, I suppose, since you are my so-called defender on the road."

"I *will* defend you—be sure of that." The dark purpose in his voice raised goose bumps along her skin.

"Pray do not concern yourself," she said curtly. "Remus is the best protector I could possibly have."

His gaze searched her, intimate as fingers grazing her face. No doubt he suspected something was amiss. Aye, Richard's ugly revelation had wounded her, but she would never give the Raven the satisfaction of knowing it. Instead she watched the wolf as he bounded off, chasing another elusive scent.

"Why does a wolf heed a woman's hand?" the Raven asked.
She felt reluctant to tell him anything, to place the weapon
of knowledge into his hands. But she could not avoid answer-
ing without deplorable rudeness. At length she spoke, be-
grudging every word.

"After my mother . . . died, and my father rode off on
crusade, I passed many hours roaming the forest. One day I
found a wolf pup, abandoned in its den."

"Abandoned? That's not common, from what I know of
wolves."

"I cannot be certain, but I believe he was outcast due to
his unusual coloring." She smiled without humor. "Wolves
are like people, monsieur. They do not abide one who stands
out from the pack.

"I brought the pup home, and why not? At fourteen I was
chatelaine of my own estates. I trained Remus by my own
hand, but he heeds me from love."

Beneath drooping lids, his gaze tracked her. "Belike you
were much alone."

Her heart contracted with the old familiar pain. Aye,
she'd been alone, and desperately lonely. Through four
long years, she'd had only a wolf and a crippled old man for
company. But those years of solitude had forged her steel
in the fire of determination, honed her resolve to prove her
worth.

Then Benedict had returned, with his wrenching tidings.
Theobold lay in his grave these four years past. She could
never prove her worth to her father now.

"I was alone in those years." To hide her sorrow, she turned
away. "All told, I preferred that to the convent where I dwelled
before, where for six years straight I was never once my own
mistress."

Ah, but I will reveal too much if I speak of that—my barren
cell, the everlasting bread-and-water fasts, the night-long vigils

*when the wine froze solid in the chalice, and the rod when I dis-
pleased them.*

She flicked a glance over her shoulder to Beaumont, still
glowering at the Raven's back. "Come up, Thierry. We will
be long on the road—let us not pass the time in anger."

Thierry spurred his charger, snow flying as he drew up
alongside. Inscrutable, the Raven yielded his place.

Thierry cast him a triumphant glance. "My lady, I have
had a revelation. I am planning how to regain your lands."

Like a dagger, the hard edge of the black knight's regard
pierced her. Her skin tingled a warning she did not understand.

"By my faith, Thierry, I should be grateful for any advice, for
the matter weighs upon my mind. I have had no response from
my petitions to the king."

The gallant brushed a golden curl out of his eyes, all youthful earnestness and resolve. *Still my Lancelot,* she thought
fondly. With God's grace, that would never change.

"My lady understands the difficulty in raising an army to
retake your manor. Are you still denied all income from
your estates?"

"Aye." She disliked discussing her penury in the Raven's
hearing. The queen paid her wages and gifted her generously,
but accepting largesse from Eleanor's coffers always smacked
of charity in her mind.

"I will not raise arms against my brother, Thierry. He is
not evil-hearted. I am certain I can persuade Benedict to do
what is right—if only that cunning serpent of a counselor
were not rearing up between us."

"Indeed, my lady. Sir Bors of Bedingfield is the crux of
your dilemma. 'Tis remarkable a nobleman like your brother
would show such deference to a commoner."

She defended her younger brother from habit. "When my
father fell, fighting the Saracens, Benedict was left alone in

a strange and terrifying land—until Bors befriended him. 'Tis easy to influence a grieving child."

"Never fear, my lady," Thierry declared. "I intend to challenge Sir Bors to single combat."

Behind them, the Raven chuffed out an impatient breath. Her sinking sense of disappointment took her aback. Hadn't she always admired Thierry's pure ideals, his adherence to the code of chivalry? If it rendered him impractical—even naive—should she blame him?

"I am afraid you do not know Sir Bors." Gamely, she swallowed her disillusionment. "He is a sly and subtle creature who would find some pretext to refuse a fair fight."

If I thought he would not, I would challenge him myself.

"But his refusal would brand him a coward! As your champion—as your own Lancelot—I vow to challenge him."

The Raven snorted. "I wouldn't recommend it, puppy. This so-called knight has an unwholesome repute. Poisons his blades. Let him but scratch you, and you'd die in lingering agony."

"Par Dieu!" Thierry flung back his head. "What would a mercenary know about an affair of honor?"

"I know death," the Raven growled. "Saw Bedingfield's work in Outremer. I'd wish it on no man—not even you."

The frightened whispers of her brother's servants hissed through her brain. They had fled Lyonstone one by one, in terror of their new steward.

" 'Tis whispered Sir Bors keeps a laboratory of lethal acids and toxins," she said, "atop his tower in Lyonstone Keep. 'Tis said his chambers crawl with serpents and spiders and other unholy creatures. He calls himself an alchemist—but my brother's serfs said worse."

"Called him a witch, no doubt," the Raven said.

"Aye, they claimed he was a warlock, with the devil's own favor." She crossed herself against evil. *And this is the viper*

Benedict clutches to his breast! "Bedingfield's presence at Lyonstone is my fault. Had I been stronger . . ."

"Can't see how it's your fault." The Raven spurred Lucifer to her side.

Reluctance gripped her throat like a fist, bottling up the painful memories. But the words broke through, fired by years of resentment.

"When Benedict returned bearing news of my father's death, I—took to my bed. He was four years dead, monsieur, and I'd never known. Never spoken a prayer nor lit a candle to ease his passing. Never paid for a single Mass to keep his soul. He took everything when he left me—even the right to mourn him."

She clenched her teeth over the flow of words, appalled by her own passion.

"By the time I recovered, my brother had installed Sir Bors as his steward. Fearing Benedict acted rashly, I protested the appointment. He knew nothing of his estates after four years on crusade. But I should have saved my breath."

"But you spoke—making you Bors's enemy." Comprehension glittered in the Raven's gaze. "He sold you to Ponce to be rid of you."

"I appealed to the king to uphold my claim, asked him for a writ yielding Wishing Stone Manor to me. But the Duc d'Ormonde moved too quickly." Memories of that night made her stomach twist. "I was awaiting the king's response when the duke arrived, eager to behold his betrothed."

"My lady had no recourse," Thierry said earnestly, "but to flee for Aquitaine and petition the queen—her godmother."

But she had never told any man what else transpired that night.

"If you will not allow me to challenge him," Thierry added, "I'll petition King Henry on your behalf. My father has some influence at court."

"Bah!" The Raven's mouth twisted. "Is that your best effort? Your lady relies on you."

She struggled to contain a spurt of annoyance—unfair to her shining Lancelot, who was doing his best. "I have already petitioned him twice, Thierry. I appreciate your willingness to champion me, but I do not see how your effort can do more than annoy the king.

"Besides"—she forced a smile—"I have need of you here."

Still circling against the lead gray clouds, a bird cawed. A raven, was it, who tracked them all this way? Reflexively she glanced behind her, across the snowy field.

The black knight spurred Lucifer to a canter. "We should make haste. With luck, we'll overtake the road to Angoulême. Our twisting course may foil pursuit."

But they'd been too exposed when they departed, and Sir Guy had shown himself to be no fool. Let word of her mission reach Henry's ears and her lands were as good as lost.

Alienore spurred her horse—as if by speed alone she could outrace her fate.

Darkness pressed down on them like a restraining hand. They were stumbling over the treacherous ground by the time they found the road. With a bitter wind howling down from the north, they hurried along until they found what the Raven sought: the blackened shell of a barrel-vaulted church, its door rotted and fallen away. Walls and a roof remained to shelter them.

Around the apse where the altar had stood, the faded frescoes of saints and angels stared in silence. Alienore's conscience twinged in protest to use this holy place for common lodging. But surely, this church had been deconsecrated long ago. Their habitation would be uncomfortable, but hardly sacrilege.

As she stood blowing on her frozen hands, a flurry of black wings fluttered through the door and perched on the roof beam. Wary, she eyed the unholy bird—a raven—as it groomed its feathers. The black knight produced a handful of seeds from his pouch and scattered them. Immediately, the bird flapped down to peck at them.

She unclenched her chattering teeth. "'Tis your creature then?"

"Not mine, but he follows me." He hoisted the saddle from Lucifer's back. "I call him Mehmet."

"'Tis a heathen name." Thierry crossed himself. "Such a bird is a black omen—a harbinger of evil. We should feather him for our supper."

"I'd as soon feather *you.*" Golden flames flickered in the Raven's eyes. "Remember that, puppy. My lady, can you make a fire?"

Hands so numb she could barely feel them, she fumbled in her pouch and struck flint to steel. While the men cared for their horses in the nave, she crouched over the fragile flame. Carefully she nursed it until the fire took hold, casting wavering shadows over the frescoes until the holy figures breathed and stirred.

Still too cold to speak, they huddled around the fire under the bird Mehmet's gleaming eye. She saw the Raven decline the cured ham with a grimace, and added the knowledge to her meager cache. He served at a Christian court, prayed to no God she could discern, yet kept a Muslim diet. Still an enigma, no matter how many hours she passed in his presence.

But the Raven produced a rare luxury—a pinch of tea seasoned with ginger and cinnamon from the east. He steeped it in a tiny pointed pot suspended over the fire. When steam leaked out, he stuffed a twist of straw into the spout to catch the loose leaves and poured the honey brown brew.

With the tea heating her slowly, like a fire in her belly, she finally managed to stop shivering. Hugging herself, she welcomed the warmth spreading through her.

The Raven dispatched Thierry to take the first watch.

The young man cast him a shuttered look but belted his rich mantle around himself and went out. With a grunt, Owain wrapped in his cloak and turned his back to the fire. Within moments, he was snoring heartily.

She would have liked to follow suit, for weariness weighed her down like a waterlogged garment. But her senses were keyed up by a litany of fearful whispers she could not silence: the fear of pursuit, of failing the queen, betraying her king, losing her lands, losing her very life for treason . . .

Absently she drew her knees to her chest. The wolf squirmed into the niche beneath her bent legs and stretched on his belly with a sigh.

Across the fire the Raven crouched, his aquiline features sharp and cruel, silky black hair raked back at his nape. When he tossed a pinch of incense into the fire, the aroma of musk and sandalwood coiled through the air. It veiled the painted saints until they seemed to close their eyes.

Sitting cross-legged, he found needle and thread and started mending a tear in his surcoat. She watched his long fingers ply the needle, deft as a woman's.

"Do you not have a squire to attend such tasks?" she ventured. "I seem to recall one from the tourney—a Saracen with an eye patch."

His gaze narrowed, and her face heated. Truly, she did not care who squired him. She busied her hands detaching a burr from the wolf's ruff.

"Aye," he rasped. "Vulgrin. Rescued him from the Saracens."

"Rescued him, you say?" Perhaps she was slightly interested, no more.

"From torture," he said harshly, scowling into the flames. "They'd taken his tongue for some offense—blasphemy or falsehood. But his one eye's sharper than most men's pair."

"Yet he is not here now."

"He's too old for these northern winters. Left him behind at Poitiers, warming his bones at a fire."

More likely he left his lackey behind to spy. But the Raven had given her an opening to ask—only for the queen, of course.

"How long did you crusade?"

"Was knighted early, due to my size and skill. I went on crusade at fifteen and fought for some fourteen years."

"So long as that?" She stared. "By the grace of God, monsieur! 'Tis a wonder you survived. Did you . . . have no home to return to? No family, no—wife and children—who waited?"

His features hardened, the lines deepening around his eyes and mouth. His needle continued its steady dip and pull. "No family I cared to claim."

"Did you never marry?" she asked—only for the queen's sake. Eleanor would value knowing his vulnerabilities.

"Briefly." The shining needle stabbed the wool. "In my youth."

A curious pang shafted through her. "And?"

His voice grated like rusted iron. "She died."

The tightness eased around her heart—but how could that be? She took no personal interest in his affairs.

"Forgive me for pressing you." She hesitated. "As you have noted, I am not known for tact."

" 'Twas a lifetime ago." He bit off his thread with a deft twist. "I'm . . . unaccustomed . . . to discussing it."

She lowered her cheek to her knee. Remus's ribs rose and fell with his breath.

"Have you no children? 'Tis somewhat rare for a man of your age to lack them."

"Aye, well," he said dryly, "among the Norman lordlings I squired with, Saracen's bastard was no fine title. I'll inflict it on no child of mine."

Bastard born—but his sire must have been a nobleman, to give him a knight's training. Keenly she wondered at which court he'd trained. Although her avid curiosity about the man disconcerted her, the mystery surrounding him only deepened. Despite the stigma of bastardy, he had won entrée to a royal court. His skill at arms was prodigious, his talent for leadership evident, his Norman French as fine as her own. Yet he swore by Allah's name, like any Saracen.

"Whom did you serve, on crusade?"

"French, Normans, Saracens—whoever paid the most." His features twisted with bitterness. "Don't mistake me for your shining Lancelot. I'm no idealistic fool, taking the cross to liberate the Holy Land. After a lifetime in that pestilential hell, I've nothing left of honor or virtue. I'm the Devil of Damascus, or haven't you heard? I'm nothing for you to admire."

She flinched from the bolt of fury and pain he'd hurled. Beneath her knees, Remus lifted his head and looked around.

"I have heard what they call you." She stared at the knight's brooding countenance. "No doubt your trials on crusade forced you to deeds that would make a lesser man quail. But you do not strike me as weak or indecisive. If the course of your life displeases you, I do not believe you cannot change it."

He stared at her, eyes raw as an open wound, scarred features stripped of his customary indifference. She looked straight through the open window of his soul. *Pain, pain and solitude, and a cresting tide of loss.*

She had never seen such feeling in a pair of eyes—except her own, staring out at her from a polished plate.

"You may still redeem yourself," she whispered. "'Tis never too late to find your virtue."

"Almost a man could believe, to hear you say it. Should've been a knight yourself. Your steel's too keen for a court-bred lady."

Self-conscious, she dropped her gaze. *Well do I know I am too direct and unpolished to make a court lady.*

"Can't win your regard by virtue—not this devil." He grimaced. "So I must fall back on other tactics."

"What tactics are those?" she asked, wary. For a dangerous moment she had forgotten what he was.

The corners of his mouth turned up, distracting her. Bared by the severe pull of hair, he possessed a compelling face—harsh, no longer young, too embittered to be handsome. But the pale scar slashing from ear to jaw, the grim lines bracketing his mouth, merely added to the impression of strength and resolve that pulsed from him. And his mouth was interesting, well shaped, with a full lower lip.

Sensual. The word whispered in her mind.

"I've a theory about the queen's most virtuous lady." His gravel voice dropped an octave. "Your regal manner, your purity that shines like a star. They're your armor, aye? To protect the beating heart of the woman beneath."

"By my faith, I know not what you mean." Caution prickled her skin.

"You're fire, not ice, with passion they must've done their damnedest to beat out of you in your convent. Do I speak true?"

"Nay! Passions of the sort you describe are . . . a dangerous thing, a—destructive force. They have brought too many women to grief. If I'd possessed any such longings, I would have banished them long ago."

His uncanny gaze pierced her. "What woman dear to you came to grief for passion's sake?"

"Jesus wept! I will not discuss this with you or any man."

"Keep your secrets then . . . until you choose to tell me."

The pulse of panic hammered in her veins. "You think to find this hidden passion you claim I possess? You are doomed to failure, Lord Raven, for I have none."

"Don't you?" In a whisper of sable fur, he rose.

"None at all." She surveyed him with a Lyonstone's imperious coldness.

"Then you've naught to fear." He circled the fire with a panther's lethal grace. Her pulse slammed through her veins. Beneath her knees, Remus slumbered, oblivious.

"What are you about, monsieur? I shall tolerate no impropriety, and I am well able to defend myself."

Step by step, he stalked her. "Your professed lack of passion's your best defense. If it's so, you're safer than a babe from my desires. I've no taste for inflicting myself on unwilling women—and that includes your damned cousin. So you should be unaffected."

She cleared her throat. "Unaffected by what?"

Stooping to the kill, he dropped to his knees before her. The aroma of musk and sandalwood clouded her senses as his dark silhouette filled her vision. She pressed her spine against the wall until she could retreat no farther.

"This," he whispered. Cinnamon breath brushed her face.

At the last instant, she closed her eyes.

When she dared to wonder—as any maid did—what a kiss might be, she never dreamed of hot cinnamon, sweet and melting on her tongue, filling her mouth like a decadent treat. She could counter any assault. She had her knife; she could have used it. But she was undefended against this gentle sweetness that tempted her, until she opened her mouth and asked for more.

She gripped his shoulders, leashed power bulging under her hands. He made her vulnerable—the feeling she had striven a lifetime to banish.

He cradled her head beneath her coiled hair, calloused fingers brushing her nape. Her heart staggered like a drunkard, and still she could not breathe. Rashly, she swept aside a lifetime of conditioning and leaned into him, yearning for something she could not name.

Beneath her knees, the wolf whined. When Remus squirmed out from under her, he dislodged their bodies and broke the kiss.

Clutching the Raven's massive shoulders, she drew a shaking breath and opened her eyes. His gold-skinned features filled her world, amber eyes glowing like banked coals.

"Allah be merciful," he whispered. "I was right about you, Alienore of Lyonstone. Tell me I was right."

She was struggling to form a reply when the wolf barked in warning. A whiplash of alarm hissed through her as the Raven surged to his feet. The sleeping Owain pushed upright with a grunt. Her gaze flew to the door as Thierry burst through at a dead run, his sword drawn.

"*En garde!* We're under attack!"

Chapter Seven

A lightning charge of panic sizzled through her body. Clutching her long-knife, fiercely regretting that she carried no sword, Alienore leaped to her feet. *Sword or no sword, I will sell my life dearly.*

Owain ran to kneel before the door and braced a steel crossbow against his shoulder. The mechanism whirred as he fired a bolt into the night. From the darkness, a horse screamed in pain, mingled with a man's rough curse.

Pressing another quarrel into place, Owain turned the crank against the ratchet to arm the bow. The weapon armed with agonizing slowness—its primary drawback.

"Surround the shelter!" a voice bellowed in English, making her stomach clench. "Let none escape. The king wants them taken alive!"

She shook off the paralysis that gripped her. "I'll not raise arms against the king! 'Tis some misunderstanding—"

"If you're taken now, you're lost." The Raven pressed against the wall, firelight gleaming along his raised scimitar. "If you carry some treachery, the best you can hope for's a merciful beheading."

"Nay," she whispered, strength running from her limbs— brittle driftwood tossed on a sea of great events. God save her, he was right.

"Saddle the horses," he said. "We flee this trap before it closes. That's our only hope."

Conflicting impulses warred within her: the urge to take her place among the fighting men, set against the instinct to obey. While she debated, a red-fletched arrow whirred through the door and thudded into the wall behind her.

The Raven's bird lifted with a caw and went winging through the door. Her wolf growled and darted after.

"Remus!" she cried, a bolt of fear striking inward.

The Raven swept out an arm and pulled the wolf to safety, while Owain fired bolt after bolt into the darkness. Outside, the screams of the injured horse tore the fabric of night. Another shaft flew through the door and impaled their piled saddlebags.

"Alienore, the horses!" Thierry shouted. "Hurry, for God's love!"

Slamming her long-knife into its sheath, she ducked among the horses and scooped up a heavy saddle. She struggled to saddle the restless beasts as arrows hissed through the air and men shouted orders outside. The horses sidled away from her, eyes rolling white, their shifting hindquarters a constant threat.

With a harsh command from the Raven, Thierry darted out with him to engage their attackers. Steel clashed on steel. Working with frantic speed, she caught a confused glimpse of the two braced in the doorway, shoulder to shoulder, in fierce combat with a flurry of shadowy figures. Fear shrieked in her mind.

She was fighting to tighten a buckle and cursing the skittish horse when a whiskered face appeared at the empty window. The soldier's gaze swept past her gowned form to find her companions crouched near the door with their backs to him. When he cocked back an arm, steel flashed from a throwing knife.

Shouting a warning, Alienore drew her blade and lunged for the armpit exposed by his lifted arm. With the force of desperation and seven years' training, she buried her blade to the hilt.

The man fell back screaming, nearly wrenching the knife from her before she twisted free. The Raven spun toward her, eyes locking with hers.

Gripping her red-streaked knife, she stared back at him as tremors of shock swept through her. Never had she attacked a man in earnest, outside the stylized confines of the tourney field.

Stricken, she looked into the Raven's amber gaze and saw the fires of hell burning in his soul.

While the kneeling Owain guarded the door, the Raven tossed her into her saddle—strong and steady even in the pitch of crisis. The others mounted beside her. Owain loosed a last bolt into the darkness and sprang for his mount.

"Make for the wood." The Raven gripped his wicked blade. "Stay close."

Before she could respond, the black knight roared a battle cry, mingling the name of Allah with a cascade of heathen syllables. Still shouting, he spurred through the door into the dangerous night.

Unexpectedly, the ancient cry of her ancestors exploded from her heart.

"For Lyonstone!"

Her mare bolted through the door on Lucifer's heels, Remus bounding at her flank.

At once, the bone-chilling cold of night gripped her. Thick flakes swirled through the air, stinging her face, blinding as they clung to her lashes. Amid billowing gusts of white, she glimpsed flashes of bright red: the king's Plantagenet guards.

So many of them. Her heart plummeted.

A strange horse crashed through the snow and hurtled into her dainty mare. Unaccustomed to such treatment, the little bay stumbled and almost fell. Struck by a flailing hoof, the wolf yelped beneath them.

"Lyonstone!" Alienore slashed with her knife. When a

gauntleted hand captured her wrist, the shock of impact jolted through her, almost crushing the bones.

Fighting panic, she clamped her legs around the terrified mare—how she missed Galahad now!—and tried to twist free. Somewhere beneath her, Remus snarled and snapped. The other horse screamed in pain, slashed underbelly dripping red against the snow.

The numbing clamp on her arm dragged her forward, dislodging her grip on the saddle. She felt herself slipping sideways—

Like an apparition, Lucifer exploded through the snow. His rider's monstrous shadow towered over him, a river of black hair and garments billowing around him, scimitar screaming through the air. Sparks flew as blades clashed, and abruptly Alienore was free.

"Run!" the Raven shouted.

His sword was a silver blur as he held the enemy at bay, blade flashing to counter their blows. Lucifer's hind legs lashed out, steel-rimmed hooves thudding into his target with lethal force. The enemy horse stumbled and went down, but another reared up in his place.

In the midst of combat, the Raven burned like a dark flame, eyes wild, white teeth bared in a grimace of effort. Blooms of Plantagenet red appeared and vanished in the blizzard as others converged. Alienore knew they beheld a terror in the night, a black devil with a Saracen sword who slew without mercy.

Determined to ward his back, she kneed her frightened mare. Fleeing while the man fought for both their lives went against the grain of everything she was. Her heart hammered against her breast, but her grip on the knife was steady.

Another mounted figure bore down on her. Screaming defiance, she whirled to meet him. Barely in time, she recognized Thierry de Beaumont's golden hair.

"This way!" Catching her bridle, he tried to haul her

away, but she fought him. She would not abandon the Raven—not while he fought like a cornered beast to hold off three men at once!

The black knight's scimitar wove a glittering net of death. Freed from its binding, dark hair flew around him as he roared.

"Go! Damn you, Beaumont, take her."

Sudden recognition flashed through her. The Raven would not retreat without her. Her cold heart splintered and swelled with remorse . . . and another emotion she could not name.

How badly she had misjudged him. How they had all misjudged him.

Releasing her death grip on the reins, she gave the terrified horse her head. Blindly they followed Thierry. A detached part of her, still capable of thought, hoped they rode toward the forest rather than the steep ravine—but she had no way of knowing. The clash and cry of combat receded, muffled by falling snow.

When the forest loomed, relief surged through her. Beneath the boughs, the storm's fury eased. Once more she could see dimly in the darkness.

The wolf limped beneath the trees, ribs heaving, and she whispered a prayer of thanks. Thierry pivoted and thundered up beside her, his stallion blowing like a bellows.

"Why do you halt?" he panted. "We dare not linger."

She strained to see through swirling snow. "Have you forgotten our companions? They may require our aid."

"We must escape the danger!" He wrenched at her bridle. "Your safety is our paramount concern. I'm certain the others would agree."

She stared straight into her Lancelot's eyes and saw fear lurking in his gaze.

"Flee if you would," she said. "I will not abandon our fellows."

"Alienore, for mercy—"

Remus crouched and growled a warning. Firing with the charge of danger, she whipped out her knife as Lucifer surged into view. The Raven's inky cloak and hair billowed as he spurred past.

"Hurry! They're behind us."

Their flight became a nightmare from which she could not waken—a flight from her king and his certain vengeance, from the knowledge that somehow she had strayed from the path of honor. They stumbled through darkness with no light to guide them.

The horses struggled through lashing branches and treacherous drifts. Cold seeped through her garments; her teeth chattered until she locked her jaw to silence them. Again and again, shouts echoed through the wood. How the Raven managed to lead them, she could not comprehend. Dimly she perceived he was making choices, leading them, twisting ever deeper into stands of gnarled oak. Gradually the sounds of pursuit faded.

Abruptly, her mare pitched down a steep embankment and skidded over an ice-locked stream. Alienore whispered thanks to God and all the saints that the river was frozen solid. Plunging into icy water would be the death of them now.

When they scrambled up the opposite bank, her exhausted mare hung her head and heaved for air, mane lying in damp tendrils along her neck. Rousing from her stupor, she rubbed the mare's shoulder and looked anxiously for Remus—nosing in a tangle of bushes near the bank.

"Let the horses breathe," the Raven rasped. "Where's Owain? He was on my heels when we fled."

She brushed ice from her lashes and looked for the bearded guardsman.

"I have not seen him for some time," Thierry ventured.

"Damn." Roughly, the Raven scrubbed his face.

"We must press onward," Thierry said.

"The man may be injured." The Raven's golden eyes hardened. "He may need our aid."

"He is a common man-at-arms. Surely he can take care of himself."

The Raven's voice was rusted steel. "Common born or no, he's our comrade. I'll not leave a man behind, Beaumont."

"Let's wait here a moment." Alienore struggled to form the words. "Perhaps he has merely fallen behind."

Now that they'd stopped, the deadly cold deepened, seeping through her clothes, reaching greedy fingers for her fading warmth. They said this was the coldest winter in living memory, and prolonged exposure to such extremes was perilous. She longed for her blanket, abandoned with everything else when they'd fled.

Breath hissing through her teeth, she checked the calfskin pouch at her waist and found the queen's missive to Castile. It burned her fingers like hellfire—a dangerous letter, a few treasonous lines that could cost them all their heads.

"We dare not wait," Thierry said, "against all the dictates of prudence. I'll escort Lady Alienore ahead."

The Raven pushed out a cloud of breath. "You'll be lost in the wood."

"I will not!" The youthful voice rose in protest. "I'll have you know I was raised in a wood. I won't lose my way."

"That so?" The Raven shot him a keen look. "Then retrace our path—and find our comrade."

Thierry's nostrils flared. "I will not leave my lady. Why don't you search for him yourself, mercenary?"

"Because I command this party," the black knight said softly. "And you've sworn to obey me."

Shivering, Alienore struggled to remain alert. She could no longer feel her feet or hands. Trying to restore the flow of blood, she flexed her toes.

Beneath the riverbank, Remus wiggled into the scree and vanished.

"Remus." She unlocked her jaw to speak. "He may have d-d-discovered a cave. I pray he does not disturb a b-b-bear."

"All we need to make this night perfect," Thierry muttered.

The Raven shot her a discerning look. "A cave may prove a lucky find. While Beaumont does his duty, you'll have shelter—perhaps a fire."

"A fire?" Thierry cried. "Have you taken leave of your senses? Why not fly a banner and blow trumpets?"

"We've shaken off pursuit for now." The Raven sprang from his saddle and landed knee-deep in snow. "The king's men'll be lost, while the cave hides our fire."

"So you think."

"Be grateful, Beaumont." The Raven eyed him coldly. "You'll have fire to warm you when you return."

Sullen, the gallant scowled.

"Thierry, will you not g-g-go?" Her entire body shuddered with cold. "Our comrade may be injured, and 'tis so c-c-c-cold."

He shot her a resentful look. "This is utter madness. But never let it be said that a Beaumont failed to honor his word."

Thierry kneed his stallion into motion. Quickly the snow swallowed them up. Staring after him, Alienore realized she was now alone in the wilderness with the Raven. The king's sworn man—or was he?

He could betray me to Henry now with little effort.

Bleakly Alienore huddled in the dark hole Remus had nosed in the riverbank. Earthen walls pressed close around her, and dried leaves rustled beneath.

She could not comprehend why the Raven had not yielded her up to the king's men, since he was a king's man himself.

His game must be deeper than the queen believed. But how could she think him so unworthy? Hadn't he risked his life on her behalf?

Presently, she hardly cared what the Raven did while she remained near the precious scrap of fire he had coaxed to life. She'd been cold for so long she feared never to be warm again. Her fingers and toes throbbed as blood returned to the frozen limbs, and she bit her lip to contain a whimper.

With God's grace, she would stave off frostbite. Remus, too, seemed content to sprawl nearby and lick his bruised paw. His keen senses would warn them if anyone approached.

The Raven ducked inside, bent double beneath the low roof. His uncanny eyes searched her, and warmth stung her cheeks. Before tonight's deadly madness had commenced, the Devil of Damascus had kissed her.

He had wagered Richard he would seduce her.

Why in the name of all that was good had she allowed it? In a single night he'd shattered the protective armor she'd forged, link by link, over the lonely years since her mother's death. A single kiss, and she burned with sinful fire.

She cleared her throat. "Are we still pursued?"

"No doubt." He crouched across the fire, a fallen angel with fiery eyes. "We're safe enough—unless Beaumont leads them straight to us when he blunders back."

Aye, her shining Lancelot had hardly weathered this crisis with knightly valor, for the Raven carried those honors. Without his savagery in battle, his unflinching courage against overwhelming odds, they would not have escaped the king's vengeance.

Indeed, they had still not escaped it.

"I'll have the truth from you, lady. What mission were you charged with, to go against the king?"

" 'Twas never my intent to go against the king." Her very wits were muddled, buffeted by dread. She could no longer recall why she must conceal her mission from him. "The queen wished only to protect the interests of Princess Aenor, who would wed—"

"How'd you intend to reach Castile? Entire peninsula's plunged into war—Christians against the Muslims. Atrocities to turn your hair white are a daily occurrence."

She swallowed hard. "I know that, monsieur."

"You know naught of holy war—thank your God for that." Fiercely he glared into the flames. "I know the hell on earth they call the Christian Reconquista. Rest assured I won't drag you into it."

"Contrary to your belief, I am not a fool." Annoyance prickled through her. "I am quite familiar with the political situation. My plan is to make for the port of Marseilles, then take ship for Valencia. From there we strike inland, avoiding the war between Aragon and Navarre."

"And be captured by pirates before we ever see Spain? The sea's a highway for cutthroats and corsairs. Alienore, she's launched you on a suicide mission."

"Her need for this marriage is great." She defended her queen, but could not silence a whisper of doubt. What was Eleanor's true purpose?

"Ever read the missive she gave you?"

"Certainly not." Her tone was stiff.

"I suggest you overcome your fine scruples."

"Read the queen's personal correspondence to a foreign monarch? I shall do no such thing." Stubborn, she shook her head.

Curling tendrils of hair slipped into her eyes. Absently she pulled off her snood and shook her hair free and worked her fingers through her tresses, skeins of wheat gold hair pooling in her lap. When she felt his eyes upon her, she looked up through a curtain of firelit hair.

In the flickering play of light and shadow, his eyes were banked embers. No battle savagery hardened his features now.

He stared at her unguarded, with a man's desire that resonated through her like a pure note struck against lute strings.

A woman's hair was the devil's snare, so the nuns always said. And he was a known ravisher of women . . . or was he?

Hastily, she bundled her hair into a braid. "You are wasting your breath, monsieur. I shall never betray Eleanor."

"Henry's ordered your arrest. Don't you wish to know why?"

He crawled outside, leaving her alone with the wolf and her thoughts.

Slowly, she pulled out the slender cylinder of parchment sealed with hardened wax, stamped with the lion of Plantagenet.

Irresolute, she recalled Eleanor's generosity, her many kindnesses, the pain etched in her timeworn features when she spoke of her husband's infidelity. She recalled Sir Guy's warning, the hideous price of treason, the heart-pounding terror of pursuit. Her jaw tightened with resolve.

She broke the seal and unrolled the parchment, crossed with slanting black script in the elegant langue d'oc of Aquitaine.

When the bushes rustled, she looked up with a guilty start as the Raven squeezed into the cave. His eyes found hers and asked the question.

"Jesus wept," she whispered. "'Tis true—all of it, though she speaks in careful circles. She seeks an alliance between Aquitaine and Castile, to supplant her husband with her sons. If this missive falls into Henry's hands, 'tis treason."

His features twisted with recognition and regret. Again she wondered why he had not surrendered her. Her fate now turned on whether he chose to betray her. Danger surrounded her, and she no longer knew whom to trust. Yet somehow, during the course of this terrifying night, she had come to view the Devil of Damascus as her ally.

Intent, he crouched before the fire. "You can't complete this mission. No one can straddle the divide between warring monarchs, even be they husband and wife. You've only one chance to avoid the charge of treason."

"Nay," she whispered.

"Aye," he said, unyielding. "You must go to Henry with what you know—go of your own will. Throw yourself on his mercy."

She clutched the treasonous missive, her stomach knotting. "But that would seal Eleanor's fate. 'Twould be the final proof he requires to condemn her. He would humiliate her before the world by wedding his paramour. And he would break the queen's heart, for she loves him."

"She's already condemned herself." His eyes brooded. "Still, she's less dangerous as captive queen than a free woman. Henry'd be a fool twice over to divorce her. Clifford's chit may lead him by the cock—but he's no fool, believe me."

Acrid smoke billowed up and she coughed, embarrassed, holding her sleeve over her hot cheeks. "You are the king's man! How can I trust your counsel?"

"You can't." His mouth twisted. "We've already agreed on that, aye? We make north—"

"Nay! By my faith, I am an earl's daughter. I will not be reduced again to a fugitive, no better than a serf who has stolen the silver."

He shifted, a mask dropping over his features. "You fled a forced marriage to an aging lecher. Some would call that an act of valor."

Condemnation and guilt knifed through her. To hear him defend her—this man whom she herself had condemned.

"They say Ponce has repented his wicked ways," she murmured. "He crawled through Jerusalem on his knees in penance."

The Raven chuffed out a breath. "He's old Hugh's eldest whelp. Leopard can't change its spots, aye?"

"If God can forgive him, then we must. Besides, 'twas not Ponce I fled. If it were only that . . ."

His sudden stillness betrayed alertness. "Wasn't it?"

The dangerous parchment fluttered to her lap as she massaged her eyelids, the warning tightness of a megrim building between her eyebrows. "I could have accepted Ormonde, if he truly repented. In the end, he was not the reason I fled. The night I left home, I quarreled with . . . someone."

She struggled to rebuild her defenses. "But that has no bearing on this dilemma. I am the queen's privy chancellor. She has placed her trust in me. I cannot simply abandon her when her need is greatest!"

"Your gallantry's misplaced. Poitiers is a death trap for you now. Show your face, and they'll clap you in irons. Sir Guy may regret it, but he'll have no choice."

"But I never intended—Surely if I send word to the king and explain—"

"I know Henry. By the time you're brought before him, his mind'll be set against you."

"I cannot abandon Eleanor without some farewell." In the morass of fear and confusion where she floundered, she found sure footing on the path of honor. "She deserves that much. She is a great and noble lady, even if misguided. She was my benefactress—she took me in when I had nothing, Raven!"

The decision strengthened her. Last summer she had fled dishonor so profound it threatened her very sense of self. She'd fled from weakness, that was the truth, and she would never forgive herself for it. Only her actions could redeem her now, and prove her to be other than what she feared.

"I must return to Poitiers and trust in God to uphold me." She clasped her hands, serenity stealing over her.

"Sheer madness."

"Of course, I do not expect you to accompany me. Under these circumstances—"

"Your bloody sense of honor's muddling your wits," he growled. "Tell me one reason I shouldn't truss you to your saddle and make straight for Henry. It'd be to your benefit."

"And to yours. He would reward you generously for netting the queen's privy chancellor, would he not?"

"Aye," he said softly, raising the hairs along her nape. "He'd reward me beyond your imagining. I have every reason in the world to betray you."

"But will you?" she whispered, aching to know his motives. "Dare I trust you, Raven?"

Beneath his eyebrows, he cast her a burning look. "Don't make that mistake. You forget what I am, Alienore."

The wolf raised his head, ears swiveling forward. Her gaze met the Raven's. Lifting a finger to his lips, he uncoiled and slithered toward the exit, scimitar whispering from its sheath.

She readied her long-knife even as conflict twisted her belly. If she raised her blade against the king's men, didn't that make her a traitor for certain? Outside, footsteps crunched, mingled with the rattle of chain mail. A horse whinnied in welcome.

When a shadow blotted out the cave mouth, she clenched her teeth over a scream. The Raven pressed beside the opening, crescent sword raised to strike as a mailed arm dragged aside the undergrowth. A hooded head poked inside—and Thierry de Beaumont looked up.

The Raven checked his blow in midswing, notched blade hovering above the intruder.

"Next time hail first, boy. I could've had your head."

"Grant pardon." Sounding weary, Thierry dragged himself inside. "These woods are crawling with the king's men. I doubled back twice to ensure I wasn't followed."

"Thank God you are safe returned." The cool tones of a privy chancellor concealed her turmoil. But fear sat like a stone in her belly. "What news of Owain?"

"Alienore, I'm sorry. The man is dead."

Remorse struck inward, piercing her heart. Now a good man lay dead on her account.

You are not worthy of such sacrifice, her conscience whispered. *You are not what they believe you to be.*

"*Inshallah.*" The Raven scrubbed a hand over his face. "So. Lady says we make for Poitiers."

"But how can we?" she said miserably. "The king's men will seize me the moment I show my face. They think me a traitor now."

Speculation flickered in the Raven's gaze as he eyed the blond gallant. "Fine surcoat you're wearing, Beaumont—most distinctive. Belike you'll make a loan of it."

Chapter Eight

She queen had betrayed her—the Raven knew it in his bones. When she dispatched the girl on that traitor's mission, Eleanor of Aquitaine had signed the order for her execution. Allah's heart, why couldn't Alienore see it?

He lurked in the queen's tiring chamber and plotted escape routes by habit: the casement too high for escape, the servants' cubby a dead end. But Alienore's blade-straight figure compelled him, her graceful silhouette etched against the fire.

Lyonstone's daughter made a damn fetching gallant. She wouldn't have stooped to the indignity of a disguise—but what a disguise it was.

She'd already flung Beaumont's surcoat aside. Proud breasts and narrow waist encased in a moss-green coat, legs sinuous in tight chausses, those masses of gold and silver hair pinned high to expose her neck . . . She was walking temptation to any man's eyes.

Alienore of Lyonstone would make one hell of a duchess.

He couldn't have wished for a more stalwart companion during their nerve-racking flight. She'd guarded his back, when she could have fled.

An unfamiliar sentiment surged through him: a fierce drive to protect her, stand between her and danger—a tenderness that shook him like an earthquake. *Careful, man, or you'll be trailing at her heels like that lovesick Beaumont puppy.*

The door swept open to admit the Queen of England, blazing in indigo over cloth of gold, her features radiating affectionate concern. As the Raven lurked in the shadows, she hurried to Alienore.

"My dear child! What has befallen? I cannot believe anything but disaster would dissuade you from your duty."

"I fear your faith in me has been misplaced, Your Grace. We were attacked by the king's own guard."

His eyes narrowed as he scanned the queen's countenance. Was her concern for the girl genuine, or did the queen care only for intrigue?

"Thank God and good Saint Thibault for your deliverance, child. By some miracle, were you able to protect my missive?"

"Aye." Alienore faltered, guilt shadowing her features.

The Raven clenched his teeth. The girl wore her thoughts on her face; she had less craft for concealment than a child of five. Usually, he found her transparency rather winsome—he'd known enough deception to last him a dozen lifetimes. Now he stifled a groan as her stubborn chin lifted.

"Madam, I kept the message safe . . . but I was compelled to burn it."

He'd insisted on that, and she hadn't even argued. That bloody letter was a death sentence for whoever bore it.

"Destroyed." Sighing, the queen turned away. Calculation narrowed her cat green eyes before she glimpsed him. In a heartbeat, her mask slipped into place.

"*Depardieu*, my lord Raven! Have I you to thank for saving my godchild from enemy hands?"

"The king's hands, Your Grace." He bowed. "I'll speak plainly, not to squander time."

"By all means, monsieur."

"Your game with the lady's played out. Henry will soon know it—if he doesn't already. For her safety, she must leave your service."

"I do not agree." Alienore swept forward. "I have no desire to return to England until my inheritance and forced betrothal are addressed."

"You must find the king and affirm your loyalty," he said grimly.

The queen's eyebrows winged up. "Ah, but that is impossible. The counties between here and Normandy are simmering with civil war. Maine, Anjou, Touraine, Brittany—all chafe beneath Henry's heavy hand.

"Wherever Henry may be at the moment, you may be certain he is where the fighting is hottest. *Avoi*, monsieur, I am astonished you suggest it."

Treacherous lady—the queen's allies rebelled, at her command.

The Raven scowled. "Be certain I'll ensure her safety."

Alienore's chin lifted in her imperious way, her eyes molten silver. "By my faith, that is entirely unnecessary, Lord Raven. If I am given leave to go anywhere, I shall arrange my own escort."

"For the moment," the queen said, "no escort shall be required. My godchild is far safer here at Poitiers than tramping about the countryside in a futile bid to locate Henry."

"Madam, she's exposed," he gritted. "Does her safety mean so little to you?"

"It means a great deal to me—enough, monsieur, that I deemed it prudent to conceal her departure. With her tiring woman's assistance, we have put about that illness confines the lady to her apartments. Imagine the joy that will greet her recovery when she appears like the risen Christ."

His dangerous rage ignited. For all her so-called affection, the queen would see Alienore's head roll for treason. "You'd risk seeing her charged with sedition?"

"She can hardly be accused of sedition when none can prove she left Poitiers."

"Nothing can be proven against me." Alienore's level gray eyes regarded them. "Unless I flee like a witless rabbit."

"As always, privy chancellor, you grasp the situation perfectly." The queen inclined her head.

At last, a crack appeared in Alienore's controlled facade. Her tone turned brittle as her fingers knotted, hard enough to whiten her knuckles. "Then it seems I can do naught but wait, like an insect caught in amber—as I have done these many months." She strode to the casement and stared out, her back rigid.

Aye, she chafed at inaction. He knew her well enough to guess she'd rather don armor and challenge her accusers than maneuver among these mazy intrigues. Maybe he could use that reckless courage of hers. But he knew what it would cost her, with her damn bloody honor, to go against her sovereign's bidding.

He spoke quietly, so Alienore couldn't hear. "Cleave to this course, and you'll destroy her."

"A wise ruler never falters, nor admits to an error." Eleanor lifted guileless eyes to his. "I learned that lesson from my husband."

Pity you learned no more from him—like loyalty.

"Alienore, my dear?" The queen smiled tenderly. "You do not mind allowing me a moment's privacy with your champion, do you?"

Alienore studied her sovereign with troubled eyes. Holding his breath, the Raven silently urged her to defy the queen—but Eleanor of Aquitaine had tied her hands.

"Lord Raven is not my champion," Alienore said low. The bitterness of defeat flooded his mouth. "As he is the first to admit. But it seems the matter is settled, is it not? I cannot leave Poitiers against your will—not when I swore to your service."

Yet as she left, a worried crease deepened between her eyebrows.

He should have tossed her over his saddle and made for

Normandy while he had the chance. Instead, like a fool, he'd let her sway him with her prattle about honor and duty. Now he must devise some other scheme for smuggling her out of Poitiers, with the queen on full alert.

Eleanor concealed her triumph behind faultless courtesy. "You have survived a taxing ordeal. Will you take wine, monsieur?"

He inclined his head, and she poured a dark torrent of burgundy into silver cups, managing her trailing sleeves with elegance. Claiming his goblet, he steeled himself for a battle of wills.

Serenely, she smiled. "Let us drink to Alienore's good health."

"Gladly." The wine was an uncommonly fine Bordeaux— forbidden to a Muslim, but he'd broken that edict long ago. Savoring the illicit pleasure, he inhaled the spicy bouquet.

The queen strolled to the casement and rested light fingers on the glass. "You will pardon my directness, but I cannot avoid noticing that you take an uncommon interest in my godchild's affairs."

"I do as I'm bidden. It's the nature of a mercenary."

"Ah, but you are no mere mercenary. You must not be so self-effacing, monsieur! I know precisely who you are and have known for some time. Only I am allowed the privilege of keeping secrets at Poitiers."

His blood turned to ice, though he kept his face impassive. "I'd expect no less."

"So you are Henry's man." She shrugged. "Or, at least, so you claim. Yet my pious former husband, the French king, writes you are to be trusted in our scheme. He believes you intend to betray Henry and let the French army come pouring into the Vexin."

He admitted nothing.

"You play a dangerous game, monseigneur," she murmured,

giving him a lord's title. "I wonder if even you are quite certain what you intend. Yet I cannot doubt the nature of your interest in the Lyonstone heiress."

He inclined his head, a muscle flexing in his jaw. Let her interpret that as she would.

"You may well imagine the lady's reaction," she said, "when she discovers your identity."

Tension churned in his belly. The queen smiled coldly.

"Fortunately for you, monsieur, I too can be discreet. Follow my lead, and I may find it expedient to advance your aims. Be clever and cautious, and you may yet finish this game to your liking."

Pensive, he swirled the wine around his mouth. Did she truly know him, or was this a bluff to smoke him out? He'd commanded men for Henry in the troubled Vexin between France and Normandy long before Henry gave him lands there. Let the queen drop a single hint, and he was undone, and all his grand hopes with him. Forthright Alienore, proud Theobold's daughter, could forgive a man anything but deception.

Yet if she remained at Poitiers, she would die a traitor's messy death.

He dared not oppose the queen openly, damn the woman. Notwithstanding Sir Guy's vigilance, she held all the power at Poitiers. One word of command, and the Raven would find himself tossed out on his rump, all his careful plans in ruins.

And Alienore would be unprotected, at greater risk than before. For both their sakes, he must bide his time.

He spoke into his goblet. "Grateful for your discretion."

"Then, monseigneur, we are agreed? The anonymous knight called the Raven will continue to serve as my master-of-arms, while Alienore remains my privy chancellor. We shall countenance no further talk of sending her to Henry."

He bowed himself from the royal presence, curtains of hair falling forward to obscure his wrath.

Now a new strategy was forming—risky and underhanded, leaving a sour taste in his mouth. Undoubtedly Alienore would hate him before it was finished. He told himself the end justified the means and went to find Prince Richard.

A woman's cries of passion seeped through the closed door, coupled with a man's groans. In the corridor, the Raven cast a wry glance toward the guardsman he'd bribed. The man grinned companionably and shrugged.

He had no bloody time for this. Impatient, the Raven waited while the rutting mounted in fervor. The instant it ended, he struck his knuckles against the door and strode in.

Within the royal boudoir, a sea of candles blazed around a dishelved bed draped in Plantagenet crimson. The reek of sex hung heavy in the air. He glimpsed a pair of shapely white legs; a tumble of red curls spilled across the bedclothes.

Richard Plantagenet raised his head from a pillow of plump breasts. "*Mon Dieu*, you're supposed to be in Castile, man! You find me at a disadvantage. Unless you wish to join us, eh?"

These bloody southern French. The Raven betrayed nothing as Rohese de Rievaulx scrambled under the coverlet. "I was compelled to return. Apologies for disturbing your . . . rest."

"Well, I'm feeling benevolent." Unconcerned with his nakedness, Richard rolled on his back and stretched—a lion lazy but dangerous in his den. "Though if you'd arrived a moment sooner . . ."

The Raven twisted his lips in a smile, disgust churning in his belly. His eyes flickered over the Rievaulx girl, all outraged modesty as she clutched the bedclothes to her breasts and glared at him.

For this Alienore had challenged him, risked her honor, her very life—to defend a lying whore who reeked of passion. One more stain upon his name was nothing, but Alienore . . .

When she'd learned Owain's grim fate, sorrow had shaded her silver eyes to lead. He'd burned with the need to console her in his arms and cursed his own weakness.

What, an earl's proud daughter take comfort from you— infidel, sell-sword, a Saracen's bastard? Yet she'd never faltered as they crept through the forest, alert to every snapping twig, bound for Poitiers despite his every counsel.

"I need a moment." He didn't apologize for the road mud that daubed his boots, the stink of horse that clung to him. Richard would think his mercenary lacked breeding, which suited him all to the good. He hadn't had time to wash.

"Consider yourself indulged." Yawning, the prince reached for his wine cup.

"Alone, if we may?"

"You put yourself forward, monsieur," Richard said amiably, reaching for his braies. "But you amuse me, which has a price beyond rubies. I confess myself intrigued by this nocturnal visit."

Ignoring the Raven, the girl turned her jade-colored eyes on the prince. "Richard, are you leaving me already?"

"That would be impossible, *chérie.*" The prince bowed gallantly. "Cultivate the virtue of patience, eh? We have hours yet to play."

Mollified, the girl reclined, lips curling in a smile of triumph.

For this Alienore risked herself? The slut's not fit to wipe her boots! With a contemptuous glance that made her smile falter, the Raven stalked to the hearth.

"And so." The prince flung himself into a high-backed chair. "What can possibly be so pressing?"

"A matter of money, Your Grace." The fire's hostile heat pressed against his skin and crackled with hunger. "I come to collect on our wager."

"What wager?" For an irritating moment, the prince

looked blank. Then his cobalt eyes narrowed. "You mean the demoiselle Alienore?"

The Raven quashed a lifetime of conditioning. Not an outright lie, no violation of his oath, but he would mislead his prince. The end justified the means. Propping elbows on knees, he hunkered forward.

"We were alone together for a night." He pitched his voice low—knowing the girl was straining to hear. "I took advantage of every moment."

"*Mon Dieu*." Richard stared. "What of Sieur de Beaumont? He accompanied you, *oui*?"

"That puppy? Left behind in the forest." With a shrug, he consigned Thierry de Beaumont's reputation to the dogs.

"Ah! This is what comes of sending a boy to do a man's work." The prince, all of sixteen, gestured in disgust. "But the demoiselle—she allowed you . . . ?"

"The girl's an innocent." Allah gild his tongue if the man pressed for intimate details about his alleged encounter! "The queen ordered her to accept my . . . protection."

His blood smoked to recall the lush feel of her mouth, opening to his kiss—

"Remind me to thank my mother for that." The prince's chuckle held an ugly edge. "So Lady Virtue has tumbled from grace. She beds a common mercenary, yet spurns a prince?"

So the rutting goat had tried, damn him. The Raven clenched his jaw over the murderous rage that boiled on his tongue, and twisted his lips in a chilling smile.

"You recall what we wagered? I've come to collect."

"Ah." Richard's fist clenched around his cup. "Never let it be said a Plantagenet failed to honor his word."

The Raven treaded carefully, the scent of his prey filling his nostrils. Irritated by the smoke, his throat itched for wine, but he wouldn't risk clouding his wits now. "Can't carry on a proper liaison here. Poitiers crawls with spies and talebearers. I'd spirit the girl away—to some place more private, aye? Some chateau or hunting lodge, far from her chancellor's duties."

Richard scowled into the fire. The Raven's hand twitched, missing his sword—left despite his misgivings with the sentry outside. No man bore steel before his prince, but he'd kept the curved dagger. His fingers ached to draw it.

The bedclothes rustled as Rohese slid to her feet, revealing a sensuous glimpse of pear-shaped buttocks, and wrapped a surcoat around her voluptuous figure. He gritted his teeth as she sauntered toward them, the open robe offering glimpses of pale legs and pouting breasts.

Once she'd seemed fetching enough, at least for an hour's diversion, but no lust tightened his loins now. Wrapping a careless arm around her, the prince tumbled her into his lap.

Bloody hell—a seasoned harlot. If Alienore knew, the shame would kill her.

"Your bed grows cold." Rohese cast the Raven a coy glance. "And so do I."

"You, *chérie*—cold?" The prince laughed. "*Par Dieu!* If Alienore welcomes your attentions, monsieur, who am I to stand in love's path? But I'll have a favor from you as well."

Not the terms of our bargain—but this is Richard Planta-genet. The man was Duke of Aquitaine, and heir to the English throne if his brother died without issue. Any man would be wise to recall it.

"Her newly pious duke will want nothing to do with the bitch now that you've had her." Malice twisted the prince's face. "What noble lord wants a commoner's leavings? Not even her lands and dowry will sweeten that bitter brew. Truly, now, one man to another—don't you think we owe him the truth?"

He misliked where this was headed, but kept it from his face. "The lady spurned his suit."

"But not to his face. By all reports he lingers in her hall

like a lovesick swain, drinking her ale and wenching while
he awaits her return." The prince bared his teeth in an unfriendly grin. "I'll arrange your little love tryst, make it right
with my mother—*mon Dieu*, I'll even lend you my own hunting lodge. How's that for generous? But first, you'll grant me
my pound of flesh. Get me the Duc d'Ormonde."

The Raven's suspicions exploded as alarm jolted through
him. Gripping his chair, he restrained himself—barely in
time—from surging to his feet. Did the prince too know
him? Or was it only spite from a spurned suitor?

The Raven bit out the words. "Highborn lords don't come
and go at my bidding."

And Ponce least of all, when it comes to that.

"Use your wits, man—you're clever enough. Lead Ponce
d'Ormonde to his fugitive bride, and let her deal with him."

Richard Plantagenet narrowed his gaze on the girl in his
lap, her eyes wide with dawning awareness. "And you, my
sweet, will breathe no word of this to your sainted cousin—or
suffer my grave displeasure."

Chapter Nine

The blind man flailed, groping for the tormentors who hovered beyond reach. One bold fellow darted in to tug the victim's jasper-studded surcoat, then danced back to howls of laughter from the drunken crowd.

At the high table, a bored Prince Geoffrey pelted the blindfolded gallant with a steady hail of nuts. In his wild efforts to avoid the stinging rain, the gallant knocked over a bench. The missile skidded into the legs of a kitchen churl, whose tray went flying, spattering ale across the floor.

From a lower table, Alienore looked for the chamberlain to end this unseemly brawl. But excesses that earned rebuke on other occasions now passed without remark. On Shrove Tuesday, the day of mischief before the long, somber twilight of Lent, intemperance was forgiven.

Unhappily she pondered the volume of royal correspondence that awaited her. Yet she felt a troubling ambivalence toward her duties.

Eleanor is proved a traitor by her own hand. Now her disloyalty taints me as well. She felt sullied, as though by the stinking refuse of a chamber pot. She could trust no man or woman at this treacherous court—save one. Yet the Raven had gone away.

She was at a loss to comprehend the enigmatic knight. An embittered crusader who practiced Saracen customs and swore in Allah's name. The king's trusted man who protected her from the king's vengeance. Over a sennight since he'd vanished, and still he commanded her thoughts. Hidden facets of his character glittered like blood rubies in darkness.

The unflinching courage that flung him between her and her enemies, teeth bared as he battled to save her.

The relentless resolve that guided them through the mazy forest.

The self-contempt that scorched his ruined voice. *I'm naught for you to admire,* he had hurled at her. She knew that pain too well—the white-hot lash of disgrace.

And the molten heat of his kiss, pooling in her belly until she ached for him.

By her faith, she knew him not at all. Yet she found herself powerfully tempted to trust him.

A feminine shriek recalled her to the game. The blind fool had captured Rohese, flushed and pretty in yellow silk, red curls tumbling from her chaplet. Despite her noisy indignation, the damsel paid her forfeit with a kiss. Before the drink-blurred eyes of all the court, the gallant played it to the fullest, hands straying everywhere.

Alienore turned away from her cousin's disgrace. Saint Swithun save her, the Raven had told the truth. She no longer took him for a lecher, inclined to rape an innocent maid on the eve of a holy feast. Sighing, she rose.

The movement caught Rohese's eye. "Nay, Alienore, you cannot slip away! You've not taken your turn."

Alienore made a courteous demurral. She never played such games. She, romp like a child with this throng of mischief-makers, when she had work to do? She could not comprehend why Rohese should suggest such a thing.

Unfortunately, Prince Richard seized upon the cause. "Nay, don't spoil our sport! Come into the circle. I, your future king, command it."

With an indulgent smile, the queen touched his sleeve. Yet Eleanor of Aquitaine said nothing to spare her this humiliation.

Are they not content seeing me branded a traitor? Nay, I must become a jesting stock as well. Anger seethed in her soul as she whisked the blindfold from her cousin and tied it in place.

As she blundered about with arms extended, groping after fools, the acid knowledge seeped through her. This senseless game mimicked her life at court. Like the village idiot, she stumbled through her part, blinded from the truth by her own narrow perceptions.

"Hsst!" A hand caught her wrist, yanked her through the crowd. For a foolish instant she thought it was the Raven, come to rescue her. Her heart leaped with a mad jubilation.

Then she scented cloves and lavender. Whoever he was, her rescuer was not the Raven. The very air did not hum with the leashed vitality of his presence.

"This way, my lady!"

Groping, she brushed a marble pillar. Her rescuer pulled her behind it, blocking them from the court's unfriendly eyes.

"Thierry?" Ah, her Lancelot—at least he had not abandoned her. She loosened the blindfold, but he caught her hands.

"Listen well, my lady! I overheard Prince Richard conversing with Her Grace. Alienore . . . Ponce d'Ormonde is coming."

Ponce d'Ormonde. The name whelmed her chest like a tourney lance, knocking the breath from her lungs.

"You were not to be warned, by the queen's own order! Ormonde must have thrown his support to her cause. Alienore, she has sold you out."

"Nay, that is impossible." She trembled with shock. The sickening enormity of this betrayal surged through her. "I cannot believe that."

"Believe it! I risk my own place by telling you." He pressed his lips to her shaking hand. "For your sake I risk all, my brave Guinevere. You must fly to my father, the Comte de Beaumont. He will shelter you."

"Nay." She squared herself against the ugly truth. "So Ponce d'Ormonde would stoop to treason, consorting with the queen. When does he arrive?"

"By nightfall. I heard Richard say it."

Fresh alarm spurted through her. "God save me, that is no time at all."

Beyond the pillar, a tide of voices mounted, salted with complaints over the delay.

"Fear not, brave lady." Thierry gripped her fingers hard enough to crush them. "You shall flee to safety, while I challenge for your hand."

"Alienore, come out!" Richard bellowed. "Else I shall be owed a forfeit—"

"Imbecile." She hurled the word like a spear toward her drunken prince. They had both betrayed her, mother and son, to win the Norman duke's allegiance. Yet beneath the winds of crisis, the swirling fog of days cleared away. Her thoughts marched through her brain with relentless logic, telling her what she must do.

Her command rang clear as a war horn. "Thierry, you are to do nothing on my account—nothing at all, do you comprehend me?"

"Nay, Alienore, don't you see? I'll challenge him for your hand! My father is the king's man. He'll petition Henry. We can be married by Easter, only think of it!"

Beyond the pillar Richard's voice rose, a taunting singsong, drawing closer. Apparently he had come down to roust her out of hiding.

"Thierry, I do not wish for that." As she spoke, her certainty crystallized. The flimsy edifice of her self-deceit shattered. "'Tis a great honor you would do me, but—I cannot."

"What are you saying?"

"Jesus wept, there is no time! You need only remain silent until I can act. Swear it on your honor as a knight."

"My lady, are you refusing me?" His grip would splinter

the bones in her fingers. "Was it all no more than a game to you? You knew I sought a noble bride, knew I would have nothing if I did not marry well—"

"I made you no promises." Desperate, she wrenched free her throbbing hands. "How could I? I am bound already by one betrothal I do not desire."

To that he said nothing. Even so, her conscience pained her. Had she encouraged him unfairly these many months? Well, she must examine her conscience another time.

"Swear to do nothing," she whispered. "Swear it on your love for me, if ever you did love."

"Alienore—" He choked. "Very well, if you insist. I swear it."

She wrenched away, into the open. A drunken roar heralded her appearance. Rough hands gripped her shoulders. Stumbling, she clutched the encircling arms, fingers spanning a fighting man's biceps. It ended the accursed game, God be praised, for she'd captured someone at last.

"Too late." Wine-sour breath washed over her, an instant's warning before Richard's mouth came down. Eager lips squirmed against hers as she strained away. A wet tongue nudged against her lips.

Vivid memories rushed through her of another kiss, another man, the tingling thrill of unknown sensations coursing through her. How could two kisses be so unlike? Revulsion for this one made her flesh creep.

Burning with shame, she twisted away and snatched off the blindfold.

"Still playing the virtuous maid?" Richard leered. "Mon Dieu, but I know better."

"Your Grace, this behavior is unworthy of you—and of me." With a shaking hand, she found a handkerchief and wiped her lips. "I fear you are much the worse for drink."

"Nay, wine but improves my performance! You can ask your pretty cousin about that."

"Very well, *carissime*." The queen's cool voice sliced through the ruckus. "You have claimed your forfeit from my most virtuous lady. Unhand her now."

Drawing a mantle of dignity around her, Alienore curtsied stiffly. Fury and shame scorched her. By God, if only she were a man! She would challenge them all—but nay.

They were her sovereigns. She could only reproach their ill use with cold courtesy.

"With pardon, Your Grace, I take my leave."

"We'll see who does the taking this night," Richard muttered. "*Avoi*, we'll see how well you play your little game then."

So Richard Plantagenet stood her enemy. He'd sent for Ponce—she knew it now as clearly as if he'd told her. Still, it was not too late. Not if she kept her wits about her.

"Ooh, milady, such a turrible thing!" Nesta's freckled face hovered before her as Alienore burst into her apartments. Bounding through the open door, Remus planted paws on her shoulders and slathered her with an exuberant tongue.

"There is not a moment to lose." Drawing comfort from his nearness, Alienore scrubbed the wolf's ruff. "Where are my saddlebags?"

"Here. But, milady—" Nesta wrung her hands as her mistress burrowed into the wardrobe. Alienore's fur-lined pelisse and boots came tumbling to her hand. "There's a soldier—"

"Not now, Nesta." Pawing through the chest, Alienore tossed shifts and stockings to the floor. "Run down to the kitchens. And I do mean run, with no stopping for chatter along the way."

"I never—"

"Bring me bread, cheese, apples, whatever they have. Then find Luke—him and none other—and tell him to saddle Galahad."

Her hand closed around the slender length of her broadsword: gray steel wrapped in leather, with no glimmer of wealth to betray her in the tourneys. In its familiar haft she found her strength.

"Nesta, this is most important. Tell Luke it must be done quietly. He's to meet me at the postern gate."

"But, milady!" The girl wiggled with agitation. "This soldier, I ran across 'im in the buttery. He's a lad from 'ome."

Arrested as she burrowed for her gloves, Alienore stared. "A courier from home, after all this time—for me?"

"Nay, milady, not for you. He's chance-come, bride-hunting for the young earl."

"By my faith, Benedict is *here?*" Her heart contracted. "Does he seek to mend our quarrel?"

God save me, has he ridden with Ponce?

"Nay, milady, the earl stayed 'ome. But the soldier was all agog to see a familiar face." Nesta hesitated, her brow furrowing. "'Tis a hard winter there, he says. Scottish bandits are a-raiding, and I—I'm scared."

Starving for news from home, Alienore trembled with the urge to shake the addle-witted girl until the words tumbled from her mouth. With an effort, she restrained herself.

"Calm yourself, Nesta. Matters cannot be so grim. We have no word from our faithful Raoul d'Albini . . ." Her voice wavered. Her only friend after Marguerite's death, more father to her than the crusading earl. "I wrote him a letter when we came here, Nesta, and said where to find me. Yet he has not replied. Raoul would send notice without fail, if . . ."

Wouldn't he have written to warn her when Ormonde tired of waiting? No matter what had passed between them the night she left.

Alienore cleared her throat. "What more did this soldier say?"

"He said yer brother claimed yer crops, milady, leaving naught for our folk. The livestock too—yer own good sheep, he's claimed. Says ye're never coming 'ome, and yer lands are his now."

"By what right does he dare?" Rage coursed through her. "How will our people survive without their livelihood? God's mercy, I should never have left them."

"What do we do, milady?" Nesta's hands twisted in her woolen kirtle. "I'm worrit for me mam and da. Are we going 'ome?"

Nosing her skirts, the wolf whined. Bleakly Alienore hugged him and rested her chin on his head.

"I cannot go home, Nesta. Until the king rules on my petition, I am powerless. Once again I must flee Ponce d'Ormonde like a thief from the gallows. I have no allies here—not even the friends I thought were mine."

"Why, we all stand by ye, all the folk from Lyonstone. I'd follow ye to the grave, milady, after what ye done on my account—and me no more than a wee lass when that devil bailiff would have his way. I'll go with ye, wherever ye're going."

"You are beyond good to say it. I do not doubt your courage, but I will not have you flee into the wild. This time, I must go alone."

"Alone?" Nesta propped hands on her hips. "Ye mean—without me? Ye'll not manage on the road without yer Nesta."

Alienore smiled wanly. "You are terrified of horses, and I must ride at speed."

"For yer sake, milady . . ."

Aye, for her sake Nesta would screw up her courage. But the tiring girl would slow her—and that, she could ill afford.

"Nesta, I have greater need of you here. I have a letter for the queen that she must not receive until I am well away. I dare leave it in no hands but yours. No matter what she has done, I will not abandon Eleanor without a word of explanation. May I rely on you?"

"Aye, milady." The tiring girl stood straight, pride shining from her eyes. "But where will ye go?"

Pinning a snood over her hair, Alienore stared at her reflection in the polished plate: pale, freckles standing out across her nose, chin set with determination. But her eyes glowed like stars.

For the first time since she'd fled home, she felt like a Lyonstone.

"All depends upon the king now. 'Tis there I must go—to King Henry's court." She thrust her sword into her saddlebag. "And I dare not tarry, with Ponce d'Ormonde on the move. I must leave this very hour."

Henry shall have the truth from my own lips. And I shall have a ruling on my inheritance, and this would-be husband.

Galahad cantered along the road beneath a sky glowing red with sunset. Beside them, the river slept beneath a blanket of rotting ice, winding north toward the troubled counties where the ember of war smoldered.

Henry might be anywhere, reducing a rebel castle or staving off the French king's assault. Alienore hoped to learn his whereabouts in villages and abbeys along the way.

Despite the danger, her heart thrilled as she rode. On a dripping bough, a robin warbled to welcome the thaw, sweet as the certainty that thrummed within her. For the first time since Benedict returned from crusade bearing news of her father's death, a shoot of hope unfurled in her breast.

In the crisp air, sound carried. Galahad's ears swiveled forward as Remus halted, head cocked to nose the air. On guard, she drew rein, so that she too could hear. Through the trees, distant cries rose and fell on the wind: the belling of hounds.

The fine hairs along her body rose to stand on end. She told herself there were many sorts of prey those hounds could be hunting. Still, Ponce d'Ormonde must have reached Poitiers by now. No doubt her flight had been discovered.

Well, no matter. I am no cutthroat or runaway thief. 'Tis folly to believe he'd set hounds to track me—and folly to believe he will do nothing.

The tales of his past depravities would send chills down any woman's spine. He'd coupled serving girls with his hunting hounds, so the rumor ran. And set those same hounds to hunt his runaway serfs, to the bloody finish. Either he was corrupt as Lucifer, or he was mad.

Even if he had repented in his old age, she could imagine the duke's rage when he learned his coveted heiress had slipped his grasp again, after he'd crossed an ocean and two war-torn countries to claim her.

She clapped her heels into Galahad's flanks, and the stallion surged ahead. He could run half the night without tiring. Still, she disliked the notion of barreling blindly along. If Galahad put his foot into a rut, he could break a leg—or her neck, when he threw her.

Again she drew rein. For a tense moment she heard nothing . . . then the baying of hounds split the air. Shivering, she peered behind her, where the road tunneled beneath darkening trees. If Ponce had loosed his hounds—runaway serf or runaway bride, what difference to him?—she would do well to leave the road. Yet she didn't fancy the notion of blundering through the pitch-black wood. Undecided, she worried as Remus milled around the stallion's legs.

A frenzy of distant barking prodded her to action. She swung a leg forward over the pommel and jumped down—a knight's careless dismount rather than a lady's. But none would disapprove on this bleak road.

Pulling Galahad behind her, she crept down the sloping bank. At the river's edge she hesitated. Shrove Tuesday had brought a thaw, but this winter had been the coldest anyone

could recall. Cautious, she prodded the ice with a branch—
solid, so far as she could tell. When she leaned into it, ready
to spring back, it held her weight. Leaving the warhorse behind, she eased onto the ice, alert for cracking. The wolf ran
past her and lapped fresh water from standing puddles on
the surface.

*God's mercy, the hounds will be here soon. Where is your
courage?* Shuddering, she urged the reluctant warhorse onto
the ice. It stretched away before them, beneath a ghostly
moon.

Perhaps the river would save her. Confused by the jumble
of scents, the hounds might miss her.

Behind her, a twig snapped. Remus growled, muzzle skim-
ming back to bare his teeth.

She hissed to quiet him. The wolf subsided, red eyes trained
upon her. Galahad snorted, and she pressed her hand against
his muzzle. Silence seeped through the forest.

At last she crept forward, wincing at every clop of the
stallion's hooves. Increasingly agitated, Remus wove back
and forth before her legs, whining, nearly tripping her. Then
the stallion picked up the wolf's unease and balked. Peering
behind them, she tugged on the bridle.

Suddenly a sharp percussive crack sounded, followed by a
splash. A stab of terror pierced her heart when she spied the
jagged hole in the ice. In the black water, Remus floundered,
immersed to his snout. His paws churned for purchase, but
found none.

Panic clawed at her chest. Forcing back the clamoring
fear, she tore open her saddlebag, and jerked off her gloves
when she could not find what she sought. The wolf yelped as
he struggled against the deadly current.

Struggling to keep her head, she sobbed with relief when
the coil of rope materialized. Hastily, she looped an end
around Galahad's pommel and tied it, while every instinct
screamed for speed.

At last, she looped the rope around her waist and edged toward the dangerous hole where the wolf fought for his life.

Beneath her, the thin ice cracked. Gasping prayers to every saint she knew, she dropped to her knees and crawled. Icy water seeped through her stockings and bliaut as she inched forward, calling encouragement to the wolf.

She had nearly reached the edge when a snap split the air. Between her hands, a fissure opened. She teetered between unsteady plates of ice—and knew she could proceed no far-ther. Her valiant friend struggled against the deadly current, white-rimmed eyes imploring for help.

Blinded by tears, she screamed, "Remus!"

"Allah's blood, Alienore!" a hoarse voice shouted. *"Don't move."*

Frantic for the wolf, she did not even wonder at the miracle of the Raven's appearance. He strode toward her as she spread herself precariously over the widening fissure.

"Knot the rope around you!" The Raven gripped Galahad's bridle. His steadying presence infused her with a tincture of strength. "I'll pull you out."

"Help Remus!" The wolf yelped and vanished beneath the waves. Her heart lodged in her throat until his wet head emerged. "He cannot hold out much longer."

"After I help you," he said.

On the edge of hysteria, she screamed out the unvar-nished truth. "That wolf is the only creature on earth who loves me! *Help him.*"

"I swear on my life, I will. Alienore—trust me this once."

Conflict twisted her stomach. Knowing she dared not squander precious seconds by arguing, she clung to the rope as it pulled her to safety.

Catching her beneath the arms, the Raven hauled her to her feet, then dragged her against his muscled frame. She clung to him, massive shoulders knotting beneath her grip, and caught a bare glimpse of his scarred features, pitch black hair raked back, amber eyes flaming.

"Bloody reckless woman." Cradling her head, he crushed her against his chest. "Are you injured?"

"Nay," she whispered, feeling his arms around her, pressing her against his strength as if he would never let go. For a mindless instant she sheltered there, safe within the bastion of his body.

A yip of terror shattered the spell. With a rough exhale, he released her.

"Help Remus." Sobbing, she fumbled at the rope.

He knotted it around his own lean waist. "Alienore, if I fall in, you must pull me out. You've the strength to do it."

Nodding, she gripped the rope. He edged onto the dangerous surface. With feline grace, he crawled toward the struggling wolf. Somehow, one limb at a time, he slithered to the broken edge. Looping the rope around her body, she braced to support his weight.

The Raven stretched flat over the fragile ice and reached for the wolf. Obscured by darkness as clouds swept across the moon, he plunged his arms into the freezing water. The frantic wolf struggled, dragging him toward the water. Immersed to his waist, the man held steady, legs straddling the ice.

"I have him," he rasped.

With all her strength, she pulled.

In a flailing scramble, Remus heaved from the water. She sobbed with relief as he trotted to her side. On solid ground, he shook himself, sending a shower of droplets flying.

She could not spare him a moment, her weight set against the drag of the Raven's mighty frame, poised on the broken edge. With no leverage to free himself, the knight lay submerged, risking no further movement. He had to rely upon her to pull him free.

She set her weight against the rope and heaved. His substantial bulk did not budge, and a sob of frustration burst from her. Snugging the rope around Galahad's pommel, she urged him toward the shore.

Beneath their pull, the Raven slid onto solid ice. She urged the horse onward and dragged the knight to safety.

At last she could kneel and fill her arms with wriggling, soaking-wet wolf. She hugged Remus and cried as he covered her face in sloppy kisses.

Thank you, God, for sparing him.

Recalling the Raven, she rose to see what assistance she could offer.

His appearance shocked her to the core. The knight had stripped off his soaking coat and shirt. Naked to the waist, he stood beside Lucifer, his back to her, rummaging for dry garments in his saddlebags.

The sight of his unclothed body seared into her: the raw power that shouted from swelling shoulders, twin columns of muscle plunging down his spine, tapering to a lean waist and leather-wrapped hips. Knotted muscle bulged in his biceps as he worked.

Paralyzed by longing, flooded with heat, she could only stare at him.

At last he pulled a dry coat over his head and tugged it over that sculpted torso. He settled his hammered belt and reclaimed his Saracen sword. Its topaz ember shimmered as he turned toward her. Across the distance between them, their gazes met.

"Lord Raven. Words cannot convey the extent of my gratitude. I can only thank you . . . from the depths of my heart."

Still she could not tear her eyes away.

It has to be said, her honest nature insisted.

"I hope you may forgive me, for . . . for the falsehoods I believed of you. That business with Rohese was a grave injustice. I—misjudged you."

He looked away, brow furrowed. A hint of discomfort deepened the lines around his mouth. Once she would have called it guilt. But she would trust him with her life now. So she attributed his brooding unease to the cold, and watched with a full heart while he tossed the surcoat around his shoulders.

She busied herself with her saddle. "I dare not linger here. Those hounds—Since you were abroad, you cannot know it. I am fleeing the Duc d'Ormonde."

Over his shoulder he cocked her a startled glance, not quite meeting her gaze.

"You fancy Ormonde would loose his hounds on you?"

"I do not know." She sighed. "But he has come to claim me. To find me missing again . . . well, he has waited six months to bring me to heel. Even a saint's patience would be strained by now."

"Alienore." He scrubbed a hand over his face. "Those hounds aren't his."

"How can you be certain?"

"I'm certain." He chuckled grimly. "Broke my journey at Poitiers."

Suddenly she recalled his unexplained absence. Now that she had a moment to think, she wondered why he'd been roaming the woods—at this late hour—to stumble upon her. She drew breath to ask, but his next words sent the thought spinning from her head.

"Eleanor's seized her moment. With her guard made drunk for the holiday, the queen's escaped, her sons with her." He cast her a hooded look. "Those hounds answer to Sir Guy. If he doesn't retake her, his head will roll."

Riveted, she stared. "The queen has escaped?"

"Aye." He swung into his saddle. "Men will die now without fail. Nothing can stop it anymore."

"But King Henry—"

"Has been too lenient." Inscrutable, he pivoted Lucifer and looked down on her. "He must answer this, else his enemies take it for weakness."

"'Tis imperative I reach him." Desperate for haste, still she made herself pause, as he had done, to find a cloth in her saddlebag and towel herself dry. No sense freezing to death when a moment's care would prevent it.

By the time she vaulted into the saddle, a fragile hope fluttered within her. "Do you—would you escort me to Normandy? These are perilous times, and I—I can pay for your service."

For an excruciating interval, he said nothing. Heat crept into her cheeks. A muscle flexed in his jaw, making her wonder what he thought. At last, a corner of his mouth curled up in a mordant smile.

"Aye, Alienore of Lyonstone. I'll take you."

Relief spilled through her, mingled with unsettling excitement. "As to the matter of your payment—"

His eyes were bitter as he spurred past her. "We'll both pay in full for this night's work. Believe me."

Chapter Ten

His plans were ripening faster than he'd hoped. Yet the Raven brooded as they galloped side by side in the moonlight beside the treacherous river that had nearly claimed her life.

He could have lost everything when she startled into flight—but nay. Though he'd never wish harm on the wolf, Remus's mishap had won her trust. Alienore of Lyonstone saw her world straightly, etched in black and white. Now she'd decided to trust him, she'd believe in him as she believed in God.

Aye, she'll believe—until I give her certain proof of treachery. I deserve no one's loyalty.

He'd gambled the threat of marriage would accomplish what persuasion had not, that Alienore would flee as a hart flees the hunter. But he'd failed to anticipate the speed she'd bolted with. Someone had spilled the news too soon. An hour later, and he might never have caught her.

Now the tall beauty rode beside him, valiant as any knight, fierce as the lion that clawed from her knife. Her purity of soul shone through her eyes, unflinching as Damascus steel. When he'd found her crouched over death on that perilous ice, a surge of protective instinct had stopped his heart.

Dangerous nonsense. He crushed his reins until Lucifer snorted in protest. Since Isabella's death, he'd been scrupulously careful never to initiate any liaison beyond the most casual encounters, the rules understood by all.

Never again would he wake sweating with terror on a woman's account. Never again would he stand over such horrors as his grief had wrought in Damascus. Never again would he howl like an animal with anguish—

"There!" Alienore called. Forcing back his hellish memories, he found the silhouette of a ruined watchtower perched above the road.

"The keep that stood there was reduced long ago," she said. "But enough remains for shelter while the horses rest."

"There's a village near, aye? An abbey to shelter travelers."

" 'Tis the hamlet of Châtellerault." She cast him a guarded glance. "But these lands are loyal to the queen. I would not break cover until we leave Aquitaine well behind."

"The tower then." He reined Lucifer into the turn. Despite a roof open to the sky, the walls stood intact, easy to secure.

They stabled their horses on the ground floor and worked side by side in companionable silence. Covertly, he watched her—a constant surprise. The earl's daughter was capable as any squire, courage and resolve emanating from her. Confident and graceful in split skirts and high boots, she hummed under her breath—her smoky contralto, her boudoir voice that set his blood seething.

When would he see her in his bed, long limbs wrapped in furs, burnished curls tumbled around her face as she took him in her mouth?

Hard and aching with desire, he climbed the winding stair to the roof, its crumbling walls framing open sky. A lambent moon gleamed in the bowl of night.

While Alienore spread her blankets in a dry place, he put his back to the wall, where he could watch the stair. Remus curled at his mistress's feet. Soon the wolf's ribs rose and sank with the rhythm of sleep.

While the Raven kindled a fire, she sliced brown bread and sharp cheese—meager fare, but fresh. *Bismillah*, he'd eaten worse. As their meal progressed, the pensive line between her eyebrows deepened. Gradually, her gaze hardened to steely resolve. At intervals, for no apparent reason, a blush suffused her fair skin and her eyes faltered, lashes sweeping down to hide her gaze.

Is she thinking of a man? By the Prophet, Ormonde would suffer no lingering affection for Richard Plantagenet or that Beaumont puppy once she married.

She hugged her knees to her chest. "My unwelcome suitor has hunted me like an animal from England to Aquitaine. Somehow I must persuade him to abandon me."

"Can't see how you'll discourage him." The Raven's eyes hooded. "Sees you as his salvation, maybe."

"I am no priest to absolve his sins." Uneasily, she shifted. "We must expect him at court, sooner or later."

"Likely sooner."

"Yet I am confident of the outcome. I shall persuade the king of my loyalty and regain my inheritance. Ormonde's suit I shall consider in due course."

Trouble was, Ormonde couldn't afford to wait for a marriage-shy maid to arrange her affairs and consider him in due course.

"Still, I will not leave the question to chance." Her silver eyes flashed. "I must ensure I am such a woman as no proud Norman lord will marry."

Oho, clever girl, what scheme do you weave now?

"Do you plan to surrender your lands?" he asked casually. "Donate your inheritance to the Church?"

Let her not consider it.

Eyes blazing, her proud head lifted. "Surrender my father's legacy for my own comfort? I think not."

"How then?"

For a long moment that quivered with intent, she held silent. "The duke has bragged on the virtue of his bride. How then if I am shown to be . . . tainted?"

Cold fury washed over him. *Allah's blood, did Richard—?*

"Do you . . . comprehend what I am suggesting?" Her eyes eluded him as she stroked the wolf.

"Speak plainer."

"Oh, Raven," she sighed. "If you would have me speak plainly, then so I must. By the time we reach court . . . I would be . . . no longer a virgin."

He pushed out a breath, waves of jealousy crashing through him. *Beaumont, it has to be. By all that's holy, I'll kill the puppy!*

"What lucky fellow's chosen for the deed? Or would any willing blade suffice?"

Crimson flooded her skin, but her eyes met his without flinching. "My lord, you swore to seduce the queen's most virtuous lady. I am offering you the opportunity to win your wager."

Unease rippled through him. "My wager?"

"From shame your noble heart shrinks to confess." A wistful smile curved her lips. "Aye, Richard told me everything. You wagered to seduce me."

That was not everything, for no doubt Richard left out his own role. Shame over that thrice-be-damned wager clenched his belly. "Why *me*—of all men living?"

"I am aware of your besetting sins. Women are clearly your weakness, along with a fondness for drink. But there are worse faults a man may have."

He was strangling on the dry bread and cheese of their supper. "Oh, I've worse—"

"Despite your shortcomings, you have shown yourself to be a man of honor." She inclined her head, gracious as a queen.

Nay, that he was not. The Raven gritted his teeth. "Many maids would seek more in a lover."

"Well, one must grant that your hygiene is satisfactory. I cannot deny that is a point in your favor." Her lashes dropped. "Also, Lord Raven, you are not . . . unattractive."

Her whisper ignited him. Since the night he first saw her in all her glory, a costumed goddess at Richard's masque, passion for Alienore of Lyonstone had possessed him like a demon. He burned to claim her, to trumpet his possession to the hopeful gallants who worshipped her. He burned to strip away that cool composure and fire the ardor of the woman beneath.

He sought her gaze. She met him like a knight on the tourney field, all courage and resolve—and a feverish exhilaration that made her eyes glow like lamps.

"Aye, 'tis a mortal sin," she said huskily. "Yet we shall both obtain what we desire. You shall win your wager, and I shall win my freedom."

She would surrender her maidenhood on the basis of a lie. A bolt of guilt shafted through him. She was too good for this, too honorable and brave and fair; she did not deserve this betrayal. Still, whatever her misguided purpose, he'd be a fool to waste this shining opportunity fate tossed in his lap.

A lightning charge of anticipation sizzled through him.

"Intriguing plan, lady. But I've a condition of my own."

"Why, what more can you desire?" Innocent, so innocent, her eyes lifted.

"Pleasure, Alienore. Let's grasp as much as we may tonight."

Staring at the Raven, who lounged like a panther on the floor, Alienore could scarcely believe she'd made this shocking proposal—offered herself like a wanton to the Devil of Damascus.

It had been pure impulse, temptation sprung full-blown as she watched him: dark and deadly as sin, scimitar lying across his knees, ready to defend her always. She placed her mortal soul in jeopardy to protect her honor—and surely for no other reason. By his own admission, he wanted her. Was it so wrong to use that? His passion, her passion, the frisson of raw need that arced between them when they kissed?

She submerged unruly excitement beneath a sea of cold logic. "Pleasure is not our purpose. That is to say," she hurried on, face flaming, "I do not begrudge *you* whatever . . . physical fulfillment . . . you may glean from the undertaking. I warrant some degree of . . . ah, pleasure . . . on your part is needful."

"Aye, it's needful." Swinging his scimitar aside, he uncoiled from the floor. "And not only on my part."

"Wait!" Her hands flew up to keep him at a distance. Now that she'd removed the bastion of propriety that stood between them, the cold composure of the queen's minister deserted her, leaving her red faced and stammering as any maid.

"Ah, certainly that is a noble impulse, Lord Raven. But I would prefer not to linger in the vain pursuit of . . . carnal pleasure." Her voice wavered. "By my faith, I am convent reared, and hardly capable of such."

"You're capable." His amber eyes kindled. "Believe me."

"Nay! I would have you commence the deed swiftly— once I am fully prepared—and thus bring the act swiftly to completion."

"Do I comprehend you?" He spoke with deceptive softness. "I'm to fall on you like a beggar at a Yule feast—once you've braced for my assault—then barrel through the act with no heed for your pleasure?"

"Aye." She set her chin. "I prefer to forgo delay, which only encourages timidity and vacillation."

"You'd find it unpleasant, Alienore—and downright painful."

"Jesus wept! How painful can it be? Most maids survive the experience. Why, even if 'tis painful, I do not fear that."

Chuffing out a frosty breath, he vaulted to his feet and prowled the chamber. "This isn't some challenge to conquer on the tourney field."

She willed her pulse to slow its headlong gallop. If only he looked less like the devil they called him, a lithe shadow sweeping before the fire.

"I have offended you," she said, contrite. "I meant no slur to your . . . abilities. I withdraw the offer—"

"Nay!" He pivoted, surcoat billowing, and speared her with a gloved finger. "I'll do the deed, Allah have mercy on both our souls."

She hardly knew whether to feel relieved or horrified. "Then I suppose I must . . . thank you? I hardly know what to say—"

"Not one damn thing. If you intend to do this, we go about it my way."

Uncertain, she eyed him. She'd supposed this man of the world would accept a lady's advances with greater polish. Instead, he smoldered with contained wrath; she'd grown too accustomed to his restraint. Now she was thankful to have space between them, though she knew with a fluttering in her belly that soon he must come much closer.

No other strategy would save her from Ponce. Bravely, she swallowed her misgivings. "I shall not counsel you."

Indeed not, for what shall I do if he changes his mind?

She conquered a last desperate clutch of modesty. "I fear you must—instruct me how to proceed. Shall I—shall I disrobe?"

Across the chamber, he searched her features. She could not read him, but the harsh cast of his features softened.

"Don't be so hasty," he growled softly, sending chills scudding across her skin. "Let's take some wine. Happens I've a vintage, very rare and . . . special."

"By all means," she said, relieved.

He stalked to their possessions and produced a copper flask. When he poured her a tiny cup brimming with golden wine, the heady aroma of honey and cardamom curled out.

Senses swimming, she tingled when their fingers brushed. "Is this something you brought from Outremer?"

"Long ago." He dropped down beside her. "I was saving it for you, Alienore . . . though I never knew it."

Her heartbeat quickened at this familiar use of her name, which she had more than invited. But he stretched out without touching her, laid his sword within easy reach. Clearly, he would not pounce on her just yet.

The wine coated her mouth in sweetness. Tendrils of heat unfurled in her belly. Liquid warmth pooled and pulsed between her thighs.

"'Tis . . . pleasant." She hoped he would attribute her blush to the fire.

"Ah, but you care not for pleasure. Tell me, what do you fear?"

His proud profile was etched against the fire, his sensual mouth framed with lines of bitterness and pain. White against bronze, the thin scar slashed down.

Once, she'd thought his face betrayed cruelty and dissipation. Yet now she saw only the strength carved by suffering, the wisdom of experience, and the relentless resolve she'd grown to admire. He was valiant and baffling, her unlikely savior—a crusader without a Christian name.

Eased by the wine, her question slipped out. "Did you ever meet my mother?"

"Nay. I came not to court."

He alone might understand her tangled knot of grief and secrets—this disgraced knight who, despite his public shame, had kept his secret honor.

"She was one of Eleanor's ladies when Eleanor was Queen of France and called the most beautiful woman in the world. My mother too was beautiful, and high-spirited— like Rohese."

She hesitated. "But my mother kept her virtue . . . not like Rohese after all."

Her contrite glance absolved him of the sins she'd heaped upon him, but his scowl only deepened.

"My father fell in love with Marguerite the moment he saw her and besieged her with wooing until she agreed to wed." She closed her eyes against the memories, her parents laughing and loving in her childhood. Then later, drawn with suffering and hostility when her father turned against her dying mother.

"Did you never hear how she died?" Her throat ached with unshed tears. "I have never been certain how widely the tale is told."

His breath brushed her ear. "I was in Outremer. Tell me."

"She was badly injured when a tower collapsed in a deserted wing of the castle. She should not have been there." She swallowed. "The stones . . . crushed her spine. She lingered in a sort of twilight for nearly a year, but never left her bed again."

She forced herself to speak of it, her deepest shame. "Someone else was in the tower that day—my father's arms master, Raoul. 'Twas said . . .'twas said they were trysting, that they were lovers. But my mother swore to me, over and over, that it was not so."

Astonishing to reveal this dreadful secret to the man she'd viewed as her enemy. Yet he was her true champion as Thierry had never been—her light in the wilderness, with darkness all around.

The wine's warmth was spreading like ripples in a pond, lapping at every nerve.

"You believed the rumors?"

"My father did." She sighed. "Afterward, my parents never spoke a word without rancor. I believe she died of a broken heart, mourning the death of their love."

"Your father believed," he whispered, breath licking her ear, running like flames along her neck. "But did *you* believe?"

"Never! Not because my mother denied it, but Raoul . . . . he was her cousin, like an uncle to me. After my father and brother took the cross, Raoul was the one who stayed. His legs were crushed when the tower fell. To the end of his days, he shall only crutch along with walking sticks. But Raoul denied the rumors—and him I believed."

"You fear your mother's weakness. Fear the same willful passion that destroyed her will destroy you."

She had never admitted it—never acknowledged that she had donned her armor of virtue to defend from Marguerite's indiscretions.

Recklessly she swallowed the last sweet drops. The wine burned all the way down to the woman's place that nestled between her thighs, swathed in layers of wool and linen. That hidden place throbbed gently, like a beating heart.

"I have no such passions, for I am no mere Rievaulx. I am a Lyonstone first."

"Whatever you are, you don't lack passion." His lean features filled her vision, copper skin framed by the night black spill of hair.

"I shall never acknowledge such passions, Raven, no matter what was in that wine."

"Think I'd drug you?" His mouth twisted bitterly. "Well, no wonder."

"Nay, I only meant—"

"It's a potion to relax you, no more." Deftly, he hooked his fingers in her snood and pulled it free. The sensuous slither of hair unraveled down her back.

"Place your trust in me, Alienore. Trust me this once."

"I trust you, Raven," she whispered. "But I shall feel nothing in your arms—neither fear nor passion. I'll lie with you to defeat my enemies, nothing more."

"Nay, brave one. Let yourself know pleasure now." His golden eyes seared through her, through the dizzying plunge of falling, the world revolving around her. He caught her gasp with a kiss.

His mouth was a warm vortex drawing at her resolve, flavored with spice and honey. She gripped his surcoat to anchor herself—the panther's lush pelt sheathing his fierce heart. His arm swept around her and pulled her into him.

She splayed her palms against his chest, her entire body thrilling with danger. She who feared no man, who defeated armed knights in battle—now overwhelmed and powerless, disarmed by a kiss. The languorous pulse between her thighs waxed and waned. God save her from this heathen wine!

She clutched his massive shoulders. His arm was sheathed steel against her spine, yet still she was falling. He alone could save her.

"Stop, Raven! This was not what we agreed."

"Too late—far too late. Tell me now you feel nothing."

"I feel nothing! 'Tis only the wine. Do you think I don't know?"

"Brave as a lion," he muttered, curse and endearment mingled.

Above, the star-filled heavens shaded from black to cobalt, for dawn was coming. A bird's silhouette perched on the wall. Skilled as a troubadour, the Raven plucked the lute strings of her flesh, kissed the pulse that hammered against her throat. A glissade of gooseflesh raced along her skin.

In that instant she understood, with piercing clarity, the sweet beguilement of sin. She would sell her soul gladly to prolong this exquisite cascade of the senses.

Was this what Marguerite had felt? Was this what condemned her? She shuddered as his lips found the hollow below her ear, stirring ripples of shivery pleasure.

"Does this please you?" he whispered.

At last, she'd found a man who matched her strength. A man whose powerful sense of honor guided him like a rudder through the treacherous shoals of life, a man she could admire . . . even love.

His fingers brushed the wool-sheathed curve of her breast. A shock jolted through her. "My God, Raven . . ."

All the blood in her body was rushing to that point, her

breast swelling to fill his hand, rising to a peak. Extraordinary, these ribbons of sensation unfurling to her center.

She struggled to speak, voice so husky it sounded like a stranger's. "This is indecent."

He chuckled like the devil himself, his thumb brushing back and forth over the swollen peak until she could bear no more, the heart of her body throbbing.

When he tugged at her lacings, she clutched his shoulders.

"Wait, Raven! I am no longer certain this is a wise notion."

"It isn't," he murmured. "You deserve a better man."

A warning whispered through her, forgotten when he kissed her, and fueled the slick throbbing where her thighs pressed together. When their tongues twined, his breath caught. For the first time, she knew the heady rush of feminine power, to render this fearsome knight helpless with a touch.

A seam of cool air opened along her spine as the gown slipped from her shoulders. The curves of her breasts stood outlined, pushing boldly against her linen shift. In his face, she surprised an expression of brooding tenderness, foreign to his hardened features—affection, shadowed by remorse. She wondered at it until his fingers teased and stroked again. Until she closed her eyes, forgetting.

"Alienore, you're ready for this, brave one. I've waited for you forever . . . far longer than you know."

In a sudden rush of modesty, she gripped his hands.

"A moment," she whispered, seeking some last reassurance. "Tell me your true name first."

A raptor's lids slid down to hood his eyes. He went utterly still, face closing around his secrets, and she knew he would not answer.

Then his gaze probed hers as if searching for her soul. His breath released in a sigh. As though the tower were filled with people, he pressed his brow to hers and whispered.

"My Christian name was . . . Jervaise."

"Jervaise." He trusted her with his secrets, as she trusted him with hers. "'Tis a beautiful name and naught to be hidden."

When he tugged her shift gently, the lines of her body were revealed. How could he like what he saw: the ripple of muscle honed by years of sword-play, her breasts too full, as she'd always thought? Suddenly, she was torn between an abashed desire to cover herself and the need to pull him closer.

He eased her back on his cloak, warmed by his body and fragrant with musk. The plush fur caressed her naked skin. Though she could not say what she desired, her fingers spoke for her, trailing along his coat.

He unhitched his sword belt, swung aside the sheathed crescent—disarming himself in her presence, trusting her that much. Then he peeled off his coat and bared the colossal physique that stole her breath.

Bronzed by the dying fire, his skin stretched tight over slabs of muscle, dusky male nipples, torso crossed by the pale slash of old scars. The double column of his abdomen plunged down into his braies. She dared lower her gaze no farther just yet.

Her curious fingers traced the bulge of his arms. His skin burned with fever, heat radiating in waves she could almost see. She had never thought a man's skin could be smooth and supple as doeskin. The feel of him fascinated her, the contrasts between smooth and rough, fierce and gentle.

Suddenly she longed to feel him everywhere. Smiling, she pulled him toward her.

He laughed deep in his throat and bent over her—

The harsh caw of a raven did not alarm her, even when the ripple of warning ran through the Raven's body. The wolf raised his head and growled. Too late she heard the clump of booted feet on the stairs.

Behind the Raven a torch flared, illuminating the men who followed: guards in Plantagenet crimson, eyes flying wide with speculation, an incredulous Sir Guy Aigret. Bringing up the rear, scarlet with mortification and betrayal, stood Thierry de Beaumont.

Stunned, she remained where she was. Surely the Raven would leap up, his scimitar flashing to defend her as always. Yet he made no move for his blade.

His words pulled the scales from her eyes at last. He pressed his brow to hers. "Alienore, I'm sorry. You left me no choice."

Chapter Eleven

Sadly the church bells tolled, clanging through the keep where the king's men were holding her. Yet it was not the hour for prayer. Frowning, Alienore rose from her stone-cold hearth.

A pity Sir Guy could find no better prison for the queen's privy chancellor. Since she'd been taken into custody, she had grown weary of this drafty chamber, the lumpy pallet where she tossed at night, the limited view of muddy streets below.

Now the view remained unaltered. Judging by the bells, she'd expected some catastrophe, a conflagration or plundering army.

Shivering, she hugged herself, detesting the grimy feel of her gown. She'd been wearing it since Poitiers, three full days past. The teeth of worry gnawed her. Somehow she must speak with someone, learn what was happening beyond these walls, or go mad.

Pious Ponce—where are you now, my twice-jilted suitor? Have I discouraged you at last with this latest shaming? And the queen—God save her, where was the queen? Did Eleanor believe she'd betrayed her?

Restlessly she paced, breath puffing white, her route made wearisome by repetition. When she stooped to hug Remus for comfort, she caught a whiff of the malodorous bucket.

The wolf was allowed out to relieve his needs, but she was not. Sir Guy would take no risks where Eleanor's privy chancellor was concerned.

I should have swallowed my accursed pride when he came

upon us—the Devil of Damascus and the queen's most virtuous lady, tumbled on the floor like a pair of rutting peasants. Fiercely, she banished the memories that pulsed with banked desire. Better she should flog herself for the appalling breach of judgment that landed her in that reprobate's arms, and now in this current disaster.

I should have explained, but I was too proud to defend myself before the king's leering men.

And Thierry, her disillusioned Lancelot, had been so furious he would not even look at her, all that dreadful ride to Châtellerault. She'd known no other way to withstand the scorching shame of being discovered with a known libertine in the tatters of compromised virtue—no other way but to hold her head high and ride in imperial silence. Sir Guy had ordered her captivity and thundered off in pursuit of the fleeing queen, with no time to spare for a dishonored maid.

The church bells crashed, great deep-throated alarms that set the world trembling. Heart lurching, she hurried to the arrow loop and fretted to find the same view.

What if Louis had sent French troops to support Eleanor's rebellion? Or was it wrathful Ponce, come to appease his wounded pride?

If it's Ponce, praise God they did not take my long-knife.

The thud of a heavy fist sent her spinning toward the door, the knife flashing free in her hand. Then she chided herself for a fool. If soldiers had taken the town by force, they would not knock politely before bursting in.

"Enter," she called.

Sir Guy pushed in, clad in mud-spattered riding clothes. He avoided her gaze, and she fought down a hot blush. This good-hearted Englishman, her father's friend, had seen her half-naked on the floor in a wastrel's arms. She could scarce bear to contemplate what he must think of her.

Yet not for nothing was she an earl's daughter. She sank into a stately curtsy.

"Bid you good evening, Sir Guy."

"Milady." Speaking their native English, he darted her an uncomfortable glance. "I thought ye'd wish to know. The queen's been captured."

Ah, the bells! They ring the queen's doom. Her heart sank to her boots, but she spoke steadily.

"Has she been allowed to account for herself? Perhaps there is yet some reasonable explanation."

"Bah!" No man to waste words, he grimaced. "She's proved a traitor to any man's satisfaction—even a wronged husband. We caught her, disguised as a man, riding hard to Paris. Her saddlebags were bursting with treasonous papers and half the wealth of Aquitaine."

The chamber dimmed around her as the last flicker of hope sputtered out.

So the queen is a traitor after all. My faith in her was as misplaced as my faith in that wastrel knight. God's truth, I must be a fool indeed to possess such appalling judgment.

Eyes stinging, she spoke in muffled tones. "And her sons?"

"Those whelps of the devil?" He snorted. "Richard and Geoffrey made good their escape, God rot their treasonous souls. By now, they'll be in Paris with their worthless brother, swearing fealty to French Louis."

So must all honest Englishmen think of their princes now. She swallowed past the ache in her throat. "I pray you, what will happen to her?"

"She'll not see the light of day again, except through iron bars—never go free while our king lives. Maybe he'll divorce her, for never had a man greater cause."

"He'll not divorce her and risk losing Aquitaine," she whispered. "But how she will hate being imprisoned."

Even after all the queen had done, a rush of compassion nearly undid her.

Whatever she is, whatever she has done, I love her. Just as I loved my mother.

"Where will they take her?"

"King's issued orders to hold her at Chinon. Those lands will hold loyal—not like Aquitaine."

"Chinon is in Anjou." A spark of hope flared in her battered heart. "A day's ride from here."

"I set sail by river at dawn. Now this thaw's rotted the ice, it's easier than wading hip deep through the mud. God knows I'd enough of that business while we hunted her down."

"Sir Guy." Clasping her hands, white-knuckled, she lifted her eyes to his. "I know you've no cause to think well of me—now. Nonetheless, I would ask a boon."

Embarrassment furrowed his brow at this oblique reference to a lady's shame. He scrubbed his face with a calloused hand.

"Aye, well, ye may ask."

She drew a careful breath. "Her Grace will be devastated, with all her poor hopes in shambles. I am her godchild, and . . . 'twould mean a great deal to be allowed to see her."

"Christ, milady." Groaning, he stumped to the dead fire and scowled at the bucket with its foul contents.

"Ye've been kept in poor comfort, haven't ye, lass? I'll ask yer pardon for that. Theobold's daughter deserves better."

Her cheeks burned to hear the words of condemnation he did not utter. This was her own doing. If she'd remained with the queen, she might have prevented—

With difficulty, she quashed the thought. "I know what it must have seemed. What you must have thought when I fled without a word and then . . . later."

Her voice nearly failed her, but she forged through the burning wall of shame. "I swear to you, upon my mother's soul—I was going to the king. I had naught to do with the queen's escape, I swear it!"

He puffed out a skeptical snort.

"I left a note to bid her farewell. You may ask my tiring girl. By my faith, I am no traitor!"

Though he refrained from heaping his doubts upon her head, the forthright old soldier avoided her gaze. "Aye, that Raven said the same—defended ye. But what else could he do, the way we found ye?"

The Raven had entrapped her, compromised her, coldly planned her humiliation like a military campaign, then dared to apologize as the king's men took her. She'd not glimpsed the wretch since her imprisonment. But she would not ask her guard about him for all the riches in Outremer—those selfsame men who'd found her in his arms.

Jervaise. Is that even your name? She had nothing to occupy her mind save thoughts of him. No doubt that was why she could not forget him.

Sir Guy stabbed the ashes with his poker as if wishing he could run the man through. "The Raven—ha! What manner of godless name is that for a Christian knight? Damned if I know what to make of him." He fixed her with a shrewd eye. "He claims he's the king's man now."

"So he has always claimed."

"But I can't disprove it, can I, without the king's word? And well the villain knows it. So I'm holding him under guard."

The Raven held captive! Savage vindication speared through her even as alarm knotted her stomach. Her muddled reactions to the man infuriated her. Surely that unprincipled knave deserved whatever befell him. He had betrayed her, betrayed Eleanor, betrayed his country and his God when he fought for the Saracens. What would prevent him from betraying Henry too? If Sir Guy threw the Raven into the deepest pit in Aquitaine and left him there to rot, it would serve the man right.

Still, there was justice to consider. Whatever his motives, he'd saved her on the road to Castile, saved Remus from drowning too. She owed him something for that.

"I suppose he must be allowed to clear his name, Sir

Guy—if he can. We shall address the king when you take me before him."

The old knight threw her a cross look. "I thought 'twas Eleanor ye wished to see."

"Both ends may be accomplished with one stroke. Chinon stands north between here and Normandy by almost any route. I would see Her Grace, offer what comfort I may, then accompany you to the king."

"I planned to leave ye here." He scowled at the cold hearth. "Devil take it, this is no fit lodging for a lady! I'd clear yer name, lass, if I could—for Theobold's sake."

"My good man, it shall be cleared," she said more surely than she felt. "I shall give you no cause for dismay. You have my word of honor."

"See that ye don't," he grunted. "I'll leave orders. Be ready to sail at dawn."

A thrill of triumph sang through her veins. If they traveled swiftly, perhaps she would yet manage to reach the king before Ponce found her. That much of her plan she could still salvage. When the duke finally overtook her, her rumored defilement must surely cool his ardor.

Yet conscience prodded her toward her duty—such as it was—toward the scurrilous knight who'd entrapped her.

"If I may inquire, what do you intend to do with Lord Raven?"

Halfway to the door, Sir Guy halted. "What do ye think? There were enough eyes to see what I saw. I can't still so many flapping tongues, no matter what I threaten."

And that must suit her all to the good. What use to sacrifice her virtue, if she concealed her ruin?

She drew the shreds of her dignity around her. "Do you mean to present his case to the king?"

"I suppose," he said, without enthusiasm. "Until then— God's truth, I hardly know what to do with him."

Well, she would ensure his case came before Henry—
which was more than she felt like doing in her current
temper. If the villain was what he claimed, the king would
restore him. Her honor would allow no less, for the debt she
owed him.

Still, he had schemed to betray her. She'd been a sparrow-
brained idiot to fancy herself in love with the Devil of
Damascus.

The bells had fallen silent, smothered by gathering night.
Kneeling beside her pallet, Alienore composed her anxious
heart for prayer.

A covert rustling, like a mouse's scurry, whispered in the
corridor. Remus uncurled from the hearth, a growl rumbling
through his chest. Her heart lodged in her throat as the door
eased open, admitting a slender shadow.

She could not discern the intruder beyond her circle of
candlelight. But the Raven's bold features sprang to mind.
And why should that villain make her heart race—except
with rage at his betrayal!

Warily she rose, one hand slipping to her knife. "Who
goes there?"

"Quietly, my lady!" the shadow hissed.

Her heart sank with an odd disappointment. Her nocturnal intruder, whoever he was, lacked the Raven's unmistak-
able sense of presence. Remus bristled protectively before
her, snarls rumbling behind his teeth.

"Who goes, I say?" Her knife gleamed a cold warning.
"Identify yourself."

"Call off your beast!" he whispered before the wolf's crouching menace. "For mercy, Alienore."

"Thierry?" Grimacing, she knelt to restrain the wolf. Remus
had never cared for him—unlike the Raven, to whom the wolf
had quickly taken. She'd trusted the one and despised the

other, but now her heart had turned topsy-turvy. She could no longer follow the compass of her instincts.

"Sieur de Beaumont." She gathered her composure. "Why have you come?"

"Am I not welcome?"

"Let us say, you are not expected." Dryly, she glanced at her threadbare surroundings. "I can hardly receive you properly."

"This is no social call." His surcoat glittered as he slipped into the light—every inch the comte's son, with all the surface splendor that had dazzled and blinded her to the character within.

Truly seeing him for the first time, she searched his boyish features and wondered why she'd never noticed his weak chin. She'd been too enchanted by the idea of him. Now it amazed her that she'd mistaken girlish infatuation for the tumultuous pull of love.

To behold him now, she felt nothing—only impatience for the silly child she had been, to believe this pretty youth could save her. She hoped she'd not made too great a fool at court—the Earl of Lyonstone's daughter, throwing herself at this boy's head.

"Well?" he asked, tight-lipped. "Have you nothing to say?"

Sighing, she squared herself for an unpleasant encounter. "What would you have me say? I am condemned by all as a traitor, it seems. Therefore I cannot be trusted."

Perhaps he had never loved her, but a puzzled hurt lingered in his turquoise eyes—as in those of a kicked puppy.

Thierry shifted the bundle he clutched—her saddlebag, kept from her since her capture. It held nothing to incriminate, except her sword. She prayed they had not taken it.

"I see they have given you my travel pouch. Am I now to beg for the return of my own possessions?"

"You needn't beg." A blush colored his cheeks, but he spoke

with awkward dignity. "Sir Guy said they might be returned, since they yielded no contraband."

"Saint Swithun grant mercy for that. I shall have a fresh gown, at least, in which to face the world. You may have noted I am in sore need of one."

"I'm amazed you are not shown the courtesy due your station." He gripped the pouch as if uncertain how to bestow it. "I'm told you're to be taken before the king."

"Aye, to clear my name. Since I cannot prevail by force, I must rely upon him to end this so-called betrothal."

"You should have turned to *me*."

"And how would you have aided me?" Six months of frustration rose to the fore. "That has never been clear to me, for all our discussions on the subject."

"I would have married you!" He flung down her saddlebag. "We would have claimed your dowry. I would have shared your title. But nay, you would not hear me. Instead you turned to the Raven—him of all men. You fell into his hands like a ripe fruit!"

A flood of shame washed through her. "I was wrong to trust him."

He hesitated. "This peculiar rumor of Ponce's arrival that I gave you, at risk of my own allegiance. Alienore . . . he never came."

"Never came?" Blankly, she stared. "What do you mean?"

"I mean that I left Poitiers this morning with still no sign of the man nor word of him."

Stubbornly her mind refused to grasp his meaning, even as suspicion flared. Once he had been her Lancelot, her shining knight. Weak willed he might be, but outright deceit had no part in his character.

She clasped her hands to still their tremor. "I do not understand."

"Nor did I—at first. Someone *lied* to Prince Richard about his arrival. Ponce d'Ormonde is nowhere near these parts.

Likely he remains at your manor, fasting and praying, or what have you."

"But that does not make sense," she whispered. "Why should anyone lie about such a thing, unless—"

Comprehension struck her like a blow. Unless someone would trick her to undertake what she refused to do otherwise—desert the queen in her hour of need. The Raven wished her gone from Eleanor's court. And so she'd gone, bolting like a frightened rabbit.

The sickening truth sank like a stone in her gullet. The Raven had guessed she would flee, guessed she would be followed. How well he had plotted her downfall.

Alienore, I'm sorry, he'd whispered.

She had admired him, trusted him—even loved him, for a moment. Inconceivable that he'd betrayed her so thoroughly—a man with his unflinching valor. Unless that too had been subterfuge, all of it: his defense of her, Remus's rescue, even his willingness to bed her. All coldly engineered to win her trust.

But why? So he could bring her to Henry for gold or recognition? To win his wretched wager? The pain of betrayal twisted her heart.

"What a simpleton I have been." Tears blurred her vision, but she blinked them back. She would show no weakness until she was alone.

"I know you . . . valued him." Thierry hovered, hand extended as if to help her—ineffectual even in this. "He showed his true character when he dishonored your cousin, didn't he?"

"Aye," she said numbly. She had even believed his scurrilous claim about Rohese's easy virtue—believed him before her own blood kin. "How blind I have been! A blind, stupid fool."

"Wiser eyes than yours were taken in—even the king, apparently. Alienore, if I may somehow assist you . . . ?"

Faintly she smiled, though her heart was splitting in twain. "You are kinder to me than I deserve."

He turned aside, a strained note in his voice. "Consider it a final courtesy."

"A final courtesy? How so?"

"I am leaving the queen's court. There is no need for her courtiers now."

No need but loyalty, chivalry and Christian kindness toward your queen.

From courtesy more than interest, she asked, "Where will you go?"

"My father summons me home. He is most displeased that I have not yet married."

"I shall be sorry for it." Indeed, she felt a moment's grief for their childish love. But that was past, and her innocence was ashes.

He cleared his throat. "Your cousin Rohese is to return home as well. Her family estates lie near the Beaumont lands. Of course, I've offered to escort her."

"Of course." She eyed him. "Her only brother died on crusade, so she has a generous dowry."

"I would have preferred to marry you, but that is no longer possible," he said stiffly. "With the stink of scandal clinging to your name, no lord would wed you now."

She fought down the scalding shame—still an earl's daughter, despite everything.

"If only Ponce feels the same," she murmured, "I swear 'tis worth it to be rid of the wretch."

Chagrin flashed across his features, and she knew he regretted their sharp exchange.

"Never mind, Thierry. You were kind to tell me, though I have given you little cause for kindness."

Thierry hesitated. "I should make my farewells. Lady Rohese awaits me."

"You may rest easy." She struggled against a tide of regret.

"When I depart, the Raven remains here. I shall never lay eyes upon him again."

Fog swirled over the river and wound through the trees. Only the muted tramp of boots disturbed the dawn. Alienore shivered as she hurried along, Remus trotting at her side, enclosed by a phalanx of Plantagenet guards. Sir Guy was taking no chance she might escape.

Did the man not know all courage had fled her? The compass of certainty that steered her life had skewed awry the night she abandoned her queen. Now she lacked a guiding star to set her course. She was adrift, clinging to the twisted wreckage of her life.

At least her virtue remained intact. She thanked God that Sir Guy had interrupted their ill-starred encounter.

The tall mast of a boat pierced the fog. Its hull scraped against the dock with a hollow sound. Shadowy figures appeared and vanished on the foredeck among the tethered horses. Her dappled Galahad whinnied a greeting when he saw her and brought a wan smile to her lips.

Let no man guess my heart is broken. She'd donned severe black velvet—the color of austerity—hair coiled low on her neck, black silk ribbon twined through the braids. Squaring her shoulders, she marched forward like a prisoner to her execution.

The barge loomed before her. Remus bounded across the gap, causing a flurry of consternation as he wove grinning among the guards. She gathered her skirts and reached for the rail.

From nowhere, a cold breeze sprang up, stirring the iron river into anxious ripples. Overhead, a raven cawed. The fog billowed and parted before her.

Heat swept through her in a scalding rush as the black knight stalked toward her, boots striking the deck like the hammer of doom. The world fell silent with dismay.

Within the hood, his scarred features were intent, fixed on her like a loaded crossbow. His burning eyes were arrows of fire, targeting her heart as he reached—

She snatched her hand away. A shaky breath spilled out as she spun toward Sir Guy.

"What is the meaning of this?" she demanded. "We both agreed this man was not to come."

"Milady." Looking harassed, Sir Guy ducked a bow. "I can't twist my plans this way and that to suit a maid's fancy. We're about the king's business here. Lord Raven—hah!— sails with us as far as Chinon. Then we'll see."

She stiffened her spine and looked down her nose at the Englishman. Discomfort and belligerence warred in his face as he glared back.

If she allowed her armor of ice to thaw, she would hurl accusations at the Raven that blistered every pair of ears in hearing.

"I refuse to travel with this unprincipled varlet," she said coldly.

"It's that, or return to yer cell." Sir Guy glanced uneasily at the Raven.

She was not so great a fool to fight a lost battle. Raking the Raven with a frigid glare she hoped would freeze the extremities right off him, she swept her skirts in a disdainful hand and leaped aboard, ignoring his extended hand.

A plump wren of a girl, rosy with smiles, popped up before her. "Ooh, milady, ye look chilled right through! But we'll put ye right."

"Nesta!" Relief sweeping through her, Alienore embraced her tiring girl. "I thought not to find you again."

"Sir Guy brung me here—the queen bein' gone and all. Did I do right to come, milady?"

"You did." Alienore smiled into the worried brown eyes.

"Well, ye may not think so for long. Ye'll recollect how

seasick I was during the Channel crossing. I'm already feeling a bit green around the gills."

With the girl's assistance, Alienore found a protected seat out of the wind. The crew cast off the lines and the current tugged them forward, sweeping them past the bulk of Châtellerault toward the mighty Loire, and eventually the sea.

Ranks of oars dipped into gray water to propel them. At such speed, they should make Chinon in no time—the sooner to rid herself of the Raven's repellant presence.

As if conjured, he emerged from the mist. Beneath the hood, his saturnine features were drawn tight, as if he squared himself against a difficult task. Nay, it could never be shame flickering in those heathen eyes. She must no longer deceive herself.

Pointedly she turned away, watching the trees slide past. If only her heart would ease its frantic tumble . . .

"Three days past, I was your champion." His raspy voice was acrid with bitterness. "Today I'm the villain, fallen from grace."

And do you wonder why! She wanted to scream at him. She wanted to pound her fists against his chest—the same chest she'd caressed with curious fingers, hot bronze skin stretched over muscle.

Somehow she contained the furious words bubbling on her lips. She would not lower herself by engaging him. Instead, she glared toward the shore, though she could not have described what she saw there.

Pushing out a breath, he hunkered down. "You're right to be angry. I deserve all your curses. For whatever it's worth—your disgrace was never my aim."

Oh, how she yearned to shrivel him with a scathing denunciation.

"Alienore—I'd remedy this, any way I might. You comprehend me?"

He reached for her, and her composure snapped. Furiously, she turned on him.

"Can you remedy the fact that you are a liar and a knave? That your only intent in aiding me was to trick me into trusting you for your own shameful purpose? Can you restore your honor and mine with words?"

"Nothing I can do would dull the bright blade of your honor," he said low. For a heartbeat, the keen beam of his eyes looked straight into her soul. "Any claim to honor, I lost long ago. But I never wished you ill."

"You planted the lie that Ponce rode to Poitiers, did you not? Knowing what I would do . . ."

He stiffened. "How—?"

"Do not think to deny it! 'Twas a ploy to send me bolting, so you could play at being my champion, to make me—trust you." Her voice broke, but she steeled herself to finish. "Ponce never set foot in Aquitaine, did he? Thierry de Beaumont told me."

He searched her face as though waiting for more. When she said nothing further, his broad shoulders eased. "Beaumont again."

"How pleased you must have been! How you must have gloated to see me tumble into your arms like a foolish maid."

"I never gloated, Alienore." He glanced aside, one hand scrubbing his lined features. "By the Prophet, I regret my choices—all of them."

"But you do not deny it?" She felt an odd stirring of disappointment. Surely she had not expected him to redeem himself, explain it away at this late hour?

He frowned into the distance. "I don't deny I wished you free of the queen and safe."

"Do not dare claim you lied for my benefit." She drew on the well of courage, that unflinching determination to know her adversary. "Why did you do it? Was it so vital to win your wager?"

"Damn the bloody wager," he growled, flinging back his hood with contained violence. "You think this is all for that?"

His hard-edged beauty burned her, all feral eyes and raking cheekbones, sin black hair pulled sleek at his nape. Her treacherous heart turned cartwheels.

"I never spoke you false, Alienore. Yet I've lied all the same, aye? The truth'll come clear soon enough. I've played this game out."

"How disappointing for you." She turned away. "Your grand amusement shall be over."

"Alienore—"

"Do not call me so!" She willed away the tears that betrayed her. "There is nothing between us—nothing at all, do you hear?"

Softly he said, "Now it's you who lie."

He was not the man she'd believed him to be. She had loved a lie, a mirage that did not exist, except in her dreams.

"Leave my presence, or I shall ask Sir Guy to remove you." She steeled her voice. "After we come to Chinon, I do not wish to see you again."

The world held its breath while he uncoiled to his feet. Regret darkened his tone.

"You may find that difficult—Allah help us both."

Chapter Twelve

Shrouded in cobwebs, the chamber made a better crypt than a chapel. The fusty smell of mildew lingered in corners no servant had aired, so suddenly had the queen arrived.

A tiny island of candlelight burned in a vast sea of darkness. The Queen of England knelt at prayer, her slender back straight as an honest intention. But her head was bowed—too heavy a weight for the fragile neck. By that tiny clue, Alienore sensed her sovereign's despair.

Unwilling to intrude, she hovered near the door, shutting out the impersonal eyes of the Plantagenet guards. Indeed, she welcomed privacy for her own unruly emotions: the sharp spear of her queen's betrayal, set against a sneaking sense of guilt. If she had not abandoned Eleanor, could she have counseled the queen to stay?

"Your Grace." Alienore fell to her knees. "God and Saint Swithun uphold you."

"It would take nothing short of a miracle to uphold me now. But our cause is not lost." Green lightning flashed in the queen's eyes. "For my sons remain at liberty. Soon or late, their army shall restore me."

"Madam, do not speak such words, even to yourself! Your enemies would construe them as treason."

The queen crossed the chamber in a rustle of blazoned brocade. Bending gracefully, she clasped Alienore's hands and raised her. "I did not grant this audience to speak of my plight, but of yours."

Within Alienore, the bubble of guilt swelled and burst. A

sob clawed from her throat. Kneeling again, she kissed the signet ring of Aquitaine.

"Your Grace, my plight is nothing that cannot be made right. I am here for your comfort. We must pray—"

The queen's hands tightened in warning as the door scraped inward. The hammer of recognition whelmed her heart.

The Raven filled the doorway like a dark angel, draped in the black wings of his surcoat. When he bowed, inky hair slithered around his grim features.

"Ah, Lord Raven." The queen smiled. "We appreciate your swift response to our summons."

Suspicion tingled through Alienore as he joined this private audience, turning to keep both doors in sight—as if he suspected assassins, even here.

The door boomed closed. The candles fluttered in their sconces like fading hopes.

Glaring at him, Alienore dashed away her tears and rose. Could she not even beg her sovereign's forgiveness without his involvement? Oh, she was still angry—blindingly angry, stung by the bee of wounded pride and the ache of her lacerated heart.

This man had unclothed her . . . touched her . . . in ways no other man had ever dared. And she'd responded, flamed to blazing life. Even loved him, for a heartbeat.

"*Avoi.*" The queen's eyes lingered on her struggling features. "Sir Guy informs me you are bound for the king in Normandy."

Alienore knew how damning that must look. "'Tis not as it appears—"

"Is it not?" the queen said mildly. "And what say you, Lord Raven?"

"I fixed my course long ago," he rasped. "I say it's over late to change it."

"You speak more truly than you know. You may find Henry to be less favorably disposed—shall we say, less predictable—than you expect. Before you beard that lion in his den, I am resolved to defend Alienore from scandal."

Unlooked-for hope reared up, warring with bitter irony. The queen had not defended her loyal chancellor, but she would act now for the guilty fugitive who'd abandoned her?

The Raven studied Eleanor of Aquitaine as a man studies a strange dog, ready to defend himself if it seemed likely to bite him.

The queen glided to the window, tinged with the ruddy light of sunset. "Sir Guy has explained the circumstances in which he . . . found you."

Alienore burned with humiliation. Her disgrace was common knowledge—she must accustom herself to it. But her shame would save her from pious Ponce when he ran her to ground. "Your Grace, I shall not make excuses for my abominable conduct. I made full confession to the priest, who gave me penance—"

"By good Saint Thibault!" Wearily, the queen bowed her head against the glass. "Did you think I would reproach you?"

"How can you not? I reproach myself hourly for this debacle."

The Raven's face tightened, a muscle flexing in his jaw.

"Oh, Alienore," the queen sighed. "Normally I would rejoice to see that icy heart of yours melted by ardor. You might say it restores my faith in the frailty of human nature. However, this public scandal has cost you dearly."

The Raven gripped the curved dagger at his belt. "I'll make amends for that."

Alienore shot him a wrathful look. "I want nothing from you."

"*Voire*, monsieur!" the queen exclaimed. "You shall have your hands full with her. Even so, I rely upon you to keep your word . . . this time. I do not view lightly this shaming of my virtuous lady. You cannot restore her virtue by slaughtering any man who dares question it. Normandy is not Damascus, Lord Raven. Your usual tactics are sadly unsuited to any civilized land."

A chill radiated from him. "I'm aware of that."

"Indeed, I can think of nothing that may repair the damage you have wrought . . . but wait."

An instant before her fate was sealed, Alienore knew what the queen would say. A bolt of stunned disbelief smote her, so she could not speak. The queen met her horrified gaze with something like compassion.

"Monsieur, it is our will that you marry my privy chancellor, Lady Alienore of Lyonstone, to restore her good name and honor."

Alienore was strangling on the bitter bile that rose from her stomach. Emotion knotted her innards like colic. Past all caution or restraint, a shout burst from her lungs.

"Nay, I will not marry *him!*"

Before her queen's astonished glance, she mustered an army of words to defend herself. She must order a legion of logical objections Eleanor's rational mind would accept.

"Your Grace, think what you are saying. I, an earl's daughter, to marry this . . . this villain, this wretch? There is no name black enough to call him."

The queen elevated her eyebrows. "It is our will."

"Nay!" She strove to master her tone. "I—I cannot marry him. I care nothing for my tattered reputation. I care nothing for . . . dishonor. Why, better even Ponce than—"

"Alienore." The Raven's fists clenched at his side.

Blinded by fury, she turned on him. If she saw triumph gleaming in his eyes, she would kill him where he stood. What a coup this would be for him, far better than any wager!

Yet his eyes were grim as ashes. "For you, of all women, to claim you care nothing for honor."

Swiftly she turned away. Aye, once she'd prized honor

beyond everything. But for one misguided moment, she had trusted her heart instead.

"Alienore." He addressed her stiff-held back. "When we were found and you . . . compromised, I would've offered marriage. By the Prophet, this very morn I said—but it was futile. You wouldn't hear me—"

"Futile?" She whirled to face him, so angry she could barely form the words. "'Tis utterly impossible. If for no other reason than who you are and who I am! How should I marry a wastrel who claims not even a Christian name?"

"Depardieu," the queen sighed.

Startled, Alienore swung toward her. In her fury, she had almost forgotten the royal presence.

"I would never sanction such a match as she describes for an earl's daughter," the queen said, "no matter the circumstance. Monsieur, I fear you have played out your game. You had better reveal who you are."

Alienore stared from one to the other. So the queen had known him. And why should it surprise her? As she watched him, scar blazing white against sun-bronzed skin, the rat of suspicion nibbled at her mind.

"Aye, pray tell." Her words echoed, as if from far away. "If *truth* is a word whose meaning you know. What man are you?"

He expelled a harsh breath. "It won't please you to hear. I'd rather have told it my way."

"Belike that would have been never," she said coldly.

Her blood pounded against her temples, the ominous tightening that preceded a megrim.

"Half my life, I hid my name." White-knuckled, he gripped his dagger. "In its place, men gave me another—one all the world knew. Then I won the duchy—"

A strangled blurt of sound slipped past her lips. His bitter mouth twisted.

"Lady." He grimaced as if the words soured his tongue. "I'm the Duc d'Ormonde."

"Ponce," she whispered. But how could this be? She'd seen Ponce in England, if only from a distance. The coil of tension around her temples clenched tighter. *God save me, I swooned into his arms like a serving wench! I even fancied I loved him—*

"Not Ponce." His eyes hooded. "Ponce is dead, these four months past."

"Dead?" Her mind reeled.

"Dead of a broken neck when he plunged down your manor stairs. Dead and buried, but not mourned." He smiled without humor. "With no heir from his loins, his bastard brother was ennobled."

"But who—?" She could not seem to grasp it.

A mocking hand swept over his travel-stained form. "Jervaise de Vaux."

So he had not lied about his name, at least. But Ponce was dead—the reformed drunkard, the repentant lecher, the fate she'd dreaded these many months? Why, in God's name, had Raoul never written?

Hope sparked within a sea of despair. "But . . . if you are not Ponce, you are not bound by the precontract of marriage signed without my consent. You are not required to assume his obligations—"

"Nay, not required." His harsh voice gentled. "I committed to it full willing. Beyond willing—I desired it."

Desired it, but he did not say he desired *her*. For he'd chosen her sight unseen, had he not? He'd schemed for her before he ever came to Poitiers.

"You desired my fortune, do you mean?" Proudly her head lifted, lightning pain flickering at the edge of vision. "Let us call the thing what it is, at least. Not desire, but sheer avarice."

His scarred face tightened. "I've never been wealthy. Now I'm more beggar than duke. My esteemed half brother ran the duchy into the ground. Pity he found his piety only after he lost his fortune."

Pain speared through her skull and split her thoughts. "So you require a fortune—*my* fortune, the revenues from my Wishing Stone lands."

"Aye." She almost fancied an apology in his expression, but his words dispelled it, spoken brutally as if he flogged her—or himself—with the truth.

"I need the dowry your brother will pour in my coffers. I must have it." Absolute conviction burned in his eyes. "If you want naught to do with me afterward, I'll not force you."

Had she actually expected him to deny it, to reveal somehow the nobility she'd fancied he possessed? If so, she was a fool thrice over.

Ponce d'Ormonde was dead. But like the many-headed hydra, the monster had sprouted a greater threat in his place. The infidel duke called the Devil of Damascus would make her the worst husband she could possibly imagine.

In mute entreaty, she turned to the queen. Eleanor watched her with sympathy and understanding, but also with resolve.

"Your Grace—"

"My dear child, this is the only course you left yourself when you fled my keeping."

Jesus wept, was this motivated by revenge? Was this how the queen punished her? The queen she loved could never be so heartless.

Relentlessly the royal decree rang through her throbbing skull.

"I have sent for a priest. At Prime on the morrow, my beloved godchild, Lady Alienore of Lyonstone, shall become the Duchesse d'Ormonde. I intend to witness the ceremony myself, so that none may question it."

With an ironic smile, the queen turned to Jervaise. "So you see, monseigneur, I have kept my promise to you, even when you betrayed yours to me. I trust you will not forget my benevolence when you claim your lands on my husband's border."

Dully the bell tolled, a muffled clang that summoned the faithful to prayer. The sullen red of dawn shimmered in a gray mist of rain.

The whole world weeps for me.

Alienore had passed the night writhing in the hell of an agonizing megrim while faithful Nesta bathed her brow with cool cloths soaked in lavender. The wolf had lain across her feet, a distant comfort, whining with distress.

Heartsick, she felt the crushing tension ease its grip on her skull before dawn. She had sunk into exhausted sleep, Nesta dozing facedown across her knees, when the queen's messenger arrived.

Eleanor sent one of her own gowns for the ceremony. Tall and slender as the queen herself, Alienore stood rigid while Nesta laced her into it: ice blue damask crusted with pearls, draped over samite worth half a kingdom. Beneath a silver chaplet, her hair rippled free to her waist. Nothing she wore was her own, except the swirling moonstone of her mother's wishing ring.

She stared hollow eyed into the polished plate. In her white-faced image, the light of battle kindled until her eyes burned like stars.

"Are ye well, milady?" Nesta ventured.

"I am betrayed on all sides, cornered like a rabbit, my reputation in shreds." Alienore's chin came up. "I may have lost this battle, but I have not yielded the war."

In the corridor, a familiar figure stumped forward.

"I'll give ye my arm to the altar, lass," Sir Guy said gruffly, "if ye'll have it. It's what Theobold would want."

Belligerent, he glared up at her as if expecting her to protest. But she harbored no resentment against the blunt old man. He'd been a good friend to her father and a faithful servant of England, and as kind as he knew how.

She sank into her deepest curtsy. "I should be deeply honored."

The old knight thrust out his chest and offered his arm. Together they walked forward to confront her fate.

The chapel blazed like a benediction, with ranks of glowing tapers dazzling her eyes, making the blue-mantled statue of the Virgin swim in a sea of light. A ruby sunrise poured through stained-glass windows. Massed golden flowers—the season's first blooms—drenched the air with sweetness.

Her gaze slid past the nervous priest, past the Queen of England, kneeling in her pew.

There before the altar, like a wrathful demon, stood the Raven—Jervaise de Vaux. The infidel duke who would shortly be her husband.

Her step faltered, but Sir Guy patted her hand as if she were a child. The gesture was so like her father's that tears pricked her eyes. Step by step, she advanced, eyes fixed on the man who waited.

For the first time, he wore other than black. Now he stood unmasked in a surcoat of deep garnet, all flame and shadow, bright belt knotted around his hips, its heavy ends swinging against his knees. A brooch gleamed at his shoulder, the leaping form of a wolf in flight—the talisman of Ormonde. Defiant, she met his gaze. For a bare instant, his Saracen features fired with emotion.

She could scarcely breathe against his dark intensity. He stared as though she brought him something he'd craved forever—yearning and regret and burning resolve all mingled.

He stared as she'd stared at the Virgin, aching with the longing to prove her worth.

He stares at me in triumph. Her stomach fluttered. *And desire.*

Aye, he married her for her fortune. But she knew he

wanted her as well. He wanted to finish what they'd begun that night when she offered him her virtue.

No doubt this very night he would seek to claim his prize. So she understood it to be between maids and their husbands on the bridal night. Holding her resolve before her like a shield, she advanced to confront her nemesis.

He'd not darkened a church doorstep since his knighting, a lifetime ago. But oh, she was worth it—this and more.

Jervaise stood now before the God he'd renounced. Three windows large enough for a crossbow bolt behind him, then the yawning cave of the confessional, where an assassin could crouch. For once, he paid little heed to cunning, but stood thrumming like a drawn bowstring as his bride approached.

Alienore wore nobility like a queen. Glittering finery encased that matchless body she'd bared to him so bravely the night he betrayed her. With head high she walked, her gold and silver hair like an aura. In all that blazing beauty, the steel of battle flashed in her eyes.

No doubt she'd passed a wakeful night—the same as he. Frailty lingered in the violet skin beneath her eyes. But even this crushing setback had not weakened her tempered steel.

Sir Guy trotted beside her like a faithful watchdog. Jervaise hadn't wanted to reveal his identity, but the old warrior had been ready to leave the nameless Raven rotting in the dungeon in Châtellerault if he'd held silent. Revealing himself had been his only option. Skeptical at first, the man had ample cause to believe him now.

But not to love him, after he'd ruined the earl's daughter.

Sir Guy had clearly swung around to Alienore's cause. That was one of her gifts, to inspire this blind devotion. Easy to see why even a prince had coveted her.

Yet that idiot brother of hers would have thrown her to the tender mercies of a man like Ponce, careless as a man tossing a bone to a mongrel. Allah's blood, that marriage would have been a disaster. She'd done well to flee. He could afford to admit that now. And his brother had died—under bloody odd circumstances—before he could pursue her.

She belongs to me now. Satisfaction flooded through him. She was his, and he would keep her.

She released the old knight with a gentle word of gratitude—noble even in this to the jailer who dragged her to her fate. For her sake, Jervaise bowed low, as he would for the sultan himself. A whiff of her lavender fragrance—pure and beguiling—teased his nostrils.

She surveyed him through eyes that pierced like spears, cold and bright as courage. Then spoke in her boudoir voice, low but clear.

"Monsieur, let me speak plainly. I will utter the travesty of these marriage vows since the queen commands it. But no oath spoken under duress is binding. 'Tis fair to advise you I do not consider this matter resolved."

Of course she was too honorable not to declare her intent, even when discretion would serve better. No doubt she would appeal to Henry. He would be astonished if she didn't. Yet he beheld her bright beauty under that glorious banner of hair, and an aching tenderness squeezed his heart like a fist.

So the Devil of Damascus claimed his bride. She quivered with tension like a drawn bow beneath his hand—but bided her time.

Let her protest to Henry, his warring sons, French Louis and the pope himself. By Allah, by Allah—I swear I will keep her.

His arm was coiled steel beneath her hand, knotted under garnet velvet. A fleeting memory stole her breath: his taut bronze skin in the firelight. She had touched him only once, but she knew she would never forget it.

Sternly she chastened her unseemly thoughts and turned to the priest. "Good Father, I trust we are permitted to make confession before Mass."

Jervaise stiffened, breath hissing through his teeth. Belatedly she recalled his habit to shun the Mass. No doubt like any devil, he feared the wrath of God. Suddenly she wondered how many years had passed since he prayed. How many years of death and crippling hardship while he fought for whoever would pay him?

"Didn't you confess two days ago?" he muttered. "Can't have committed so many sins since."

"Fie, monsieur! I will not stand before God without shriving my soul. Am I not correct to say so, Father?"

The nervous priest stammered assent, cringing from Jervaise's grim regard. "Ah, my lady is correct, mostly correct, though I—I am given to understand the matter must proceed without delay."

"Surely you of all men will not deny me the comfort of my faith?" she demanded, outraged.

"Well, nay," the priest stuttered. "That is to say, there should be no objection if—"

"Let her confess, if she wants it," Jervaise said in a voice like rusted steel. "I shall not."

His jaw was knotted as he stared ahead, as if he confronted a mortal foe. Was that how he'd come to view his God? Beneath the roiling sea of betrayal, an unexpected current of compassion welled up.

The condition of his soul was hardly her affair. Still, she felt troubled as she followed the priest, her thoughts not lifted to God, but lingering stubbornly on the man she must marry.

What wounds festered in his soul? What bitter pain had he shown her when he called himself a devil who knew nothing of virtue? He'd flung the words like weapons, but somehow she did not think him indifferent to the state of his soul. He'd been a Christian knight; once, he must have cared desperately. What had happened to him in Outremer?

When she returned to the altar, her soul little eased by

the sacrament, he had regained control as if that gaping cre-
vasse had never cracked him wide. Resolve resonated from
him as he rasped the marriage vows, face set in stone when
he spoke the name of God.

When her time came to speak, she hesitated. She stood
before God and perjured herself with these dutiful promises
of submission, while her soul stood in violent opposition.
Yet she would not have him think her fearful—or conquered. So she stood arrow straight and said what she must
without wavering.

It could still be undone. Yet she could not seem to stop
shaking.

When she spoke the last word, Jervaise de Vaux turned
toward her. The intensity locked behind his features riveted
her. She could not look away.

No doubt he is exultant. She swallowed the bitter taste of
defeat. *'Tis his moment of triumph—or so he thinks.*

Somehow she found her hands gripped in his. The heat of
his sword-toughened palms seared her fingers.

"I know what this marriage costs you," he said. "Your honor,
your pride—your very self, aye?"

"As you say," she whispered.

"*Inshallah*, you'll find no cause to regret it."

She lifted her chin. "Make no mistake. As long as I live I
shall regret this day—until it is undone."

His face tightened as if she'd struck him. Fleetingly, she
felt ashamed for her churlish words. For the first time, her
eyes faltered, lashes falling.

"My dear child," the queen murmured, shattering the spell.

Alienore sank into a confused curtsy. But the queen embraced her, smiling as she pressed kisses against her cheeks.

"*Depardieu*, I must now address you as a duchess! You
have risen to one of the highest titles in the realm, a rank I
may say you richly deserve."

"I deserve nothing." Distrust and regret swirled through

her as she returned the embrace stiffly. Had she betrayed Eleanor, or had Eleanor betrayed her?

"You shall keep the gown and jewels as gifts from your loving queen." Eleanor looked into her troubled features and sighed. "Although I suspect you are unlikely to believe me, I wish you happy in your marriage, child."

"Grant thanks for your kind wishes."

The queen glanced at Jervaise as he accepted Sir Guy's gruff felicitations with a wry smile. "He is not so great a mis-alliance for a woman such as you. Jervaise de Vaux is cunning, resourceful—one of the most feared knights of the entire Crusade. A strong man to defend your lands, despite his dark and difficult past."

"Difficult? The man is the devil himself."

"He is devil driven, that much is certain." The queen sighed. "*Voire*, the two of you may find yourselves well suited in the end."

"Formidable he may be, but he knows nothing of honor or virtue." Alienore threw a bitter glance at his towering back, cloaked in that sheet of midnight hair. "How can we be well matched?"

Thoughtfully, the queen studied him. "Ormonde's honor and virtue are well hidden—especially from himself—but I do not believe they are lost. Perhaps, with your assistance, he will find them."

A sudden image assailed her: the Raven's powerful body stretched over broken ice, straining to hold Remus above the deadly water.

At least she had not married a coward. Once he had saved her, whatever his reasons. But if her plan succeeded, she would never return the favor.

The thought dropped like a stone in her belly, spreading bleakness in its wake.

Chapter Thirteen

The abbey at Tours left a great deal to be desired. Alienore would gladly have ridden through the night to avoid it . . . and what awaited her there. But her husband controlled her choices now.

God save me from my wedding night. Her stomach fluttered with nerves. Her qualms had intensified as they thundered north toward the king's court. They'd left Eleanor of Aquitaine to meet her fate. Now Sir Guy and his Plantagenet soldiers provided escort for the Duc d'Ormonde.

Alienore grimaced as she sat, arms wrapped around her knees, on a flat rock above the abbey brook. Cherry blossoms perfumed the air with haunting sweetness. She vastly preferred this damp rock to the noisome hole of the abbot's chamber, whose dubious comfort he'd offered them.

The thought of that chamber, and the bridal bed that waited, made her seethe with agitation. Marriage vows or nay, she would not yield the fortress of her person. She knew enough of Church law—had made it her business to know—to recognize no marriage could be binding unless it was consummated. She would use that leverage with the king.

A twig snapped, loud in the twilight. She glanced toward Remus. Mud flew from churning forelegs as the wolf dug vigorously.

Suddenly Jervaise de Vaux towered over her, a curtain of hair framing his shuttered eyes. Her dove gray mantle lay over his arm.

"Can't blame you for preferring clean air to that verminous abbey," he said. "I envy Vulgrin his place."

His mute Saracen squire had arrived and would sleep in the stable, where he could keep an eye on their expensive horses. Certainly he would sleep more comfortably than she.

Jervaise draped the mantle over her shoulders and hovered behind her like a half-remembered dream. Her nerves tightened. He must be thinking of it, just as she was—that unavoidable moment when they were alone in the bridal chamber.

She broke the silence that thrummed between them. "You need not fear for my safety, with Remus here. I shall retire in due course."

"So I'm dismissed, like any court lackey."

Startled, she turned toward him. Conflicting urges churned within: her customary shield of courtesy, set against the powerful sting of betrayal.

"Unlike you, I have no talent for pretense." She layered her voice with steel. "You trapped me in this arrangement against my will . . . at least for now. I see no reason to pretend 'tis by choice."

He circled the rock and sat beside her—too close, but she would not give ground. She stared straight ahead, his restless heat licking against her skin.

He too stared into the dusk. "You'll petition Henry to undo the marriage."

Aye, and why am I reluctant to admit it?

"You'll know Henry is in poor standing with Rome." He stretched his legs, bound in leather chausses, and studied his boots. "This business of Becket's murder—though by all accounts Henry's men bungled it—has offended your pope."

"It offends all good Christians." Her eyebrows drew together. "The pope has rightly canonized Thomas Becket. Often I have wondered if Eleanor's disaffection with Henry sprang from that moment, when his knights cut down the holy bishop as he prayed."

But that was Eleanor's business. She would not share it with this infidel . . . this crusader who'd turned his back on God.

"Becket opposed his king. Never wise." Gold eyes glittered beneath his lashes. "Whoever ordered the killing blow, the bishop died for it. Even if Henry heeds your plea, there's little he can do 'til the rift with Rome's repaired."

"I will petition Rome myself if I must! Between my brother's pandering, your greed and the queen's malice, I have been ill served in this affair."

"Don't forget your own passion." His gaze slid down her body. "Once you wanted me. Have you forgotten?"

Heat pooled between her thighs. "You twist my actions to serve your purpose. Passion played no part in what occurred that night."

His eyes smoldered. "Never known you for a liar."

"I am no liar! If you would say so, you have never known me at all."

"Oh, I know you, Alienore." Scarred features intent, he studied her. "Well enough to know you'll make the finest duchess Ormonde ever had. Pity you're matched with a man like me."

Bitterness laced his words and halted her angry torrent of accusation. Once, he would have been worth knowing. Once, before a sojourn in hell destroyed him.

Unwillingly, she asked, "How does a duke's son come to be a mercenary, anyway? You learned the knightly arts in a noble court, or I am much mistaken."

He bent to knock mud from his boots, a curtain of hair sliding forward to cloak his features. "That tale's long to tell."

Stubbornly she waited for it. After all, he was her husband—if only for a short while. Did she not have the right to ask?

He glanced up at her silence, eyebrows lifting. "Come in to the fire, then. I'll spin you a story you won't have heard."

Guarded, she backed away. "I would have the truth or nothing."

"The truth then."

He offered his arm. She felt loath to take it, unwilling to retire to their bed, but she could hardly remain outside all night.

When she whistled for Remus, the wolf bounded over. Resigning herself to the mud that would coat her mantle, she braced herself. Instead, the wolf galloped straight to Jervaise and launched against him, planting massive forepaws against the knight's chest.

An unaccustomed grin creased his face as Jervaise scrubbed his ruff. At last he pushed the wolf gently down and rubbed dirty hands against his chausses.

"I'm no fit escort for a lady now."

An unexpected gurgle of laughter escaped her. "Had Remus chosen to greet me, I'd be no fit lady for your escort. Pray do not trouble yourself."

He cast a strange look at her laughing face. Something like wistfulness surfaced and sank in his features. His expression caught her like a net, and her smile faded as she stared up at him. God save her, he was beautiful—savage and proud and deadly. Those lines of hardship and disillusionment merely enhanced the sensual appeal that made the ladies swoon in Poitiers.

She wondered how that mane of hair would feel spilling between her fingers. How the narrow planes of his face would feel if she traced them.

"Come inside," he urged.

Disconcerted, she accepted his arm, his knotted bicep swelling under her fingers. They strolled through the orchard as Remus frisked around them.

"Hugh de Vaux sired a devil's dozen of bastards—like

father, like sons." Jervaise scowled as if the words tasted sour on his tongue. "Gave us all a knight's training. Mine was at Mortain, on the Norman coast. I was determined to make good."

"Mortain—was that your mother's place?"

"My mother was a Saracen slave girl Hugh brought back from Jerusalem," he said roughly. "Yasmin."

Bastard to a Norman duke and his heathen concubine. She nearly recoiled, before her conscience smote her. A man's birth did not define him—so Raoul always said. But had she ever truly believed it?

"She was a gentle soul. Loved her son and heeded the pillars of Islam." His face was hard as he strode along. "I strove to please her and please my distant sire. Make them both proud. I was knighted at fourteen."

"Truly?" Surprised, she glanced up. " 'Tis early for it."

"Hugh offered me a place. Like a fool, I was exhilarated. A chance to prove myself, I thought. It's why I followed him on crusade."

"What said your mother to that?"

"I stopped to see her on the way. She'd died—months before. No one troubled to tell me."

Her heart clenched as old memories reared up. They had not seen fit to inform him, no more than Benedict had informed her when her father died. Hadn't they thought she would want to know—that Theobold's daughter was worth telling?

But those secrets struck to the heart of her hidden pain. She was not prepared to share them.

"I was sixteen, defending a castle near Antioch." He bit off the words. "It's hot, thirsty, bloody business—making war in that inferno. But we were soldiers of Christ. One night while we slept, Saracens doused our walls with Greek fire. Hugh was trapped when the gatehouse burned."

"Nay," she whispered, the hellish image flaring to life. God's mercy, had Theobold died thus? "What did you do?"

"Soaked my mantle in water and wrapped it around me—forced my way in through a murder-hole. There was never love between us, but he was my father, though a damned poor one."

"Did you . . . ?"

"Shouldn't have bothered." His mouth twisted. "Before I could drag him out, the burning roof crashed down on us. Hugh was pinned under a beam too massive to lift, though I near killed myself trying. When I realized, I had to decide—whether to save my own life or die with him."

"God save us." Too vividly she could see him, the young Jervaise, raging at God and fate as he bent double with coughing in the noxious fumes.

"I would've suffocated or roasted. Neither death's an easy one. You can hear to this day what those hell-born vapors did to my lungs. So I did the only thing I could. Hugh lay writhing in the flames, screaming and cursing me for failing him. What could I do but ease his passing?"

Horror crawled through her. "Did you—?"

"Slit his throat with my own sword," he said through clenched teeth. "My own father, Alienore . . . the man I lionized and feared and hated all my life. He bled like a pig and died cursing my name."

Wishing she could say anything to ease his tortured soul, knowing no words could comfort him, she squeezed his arm with both hands. A lifetime of anguish beat out at her.

"You tried to save him, Jervaise, at risk of your own life. That you lived is no dishonor."

"It was in my mind!" He bared his teeth. "I failed him, Allah, myself—betrayed my oath and my pledge to defend him. And how they all whispered. All the filthy rumors and innuendos, saying I abandoned him from cowardice to save my own skin."

"How could they think so?"

"I was the bastard of an infidel whore," he said viciously. "That's what they always called me. I was—shamed by it, by my failure. So I gave up my name and my broadsword as atonement. It's how I came to bear a Saracen blade and the name Raven."

To give him some respite, she retreated to safer ground. "Your half brother inherited the duchy. Did he sire no sons, after all this time?"

"Ponce's heirs were his bastard brothers. His first duchess died without issue—some say from a broken heart. Perhaps it was a mercy. He would've been no easy husband in those days."

He cast her an oblique glance. Ponce would have been *her* husband if she hadn't fled.

"Did you know your brother well?"

"Nay. I was beneath his notice, like the others."

"Others," she said, with a thoughtful smile. "Are they much like you?"

"Devil's spawn, the lot of those I knew. When Ponce died, they put themselves forward, each perjuring himself to malign the others. Two of them were done to death by a third—a knife in a dark alley. I was the only one the king trusted."

"Small wonder."

"Henry couldn't risk another lord of uncertain allegiance who might join the rebels. He was sure of my loyalty. It's the reason he chose me, despite Damascus."

Aye, Damascus—where he'd earned his notoriety. Questions sprouted like wildflowers in her mind. But the abbey loomed before them. From the refectory, voices shouted and crockery clattered. The greasy odor of the fish soup they served for Lent made her stomach heave. By her faith, the place sounded more like a drinking hall than a house of God.

On the threshold, she glanced up at him. "How is it Henry feels so certain of your loyalty?"

"Saved his life once." He shrugged. "Though it would've been to my advantage to let him die."

Surprise flashed through her. "But how——?"

"That story must wait." His face closed like a door, sealing away his grief as though it had never been. "They're expecting us for supper."

She had misjudged him.

Alienore sat in the high-backed chair, bare feet stretched to the brazier, while Nesta drew the brush through her hair. She sat in her bridal chamber, chilled in her night rail and pelisse, and recalled everything she knew—and did not know—about the man she'd married.

He'd claimed his share of honor once, yet that could change nothing. This outcast knight had lied to her, schemed to win her fortune. No doubt there remained much he had not told her. He'd said naught of Damascus, for one thing.

A soft sound snatched her attention. Hands clenching on the chair, she looked up.

Jervaise filled the doorway, a slice of night that prowled and breathed. Darkness entered with him, wrapped around the crouching furniture. Shadows limned the crucifix against the whitewashed wall, pooled under the canopied lair of the bed.

She lifted her chin to show she did not fear him—though that would be a lie. Her heart thudded against her ribs hard enough to make her dizzy.

Nesta bobbed a curtsy. "I'll just be takin' me leave."

"You had better sleep here, Nesta." Alienore rose. "I dislike the look of that merchant's son without."

"Ooh, milady!" Nesta's cheeks turned pink. "I'll find me own place *tonight*."

Alienore blushed fiercely at the unsubtle emphasis.

"I bespoke the tanner's wife on your account," Jervaise told Nesta. "She'll expect you to share her pallet. Appeal to Sir Guy if the need arises."

Scurrying out, Nesta cast her mistress a coy glance that made Alienore clamp her teeth around an irritated rejoinder. Her tiring girl had been overwhelmed by the excitement of these nuptials. Happily discarding the better part of a year's anxiety, Nesta viewed the entire wretched affair as a love match.

Watching the girl abandon her, Alienore suppressed a sigh. In truth, she hadn't believed Jervaise would be daunted by a servant's presence. When he bolted the door, she swallowed against a bone-dry throat.

She resolved to take command of the situation. Yet she could not seem to frame the words in her mouth. In mounting agitation, she watched him discard one boot, then the other. His bare feet were strangely elegant, as were his hands as he unknotted his sword belt.

Suddenly, he glanced up. "Some wine before bed?"

Her composure unraveled. "I think not. I shall not be drugged into submission . . . this time."

His mouth curled wryly. "There's the abbey's wine, poor vintage though it is. And I'm no man to drug a woman into submission."

"Are you not?" Her nostrils flared. "I vow that has not been my experience."

"That wine was meant to ease your fears, no more. The rest was your doing. You offered yourself to *me*—remember?"

She maintained her scornful silence, for she would not bandy words with him. But her composure slipped further as he swung off his belt, scimitar thudding against the chest with muted menace.

He peeled off his surcoat. Before he could disrobe to the skin, she gathered her resolve.

"Monsieur, I would have a common understanding between us."

"Indeed, wife," he said softly. "Let's have that."

Her spine stiffened when he called her wife, fortifying her to say what she must.

"I am your wife unwilling, as you fully know—your bride in name only. For propriety's sake, I am resigned to the unfortunate necessity of sharing your chamber. But that is all this shall be. Do you understand me?"

"Let's say I don't." Still as a crouching panther, he watched her. "What do you see between us, wife?"

"I am *not* your wife—except by name. I do not intend to allow any . . . intimacy . . . until I petition the king."

Her words rang boldly, yet she felt anything but brave. Concealed among her saddlebags, her sword would enforce her will if it must, though she was averse to baring steel in their bridal chamber. Still, she would do what she must, if reason and persuasion failed.

"You'd claim lack of consummation." His voice scraped out. "To annul the marriage."

"That, and my lack of consent to the match."

"*Bismillah*, do I seem a lackwit, to give you that weapon?"

A frisson of warning slid down her spine. Refusing to show fear, she lifted her chin.

"Chivalry alone demands it and your honor as a knight. Have I not made it plain? I am unwilling!"

"*Chivalry and honor?*" His voice roughened. "You mistake me for a true knight. I prefer a willing woman, aye. But too much swings in the balance to be swayed by sentiment."

Fury coursed down her spine and flooded her with reckless courage. She drenched her words with all the contempt of an earl's daughter. "Then you'd resort to rape to serve your purpose. To serve your greed."

Roughly he dragged the coat over his head along with his linen shirt. For a sizzling instant she reeled beneath his impact: the chiseled strength of a fighting man, the broad planes of his chest gilded by fire, knotted column of muscle plunging down to his trews.

"This'll be nothing like rape." Eyes hooded, he met her gaze. "You'll be willing enough."

Battle heat seared through her. He declared his intent as clearly as a blown trumpet. Abandoning persuasion, she fired into motion and lunged for her saddlebags. If he forced her to the sword—

The impact of his body knocked the breath from her lungs. She landed facedown across the bed, his heavy frame on top. If he hadn't caught his weight on his arms, he would have crushed her. Straw scratched her skin through the mattress as she twisted, seeking a better placement. When she rolled over to confront him, the dizzying scent of musk and sandalwood filled her head.

The hard lines of his body thrust against her, pressed her into the scratchy bedding. He pinioned her arms beside her head.

The breath rushed from her lungs at the searing imprint of his body. Her pelisse had twisted beneath her. Through the thin shield of her night rail, the stiffened blade of manhood nudged her thighs.

She stared into his saturnine features as his hair poured around them—curtaining them in a private world. Her brain seethed with panic. "Will you truly sink so low?"

"I've wanted you since the day I looked in your eyes." Sweet with cloves, his breath brushed her face. "And found a woman strong and fierce as a lion, who'd challenge the devil himself. I've wanted you my whole life . . . searched for you without knowing it."

Blindly she shook her head, hair flung against the mattress like a fallen banner. "It will be rape."

"Nay—not rape," he muttered, and captured her mouth.

Chapter Fourteen

She'd yearned for this—his mouth, his taste, the urgent press of his hands on her body. Her own desire, too long denied, lanced through her armor like a fine-honed blade.

His kiss stormed her defenses like a charger at full gallop, demanding her surrender. Their tongues sparred in combat, the insistent nudge of aroused manhood against her womb.

She strained against him, a contest of strength, hands fisting as he pinned her wrists to the bed. Her scalp tingled as ribbons of hair snagged beneath their bodies, the pain bringing tears to her eyes.

Senses reeling, she dragged air into her lungs. "Cease, you villain!"

"Jervaise." Turning his rough-shaven face into her throat, he rubbed like a cat against her skin. "I've waited long to hear you speak my name."

Tendrils of awareness uncurled below her belly. He commenced a subtler assault, tasting her skin where the fine dew of sweat sprang out. Her pulse struggled under this new offensive.

"Stop," she whispered.

"Never," he muttered, nuzzling the vulnerable nexus of neck and shoulder. Pleasure arched and stretched within her like a waking demon.

Aye, fight him. Fight for your Christian soul. So she fought, but still she desired him. Caution swirled through her brain like wind stirring a pond and vanished as quickly. His hand brushed her breast, swelling like a ripe apple, veiled by white linen. Her breath rushed out as he found the stiffened peak, already tingling with expectation. She moaned deep in her throat as he teased her to swollen readiness, despair and delight mingling.

She clung to the cracked shield of her resolve. "Jervaise . . . I do not want this."

"It's no sin, Alienore. We're man and wife."

Her fierce denial faded as his open mouth found her through the fabric. Darts of pleasure spiraled inward as his tongue stroked her, suckling like a babe. Surrender could only lead her to ruin, strip her of both lands and independence. Yet she could not deny him. She gripped his shoulders—to hold him back, or draw him closer?

Sweet mercy, somehow I must stop this. If she did not, she'd find herself bound to him by flesh as well as marriage vows. Even the king could not save her if Jervaise de Vaux planted his child in her womb.

Desperation fired as she heaved beneath him and resisted the carnal urge to rub against him like a wanton.

"Allah's heart." His hand hooked in her night rail. Cool air shocked her fevered limbs as he peeled it up. Barely in time to preserve her modesty, she trapped his hand against her thigh.

She'd braced for a contest of strength, but he was too clever for that. His sword-roughened palm found the virgin skin of her inner thigh, where no man had ever touched her. The sheltered opening between her thighs flared into throbbing life. She dared not move nor even speak, lest she betray herself. His hand claimed her terrain, one breath at a time.

When he found her petal-soft folds, smooth as any lady's, a hot rush of urgency pulsed through her. She panted like a winded fighter as cool air teased her thighs and squeezed her eyes closed in an agony of embarrassment. She would squeeze her legs together if he weren't sprawled between them.

"Bloody hell, Alienore. I've dreamed of this."

The musk of salt and arousal teased her nostrils—the scent of her own body. The tender channel of her womb clenched, as if to grasp him.

"Stop this." She trembled. "I cannot—I *will* not—"

"Oh, you will." He spread her wide. "And revel in it."

As her last bastion threatened to crumble, she leaped for her final chance.

"I am revealed to your eyes," she whispered, "yet you hide from mine. Would you demand more than you are willing to give?"

It smacked of trickery rather than the clean strength of defiance, and she reviled the lie. Yet he stilled, poised to spring.

"I'd give you all I own." He paused. "Nakedness between lovers is no sin, Alienore. I learned that in Outremer."

He knelt between her knees, eyes sweeping her body, and the knowledge of what he saw seared through her. Legs supple with unwomanly strength, the brazen exposure of that place between her thighs, sweat-damp linen clinging to her breasts, cheeks flushed with libertine passion.

Now he sees the truth of me: my lack of a maid's softness, and the wanton lust of a Rievaulx. Yet to unlace his chausses, he released her. It was enough, more than enough opportunity for a woman with her skills.

Lightning swift, she rolled away from him. Her bare feet smacked the floor. Pushing out a harsh breath, he leaped for her and snared her pelisse. She twisted out of it, leaving the garment trailing from his fingers as she dove for her saddlebags.

He was already springing from the bed with a curse, already lunging across the floor as she dragged her sword free. With one hand she flung the sheath away, and swung the broadsword up between them—barely in time.

He twisted into stillness a blade's length away, half-bound chausses entangling him. He eyed her ready stance, feet spread and weight balanced, both hands gripping the broad-sword. Firelight seared along the blade.

She itched to put distance between them. Yet she dared not move, lest she tangle her feet in her own garment. She watched his chest rather than his face, ready for any flicker of movement.

"If you love life, monsieur, do not approach."

Black humor threaded his ruined voice. "Never knew such sport could be found in the bridal bed."

"There shall be no bridal bed for us." She held the blade extended, its tip grazing his sternum. "I tried to spare us this moment, but you refused to listen."

"Think you could best me? I'd overcome you in a heartbeat."

Nay, she was not so great a fool.

"I believe there is something left of the Christian knight you were." She prayed she had not misjudged him. "I believe you would not rape an unwilling woman."

"That's your mistake." Sparks flared in his eyes. "I learned long ago not to harbor a tender conscience—or I'd be dead."

Her shoulders burned as she held the heavy blade extended, but she dared not betray weakness. She swallowed against the knot of dread and stared coldly down the sword. "If you are truly as despicable as you claim, then at least I shall know it."

As always he was difficult to read, emotions sealed away behind saturnine skin. His eyes narrowed, his scarred features hardening.

"Say I agree to delay until we find the king. Say he refuses to see you, or denies your petition. What can I expect in exchange?"

The knot of fear tightened in her chest. Her arms and shoulders were screaming from the sustained effort of holding the blade. Aye, he was negotiating, but they had not come to terms.

He had stated what he was prepared to offer, and she did not care for it. But if she won some small respite, she was certain she could persuade the king. She was a Lyonstone, after all.

"If you agree to delay this matter until I have petitioned the king," she said carefully, "and he refuses me, then I will know there is no hope. In that case, I will . . . allow you to share my bed."

"Nay," he said, intent. "I'll have more from you when the time comes than stoic endurance."

"Would you have me behave like a wanton?" Her nostrils flared with outrage.

"Not a wanton. Like the woman you are, Alienore. Don't deny your nature or the pleasure you find in my arms."

The pleasure you find in my arms. His words slid over her skin like a caress. Standing barefooted in her night rail, she shivered.

"You are deeply mistaken about my nature." With all her being, she strove to believe it. "But if the king refuses my petition, I will . . . oblige you. You have my word of honor."

He searched her features. "Then you've mine—whatever that's worth. Your willing body in my bed's a prize worth the wait."

Heat flooded her face at the dark promise in his tone.

"Lower your sword, my lady," he jeered. "Your virtue's safe from the devil . . . for now."

Her mind was far from easy, but she could hardly maintain her vigilance all night. With a sigh, she lowered the blade, point resting on the ground between them. Relief flooded through her trembling limbs. She had held him off, for the moment.

I was right about him. By my faith, I was right. Whatever he said to the contrary, Jervaise de Vaux would not force himself upon an unwilling woman. He was not the conscienceless monster he painted himself—not quite.

Before her visible relief, his face twisted. With knife-sharp motions he retied his chausses, then jerked on his boots. Still gripping the sword for insurance, she retreated to the brazier and gave him a wide berth.

He dragged his coat over his head—never mind the shirt—and flung his surcoat around his shoulders. Without a glance at her wary figure, he strode for the door.

"Where are you going?" She could not help asking.

He wrenched the door open without looking back. "To hell."

Fear gripped her belly as he strode across the threshold and slammed the door behind him.

She should be pleased to be spared the devil's attentions.

For the hundredth time, Alienore reminded herself what she should be feeling as she knelt in the abbey church. She should be singing paeans of thanksgiving for her deliverance. Instead, she'd spent her wedding night tossing in the abbot's scratchy bed while she awaited Jervaise. But he had never returned.

Certainly he had not appeared for Mass. Behind hers, the pews were crowded: the dutiful monks, her yawning Plantagenet guards, a motley band of travelers. But Jervaise was not among them.

The rumble of hosannas rolled from the monks, her contralto rising above them. Beside her, Sir Guy hoisted himself up with a grunt, knees popping. She cared not to think what he must be speculating. No doubt Ormonde's raging emergence from the bridal chamber had not escaped notice. In all likelihood, Sir Guy knew where Jervaise had slept. But she would not lower herself to ask.

In a cloud of incense, the abbot swept past, bearing the heavy penance candle. All would be dolorous throughout Christendom until Lent gave way to Easter. Sighing, she crossed herself and followed the procession.

The dripping gray sky did not lift her spirits. The muddy

yard was crowded with milling horses. Near the gate, a black-clad figure murmured to his turbaned squire, Remus panting at their feet.

Her heart gave a bound of pleasure and relief. As if she'd cried out, Jervaise turned toward her.

Bareheaded in the rain, he'd clubbed back his hair to bare his feral profile. The lines around his mouth and eyes were deeper chiseled, as if with hardship. But he was stalking toward her like the predator he was. She must compose herself. She clasped her hands and waited.

"Bid you good morrow." She was pleased with her distant courtesy as she ruffled Remus's fur.

"I've seen better morrows." His eyes raked the yard, scattered with bedraggled chickens. "Restful night?"

She looked down at the wolf, her cheeks scalding. "I am prepared to resume our journey."

"Good. We break fast in the saddle." He pitched his voice loud enough to reach Sir Guy, hovering watchfully nearby. "A royal courier just passed. The king keeps court at Le Mans—no more than a day's ride."

"Le Mans?" Excitement and dread fluttered in her stomach. "Then Henry is far closer than we believed."

"'Tis surprising." Sir Guy stumped forward to join them. "They're naught but a nest of rebels and traitors in Maine, curse them. 'Tis a wonder Henry closes his eyes to sleep . . . if he does sleep."

"Even Henry must sleep." Jervaise's mouth twisted in a mirthless smile. "If the roads allow, we'll share his roof tonight."

"Le Mans is not so close, lad." Sir Guy frowned. "Ye'll founder the horses to arrive today, if Henry's even there. He's like to uproot his court and travel thirty miles at a moment's notice."

"We'll follow him to Outremer if we must," Jervaise said grimly. "My lady and I have cause for haste."

She recalled the utter lack of triumph she'd felt when he flung himself from their chamber. Why this reluctance to see the matter concluded? Surely she did not fear the outcome. The righteous cause would triumph . . . didn't she believe that?

Unless it was that which she feared.

"Indeed, monsieur, I would see this matter resolved. Let us make haste."

Chapter Fifteen

The great hall at Le Mans reeked of treasonous intent. Alienore's skin prickled as she edged through the throng: the queen's chancellor, come to the king's court. By the warmth of their greetings to her, these elegant monseigneurs with their careful smiles betrayed their sympathies.

Almost to the last man, these were Eleanor's supporters. In her heart, she questioned the king's wisdom in coming here. For he was indeed in residence.

Beautiful and false, the hall was meant to dazzle. Stone ribs held aloft the ceiling's crushing weight as if by witchcraft. Linen hangings deceived the eye: a lion sprawled among false trees, eyes watchful beneath a jeweled crown. The entire court quivered with awareness of its angry king.

Jervaise had driven them at a grueling pace to reach the keep before nightfall. She might have protested, but she would not have him think her reluctant—or fearful. She'd left Remus in their chamber, and she missed the wolf's presence. But Jervaise warded her back, his formidable height and Saracen sword sufficient to strike terror in any man's heart. Around them, courtiers hissed with speculation.

His nearness distracted her beyond reason, firing the reckless passion of her mother's blood. But here in the hostile court, she dared not show it.

Already the chamberlain had warned she could not expect an immediate audience. Days might pass before she could bribe or cozen a place in the king's schedule. Meanwhile, she could not sleep chastely next to Jervaise in that curtained fortress of a bed. They must manage some other arrangement, if she wished to sleep at all.

The double doors flew wide and boomed against the walls. A stir of interest rippled through the crowd. Torches leaped as a force pressed inward, parting the sea of bodies like a ship in a strong gale. She could just discern a head of flaming hair cleaving through the throng.

Now all the great lords and ladies sank low—all that malice contained in an instant behind bowed heads and deception. Alienore too sank into her deepest curtsy. Yet she could not resist looking up, eager for her first glimpse of the legend.

Before her, a gap opened, and Henry Plantagenet strode into view. King of England and Duke of Normandy in his own right, master of Aquitaine through his wife.

He was nothing like she'd expected. A brawny man of middle height—shorter than she—and clad in a huntsman's leather doublet that strained across his barrel chest. Mud clung to his boots; he wore no crown over tousled red hair. No lordly arrogance stamped his square, freckled features, but a flame of restless vigor burned in his face. Good cheer radiated like sunlight over those around him.

Yet he wore sword and dagger to the table, like a barbarian—or a man who distrusted his companions.

Aye, he had the brash Plantagenet charisma in full measure. He swept through the hall like a strong wind, blue eyes piercing beneath his brows.

He is worthy of Eleanor—a great king for a great queen. A rush of pride coursed through her. As he passed, her head lifted. While she looked upon him, Henry Plantagenet turned his head and saw her.

That penetrating gaze shafted through her like lightning. Surely he could find no fault in her appearance: deep blue over white brocade, coiled hair gleaming beneath a jeweled crespine. Proud, desperate, fearless, she met that keen appraisal without faltering.

Henry's gaze tracked to Jervaise, magnificent as a sultan with his ink black mane pouring down. Recognition sparked between the two, though the king's pace never slackened. Henry's eyes narrowed before he turned away, bounding onto the dais with a young man's exuberance.

"Friends, at your ease!" he cried in Norman French, his hoarse voice booming. "Your king is starving! Let's not delay the feast."

He flung himself into his chair. Silver horns trumpeted, summoning the guests to their places.

"Be careful." Jervaise's warm breath brushed her ear. "They'll know we're Henry's allies, once we take our place."

Aye, tonight he announced his own identity to that bowstring-taut assembly. No longer the disgraced knight, but the infidel Duke of Ormonde.

She took her place at the high table, facing the ranks of hostile diners. He slid into a chair beside her, one step closer to the throne.

Every shadowed alcove could conceal an enemy. They sat near enough to the king, and his favor, to make them targets for an assassin's bolt. But Alienore was not an earl's daughter for naught.

Calmly she held out her hands to the page, who poured scented water over her fingers into the silver laver. The butler decanted a torrent of burgundy into her goblet.

From the lower hall, a cold spear of scrutiny sliced through her. She searched the tables—and saw him. Almost hidden in the painted forest, an enemy lurked. Still as a stalking beast, with infinite patience, he waited for her.

"Nay, it cannot be," she whispered. "He would not leave my brother's side for all the gold in Outremer."

Jervaise glanced toward her, his mouth twisting. "Should've

come sooner, as I told you. Sir Bors of Bedingfield's beaten you to Henry."

The man has not changed. A shiver chased down her spine. *Save to become more unnerving, if that is possible.*

Framed by pale hair cropped straight across his brow, Bors of Bedingfield possessed a strong-boned countenance that made the ladies sigh. Roman nose, rugged jaw scraped clean of whiskers, deep-set eyes green as poison. He froze her blood with his smile of recognition. A superstitious fear crawled over her scalp like an insect.

Courteous, he inclined his head—as though he'd forgotten their acrimonious parting, when she'd flung defiance in his face.

Well, she need not acknowledge him. He was no more than a jumped-up carpet knight, and she newly made a duchess. She turned away, dismissing him. Jervaise met those viridian eyes straight on and bared his teeth in a wolfish smile.

"So he has come." She beckoned for a slice of smoked sturgeon. She had already tired of Lenten fare, though the king's table boasted the best of it. "You knew him in Outremer, I recall?"

"Knew of him." With his dagger, Jervaise speared a slice of whale. "Now the cogs of his brain are spinning. He'll wonder why you befriend an infidel."

"I find that doubtful." Her words came stiffly, fueled by cold fury. These two had conspired to trap her into marriage. "I have wedded the infidel duke, as both of you intended."

"Jervaise de Vaux was naught but a name to him. Bors knew the Raven, not the lord he wrote to arrange your marriage."

She had always seen the two as allies, pooling all their wits to overcome her. "How could you manage the marriage contract without meeting him? My brother leaves his affairs entirely to Bors."

"Thank your king." Jervaise drank from their shared goblet, the press of his lower lip against the rim a distraction. With difficulty, she focused on his words. "I was with Henry when Ponce had his accident. Benedict offered you to Ormonde's heir. But the heirship was contested, aye?"

"As well it might be," she said tartly, "with the devil's brood of brothers you have described and not one a product of the marriage bed."

"Aye, well. Henry told me of another claimant. One of my half brothers petitioned for the duchy . . . but Henry didn't know him. Offered Ormonde—and you—to me."

Her heart sank. She should have asked these questions sooner. She had been so angry and hurt by Jervaise's betrayal, she had not been thinking clearly. Henry would not easily undo a match he himself had arranged. How could she persuade him?

Strategies swirled through her head as she scanned the table, gleaming with a king's ransom in silver and gold. Restless with the confinement of his chair, Henry paced, gnawing a heel of bread and tossing remarks to his courtiers. Looking resigned, his seneschal and chamberlain puffed at his heels.

How would it be to see her sovereigns together—Henry and Eleanor—during the glorious decades of their accord? Once they had loved, or so the troubadours sang. But all that love had turned to hate.

Inevitably, her thoughts shifted to the man beside her. They had begun with hatred, she and Jervaise. Could they ever come to love?

As she stared at the king's broad back, Henry pivoted. Now the man swept down on them like a force of nature, stocky frame filling the serving aisle.

"Jervaise, my old friend!" Coming up behind them, Henry gave his shoulder a hearty buffet. "I can't tell you how pleased I am to see you treated like the nobleman you are."

"Hope your faith is not misplaced, Your Grace." The Raven bowed.

"I've already trusted you with my safety, aye?" the king said fondly. "It's fitting to trust you with my realm. Your duchy's my first line of defense against that rascal Philip of Flanders if he looks south to Normandy."

Jervaise stilled. "We didn't think it likely. If that's changed, my place is in Ormonde."

"Who can say what that greedy devil will do?" The king stood so close she could feel him, but she would not twist around. The arrangement was awkward; a king's place was on his throne, not roaming about the hall. She should curtsy, but others had not done so. Was it a familiarity he nurtured or a contempt he despised?

Henry's voice lowered as he leaned close. Alienore squeezed against the table to avoid being pressed squarely against the royal person.

"We must station you with care, Jervaise. My sources say Philip looks to England. He and French Louis would like nothing better than to draw me out and thin my defenses there, hey? They'll press the Scots to drive south—but here. It's tedious talk for a lady's ears."

This was her cue at last. "Your Grace, pray do not allow me to constrain you. The security of your realm concerns us all."

"Spoken like a loyal Englishwoman," the king said dryly, for he must have noted her Saxon accent. "God knows I've few enough of those to be grateful for every one."

She lifted her eyes—her unwavering stare too direct for a woman—and met his gaze. Even in repose, he was restless, shifting from foot to foot as nervous servers squeezed past. She saw Richard of Aquitaine's good looks in his father's strong features, Richard's confidence in his powerful frame . . . Richard's hot ardor in his flame-bright eyes.

She struggled to maintain composure. This overt appraisal

of a virile man for a woman—from a swaggering lad like Richard, it merely irritated her. Coming from Richard's father and her king, it disconcerted in an entirely different way.

"It's I who should be grateful." Jervaise captured her arm with a casual caress that heated her blood. "I present you my wife."

For the first time, she felt thankful for the title—and this politic reminder of her wedded state.

Henry threw back his head and roared with laughter. "What, the Lyonstone wench? God's eyes, man, I did better by you than either of us realized, hey? Christ, when I think of your reluctance!"

A spark of anger flared within her. Pride kept her spine straight and her head unbowed.

"I am Alienore of Lyonstone," she said coolly. "Theobold's daughter, Your Grace—who died a hero's death, taking the cross in your name."

Henry sobered and crossed himself. "He was a brave man—I recall him well. We are grateful for his sacrifice."

Gravely she inclined her head.

"By God, you put me in mind of your father. Alienore, was it?" Henry frowned. "Not a name that brings joy to my heart these days. And loyal to my wife, I'm told. My counselors speak ill of you, madam."

Another woman would have quailed. Alienore lifted her chin.

"I was honored to serve the queen and proud to do so. But I relinquished the post when I married. Otherwise I would not have forsaken her or allowed her to be led astray."

"God's eyes, an honest woman!" The king's eyes crinkled, deepening the lines that rayed outward. "A rarity at this court, believe me. Eleanor must be devastated to lose you, not that it grieves me. As for your allegiance . . . well. You're Ormonde's bride, so your loyalties should be his, hey? For his sake, I'd give Saladin himself a second chance."

Caution tiptoed across her skin. She knew his tolerance would last no longer than her first misstep.

"Now or ever, Your Grace, I shall not betray your trust. You have the word of a Lyonstone for that."

"You're not pleased by this fellow I've given you, are you, my proud lady?"

She restrained the impulse to pour upon her monarch's head the torrent of angry grievance that festered in her heart.

"Your Grace, this is not the appropriate time to burden you with my affairs. You are weary—and, no doubt, hungry." Her eyes flickered toward his vacant chair. "I would welcome an opportunity to address the matter privately, if it please you."

Jervaise scowled into his wine, but said nothing.

"You wish to discuss Lyonstone business?" Considering, the king rocked on his heels. "It's a popular topic, madam. Your brother sent an envoy here for the same purpose. Should I hear the two of you together?"

Apparently Sir Bors, whatever his business, had not yet gained the royal ear. Or perhaps Henry said it to test her.

"For reasons I do not comprehend," she said, "my brother trusts an insignificant knight of doubtful repute to manage his affairs. You will understand, Your Grace, that I cannot discuss intimate matters before him."

"You don't object?" he asked Jervaise. "She'll exclude you as well, hey?"

She would not lower herself by begging. Yet Jervaise could always read her, one of his talents that vexed her the most.

He exhaled through his nostrils. "She'll find no solace 'til she wins your ear. I'll not oppose it."

So he would adhere to the terms of their bargain. She had misjudged him—as she misjudged everyone, it seemed. Jervaise's bitter eyes locked with hers and he lifted their goblet in mocking salute.

Henry hoisted his eyebrows. "In that case, madam, I'll instruct the reeve who maintains my schedule. You'll be sent for, so be ready."

Sensing the precise moment when the king's regard shifted, his seneschal slipped forward to murmur in his ear. Jerking a nod, Henry Plantagenet strode energetically through the hall. Around him courtiers floundered with surprise, some rising while others did not.

Alienore burned to ask Jervaise why he had not opposed her private audience. Was he truly so confident?

But she was weary of forever quarreling with him. Within days, this misalliance of a marriage would be dissolved. By her faith, why was she bleak at the prospect?

Chapter Sixteen

A thousand pardons, good lady. Are you the Duchesse d'Ormonde?"

Alienore glanced at the liveried page. Did the king summon her already? She searched the crowded hall for Jervaise, but he was nowhere to be found.

God's mercy, she felt exposed among this throng of hostile traitors—naked without Jervaise's warding presence. She hoped she had not grown craven, to cleave to male protection like any weak-willed woman.

Proudly her chin came up. "I am the Duchesse d'Ormonde. Have you a message?"

"You are summoned by . . . a certain gentleman." The boy bowed. "You are to follow me, if you please."

Evading her attempt to detain him, the lad slipped into the crowd. Eyebrows lifting, she waded after him and strained to keep him within view in this colorful sea of damask and velvet. Without success, she searched for Sir Guy. It would comfort her to find a loyal man in this treacherous crowd—one man whom Henry's ruthless scorched-earth policy against the rebels had not mortally offended. But she could not spy Sir Guy's balding pate among the bobbing heads around her.

Waves of heat rose from the close-pressed courtiers. The odors of sweat and stale perfume made her belly churn. A niggling unease fluttered in her stomach.

She almost lost the boy when he ducked between two pillars. Then his small hand darted out, pulling her into the dark corridor.

"Wait!" She hurried after him past a row of curtained alcoves. The nape of her neck prickled.

You are being foolish. Worse, you are become fearful. What danger would threaten you in the king's own court?

"This way, madam." The page held aside a spill of dusty velvet.

Inside, candles burned like flaming eyes in a dark cave. A broad-shouldered figure stood before the casement, gray moonlight streaming over a powerful physique. A dry aroma fired her nerves: the bitter essence of thyme and wormwood.

Breath hissed between her teeth as her long-knife flashed free in her fist.

The candles bled light over rugged features under a fringe of ice blond hair. Thin lips parted in a smile of welcome.

"How good of you to join me, dear lady."

Instantly she fell back, on guard, searching for hidden assailants. She saw no one and nothing, save him—yet he was threat enough. The throwing knives sheathed in his boots glinted as he glided forward.

"Why, how is this?" His mesmerizing voice tugged her like a confiding hand. "Surely the lady of Lyonstone fears no man . . . only the righteous wrath of God."

She held her courage like a shield before her.

"I fear no man, Sir Bors, but that does not mean I am stupid. Are you here for my brother or for treachery?"

His poisonous eyes slid to the corridor. Swift as a striking serpent, he flipped a coin into the shadows in a glittering arc. Her eyes followed it by instinct, like a magic trick. The coin never struck the ground.

"You have done well for your master." He smiled. "Bring wine for the duchess—and not that reprehensible swill served in the hall. And make certain we are not disturbed."

For an eerie moment she thought he addressed the darkness itself. She recalled the page only when his running footfalls receded. Fear thickened like smoke in her lungs. But she would never give him the satisfaction of knowing it.

She seized the offensive, flinging words at him like weapons.

"What think you of my husband?"

"Do you mean to ask, what think I of the impoverished butcher it has pleased the king to ennoble?" Green fire glowed in his eyes. "To speak plainly, which I know you are inclined to prefer, I think you are ill served."

Blinking, she turned his words in her mind. His foreign accent shaded the syllables: rolling consonants and stretched vowels, neither Saxon nor Norman. She had never been certain of his origins.

"I was ill served by Benedict's disregard for my father's will," she said, "but he is very young. I was ill served by my brother's counselor, who sought his own profit. That I will attest to."

Quietly he laughed. "My dear, I had almost forgotten your uncommon candor. I quite admire you for it—even when your barbs are launched at me."

He gestured to the nearby table and its two chairs. "Come, be at ease. We have important business to discuss and little time."

Her eyes followed the sweep of his hand, rings glittering: a square-shaped emerald the size of his knuckle, a round onyx whose depths swirled with darkness. Dizzy, she averted her eyes.

"I cannot imagine what business we may have in common." Stubborn, she stayed where she was.

"Oh, come now," he chided, fond as a boy with a beloved hound. "We have Benedict of Lyonstone and his lands—and *your* lands. Can we not discuss our common interests in a civilized fashion . . . for once?"

He stood with hands on the chair, ready to assist her. But she would not for anything place him behind her. Instead she circled the table, and sat in the opposite place.

A tiny crease of annoyance appeared between his eyebrows. With another thin-lipped smile, he sank into the empty chair. Turning away from the light, he angled himself so the burning candles stood behind him. The light played over the faded scars that mottled his neck and reached like pale flames toward his jaw.

"Tell me of Benedict," she said. "How fares my brother?"

"Frankly, he has fared better." Bors tented his fingers beneath his chin. "Your English winters are rather inhospitable. At Martinmas, your brother suffered an unfortunate relapse of his fever."

"Fever?" Fear shafted through her. "Dear God, what fever is this?"

"Why, the fever that plagues so many veterans of the holy wars. I myself know something of plagues and fevers, as you may recall. A loving sister would thank me for the care I showed him. I mixed his potions, fed him with my own hand. Nonetheless, I confess that his prognosis for a time was . . . uncertain."

Alienore dragged breath into her lungs. Her little brother, the bright and feckless boy she had loved. She should never have left him.

"Benedict—"

"You need not fear, dear lady. I cared for him as tenderly as I would my own son." A brief and terrifying coldness invaded his voice. "Aye, as tenderly as that. With time, he rallied. When I departed, I left herbs and detailed instruction for his care. Your brother is too important a thread in the tapestry of events being woven in England to allow any mischance."

She struggled to blunt the spike of panic. Benedict was all God had left her—her hotheaded, idealistic brother. She remembered him not as he returned from crusade—that distant nobleman with ice chips for eyes. Nay, in her mind he was still the blond imp with flashing mischief in his smile.

"I must go to him," she whispered. If he died alone, it would be her fault, for abandoning him to this monster's tender mercies. "I have been too long away."

Bors riffled his fingers, a mannerism that snared the eye. "Indeed you may go to him, and welcome—if that unfortunate husband of yours will allow it. I rather doubt it, to judge from his manner. Clearly he covets you . . . and why should he not?"

His gaze slid over her body. "A wealthy heiress, a proud and ancient name, cold beauty that burns like winter frost. Tell me, how does the infidel find your bed?"

Heat surged into her cheeks. "Why should the man not allow me to visit my own lands? Their welfare devolves to his benefit as well as mine."

The rings on his fingers glittered, green and swirling black. His elegant hands shuffled the air. "We would be fools, indeed, to think he'll allow you the freedom to spread your wings. The freedom to escape him. At least, he will not allow your wealth to slip his grasp, which he covets above all else—perhaps even more than the pleasure of your bed."

"Stop this." Her hand slashed the air. The rhythmic play of his fingers stilled, releasing her from the odd spell. "You must think me an utter simpleton! Am I to forget the poison you poured in Benedict's ears all last summer, when you forced this marriage down my throat? Am I to forget that you beguiled him to barter me away to an aging lecher, no matter my own wishes?"

Her voice strengthened as righteous anger poured through her. "You and Ormonde were allies. An unholy alliance crafted against me—and now I am to think you would work against that?"

The candles fluttered before her impassioned speech. Sir Bors gestured, air filling with an ashen whiff of thyme and wormwood. The dancing flames subsided, their wicks glowing blue.

"It grieves me you'd think so ill of me, dear lady." His voice enveloped her like a kinsman's embrace. "I do not deny I worked toward those ends that seemed best, like all men. I worked for alliance with a powerful duke—an alliance to strengthen the security of the kingdom, with Hugh d'Ormonde's rightful heir."

His eyes hardened. "Never did I foresee that Henry Plantagenet would take into his head this obscene notion to ennoble the most disreputable of Hugh's bastards. I pride myself on seeing far across time and space. But this remote chance I failed to predict."

He was lying, of course. Yet the best lies contain kernels of hidden truth. Now he echoed words Jervaise himself had spoken. She trusted neither of them.

The page reappeared, bearing a flagon and two goblets. Bowing, the lad poured a dark torrent into each. When Sir Bors sent another coin spinning across the table, the boy caught it neatly and withdrew.

Alienore cradled a goblet between her hands but dared not drink.

"Do you say, sir, you would have opposed the marriage?"

"I would have opposed *this* marriage." He leaned forward. "My lady Alienore, I entrust to you now tidings of the greatest import. *There is still another claimant for the ducal seat.*"

An anxious fist squeezed her chest. "Another bastard, do you mean to say?"

His features stiffened, skin going white over bone.

"An elder son." He shaped each word with precision. "Gotten by Hugh d'Ormonde—not on the wanton flesh of a slave girl, but to a highborn lady, gently reared with every privilege, who held a king's favor."

"Which king is this?"

"A worthy heir, descended from greatness on both sides. Given the benefits of a classical education, a soldier's training, and every advantage. Lyonstone would benefit from such an alliance. This worthy son was proposed for the duchy, but Henry chose that infidel instead."

"Henry chose a man he could trust." Anger crackled through her—though why it should anger her to hear Jervaise maligned, she could not say.

"A fine bit of trickery on the Raven's part, my dear. I was unaware of the years he spent worming his way into Henry's graces. Our plans have gone awry, I confess it. But there is still time to alter the future, if you have the courage for it."

"I remind you, Sir Bors, that *we* never held any plan in common." He proposed no more than she herself claimed to want—*did* want: to free herself of the marriage. Why she was filled with this vast distress, pressing like a hand against her throat, she could not explain.

"An unfortunate oversight." His fingers splayed around his cup. It seemed to hover slantwise, defying the pull of gravity. "I made the mistake of disregarding you, dear lady. I believed you were not a significant player, but I was wrong. Your achievements at Eleanor's court have proven you a master of the game. Are you surprised? Unlike most men, I am not loath to admit my errors. Indeed, I make it my custom to learn from every one.

"What I propose now, my lady, is an alliance: a union between the daughter of Lyonstone and the earl's chief counselor. An accord with the sole purpose of undoing this misalliance between you and the Devil of Damascus. I would restore your honor and your freedom."

Her heart beat so swiftly her head spun, thoughts whirling through her brain. She'd sought an ally to undo her marriage. Now that she'd found one—and such a one!—dread dropped like a stone in her belly.

Of course, she did not trust him, no matter what clever words he spoke. Yet the looming prospect of a future without Jervaise turned her world bleak and friendless.

"It would not be freedom for long, would it? You would

annul my marriage to the current duke and sell me to this noble claimant instead."

Firelight played on his hands, over the myriad of tiny scars that marred his skin. Not the notches of a careless blade, but divots of pale tissue, as if from burning droplets. "The future holds many possibilities, my dear, some more likely than others. It's too soon to say which of these shall prevail. Let us address the immediate problem—the devil you've taken to your bed."

The skin on her nape rose in warning like a wolf's hackles. Somehow, the man's malice seemed personal. "What of him? The marriage is already made, witnessed by the queen herself."

He bared a sliver of smile. "Marriages are unmade every day, one way or another. Surely you came here hoping for that."

A wave of despair swamped her. "I do not deny it. I intend to petition Rome, with the king's support."

"After the Becket affair? Henry Plantagenet's support would be the kiss of death to any petition that reaches the pope's ears now."

The more cordial and seemingly helpful he became, the less she trusted him.

"I must consider my options, sir. Until then, I do not care to discuss the matter."

"Consider them," he said, indifferent, rising in a whiff of dusty herbs. "Consider also, if you will, how I can aid your cause. Persuading Benedict to forgive your defection and throw his weight behind you is the least of it.

"I am a patient man, my dear, and willing to await your reply. But events in this land are moving swiftly. Do not, I pray you, keep me waiting for too long."

Restlessly Alienore paced her bedchamber, barely lit by the dying fire, mind chewing over her encounter with Bedingfield like a dog worrying a bone.

Jesus wept, where was Jervaise? She hardly knew whether to fear for his safety, with a viper like Bors hissing malice against him, or fear he'd gained the king's ear.

The rap of knuckles sent her spinning toward the sound, every nerve tingling. Alive to her fingertips, she all but ran to the door. Still, she took care to control her face. Not for worlds should he know she'd missed him or was pleased by his return.

But it was not Jervaise who waited. For the second time that night, a liveried page stood before her.

"Lady Alienore of Lyonstone? You are summoned to the king."

"The king?" She stared.

Exhaustion weighted her limbs like sodden garments. After the restless tossing sleep of her wedding night, she'd ridden miles over muddy roads. Then endured the drawn-out tension of supper and the prickling danger of Sir Bors. Now, after all that, she must address the king?

She rallied her wits for the challenge.

"Do you know if my—husband—is also summoned?"

"Nay, madam. His Grace asked only for you."

She smoothed her gown and straightened the silver chaplet that banded her brow. A glance in the polished plate showed her pallid with weariness. Then her jaw firmed, eyebrows drawing together, eyes firing with resolve.

With God's grace, I shall overcome.

They passed down a spiral stair and through the great hall, where again she searched for Jervaise. The hearth was banked, for most had already retired—or sought other diversions. Sleepy servants still toiled, piling benches against the wall, clearing a space where the lesser folk would sleep, wrapped in their cloaks near the warm coals.

He is not here. Her heart plummeted. *Sweet mercy, where can he have gone?*

"Madam? The king waits."

Squaring her shoulders, she hurried after the page, butterflies turning cartwheels in her stomach. She would require all her wits for this encounter.

Sentries with crossed pikes warded the king's bedchamber and eyed her with open speculation. She knew what they must think, to see a lady summoned alone to the king's chamber at this hour. Henry was not a man known for chastity.

Warmth stinging her cheeks, she lifted her chin and stared straight ahead. When bidden, she strode inside like a knight riding into battle.

Her wary gaze swept the chamber, stamped with the personal tokens of its master. Between bold tapestries woven with battle scenes, trophies of the hunt stared back at her: elk with antlers, boar with tusks, a bruin with a gaping jaw.

Nearby stood a writing table, a sheaf of curling parchment cascading unchecked to the floor—then the blazing gold and crimson bed, curtains drawn back to reveal its perilous depths. These were the king's hunting grounds, and the prey he stalked was she.

The man was unseemly, just as Eleanor claimed—but he was her king. He stood before the casement and the mist-wrapped turrets beyond. At least he was decently clad, still wearing the russet tunic and leather chausses he'd worn to dine. His hunting jerkin lay discarded across the bed.

Concealing her unease, she sank into a curtsy. Henry Plantagenet laughed shortly and hoisted his goblet in salute. "You didn't expect to gain my ear so quickly, hey? I circumvented my reeve entirely for you, madam. Are you grateful?"

Aware of the open door and the sentries' straining ears, she confronted the lion in his den.

"I am grateful for the opportunity to lay my case before Your Grace. But aye, I am surprised. I did not believe you would be eager to receive me—counselor to the queen you've put aside."

His cobalt eyes flashed. "Did you address my wife so

frankly? I can't believe she welcomed it—but perhaps I'm mistaken. Candor can be refreshing as rain in a royal court."

She clasped her hands before her. "Your Grace, I can only be what I am. I know no other way to speak."

"Oh, well said! I begin to see why the queen values you, Lady Alienore of Lyonstone."

He dismissed the page, and the door scraped shut—sealing them in. At least this blunted the guards' hearing, though it did naught for her jittery nerves. Unless Henry had a squire tucked away nearby, she stood very much alone in the royal presence.

She couldn't help recalling the rumors every courtier had heard. The king was lusty as a satyr, they all said. Hadn't Eleanor herself accused him of infidelity? He was Richard's father, after all.

Henry pushed away from the casement. His energetic stride swallowed the distance between them. She stood erect, hands clenched against her skirts, breath rising and falling too swiftly to hide.

Impatiently he swept documents from his chair, and wiggled his fingers to gesture her into it. Perching uneasily— for she would have preferred to stand—she braced for confrontation.

He folded brawny arms across his chest. "Will you take a cup of malmsey?"

"Nay, the hour is late. I will come direct to the matter." Wishing he did not tower over her, she steeled herself.

"Aye, madam?" Still courteous, his eyebrows hitched.

"I object most strenuously to the marriage arranged for me, against my consent, to the Duc d'Ormonde."

Eleanor of Aquitaine would have frozen her with a glance to hear the royal will questioned. But Henry Plantagenet only nodded, as if he'd expected as much.

"Do you have a religious calling, madam? I'm told you were convent reared."

"So I am. But nay, 'tis not that." She would not use her faith as a false shield.

"Then surely you must expect to marry, a lady of your station." Quizzically, he eyed her. "Do you object to the man himself? Or is this a maid's wounded pride that you were not tenderly wooed with pretty baubles and love talk?"

Discomfiting as it was, she was grateful for his directness, straightforward as the queen was subtle.

"I am no foolish maid, Your Grace, to trouble my king with girlish fancies. Until yesterday, I was a royal chancellor."

"Then what's the matter? For all his empty purse, Jervaise brings a great title and a knight's strong arm to the match. That's no small thing on the Scottish border, where your lands march." A smile gleamed in his beard. "Christ, he's always popular with the ladies. Isn't he handsome enough for you? Or doesn't he please you in the marriage bed?"

Now this was frank speaking! Heat scorched her from crown to toes. Still she strove to hold his gaze—demanding his respect.

"I object to the marriage because it violates the will of my father, Earl Theobold of Lyonstone, one of your most loyal and trusted vassals. My father bequeathed me the Wishing Stone lands and the freedom to make my own marriage. My brother, under the sway of a clever counselor, chose to violate those rights."

Her voice rang out. "As your faithful vassal, I appeal to the crown for justice! I ask you to uphold my rights, confirm my inheritance, and—invalidate my marriage, which was made under duress."

It had proven difficult to force out the last, but she'd done it. She must make him view her seriously, as a powerful vassal whose regard was worth something. Else she would have no hope of wringing any concession at all from him.

He listened to her gravely—she'd won that much. Her gaze dropped to his hands: great sun-bronzed paws horned with calluses from sword and rein, covered with a mat of curling copper hairs. Physically, he and Jervaise were utter opposites.

"Marriage is no affair of the heart, madam, but a matter decided for a woman by her male relations. You're worldly enough to know that."

"Aye, but my father—"

"Is dead these four years," he said flatly. "By wedding you to Ormonde, I give him the incentive to guard my realm as he guards my person. Now more than ever, I need loyal men around me. Why should I risk losing his loyalty to suit a lady's fancy?"

"My loyalty is also valuable. The Scots press your English flank. You've said you expect Philip of Flanders and his army to set sail any day. Between the two of them, they will crush your troops like a walnut. You stand at risk of losing your English throne."

She paused to draw breath, heart kicking like a fractious stallion. "Lyonstone is the greatest shire in Northumbria. We sit less than a day's march from Carlisle, where Scots William is certain to try you. And the north is where the English rebels hold sway. With Lyonstone to ward your flank, you may free your loyal troops to deflect the Flemish assault. I can give you Lyonstone—and by extension, I give you the north."

"I already have Lyonstone." His eyes narrowed, two beams of piercing light. "All my vassals' holdings are subject to royal jurisdiction—including yours. You offer me nothing I don't already hold."

Carefully she navigated between conflicting loyalties, struggling to bump against none of them, while she marshaled the arguments to sway him.

"Must I list those barons whose loyalties lie with your treacherous sons? Roger de Mowbray and his ambitious brother, Earl Hugh Bigod, the lords of Huntingdon and Tutbury, the bishop of Durham, and many others. All these will support the Scottish king when he surges south."

"You're well informed," the king said, dangerously quiet. "As well informed as my wife."

"Lyonstone is the key to your northern defense. The current earl is a well-meaning lad of sixteen who has never commanded troops on English soil. He places his trust in an ambitious counselor who has no reason under heaven to defend your interests—"

The king thrust to his feet and paced like a caged lion. "Even if everything you say is true, how can you aid me? Unless you plan to lead Lyonstone's army yourself, hey?"

He pinned her with his gaze, eyebrows hoisted. She itched with sudden discomfort. He could not possibly know about her exploits on the tourney field—could he? He'd merely launched a bolt at random that struck close to home.

"That is not my intent, Your Grace. There resides at Wishing Stone Manor a seasoned knight: my mother's kinsman, Raoul d'Albini. With me to enforce his authority, this great knight would lead your troops to victory."

Still he pinned her with those penetrating eyes. She prayed her anxiety did not show.

Raoul was everything she claimed him. But he was also a cripple, legs crushed by the same tower collapse that had maimed Marguerite. He could only crutch along with the aid of wooden sticks. Yet he could fight and command troops from horseback with all the skill of a whole man.

The king's thick fingers tapped against his thigh. "Wouldn't I do better to dispatch Jervaise to Lyonstone?"

"You require him in Normandy, you have said."

Henry grunted and resumed his pacing. Even at this hour, restless energy pulsed from him. She could only admire his stamina.

For her part, dark clouds of weariness hovered at the edge of vision. Flagging, she sagged in her chair, eyelids drooping. When he spoke, her eyes snapped open.

"Frankly speaking, Lady Alienore—which I'm told you prefer—that seems to me a shaky bargain. Is there nothing more you'd offer?"

She hesitated. "What does Your Grace have in mind?"

Henry bared his teeth in a smile. "Does my queen still trust you, privy chancellor?"

A wave of shock and outrage rolled through her. *God and Mary, I was a fool not to foresee this.* "If you are asking me to betray that trust and spy upon her, my answer to that is nay."

"Nay, madam? You would say nay to me?"

"I say *nay*." She poured all her resolve into the word. "Honor is not solely the province of men."

The moment the words left her lips, the implications crowded in. She might have just flung back in his face the only terms the King of England was prepared to offer. Still, there was nothing he could say that would persuade her to do *that*. Now she braced to withstand the fatal onslaught of royal temper.

He stood before the casement, one hand cupping his chin, fingers tapping against his jaw. When he met her gaze, he smiled.

"Splendid," he said. "What a magnificent creature you are, my lady. You must have half the men of Aquitaine, including a son or two of mine, at your feet."

Her gaze faltered. "I am a virtuous woman. As you have remarked, I spent six years in a convent."

"But you're no nun," he chuckled, striding toward her. "Not with your passion. It occurs to me, Alienore, there's something of value you can offer me after all."

Wary, she eyed him. "Your Grace—"

"You're a married woman, albeit much against your wishes. Jervaise's wife, of all women, but that may prove convenient."

He braced a hip against the writing table and looked at her—close enough for her to smell the forthright odor of horses in his garments. She held rigid, refused to retreat, as he caught her chin against his calloused palm.

Only the fact that he held her gently kept her still beneath his touch. That, and the knowledge of what he was: King of England, Duke of Normandy, and commander of her fate.

He angled her face so the firelight spilled across it. His fingers against her jaw were rough from the hunt, the horse, the sword.

"God's eyes, you're something," he murmured. "You must have Jervaise on his knees for you. He and I share similar tastes in women. Did you know that?"

"Nay." Her voice came out strained. "I pray you, release me."

"You must stand up to defy a king properly." Lightly, he exerted pressure beneath her chin.

Determination flooding through her, Alienore rose to her full height—taller than he, by God!

"I do not defy you. I am your loyal subject and vassal. I ask only to be treated with the dignity my rank demands."

Releasing her, Henry gave a good-natured shrug. "You must've known what was expected when I summoned you here—alone, at this hour. You're no innocent maid, a woman of your years. You've just spent half a year in Eleanor's decadent court . . . to say nothing of your nights in Jervaise's bed."

Embarrassment surged through her. Here was her moment to play that card, so lack of consummation could bolster her objection to the marriage. Yet now the moment was upon her, she found she could not do it. She could not confess to this man of the world with his knowing smile that she stood before him a virgin. He would never believe she'd deterred the Devil of Damascus from claiming his bride.

Yet now she must dissuade the King of England from his own carnal expectations—like father, like son. Anger kindled as she recalled how Richard, too, had dishonored her.

"I could hardly deny your summons, Your Grace, no matter the hour or the proprieties. Nor could I expect another opportunity if I refused this one and angered you. Pray do not read more into my presence."

She stood with the master of two realms before her. Unlike Richard, he made no attempt to lay hands on her—merely stood with restless fingers drumming his thigh and offered a rueful smile.

"Jervaise and I have shared more than a woman or two in the field. Didn't he tell you? I suppose it's not quite the thing for wooing a reluctant bride."

Inexplicably, it irritated her to hear it. She mustered what dignity she could, though her face was burning. "You have a liege lord's jurisdiction over me—my body, my estates and all that is mine—even my life. If you command me to perform in your bed, I have no choice but to obey, or fling myself from yonder window to preserve my honor."

"Good to see you understand that." He smiled.

"If I must go to your bed, I tell you plain 'twill be done unwilling, and a mortal sin! Double adultery, to say it straight out—betrayal of my husband and your wife." She pressed to the heart of the matter. "Do you intend to release me from my marriage?"

Admiration glimmered in the eyes that studied her.

"It grieves me to disappoint you, but I too will be plain. The goodwill and loyalty of Jervaise de Vaux are worth more to me than yours, Alienore of Lyonstone. You've naught to bargain with, except what you've already refused to give. The rest is mine already and with God's grace will remain so."

Henry strode to the casement where he'd left his goblet. Ice-cold to her fingertips, she watched as he tossed back the contents. Then the King of England turned toward her.

"Take heart, my lady, for one thing you have achieved. You've convinced me to send Jervaise, with you at his side, to England rather than Normandy. And I intend you to go forthwith."

She stood rooted to the floor, a riot of emotions in her heart. Bitter disappointment, anger at his cavalier treatment . . . an unnamed fear releasing its hold on her heart. She would find no easy undoing of her marriage after all. How would she manage to keep Jervaise at bay now?

She swallowed her resentment and curtsied. "I shall waste no more of your valuable time."

She had nearly left when he called after her.

"It's no tragedy being married to a man like Jervaise de Vaux. God's truth, I begin to suspect you're the perfect woman for him. I'll be interested to see what his duchy becomes, with the two of you to shape her."

Chapter Seventeen

The great hall yawned before her, a vast cavern of darkness. Avoiding benches and huddled sleepers, Alienore hurried through it—away from her disappointing encounter with the king. Rushes rustled as mice scurried before her.

Across the hall, a flaring torch marked the tower stair. She groped toward it, toward the bed and the man who waited.

Saint Swithun save her, she'd failed to persuade the king. And she'd promised Jervaise—sworn on her honor—that if Henry refused an annulment, she would yield. She heated to imagine what that would mean: the cinnamon spice of his mouth on hers, the sweep of his knowing hands, the ache of passion between her thighs . . .

The scuff of leather against stone arrested her. Straining to pinpoint that subtle sound, she froze. It came again, the rapid *chuff-chuff-chuff* of footfalls on the curving stair.

Alarm prickled through her. The stair led only to their chamber, where no other had business at this hour. The clash of steel rang out—one blow, then a clamor of parry and riposte, coupled with a man's heavy grunt.

She did not weigh her course. Instead, she unsheathed her knife and snatched the heavy torch. The reek of pitch and blazing heat struck her together, with a choking billow of smoke. Already she was charging up the stair, surefooted despite her skirts.

Wielding her torch like a sword, she raced around the curve. The scene launched her heart into her throat.

Silhouetted against the casement, a familiar form crouched

and lunged, hair swirling around him in a cloud of ink. Below him, two swordsmen battled to gain the landing, steel moaning as their blades carved the air.

And behind him, pressing from above, another pair of enemies: blond Norsemen swinging battle-axes, just beyond Jervaise's embattled reach.

Somehow, despite his perilous placement, he was holding all four at bay. He'd put his back to the wall, scimitar tumbling end over end in its deadly dance. His other hand wielded the curved dagger, vicious backhanded sweeps confining the Norsemen to the stair. With every step, they risked losing a foot to this unorthodox defense.

Jervaise fought in grim silence, eyes narrowed to slits, white teeth bared in a grimace of effort. Yet she knew he could not maintain this defense for long.

Ahead, the first pair stood with their vulnerable backs exposed. But that was not how she'd been taught to fight. Her throat split with a racketing battle cry, warning her enemies and—she hoped—alerting the sleepers in the hall.

Above, the attackers pivoted: a wiry youth and an older man, weathered face hidden behind a rusty beard. Strangers, clad in the boiled leather of common soldiers.

But their swords would still be deadly.

They gaped at her, and no wonder—a noblewoman clad in jewels and samite, gripping knife and torch in battle readiness. Recognition leaped into Jervaise's face.

"Allah's blood, Alienore! Rouse the keep."

And leave you to the tender mercies of these villains? He would be dead by the time any aid arrived.

The red-bearded brute grunted and turned his back—blatantly dismissing her. His comrade did likewise. Staring in outrage, she stood disregarded behind them. Because she was a woman, they'd concluded she posed no danger.

Jervaise pivoted left and right, his scimitar a whirling crescent of death. "Get help!"

Indecision rooted her feet to the stairs. Every iota of her moral fiber rose up against attacking a man from behind. Yet she'd given warning—and his life hung in the balance.

With a shout wrenched from the depths of her belly, she lunged, and felt the pull of fabric as her skirts tore. Her long-knife sliced up, plunging deep in the hollow behind the red-beard's knee.

The man bellowed in rage and pain as his leg buckled and sent him tumbling down the stair. She twisted aside to avoid him as he vanished around the bend.

Above, the wiry youth gaped down at her. Giving him no moment to recover, she swung the torch in a blazing arc at his knees. He leaped to avoid it.

Jervaise pivoted away, clearly pouring every drop of concentration into fending off the axes.

"Lyonstone!" Fiercely, she swung her torch. This time her flame brushed a stained shirt. The lad shouted and slapped at the smoldering fabric.

Above, a man cried out. When a dark figure pitched forward, her gut wrenched.

The battle-ax tumbled from a bloody hand, and relief swept through her as the Norseman slid down the stairs. When he bumped the distracted youth, the lad fell sprawling. Alienore darted in, and his sword went flying.

She leveled her knife at his throat. "Surrender, and you shall be spared."

Snarling, he swung an arm, knocking her blade away. Lithely he rolled aside and sprang up with a dagger from his boot.

"By the Prophet!" Jervaise dodged sweeping blows from the last Norseman. "This isn't the tourney field. *Get help.*"

"I *am* help," she gritted.

Jervaise lunged, and a spray of crimson splashed the wall. Unable to see who was stricken, she screamed and ran forward. When the youth blocked her, she swung the blazing torch with all her strength. It crashed against his head. With a groan, the lad toppled, and did not rise.

Panic-stricken, she floundered up, dragging torn skirts above her knees. Before her sprawled the last Norseman in a spreading sea of blood.

Jervaise stood panting, his scimitar red to the hilt. Somehow, he had survived.

With the danger passed, the strength ran out of her limbs. She stared at the knife in her shaking hand and did not watch the man shuddering through his death throes at her feet.

"God save us," she whispered.

"Alienore, for the love of Allah." Roughly, Jervaise dragged her against his hard body with one arm.

At his touch, the last of her strength dissolved. Long-knife and torch tumbled to the floor as she flung her arms around his lean waist and clung to him. He crushed her against him, his strength and bulk enfolding her with the promise of refuge.

"You're the most maddening, stubborn woman I've ever known. If you were hurt—"

"But I saved you, did I not?" She turned her face into his corded throat.

"Aye, you saved me," he rasped, his big hand cradling her head. "Though *why* you saved me, I hardly know."

"Jervaise—these men—"

Below, a clamor was rising, an authoritative voice bellowing commands.

Heaving a breath, Jervaise released her. "Barricade yourself in our chamber."

Indignant, she shook her head. "I shall not abandon you."

"The danger's past for now, Alienore. Let me deal with this."

Still she felt unwilling to allow him out of her sight, given the ambush he'd barely survived. Had she arrived any later . . .

He retrieved her fallen knife and cleaned it against the Norseman's chausses. When he pressed the hilt into her hand, she clutched it, the lion clawing beneath her fingers.

"Go inside." Briefly, his harsh facade fractured. "My heroic lady of Lyonstone."

Her insides fluttered strangely.

"I pray you will join me anon," she said, breathless. "I cannot rest until this assault is explained."

His face hardened as he bent to clean his blade. "I'll get to the bottom of this. Be certain of that."

When Jervaise returned to the chamber where his bride waited, his shoulders ached with tension. Long hours had passed since he'd sent her there. He was still amazed she'd heeded him.

Firelight bathed the chamber in a homey light, welcome warmth after the grim confines of the interrogation chamber. He'd spent years of his life in hellholes like that dungeon.

Must be growing soft with age and all this court living. After a night like this, his bones groaned for the softness of a bed piled with furs, well warmed by his lady's body.

Turned out his lady was not abed.

Steam rose from the wooden tub to wreathe her, graceful as a damned angel, as she knelt before the fire and combed that gold and silver splendor of hair. Bare feet with delicate arches poked beneath her robe, sparking a riot of tenderness and arousal. Inevitably, his groin tightened.

She turned to find him in the doorway and stilled—as if caught in indiscretion. But nay, not his brave and virtuous lady. Worry was written in her strained features, exhaustion in the violet shadows under her eyes.

Relief transformed her, illuminating her like a lamp. "Praise God, you have returned. I was ready to go seeking you."

He bolted the door, shutting out the darkness and the

dangers it concealed. The chamber was secure, Allah be thanked—not even a garderobe to conceal an assassin.

"I was needed in the dungeon." He grimaced. *Aye, growing soft. I've seen far worse in Outremer.* "Henry's men questioned the two who survived."

Interest kindled in her eyes. "Did you learn why they were lying in wait for you . . . or for me?"

Caught pulling off his boots, Jervaise jerked up his head. By the Prophet, she was right. Those bastards might have been lying in wait for her. Though he couldn't imagine who stood to profit by her death—beyond her fool of a brother—a wrenching fear lanced through him.

Casually he loosened his belt. Wouldn't do to frighten her any worse than those whoresons had already done. For that alone, he wanted to slit their throats.

"A strange affair," he said gruffly. "I didn't know them, but like most sell-swords, I've my share of enemies. Someone hired this lot—common soldiers—to settle a grudge."

She seemed younger tonight, less poised than the queen's privy chancellor, more vulnerable. He'd never forget how she'd rushed to his aid: resolve burning like a flame in her white face, eyes flashing silver as she battled through a wall of enemies to his side. Something twisted in his chest—a painful tenderness, too intense to acknowledge.

"By my faith, surely those men revealed who hired them? I should think fear for their hides would loosen their tongues."

"They were hired in a local inn." He shrugged out of his surcoat. "A man, cloaked and hooded, paid them silver to kill me. The same man smuggled them past the gates."

He saw the shudder run through her and clenched his fists—fiercely protective. She was his now, and he would keep her.

"If the same man opened the gates," she said, "he may yet remain beneath this roof."

He jerked a nod. "He gave no name, and they could recall no more of the fellow. Young or old, tall or short, thin or stout, any uncommon mannerisms—in short, nothing. It's as if they were bewitched."

He dragged the shirt over his head, and welcomed the fire's heat against his dungeon-chilled skin. "Henry ordered them lashed. Perhaps it'll aid their memory."

She froze, ribbons of hair spilling from her fingers. A subtle tension invaded her voice. "The king attended the interrogation?"

"Henry's a late worker, aye? He wasn't abed."

He gripped the cords that bound his chausses and wondered how much intimacy she'd allow. He'd promised not to force her until she met with Henry. But blast it, he stank of the dungeon's sweating terror.

"Will it trouble you if I bathe, Alienore? Wouldn't offend your nostrils by my stench."

"Of course." Briskly she rose, giving him her back. "Shall I send for your squire?"

"Vulgrin's not as young as he was." He unknotted his chausses. "Needs his sleep. I'll manage without."

He'd given his word, little as that was worth, and he would keep it. Yet as he shucked his chausses, he couldn't avoid thinking he would soon be naked, and she nearly so. He could ask her to bathe him—

He veered away from that dangerous thought. Her graceful hands smoothing soap over his body, caressing his naked skin, finding him rock hard and ready . . .

Damn, he couldn't trust himself. He'd wanted her too badly, for far too long. Best do what he had to without her assistance.

Rummaging in his saddlebags, he found his incense and tossed a pinch on the fire. The air grew hazy with musk and sandalwood. She busied herself near the bed, eyes averted.

His lips twisted bitterly as he dropped his braies and

climbed into the tub. Then he groaned as the hot water enveloped him, lapping his cold skin, easing his tight muscles.

Her hesitant query caught him off guard.

"Since your squire is not to be troubled, do you wish my assistance?"

Despite his good intentions, his exhaustion, the lulling effect of steaming water, his cock throbbed with painful arousal.

Thankful for the tub's concealment, he forced his breath out. "Aye."

He shuttered his gaze, not wanting to alarm her with the lust-maddened beast raging behind his eyes. But he itched to read the intent in her guileless eyes. Allah's blood, he'd take whatever she was willing to give. He was no monk—surely she couldn't begrudge him that much.

Yet he thrummed with tension, like a bowstring pulled too tight, as she knelt behind him and reached for the soap.

The delicate aroma of lavender wafted past, and he snorted. No doubt he'd smell like a damned flower by the time she was finished. But she could douse him in attar of roses if it won him her willing hands on his body.

Tentative, she touched his shoulders, and the breath rasped in his lungs. *Breathe,* he told himself as she smoothed soap into the bands of muscle spanning his shoulders. She leaned into the knotted sinews, reminding him of the strength in her battle-trained body.

By the Prophet, he needed a distraction. His voice came out hoarse as a crow's.

"You wield a blade better than many men I know. Who taught an earl's daughter to do that?"

Her hands stilled. Shameless, he prayed she'd keep touching him. When she resumed, his eyes closed in gratitude.

Her boudoir voice was a siren's song, luring him to shipwreck on the rocks. "I was twelve years old when I was summoned home to tend my mother. But aside from caring for her, I had little to occupy my time. Raoul was in similar state—our arms master, whose legs were crushed when the tower collapsed. His body was crippled, but his mind remained intact. He blamed himself for her accident."

"Your father's suspicions can't have made his life easy."

"Nor did they. I feared he would do himself an injury, without some purpose to fill his time."

"You cared for him." Jealousy shafted through him. Twelve was old enough for a lass's first love. Exactly how old was this Raoul?

Her fingers kneaded his biceps, slippery with soap, drawing those little circles that seemed destined to drive him to madness.

"You might say we were kindred spirits," she sighed. "My father seemed angry with me as well, though I could not comprehend why. 'Twas as if he blamed me for my mother's shortcomings."

She spoke lightly, but pain threaded her words. Fighting the dangerous urge to pull her into his arms—Allah save him, he was lost if he did that—he spoke curtly.

"You loved him."

"I lionized him. It devastated me to see him so angry . . . so hurt. When I asked Raoul to teach me the sword, I think it eased the guilt we both felt. Of course he protested, but I had my share of stubbornness—then as now."

Humor shaded her voice, and a smile tugged at his lips. Her hands slipped over his chest, and his heart jumped. When she hesitated, he clenched his jaw until it ached with the effort not to touch her. If she stopped now, he wouldn't be responsible for his actions.

"A cripple might teach basic swordplay, the stances and such," he managed. "But you couldn't learn to defend without a foe."

"Nay." She smoothed soap onto his chest. To his ears, she too sounded breathless.

"Raoul arranged for me to spar with this squire or that, always wearing a helm to guard my identity. Then I began to champion wronged women—the ones no knight would defend. 'Twas remarkable, how many of those there seemed to be. I suppose, in a way, I was trying to defend my mother. For there was no knight to uphold her—not even my own father."

Her voice darkened with grief and anger, a witch's brew whose bitter taste Jervaise too had choked down. He burned to cradle her in his arms, to soothe her pain. But that would send her scrambling for her sword and end this shattering intimacy that was Heaven and hell.

"It gave me a purpose in life," she said, "and Raoul as well. I doubt either of us would have survived our grief and my father's wrath without it."

"Didn't you fear discovery?" Eyes at half-mast against the rising tide of desire, he clenched his fists. He couldn't drag her hands under the water, down to the throbbing ache only she could ease.

"I was always very careful." Her fingers grazed the hardened nubs of his nipples, then flinched away. Desire sizzled through him.

"I honed the steel of my defiance in the convent. Rather than submit humbly to God's will, I grew ever more determined to forge my own path. The abbess despaired of me. I believe they were all quite relieved when I was summoned home."

She brushed his nipples again—as if she couldn't resist—and his cock jumped, curse it. He gripped her, pressed her palms flat against his chest. His heart galloped like a spooked horse.

"Alienore," he rasped, "I've sworn to you—"

"To leave my virtue intact, until I appeal to the king."

He sensed her inner struggle and braced for her withdrawal. *When she pulls back, I'll release her. I must release her—I swore to that.*

Yet she did not pull back. Her breath fluttered against his neck.

"I spoke with the king this night," she whispered.

At first, he didn't grasp her meaning. Then realization arrowed through him.

"My lady wastes no time."

Her hands stirred, restless. "I wanted to settle this."

Dread coiled tight in his belly, knotting his insides. He'd always been sure of Henry's support . . . yet he knew the man far better than he knew the king. Wasn't certain he wanted to hear the outcome, but he had to say something.

"I saw the way he looked at you." The savage beast of jealousy clawed his chest. "It's a look I've seen before when a wench catches his eye, or a willing lady or nubile girl—"

"He refused my petition. He values your goodwill."

She spoke with her signature bluntness, unflinching, as if it cost her nothing. But he knew her to the marrow of her bones, knew the quiet strength and fierce courage that fired her soul. He knew the unwavering sense of honor that drove her to tell him, rather than keeping it secret to hoard her advantage. He knew what it cost her to speak.

He distrusted these surges of emotion, but couldn't seem to control them where Alienore was concerned. Hell, didn't he remember what happened last time? Pain and grief had taught him never to love.

"Yet you saved me." He scraped out the words. "Should have let those ruffians cut me down."

"If you think so, you do not know me!"

He was ready when she wrenched away, and twisted to his feet, soapy water streaming. She resisted when he pulled her close, only her robe and the tub separating her body from his.

He met her silver gaze—incandescent with anger and pride. The force of her will met his like the clash of blades.

"I know you better than any man living, Alienore of

Lyonstone," he growled. "Better than you know yourself. I know your vulnerability and your strength."

He knew her purity and her passion, and treasured them both. Beneath the self-imposed chains of a lifetime of denial, his heart turned over.

"I'll show you passion is nothing to fear." Climbing out of the tub, he drew her close and kissed her.

She resisted him by instinct, as she'd always done. Yet he blazed like Greek fire through her senses: broad shoulders and powerful chest, abdomen taut with sinew, a lifetime of scars slashing his golden skin. The blatant lance of male arousal stood between them, and her damp robe was a poor defense.

She braced her palms against his chest. His arms closed around her, a fortress that protected her, enclosed her in a prison of her own yearning.

I thought myself prepared for this, resigned to yielding, without emotion.

Yet nothing could ever prepare her. Every kiss was an ambush by a superior power, ranging over terrain she did not know. Still, she stood her ground. His kiss was a battle to first surrender, and defeat was the same as victory.

Yet she'd never learned how to surrender with grace, even when he swept her up and bore her to the bed. Remus scrambled away with a yip as he lowered her to the furs.

When he tugged at her robe, her head reeled. Suddenly their combat was sweeping along too swiftly, tumbling her toward the crux.

"A moment," she whispered, "for mercy."

"I know naught of mercy. I'm the devil—don't you recall?"

His words raised gooseflesh along her skin. "You are *not* the devil!"

She choked as her robe fell open in a cloud of lavender scent. A sense of abashed exposure made her squirm, even as his reverent hands spanned her body. Heat followed his hardened fingers as he traced the sides of her breasts, the dip of her waist.

"For sixteen years I've been burning in hell, Alienore. You alone can save me."

A surge of tenderness caught her by surprise, the fierce swell of a protective heart. Forgetting everything, she caught his head in her hands. His raven's wing hair slithered down, framing his lean, deadly grace.

"You are not the devil," she whispered, her throat aching. "You are beautiful to me as the angels in Heaven."

"Wasn't Lucifer the fairest of all God's angels?" His mouth twisted.

But behind his bitter armor yawned a chasm of emptiness only she could fill. Tears blurred her vision as she cradled his lined face between her hands and brought his mouth to hers.

His heat seared her, skin against skin, her breasts pressed against his chest, his pulsing length like a sword of fire between them. Her desire for him blazed, a sweet rhythm that throbbed in her womb, more insistent for being so long denied.

She arched against him, her legs slipping apart. A lifetime of restraint was falling away like a discarded shield. Without words, she asked for something she couldn't name.

Jervaise understood her to her core—as he always had. She bit her lip when he cupped her, damp with her own arousal.

"Alienore," he groaned, brow pressed against hers. "Neither one of us wants to wait. Never fear."

"I do not," she said as his calloused fingers parted her. He touched her—somewhere—and a cry of astonished pleasure slipped out. The tide of battle shifted, and she floated on the ebb. Her hands dug into his corded back, nails piercing his skin at this invasion of her innermost self.

She was certain she should not like it. But her body recognized what it wanted, drew him deeper toward her sealed womb.

"Trust me in this," he rasped. "Show me that courage you have in such abundance."

"I know 'twill be painful," she whispered. "I do not fear that. Do it quickly, Jervaise—and do not falter."

He crouched between her thighs, black hair pouring over skin burnished by firelight. Staring at his length, she wondered how he would manage to fit inside her. For her entire life she'd hidden from this. Now she would discover what she'd been denied.

When he fitted his body to hers, stiffened length sliding into her tight channel, she stretched to accommodate him—then felt the flash of pain. Red light bloomed against her closed lids, but she did not voice it. Beyond the ragged remnants of discomfort, the tide was rising. Her own body turned traitor, flinging wide the gates, sweeping away her inhibitions. Clinging to him, she strove to match him, free as an arrow soaring through the skies.

She reached the apex just as he did. Braced above her, he shuddered, rigid in her arms.

When he collapsed, he rolled so as not to crush her and brought her to safe harbor, her head against his shoulder. His chest heaved as they struggled together for breath.

"Alienore? Tell me—"

"I am well." She voiced a little laugh. "More than well. Is it always like that?"

"Not always." Gently he massaged her nape. "I'm fortunate in my bride."

That reminded her of matters better left unspoken—of connivance and betrayal. But she would not think of that now. Tomorrow would be soon enough.

A sense of safety and well-being seeped through her, despite the sticky soreness between her thighs. With a sigh she let go and sank into darkness. Cradled in his arms, she slept.

Chapter Eighteen

Alienore floundered from the depths of slumber, disconcerted to find herself curled against Jervaise's bronze-skinned body.

Remembrance blazed through her and burned away the clinging fibers of sleep.

Overhead, a man cleared his throat. The bedcurtains were thrust back, sunlight pouring through the windows. Against the blaze of light stood the King of England. The sun flamed in his red-gold hair as he peered down on them.

"Your Grace!" she blurted, horrified.

Jervaise twisted up with a grunt, furs tangling around his hips, curved dagger flashing in readiness. Barely in time, she clutched an armful of bedclothes to her bare breasts.

Grasping after her shattered poise, she sat beside her naked husband with what dignity she could manage. Struggling to contain her annoyance, face flaming, she raised her chin and faced down their royal guest.

"Pardon my intrusion, Jervaise—madam." The king's lips twitched as though the infernal man were laughing. "I would've waited until you rose of your own accord, but you both seemed like to sleep the day away. Our enemies are on the move."

Jervaise reached for his braies, columns of muscle flexing against his supple back. She'd scored his spine with her nails during the height of passion, and her face burned hotter. Indisputably, he was now her husband in the fullest sense. Unsettling to recall how eagerly she'd welcomed him to her bed.

With a single smoldering look at her dishabille, Jervaise

rolled out of bed. She caught a searing glimpse of buttocks bulging with muscle before he tugged on his braies.

"Privacy for my lady." Catching up his leather chausses, he strode away.

Henry cast an appreciative eye over the tousled hair tumbling around her shoulders and the swell of her breasts.

"God's eyes, madam," he murmured. "Last night you were all ice and outraged defiance—now this. Love play suits you."

Jesus wept! King or no, would the man ravish her in her marriage bed? She tightened her jaw but said nothing, lest she singe the royal ears. Teeth flashing, he obligingly gave her his back and strode to the hearth, where a scowling Vulgrin stirred the fire.

Nesta bobbed up beside her, rosy with excitement.

"The king, milady!" she whispered.

With a disgruntled glance at her sovereign, Alienore reached for her chamber robe. "That would have been better said, Nesta, *before* you allowed him in."

The girl's face fell, and she ducked a subdued curtsy. "Aye, milady."

"Where is Remus?"

"Gone out," Nesta mumbled. "I came to attend ye for Mass—but ye were sleeping so sound I couldn't wake ye."

"Never mind, Nesta," she sighed. "Fetch ale for the king, and any morsel you can find in the kitchens. I cannot imagine how I managed to sleep through Mass. 'Tis many years since I have been so lax."

"Ooh, milady, I'd say the answer's not far to seek!" Nesta cast a telling glance at the tangled bed. Following her rapt gaze, Alienore glimpsed a reddish stain on the linen. A fresh tide of embarrassment seared through her, and she twitched the furs over it.

"The ale, if you please, Nesta."

As the girl bustled out, she composed herself and joined

the men. Already the fire was burning away the morning chill.

Chausses knotted around his hips, Jervaise swung a chair around for the king. Henry ignored it, striding back and forth with vigor.

"I have tidings from Flanders, Jervaise. A courier rode through the night to tell me."

Jervaise's eyes narrowed. "Count Philip?"

"Aye. The grasping whoreson—your pardon, madam— is making ready to sail. He's assembling a massive fleet at Ponthieu. It's as I feared. They mean to invade England."

"They support their Scottish allies," Alienore said.

Surprise flickering on his features, the king glanced toward her. No doubt he had not expected her to counsel him, but she was undaunted. He'd come to her chamber, had he not?

"Aye, madam, and the English rebels are also on the move. Northampton is threatened—though I rely on my loyal lord Huntingdon and my chancellor de Lucy to hold them in check. Still, the situation we discussed is coming to pass."

Anticipation crackled through her like the tension that fired her on the tourney field. "You will need every loyal soldier, every sword, every grain of provender the Lyonstone lands can yield. I shall compose a message to my brother—"

"Already done." He paced. "The earl's counselor rode at dawn."

God save me, he means Sir Bors. She shivered to recall their unsettling interview—and the offer that villain had made.

Jervaise stood naked to the waist with that decadent mane pouring down, still as a crouching panther. Mercenary or nay, the prospect of war did not please him.

"Your Grace," she said, "you dare not trust Sir Bors of Bedingfield."

"There are precious few I trust. Christ, this rebellion led by my own wife and sons taught me that!" He swung to face

Jervaise. "Old friend, I know this is naught you wish to hear. But I need your support at Lyonstone."

"Lyonstone." Her husband hooded his gaze. Unpleasant things resulted when he looked like that. "How well do you trust your intelligence? How do you know it's no ploy meant to draw you from Normandy? Ormonde sits on Philip's doorstep. Perhaps my support's better deployed there."

Henry's face creased in a rueful smile. "You think I don't know how you chafe to return? How loudly those neglected lands and people clamor for your attention? Nay, my friend, I am fully aware. But I have others to rely on in Normandy. Your wife persuaded me your support's best placed in England."

Jervaise shot her an inscrutable look. "Wasn't aware you take council from my wife."

"In fact," she hurried to say, "I said nothing of how you should be deployed, Jervaise. I spoke only of my desire to return home. If you wish to return to Ormonde, I shall voice no objection."

Yet her conscience stabbed her. Only last night, she'd deployed her best arguments to annul their marriage. Now the thought of going their separate ways left her cold and hollow.

"This debate is pointless." Standing still at last, Henry drummed restless fingers against his thigh. "I have made my decision. Jervaise, you'll go to Lyonstone and assume joint command—with the new earl—of the border army. Since I'm told the lad has little experience leading troops, I expect your presence will curb any youthful rashness, hey?"

Henry clapped a hand on his shoulder. Jervaise inclined his head, inky hair sliding forward, but a muscle twitched in his jaw. He held himself still—too still.

"Honored to serve," he rasped.

"Nay, you are angry," Henry said gruffly, giving him an affectionate shake. "Believe me, I know what this means for you. You'll be back in Ormonde before the harvest—you have my word on that."

The king swung around to Alienore, speculation kindling in his eyes. She struggled to untangle her emotions: concern for Jervaise, for her lands and people, buffeted with a rising exuberance that made her heart sing.

I am going home! And Jervaise is coming with me. Nothing could puncture the swelling bubble of joy that buoyed her.

"The battlefield is no place for a gently bred woman." The king eyed her. "I'll make a place here at court for Lady Alienore. With no queen or princess to lead here, this court will benefit from her gentle virtue."

His words dissolved the smile breaking over her. Dismayed, she turned to Jervaise. His face was a shuttered mask, eyes offering no window to his thoughts.

"It's what you wanted, aye?" Jervaise's mouth twisted.

The king was handing her what she'd asked for—an ironclad excuse to be quit of the man who'd coerced her into marriage. Yet perversely, the prospect gave her no joy.

Only a fool would miss the true motive behind Henry's generosity. With Ormonde safely launched for England, the king could pursue her at leisure.

She must avoid the trap. Yet one did not lightly refuse a Plantagenet.

"Your Grace is generous." She bowed her head. "But I believe I may serve better in England—at my husband's side."

Jervaise stood impassive, fists clenched.

She groped to explain herself. "I know the Lyonstone lands and people better than anyone living, including my brother, who is newly returned from crusade. 'Twould be selfish—indeed, cowardly—to place my safety before theirs."

She felt dishonest, for she had not spoken the full truth. Aye, she wished to go home. But she would not abandon Jervaise. How could she leave him to defend her lands alone?

Probably she would never know all the devils that drove

him. But she knew this much. He was not the rogue she'd thought him, bereft of honor or virtue. He placed his life at risk, his hard-won lands in jeopardy, to defend her home. He deserved her full support.

"Spoken like an earl's daughter," the king said smoothly. "How can I do other than commend your resolve?"

So easily he gave in to her? Uneasiness tickled her skin as Nesta scurried in, bearing a flagon and goblets. The king waved the tiring girl away with an absent hand, and the girl's cheerful features fell.

"Nay, lass." Henry smiled to take the sting out. "I'll not tax you. Your lord and lady depart for England this day."

As the king strode for the door, she couldn't look away from Jervaise's dark countenance. He eyed her as he would an unknown enemy—wary, even distrustful. The knowledge twisted her heart. She'd sworn the marriage vows, yielded her body, thrown her support behind him. Yet still he did not trust her.

"Christ, I almost forgot." On the threshold, Henry paused. "What with this crisis and that—I've news of those villains who attacked you."

She tore her gaze from Jervaise's guarded features. She'd nearly forgotten last night's assault by those would-be assassins.

"They were to be lashed, so my husband told me."

"Those were my orders." Henry nodded. "Their cell was found empty at dawn, and the jailer drugged."

Alarm spiked through her. "Then Jervaise is in danger."

"Nay." Jervaise watched the king. "Say the rest of it."

"It gives me no pleasure." Henry scrubbed a hand against his whiskers. "We found the missing men an hour ago, floating heels up in the river. Not a mark on them."

A chill skittered across her skin. Chafing her arms, she moved closer to the fire. Vulgrin squatted in the ashes with the shovel, his single eye glittering.

"Dead end," Jervaise growled. "Villain's covered his tracks. Damn."

"I've appointed Sir Guy Aigret to investigate." Henry shifted as if, even now, he could not bear to stand still. "The man needs a task. But I doubt he'll find much, unless a witness comes forward. Watch your back, old friend—both on the road and in battle."

"Just like old times." Jervaise bared his teeth in a wolfish grin.

"I trust Sir Guy will investigate Sir Bors?" Alienore said. "What were his whereabouts last night?"

Eyes gleaming, the king hoisted his eyebrows. "Why, madam, I'm told he was with you."

Thus did the King of England wreak vengeance on the woman who'd spurned him. She should have expected the ambush. He was a Plantagenet, after all.

When the king departed, she turned to Jervaise, her heart sinking. His mouth twisted in a mordant smile.

"Nay, 'twas not like that." Her conscience smote her. "I meant to tell you."

But had she truly? At least she could say honestly she'd never wanted Sir Bors to kill him!

Aware of the listening servants, she straightened.

"Nesta, find me a gown for travel, if you please. You have heard the king's edict. We ride for Lyonstone this day."

She could not mute the ring of gladness in her voice. But her elation faded before Jervaise's keen gaze.

"You were busy last night, aye?" he rasped. "Couldn't find time to tell me before you came to my bed?"

Uneasy, her eyes flickered to Vulgrin and Nesta as they bustled about, too well trained to react to this tense discussion. Still, she disliked discussing personal matters before them. Though she would take oath Nesta, at least, was trustworthy.

"I would have told you, Jervaise. There was simply no occasion, with the assault upon you and then . . ."

He stalked toward her. Flustered, she turned to the window and the churning river below. In the clouded glass, the dark flame of his reflection leaped to life. His hands rose to brace against the wall, trapping her between his arms.

"No occasion?" His warm breath tickled her nape. "No chance to tell me you'd met your mortal enemy? The very man who brokered our marriage? This disturbs me."

She struggled to remain calm, to recall she had nothing to hide. "We know Sir Bors is responsible, yet we cannot prove it. He alleged there is still a rival claimant for your duchy— a rival candidate for my hand. Is it true?"

"Oh, aye, it's true," he whispered, lips brushing her ear. "Does that please you?"

The pain of his distrust knifed through her.

"Why should I wish to exchange one unwanted husband for another? I know nothing of this rival claimant. Indeed, he could prove worse than—"

Too late, she swallowed the words. He barked a grim laugh. "Worse than me—another outcast, bastard, infidel? That what you meant to say?"

"Why are you doing this, Jervaise? We are wedded now—"

"Wedded and bedded." His hands slid down her arms and curled beneath her breasts. "I gave you one gift he couldn't, aye? Made you a woman—taught you the truth of your body."

Her breath caught as his hands cradled her breasts. A flood of desire weakened her knees.

When her nipples tightened under his caress, he chuckled like a demon. Burning and breathless, need pulsing between her thighs, she leaned against him and closed her eyes.

"I want no other husband," she whispered. "None but the one I have."

"Behold the power of desire," he jibed.

"I cannot blame you for doubting." Inhaling a shaky breath, she turned her cheek against his naked chest. "You are not the unprincipled knave I called you—"

Abruptly he pushed away, ending the caresses that coaxed her to voice these dangerous thoughts.

"Don't deceive yourself. I'm everything you think me. I'm the worst of what's rumored," he said harshly. "You'd do far better with another man. Afraid you're stuck with me now, though."

Heart twisting, she watched him pull a shirt over his muscled torso. Protests spun through her head, but mindful of the servants, she said nothing. Guilt and uncertainty clouded her thinking and muddied her usual decisiveness. She needed time and the solace of prayer to clarify her feelings.

"Nesta, I have missed the Mass, but I daresay the priest will hear my confession."

As Nesta combed and coiled her hair, he armored himself in the Raven's unrelieved black. He'd withdrawn behind a wall of foreboding, devoid of any warmth or tenderness.

As if last night never happened and I mean nothing to him. Struggling for composure, she draped a veil over her hair. Her mirror showed her modest and seemly, with no sign of her sinful passions or the guilt that roiled her soul.

Her stubborn spirit reasserted itself. He called himself a godless man, but he had not always been so.

"It may be long before we have leisure for matters of faith." She hesitated. "Will you not accompany me to confession?"

He raked back his hair and tied it. "Your God and I are not on speaking terms."

"But we are riding to war! You are long unconfessed. Don't you think—?"

"Nay, I do not." He shot her a black look, his ruined voice simmering with warning. "I renounced God long ago—after he renounced me. Say no more of this."

And so, once again, she failed to persuade him. But she could not seem to cease trying. She would heal the damage wrought by his rift with his faith, an open wound grave as the one that destroyed his voice. She wanted more for him—for them—than the cool resignation of an arranged marriage, two people bound together by expediency.

She was going to save him, whether he wanted it or not.

Chapter Nineteen

Alienore twisted in her saddle to search the rolling hills curtained in gray drizzle. Aye, these were Lyonstone lands.

Despite the rain that had drenched them since they set foot on English soil, miring the roads in a sea of mud, the soft breath of spring caressed her. The Wishing Stone folk should be busy in the fields, sowing the barley and oats that put bread on the table, tending her sheep—source of the manor's renowned cheeses. Yet the fields stood empty.

She'd meant to trumpet her return; she'd thought her faithful folk would be jubilant. Yet now, as her lands huddled under ominous clouds, she shivered and pulled her mantle closer.

An uneasy silence shrouded the traveling party. Watchful eyes glittered in his hood as Jervaise eyed the barren fields. Yet he too said naught.

Indeed, that was nothing uncommon. Clearly, he was displeased by the king's edict, sending him to England rather than his own distressed lands. Only at night, in their bed, would his armor drop, during those heated hours of darkness when she burned in his arms.

She cleared her throat. "By my faith, where have they all gone? 'Tis the height of the planting season—almost Easter."

"They've gone away, milady," Nesta said, subdued. "Even my own mam and da, and all my sisters too. Their little cot stood empty."

"God save us, I should never have left." The burden of guilt weighed her down. "I fled my duty when I fled Ponce. Now God must punish me for cowardice."

Jervaise snorted. "This is no biblical curse, but mere neglect. My lands looked the same after sixteen years of Ponce's indifference."

"I simply cannot comprehend it. I left Raoul in charge. He has been my steward for years, and an excellent one at that. My reeves and bailiff have always heeded him."

"Many a servant may fail his duty, aye? Need a strong hand to guide them."

"Not Raoul." Concern tightened her chest. "God's mercy, I pray no evil has befallen him. He has never written, not once since I left. But I thought—"

Knowing how close she treaded to awkward secrets, she swallowed the words. *I thought he was only angry, hurt and upset as I was, after our quarrel the night I fled.*

Yet she tingled with awareness of Jervaise, his guarded eyes trained on her. A month ago she would have swallowed her own tongue rather than confide in him, but something had changed between them.

How not, after the intimacies we share in our bed? He knows everything about me—sinful thoughts, carnal knowledge, the secrets of my soul . . . all except one. The last one and the worst.

Bending to brush away a gobbet of mud, she spoke softly. "The night I left home, we . . . quarreled. I left without telling him whence I traveled. I thought 'twould be easier. He could swear to my brother and Ponce that he knew nothing."

Jervaise was perceptive enough, and knew her well enough, to sense when she skirted an unpleasant truth. "Difficult to write when he doesn't know your whereabouts."

"But I told him! I grew uncomfortable with the silence between us and regretted our quarrel. So I wrote him from Aquitaine. By then, I thought Ponce must know my location. Still Raoul did not write, not even to answer my queries about the manor. I believed he must still be angry and put it down to that. But now . . ."

Clearly, he sensed the words she did not say. Yet he chose not to press her.

"Coming dark soon," he called to their straggling escort. "Step lively. We're too close to the border to be safe in the open."

Chain mail rattled as the sluggish mounts picked up their hooves. When they left Le Mans, six guardsmen had seemed ample protection—a party small enough to move at speed. Now Alienore found herself wishing for more to confront whatever waited for her at home.

Against the ruddy fire of sunset, the manor house stood in blackness. Its narrow windows yawned, bereft of a spark of light. Overhead, twin turrets pierced the heavens, no sign of sentries at their post. No challenge rang from the silent battlements.

Terror bloomed as visions of catastrophe flashed before her eyes. *Jesus wept! Have we come too late?*

Alienore dug her heels and the warhorse surged forward, hooves sending up splashes of muddy water.

"Wait, damn it!" Jervaise spurred after her. But she could not heed caution now.

She thundered into the yard and headed for the manor. A huddle of outbuildings flashed past: the stables, the smithy, the buttery where the cheeses were pressed. Not a soul in sight, God save her. Had the Scots already struck?

Without slacking, she spurred Galahad onto the exposed stair. His clattering hooves echoed the fearful pounding of her heart. As the warhorse pitched up, she raised her voice to the heavens.

"Hail the house!"

Behind, hooves rang on stone as Jervaise freed his scimitar with a *shing!* He would defend her to the death; she knew it without question, just as she knew her own name. But no sword on earth could defend her from this. The brooding silence of her home extinguished her last flicker of hope.

Then the portal creaked open. Dim firelight spilled onto

the stair. It limned the bent and twisted figure who tottered there, braced between wooden crutches.

A sob tore her throat. Slipping, scrambling, turning an ankle in her undignified haste, she tumbled from the saddle and flew straight into the arms of her beloved mentor.

Raoul d'Albini teetered beneath her weight but caught her close in his gnarled arms. When she returned the embrace, his crippled frame trembled. Once so vital, burning with crusader purpose, her old friend had grown old and feeble since she'd fled.

"Alienore, my child. Is it truly you?" His deep voice was unchanged, his Norman French pure as the king's. "I had all but given up hope for your return—or your forgiveness."

"'Tis no dream," she whispered. "I have come home to you."

Recalling her manners, she released him, though hot tears blurred her vision. Looming over them on horseback, Jervaise watched the reunion in silence.

"I married the Duc d'Ormonde, can you imagine?" She offered a wobbly smile. "This is my husband. Ponce's half brother, Jervaise de Vaux."

Recognition and a flicker of discomfort—or guilt?—furrowed the old man's brow. Bracing his stooped body between the crutches, Raoul lowered his snowy head. He still claimed a courtier's impeccable manners, though twenty years had passed since he'd left the French court.

"I've heard much of you." With a courteous nod, Jervaise dismounted, though he did not sheathe his sword. "My lady's mourned your parting."

Her heart swelled at his graciousness—gentle as any true knight, though he mocked himself for it.

Raoul's eyes glittered with emotion, yet he spoke with quiet dignity. "You are welcome to Wishing Stone Manor, though I fear we can offer little in the way of comfort."

Her concerns bubbled to the fore. "Those empty villages—I

do not understand what has happened. Why did you not send word?"

In the darkened manor, a footfall sounded. A shadow moved up behind Raoul, and Jervaise's scimitar swept up to defend. A ghost materialized from the darkness: a tall Saxon warrior clad in chain mail, ax jutting over his back, blond hair tangling at his shoulders.

God save me—Father! Crying out, she grasped Jervaise's arm to stay him. Had she gone witless? Nay, not her father—

"So the prodigal bride returns." The Earl of Lyonstone bowed. "I have waited long for this moment, sister."

"Benedict," she said softly.

Jervaise lowered his sword, but did not sheathe it.

Despite all that had passed between them, a crippling surge of tenderness rolled through her. Once, long ago, before Theobold banished her to the convent, her little brother had worshipped her, and she had adored him without reservation. God help her, she adored him still.

Yet her heart sank to behold him. He regarded her with the same hurtful coldness he'd brought back from crusade. Five years ago she'd bidden farewell to a grieving boy, and he'd returned from the crucible of battle a man grown—a hulking warrior like his father, a brooding shadow of the exuberant lad he had been.

So nothing had changed between them, and she swallowed her remorse. Every inch the queen's chancellor, she spread her muddy skirts and curtsied—giving him honor, though, she now outranked him.

"Good my lord, I'm honored you venture forth from Lyonstone Keep in this wretched rain merely to bid me welcome." Despite her reservations, her voice softened. "'Tis good to see you, brother."

"'Tis surprising to see you." The young earl stared at the traveling party, clustered like muddy sheep in the yard. "I thought you would be too shamed to show your face here."

"Shamed?"

"How else, after you fled your duty and my bidding like a runaway serf? Saint Swithun's bones—"

"I sought no more than justice, only the lands our father wished me to have." A sense of futility sank her heart. Almost a year since she'd left, and still they must tread the same weary terrain? She contained a sigh. "I wouldn't have left if you'd heeded my pleas."

Aye, she'd fled like a thief. But Ponce was not all she'd fled. Her brother had become a terrifying stranger.

Jervaise's Lucifer pawed the stone—evidence of the rising tension. Against his bronzed skin, her husband bared his teeth in a hard smile.

"No man accuses my wife of neglecting her duty."

"So you're the infidel duke." Benedict cocked his head to survey him. An odd light kindled in his gray eyes. "Welcome to your new home—such as it is."

Raoul gasped in outrage at this slur to an honored guest. While the old knight cast a glance of reproach at the boy he'd raised, Alienore bristled on her husband's behalf.

"You're mistaken." With a practiced sweep, Jervaise sheathed his scimitar, cloak rippling in the evening wind. "This is no home of mine. King ordered me to defend these lands. I'll return to Ormonde by Saint John's Day."

"So again you will leave us." Her brother turned to Alienore. Something like hurt surfaced in his eyes.

"Mistaken again," Jervaise rasped. "My lady will remain mistress here. She's more than earned it."

Uncertain, Benedict blinked at him. But Alienore had no thought to spare for him now. She stood riven, as though Jervaise had struck her, and struggled to absorb the sharp spear of hurt.

He had broached no such plan to her. Was he so eager to be rid of her, his troublesome bride, now that he'd gained her dowry?

She swallowed against the hot lump in her throat. "Would you leave us standing in the rain all night, brother? We are in sore need of fire and a hearty meal."

"We are remiss in our courtesy." Raoul followed her lead, though his perceptive gaze probed her features.

She glanced around. "Where is the marshal to take charge of these horses?"

Benedict sneered at that, the fog of confusion clearing from his eyes.

"Your brother has commanded your retainers to serve him at Lyonstone Keep—all but old men and cripples with little to offer." Raoul's voice was carefully neutral. "If you wish to find your marshal, your chamberlain, your bailiff and other retainers, you must apply to your brother."

Comprehension darted through her. She advanced to confront Benedict. "What is this monstrous outrage? By what right—?"

"We've much to discuss." Jervaise's hand gripped her shoulder, fingers pressing in warning. "It's best done out of the rain. Entrust your Galahad to Vulgrin for now."

She recognized his good sense, but the hot tide of outrage still bubbled. "What of our escort?"

"They'll tend to their own," he murmured. "Come out of the rain."

Raoul cast him a grateful look and crutched aside so they could precede him.

Drawing her poise around her, Alienore lifted her chin and strode inside—then halted in dismay. The familiar antechamber was a stinking cave, straw rotting on the flagstones, the odors of urine and mildew clogging the air. Embarrassment at the manor's disreputable state burned her cheeks. That Jervaise should see her home brought so low!

Before her the hall doors stood open, limned in the dim glow of firelight. Flinging off her cloak, she marched in, muddy skirts trailing at her heels.

Here, too, the signs of neglect shouted their tale. Muddy rushes on the floor, the stench of rotting food, with no sweet herbs to soften it. The trestle tables and benches were piled against the wall, shrouded with cobwebs and dust. A struggling scrap of fire did little to heat the chamber.

But there, before the hearth, a rickety table and benches still stood. There a man uncoiled, graceful and deadly as a striking serpent. Firelight gleamed on silver hair, winked on his rings and the throwing knives in his boots.

"My dear Alienore." He showed a sliver of smile. "Your return is most timely—though you've almost arrived too late."

She strode forward to confront Sir Bors of Bedingfield. "'Tis plain to see I have been too long away. My husband and I will soon put things to right."

His poison green eyes slid to Jervaise.

"Bedingfield," her husband said softly. "We meet at last."

Bors's eyes narrowed, the skin around his eyes twitching. Firelight gleamed on the white scars at his neck.

"*Salaam alaikum.* Peace be unto you." Each pointed word flew from his lips like a dart. "Isn't that how it's said in Outremer? Quite the remarkable elevation for a bastard and infidel. A rather convenient stroke of fortune. All praise to Allah, wouldn't you say?"

Jervaise bared his teeth in an unfriendly smile. "I'll not soil my tongue wishing peace to you."

"For shame, Sir Bors!" Raoul crutched forward, eyes like lightning in his seamed features. "I shall thank you to keep a civil tongue in your head. You are not lord of this hall."

Bedingfield's eyes flickered. "I believe you forget your place, old man. Marguerite de Rievaulx no longer lives to protect her paramour."

"Silence!" Alienore's voice snapped like a whip. A transforming fury burned through her. "We have not traveled these many days, over treacherous roads and pitching seas, only to bandy insults beneath my own roof. Benedict, you had best control your vassal."

Bors laughed, his rugged face creasing with genuine mirth. "Oh, Alienore, I have missed your arrogance, even if your brother hasn't. Do sit down, all of you. We have a great deal to discuss."

She was unwilling to do anything at his bidding. But Jervaise gripped her elbow, urging her to the table.

She eyed the bare boards. "Is there morsel for weary travelers?"

"Regrettably, our larders are not as they were," Raoul said with dignity. "I will see what may be managed."

"Nay, old friend." Her heart twisted with remorse. "I do not rebuke you. How can I? I am certain you did the best you could. Nesta will go to the kitchens."

Dropping her frightened eyes, the tiring girl hurried out. Awkwardly, Raoul lowered himself to the bench.

Alienore studied her brother with worried eyes. The difficult light could not conceal his waxen pallor and hollowed cheeks. Even in the chilly hall he sweated, sunken eyes glittering with fever.

Casually, Jervaise unsheathed his dagger. Four pairs of eyes followed the wicked crescent as he honed it against a sharpening stone.

"No doubt your counselor's conveyed the king's will," he rasped.

Benedict blinked vaguely, his gaze shifting to Sir Bors. Something he found there prodded him to clarity. "That course is utter folly. The rebels are a disorganized rabble, cowards starting at every shadow! They'll never muster the courage to move openly against the king. Henry wastes his time and ours if he calls the levy here."

Calmly, Jervaise sharpened his knife. "That rabble's seized command of several major keeps: Leicester, Huntingdon, Tutbury, Durham—"

"Oh, aye." Benedict waved a hand. "These Norman barons are a spineless lot—nary a drop of good Saxon blood among them."

"You are half-Norman, Benedict," Alienore said. Marguerite's sorrowful image floated before her eyes. "As am I."

"Norman, Saxon, what do those old grievances matter now?" Raoul knocked a crutch to the floor. "Do we not all shed blood when we are struck, suffer the same pinch of hunger when raiders burn our fields? Do we not owe fealty, one and all, to our good King Henry?"

"This is not *about* the king." Benedict scowled. "We're here to assess the situation, and he is not."

"Our young earl speaks with wisdom beyond his years," Bors murmured. "England has not forgotten the strife that tore these lands apart, when Henry's uncle Stephen and his dam, Mathilda, fought for the throne."

Vigorously Benedict nodded. "I say the rebels' defiance will crumble once Henry returns."

"Let's start with fact." Jervaise's eyes narrowed. "Henry's charged us to defend these borders. He has troubles of his own in Normandy."

"Well, he should not—" Benedict blustered.

"What news of the Scottish threat?" Jervaise studied the dagger's edge. Firelight ran along the blade, outlined the dots and slashes of Outremer script.

"The Scottish . . . ?" Blinking, the earl turned toward his counselor.

"My dear lord, you recall the alleged Scottish threat." Sir Bors stroked his arm, comforting him as if he were a fractious child. "We spoke of it on the road."

"Oh, aye. 'Tis rumored some rabble is massing at the border. But Scots William will not set a toenail on English soil after the trouncing de Lucy gave him last year. Sent him howling all the way back to Edinburgh."

Seeing the feverish glitter in her brother's eyes, Alienore

ached for him. Her valiant brother—noble, good-hearted, generous to a fault, so proud of his responsibilities as heir to Lyonstone. What had become of him? The pale invalid before her who swung between apathy and braggadocio was a stranger masquerading as the boy she'd loved.

She could not speak for the tears that clogged her throat.

"*This* for your assessment." Jervaise buried his knife in the table. The sickle blade hummed with menace. "The king doesn't share your view. He believes William will surge south any day."

"But—" Suddenly, the earl looked very young.

"Tomorrow," Jervaise continued, "we assess the state of Lyonstone's troops, weapons and provisions. We assure the defense of your castle against possible siege. And we raise the levy against the Scots."

Sir Bors tented his fingers, rings glittering. "My lord has made all the defensive arrangements he deems advisable. It is long since the Norman king has burdened himself with English concerns."

"He needed to set his own house in order." Alienore's cheeks burned with guilt. Henry's queen had betrayed him, and she herself had done nothing to prevent it.

"But—what more can I do?" Benedict shot her a helpless glance. "We have mustered all the men we may. There are few to ride under my banner these days. 'Twould be folly to call more! 'Tis the planting season."

Her mouth opened, but Jervaise's leather-wrapped thigh pressed against hers—warning her to silence. His banked heat licking against her leg did indeed distract her. Suddenly she could think of nothing but the slide of bronze skin against hers, the unholy fire that kindled when he came to her bed . . .

Jervaise smiled down at his knife. "I'm keen to review the arrangements. Shall we say, an hour past Prime?"

"As you will." Sullen in defeat, Benedict glowered.

"You will have to come to Lyonstone Keep." Bors showed his teeth in another thin smile. "My lord requires his medicines to achieve a restful sleep."

"I'm no invalid to be coddled," Benedict said irritably. "But I shan't sleep in this spider-infested cave my sister calls a home."

Outraged, Alienore drew breath to protest. Again Jervaise's thigh pressed hers, consigning her to simmering silence.

"That calls to mind another matter," he rasped. "Now my lady's returned, you'll release her folk to their proper places. She needs her chamberlain, bailiff and reeves, her cook and marshal, laundress and all the rest. By Holy Friday, two days hence, all Wishing Stone folk will return to their rightful place."

Alienore shot him a grateful look. Though she'd felt reluctant to yield her authority in these domestic matters, Benedict's hostility had only grown in her absence. For the moment, such orders would come easier from Jervaise.

Her brother glanced uncertainly at Bors, whose ringed fingers riffled against the table. The flash of emerald and onyx hurt her eyes. Queasy, she looked away.

"You will find this countryside quiet as a dead man, so you may sleep without fear tonight." Sir Bors's eyes slid to the staircase that climbed to the lord's chamber. "Do have a care with your footing on that stair. With this house in such disrepair, a man could easily break his neck."

He offered Jervaise a sliver of smile. "Indeed, unless I am gravely mistaken, a man *did* break his neck in that very spot and not so long ago. That is where poor drunken Ponce had his fatal plummet. But the old man here would know more of that."

Chapter Twenty

"The knave of Bedingfield spoke truly, God rot him." Raoul shifted his old bones on the bench. The fire sputtered, untended, casting uncertain light over those who remained after the earl and his counselor departed. "By Saint George's dragon, I cannot regret it." Raoul sighed. "The former duke was a terribly determined man. He would never have given up my lady."

"'Tis my fault you were burdened with him." Alienore bowed her head. "If I had not fled—no better than a runaway serf, as Benedict said—"

"Then you'd deprive the queen of her chancellor." A wry smile slanted across Jervaise's face. "Ponce was drunk when he fell, aye? Knowing the man, I don't doubt it. He was the first to condemn me in Antioch—for my father."

"You did the best you could, Jervaise. You did far more than he, from what you've said."

"Aye, well, no love was lost between us." He turned to Raoul. "You witnessed his fall?"

"God help me, I more than witnessed it." Raoul crossed himself. "When he descended upon us, the duke was astounded not to find my lady. For weeks he waited, with maddening patience, for her return. He prayed, fasted, repented . . . as if to show the world he'd changed."

"'Tis what I feared," she murmured. "Whatever his past sins, Ponce's repentance was genuine."

"Unlikely." Jervaise scowled. "He was a monster, like his sire before him, and all his kin."

"You had not seen him in many years, Jervaise. Hardship

may change a man. Perhaps he wished to redeem himself—but I denied his chance for salvation."

"He was beyond saving." Sounding weary beyond words, Jervaise massaged his brow. "Believe me."

"If his remorse was genuine," Raoul said, "my actions were reprehensible. Ponce had been here two months when Benedict summoned him to Lyonstone. The duke rode off to meet him and returned late, in his cups."

"You see?" Jervaise said bitterly.

"It was the only time he indulged. Perhaps Bedingfield set him drunk. For when Ponce returned, he was slurring out the terms of their new agreement—a marriage by proxy. To take place the next day, with some poor lass to stand my lady's part. Bedingfield coaxed the earl to sign, and it would have been all too legal."

"The utter perfidy!" she whispered. With Benedict's consent, the ploy would have worked. She'd stood but a breath from disaster—

"Ormonde stood swaying on the stair," Raoul said, "while he explained this, how my proud lady would find herself wedded and bedded. I could not contain my wrath, to see my lady's welfare so maligned! We quarreled—and our fine monseigneur swung a fist at me, cripple that I am."

"Did Ponce miss his footing?" Jervaise rasped. "Was that the way of it?"

"I wish it were so." Raoul hung his head. "But this is no such innocent tale. Nay, Ponce did stagger when I ducked his blow, but he would have recovered. Saint George guard me—I could see nothing but my lady's desperate face, still grieving for Theobold, forced to flee like a vagabond to avoid this doddering sot! I knew after the proxy marriage, Alienore would be trapped—bound by law to the match. It flashed through my mind as Ponce teetered on the stair. The notion never struck me before that moment, I swear it—"

"Jesus wept," she whispered. "You pushed Ponce down the stair."

"God save me, I did it. And do daily penance before Christ on my knees for it. If you do not care to harbor a vile murderer—"

"Nay, how can you say so?" Shaking, she knelt in the rushes and embraced him. "You were the only soul on earth who stood between me and that marriage. God strike me dead if I rebuke you for it. Why did you not respond to my letters?"

He drew back to stare. "To my despair, I received no letter from you in all the time you were away. Nor any response to my missives, which I now discern you never received. I believed you were still angry with me over that ill-timed quarrel."

"Nay, Raoul—never that." Numb, she sank back to the bench.

Jervaise rubbed her back, and she leaned into his strength. He seemed the only source of comfort in her disordered world. Bleakly, she thought how it would be when he left her.

Alone once more, with my heart as cold and empty as my virtuous bed.

"Your letters were intercepted." Jervaise's amber eyes narrowed. "By the same man who has the earl enthralled through potions and witchery."

"Such an effort!" Alienore exclaimed. "To what end?"

"To buy time for some scheme to play out." Frowning, Jervaise dislodged his knife from the table. "Now we must learn his game."

The lord's chamber had long been neglected, but Nesta found clean linens to spread over the pallet. She beat the bedcurtains free of cobwebs and scurrying spiders. Vulgrin hauled water from the well until Jervaise relieved his bent old body of the chore.

Alienore attacked the dusty floor with a broom. When Benedict returned her household folk, they would find much to occupy them.

Now she glanced toward Jervaise, lounging with feet propped against the brazier, cradling the steaming cup the kitchens had finally produced. Beneath his legs Remus sprawled, unconcerned by the disorder as he scratched a flea.

Her husband had said nothing after the servants bedded down below. She knew he would remain thus, plunged in brooding silence, until she blew out the candle.

Cross-legged on the bed, she frowned as she sharpened her long-knife. She'd thought the marriage bed must draw them closer—for how could their souls remain apart while their bodies soared to rapture? Yet every day, he withdrew farther into that dark place where she was not permitted to follow.

Studying his grim profile, she kindled with determination.

"I was interested to learn you intend to return to Ormonde without me, husband. Saint John's Day will soon be upon us."

"It can't dismay you." Jervaise brooded into his cup. "You'll be free of your devil husband. My lands have suffered a lifetime of neglect. Much is needed to put them to rights."

"That was why you sought an heiress," she said, brittle, the old pain biting deep. "For the letters of credit I signed for you, to replace what Ponce gambled away in his wastrel youth."

"They're starving, Alienore." He hunched in his chair. "All the farmers without seed to plant, without custom on those neglected roads. I chose a new steward to replace the thief who was cheating Ponce. But my presence is needed to put matters right."

"Starving." She suffered a pang of guilt. Obsessed by the wrongs done her, she'd never spared a thought for the imperatives that drove him. "I did not know."

He tossed back his mead. "Nor troubled to ask—though I

can hardly blame you. This was what Henry ordered me to ignore when I came here with you."

Her face heated. "I stand justly accused. 'Tis a noble duty, to care for your suffering dependents—"

"World doesn't take the Devil of Damascus for a noble man," he said harshly.

"Nay, do not malign yourself!" Jumping up, she strode to his side. His shoulders were rigid, but she nerved herself to touch him. "You are not to blame for misguided rumors."

"Misguided, are they? Don't delude yourself. For sixteen years I cared no more for duty than Ponce. Free will—it's what Islam teaches. I'm damned by my own actions."

Offering what comfort she could, she kneaded his shoulders.

He stared into the fire. "When I saw Ormonde's ruined lands, those wretched scarecrows shivering in rags and despair, I saw my last hope. I hoped . . . through them . . . to redeem myself. Save my father's people, as he never did."

"Of course you would." Understanding bloomed. "'Tis a knight's charge to defend the weak, uphold the righteous, protect those who cannot protect themselves—just as you protect poor Vulgrin. Just as you protect Nesta and Remus . . . and myself."

He is an honorable man at heart, I knew it! Hadn't she sensed it beneath his veneer of dissipation? Hadn't he saved her from ruin the day they met, when he would not unmask her on the tourney field? She'd wasted so much time, blindly denying him, denying her own senses.

"Don't hurry to cloak me in a Christian knight's mantle." He leaned to stir the coals, and her hand fells away. "Giving alms, easing hardship, fighting injustice—Muslim virtues, if I had them. You don't know the weight of my sins."

"But I would know them!" She knelt at his side. "If you will not confess to God what grieves you, then at least confess to someone who . . . cares for you."

"Nay, Alienore." He scrubbed a weary hand against his scarred face. "You're worth more than that. Caring for me would be the worst mistake you could make."

Staring into the fire, he ground out the words. "Don't throw your heart away on me. I can't love you."

His words, edged in rejection and betrayal, pierced her like a sword. She'd trusted him with her virtue, and he'd betrayed that for his own ends—needs that were unselfish after all. She'd abandoned her misgivings one by one to trust him with her heart. Her voice, when she spoke, was strangled.

"What do you mean to say?"

"I think it's plain enough." Avoiding her, he thrust up and strode to the casement. "There's no love left in my heart, Alienore. I can't love you. And I won't have you love me."

How had she fallen in love with him? A disgraced knight—an infidel, of all men? For now she knew the truth of her heart. She could never have loved a weak-willed courtier like Thierry de Beaumont. The idealistic virgin she'd been a year ago knew nothing of love.

As always, she would confront the truth head-on.

"Whether you'd have it or nay, you cannot prevent it," she said, low and steady. " 'Tis too late, for I lo—"

With a violent exclamation, he flung the cup away, spraying mead across the floor. "Will you make me reject you outright? Where's your pride, Alienore?"

"Reject me if you will." She steadied her voice, though she trembled head to foot. "I will not feel shame for loving you. Not such a man as you are, Jervaise de Vaux."

He gripped the sill in both hands, his knuckles white. "I said I'll leave you, soon as the Scots are dealt with. Will you still love me then?"

She closed her eyes against the sting of tears, felt them trickle down her cold cheeks.

"Aye, even then," she whispered.

"Then you're a damn fool." Pivoting, he strode past her frozen form without a glance. His ravaged features had never looked harder than at that moment, when he flung open the door and left her.

In the dead of night, an uncanny silence shrouded the manor. Jervaise's neck crawled as he slipped into her chamber. The brazier pulsed red with sullen embers, barely lifting the shadows.

A banner of wheat gold hair rippled across the bed. By her breathing, Alienore slept—a minor reprieve from her unflinching questions and storm gray eyes, for which he thanked Allah. Their confrontation had all but undone him. The barriers he'd struggled to build between them lay in rubble at his feet.

Chilled, he shed his garments in the darkness. Below the bed, Remus raised his shaggy head in greeting. Jervaise scrubbed his ruff—wryly aware that even her damn pet wolf had wiggled its way into his affections.

He turned back to the woman curled under the furs, her capable hand defenseless as it lay palm up on the pillow. By the Prophet, she twisted his heart: the salt-crusted lashes against her cheeks, the shadow of grief beneath her eyes.

She suffers on my account—one more sin to weigh my soul. He condemned himself, unsparing, as he placed his knife within reach and slid beneath the furs. She'd knocked him sprawling with those devastating words she spoke so simply, with such candor.

She loved him.

Her Lyonstone pride, her convent virtue, her fury at his betrayal—so many barriers had stood between them. Yet somehow she'd overcome them all. With her typical courage she proclaimed her love—for the infidel, the disgraced knight, the bastard who lied and tricked her.

Somehow he must arm himself with the ugly words that

must drive her away. Love was a dangerous weakness he could not afford. Yet even while he listed reasons to reject her, he was sliding closer, gathering her supple warmth in his arms.

With a murmur, she curled against him, turned her face into his shoulder—his heroic lady, her guard lowered, now clinging and soft with slumber. Tendrils of burnished hair, sweet with lavender, brushed his cheek. With her shift between them, surely he could hold her while she slept. He could hold her against his heart for the little time left them.

Tenderly he kissed her brow, and sank into uneasy slumber.

Fire crawled up the walls of Damascus. Black smoke stung his eyes and throat, the sulphurous stink of Greek fire. The screams of innocents floated on the wind: elders slaughtered in their beds, women raped as they fled. Steel flashed as men butchered children and blood ran in the streets. While he watched the carnage through a fog of rage and misery—watched, and did nothing to stop it.

The tearing grief for his own Isabella, his love, his beautiful wife, belly rounded with their precious baby—her blood staining the sand, already rotting in the accursed desert sun.

He'd warned her not to follow him, but she'd left her disapproving family for him—no place else for her to go. He'd been the death of her, the death of their unborn child, and he would never forgive himself or a monstrous God for it—

"Jervaise? God's mercy, wake up!"

With a hoarse cry, he surfaced from the nightmare to Alienore's desperate voice, her insistent hands shaking him. The wrenching images dissolved as her face hovered before him, drawn with concern, that torrent of gold and silver hair streaming down in disarray.

"All's well." Forcing his locked muscles to loosen, he dragged a clumsy hand across his damp face and dropped the dagger he'd drawn by instinct. Another nightmare, no more—only the memory of what he'd lost a lifetime ago.

"You were thrashing and shouting in your sleep." Gently, she stroked his scarred cheek. "I know you suffer nightmares— there were several on the road—but this one seemed worse than the rest."

He grunted and pushed himself up, bedclothes tangling around his hips. This revelation that she knew his nightly torment disturbed him more than he wanted her to see.

"Didn't realize my restless sleep disturbed you."

"I did not ask, for I feared to invade your privacy." Flushing, she sat beside him, and straightened the twisted furs. "I thought . . . in time . . . you might tell me of your own accord."

Tell her of murdered Isabella, of his innocent murdered babe, of the white rage that had blinded him to all save the need for vengeance against the men who slaughtered her? Allah's heart, she was far too innocent for that tale of butchery. So he stared straight ahead, knowing his reticence must wound her again.

But this was Alienore, stubborn and determined as a king on crusade. "You cried out in a foreign tongue. Was it the Saracen tongue?"

"Aye," he said harshly. His mother's language, which he'd learned at her knee along with her religion, before Hugh d'Ormonde fostered him away for a Christian knight's training. His Isabella had not spoken English or French. Too painful to share this last secret, no matter that he yearned to do it.

"Alienore." He sighed. "I shouldn't have disturbed you. I'll find a place in the hall."

"What disturbs me is your continued refusal to trust me. Have I ever given you cause for distrust? Have I faltered or fallen short in our marriage vows?"

"Nay." Remorse twisted his heart. He'd given her every reason in the world to distrust him—and yet she loved him, or thought she did. He'd pushed her away to protect her from him. To protect her and those she loved from the raging demon that had possessed him in Damascus.

"I cannot demand that you tell me," she said. "But I would like it very much if you did. I will swear to keep it silent as the grave, if that troubles you. You may trust my oath."

"Alienore—it's not you I distrust." His voice roughened. "There's no one on earth more worthy of trust."

Before the pain in her eyes, the stubborn hope that flamed beneath the shimmer of tears, he felt his resolve slipping, damn it. Perhaps he should tell her after all. No doubt when she learned, she'd know herself well rid of him. Tell her, then, what he'd never told another soul—so she could recognize the monster she'd married.

"I told you I was married. Long ago and briefly, in my youth."

"Aye." Fierce interest kindled in her features. She held very still, as if she feared any movement would silence him.

"She was a Saracen girl, young and beautiful, like my mother. Met her on crusade—after my father's death." The words, long contained, tore his damaged throat. "We fell in love, though her father forbade it. She . . . Isabella . . ."

How many years since I spoke her name?

"Left her family for me, left wealth and comfort to follow me into the field. I married her, of course. When her womb quickened, I believed Allah blessed our union. But that was a foolish hope."

Quickly, without sentiment. Tell her the rest. Then she will know.

"We were besieging Damascus, and the gates had finally weakened. While I led the assault, the defenders sent out raiders by a secret exit. They found our camp and they . . . killed everyone they found there—women, children, the wounded. All of them."

"Oh, Jervaise." Her voice went throaty with compassion. She laid a comforting hand on his arm, but he pulled away.

She would shrink from him in loathing when she heard the rest.

"When I returned and . . . found her"—he pushed out the words—"I was . . . blinded by rage and grief. I lost my sanity, the discipline that was my duty as commander. My men were . . . likewise driven."

"I can imagine," she murmured, gray eyes liquid with sympathy.

"Perhaps I couldn't have held them, but I never even tried. Instead I urged them on. When we broke through the gates, the men went berserk. They slaughtered the defenders, ravened through the streets, fired the houses, killed everyone—killed women and children—just as the devils killed ours. And I did naught to stop it."

She sat white and silent, her gaze unflinching. Soon she would recoil in disgust. How could she do otherwise, his honor-bound lady?

"When I returned to my senses, they'd . . . butchered them all . . . everyone we found inside those walls. I ordered it stopped, but too late. Due to my poor control—my failure—they lay like slaughtered lambs in bloody heaps around us. The Saracens recall it to this day. It's why they call me the Devil of Damascus. That day strengthened their resolve to resist the Christian conquest."

"This was why you resigned your command," she whispered, with sorrowful eyes. "This was why you renounced God to become the Raven, a nameless mercenary. 'Twas in penance for that day."

"I can never do penance enough." He stared at her, self-hatred churning in his belly.

She stood against it, chin lifting with that swift pride of hers. His heart swelled for her courage, even while he said the words that would drive her away.

"I can't allow that to happen again. My so-called love destroyed everything decent, in Damascus. Now you see the truth of me, this wretch you were forced to marry. Give your love to another man, Alienore—one who's worthy of it."

"Nay!" The pure light of faith shone from her like a lamp. "You have never forgiven yourself for that day. But Christ's power to forgive—by whatever name you call him—exceeds our capacity. If you ask for forgiveness, Jervaise, if you ask for grace and mercy, you will find the salvation you seek."

Incredulous, he stared at her pleading face. After all he'd told her—after the horrors he'd never revealed to another living soul—still she persisted in this asinine belief? Somehow he must make her understand.

"So your convent nuns would say," he jeered. "Don't deceive yourself, Alienore. I'm beyond salvation."

"You seek it daily," she whispered, tears spilling from her eyes. "What else drives you to save your people? What else led you to save Vulgrin from his captors, save my life, save Remus, serve your king with such dogged devotion? With every day that passes, you receive another sign of God's grace at work in your life. Do you not see it? He will give you the forgiveness you seek, but you must also forgive yourself."

"Impossible." Anger erupted at her stubborn faith in her God—and him. "Why waste your love on a man like me? Can't you understand I'll leave you? I tell you I'm beyond saving!"

"Have no fear." Through the tears shining on her cheeks, she gave him a tremulous smile. "If you will not save yourself, Jervaise de Vaux, then I shall save you."

To his stunned disbelief, she wrapped her arms around him and kissed his cheek. Fiercely resisting the comfort he would never deserve, he tried to push away. Yet his accursed flesh would not obey him. Instead of pushing her away, he crushed her in his arms.

He felt the strength of her warrior's body, her yielding softness as he dragged her against his chest and kissed her. Tasted the salt dampness of tears as her lips parted, giving herself to him. Blocking out the voices of guilt and grief, he plundered her honeyed sweetness, and her mouth welcomed his. A shudder swept through her as she clung, her lavender fragrance filling his head, the tight nubs of her nipples burning him through her shift.

Even while the dark voices screamed at him to release her, he was fumbling with her shift. Allah save him—she was helping, kneeling to straddle him, breaking the kiss to pull the shift over her head and toss it aside, casting aside a maid's modesty to push him back against the mattress. Naked, she crouched over him in a fever of madness, tasting and nipping down his throat.

Helpless to deny her, he skimmed her supple back, muscle rippling beneath his touch. When he pulled her against the insistent throb of his cock, she let him, her breasts searing his chest. With a growl he pulled her forward, cupping, kneading her fullness. Suckled hard, flicking with his tongue and biting gently until she cried out.

"Sweet mercy—" Her fingers gripped his hair until his scalp burned.

Then her hand circled his engorged length and blasted every coherent thought from his brain. Never had his virginal bride displayed such boldness in their bed. When she brushed his swollen tip where moisture gathered, he strained against imminent release.

Her confidence grew as she cupped his aching member and tightened her grip. He leaped and pulsed in her hand as she stroked, finding a pressure and rhythm destined to drive him mad. To prolong the pleasure, resist the impulse to roll her beneath him and bury himself inside, he continued to suckle, drawing hard until she panted.

"No more of this torture," he rasped. "Put me inside you, love."

With gritted teeth he contained himself while she fitted him to her womb. She fumbled a bit, his manhood sliding against her hot, slick folds. The musky odor of their shared arousal perfumed the air as she took him into her tight passage.

His deep groan of pleasure mingled with hers as he thrust. She gripped him, slick with their shared pleasure, and rode him. She learned the rhythm as she'd learned the sword, hair streaming in golden disarray, head tilted back, eyes lidded with desire. He reveled in her sensuality, her new boldness. Yet he would wait until she found her own peak.

He thrust deep, every nerve attuned to her, the focused intensity of her features, the pattern of her quickened breath. Until she shuddered violently and cried out. Spasms of release swept through her, and he surrendered to his own release.

When she collapsed upon him, their bodies still joined, he closed his arms around her. Her fragrant hair tumbled over his face.

He had failed her utterly. His confession had not discouraged her love. To the contrary, she embraced his sins—and sealed his fate. Against all his intentions, flying against a lifetime of bitter regret, he'd fallen in love with his lion-hearted duchess.

Allah help him. He would leave her to save her, before his love destroyed them both.

Chapter Twenty-one

Jervaise left at dawn, but the closing door roused her from slumber. As sunrise spilled into the sky, Alienore watched him canter away with his turbaned squire.

Today was Good Friday—the darkest day, the ultimate trial, the day Christ died for men's sins. A surge of foreboding broke over her.

Mooning after your husband like a lovesick fool! He only goes to Lyonstone to raise the king's levy.

Shaking off her qualms, she squared herself to put her shabby home to rights.

Before noon, her household came streaming back—released to her service, as Jervaise had demanded. Their careworn faces familiar as her own reflection, her only family during the lonely years after Theobold rode off on crusade, taking her brother with him. Cries of joy proclaimed their return.

"God save us, milady!" Egfrida the cook folded Alienore against her ample bosom. "Young master told us ye'd never coom back. Right glad we are to see him proved wrong."

Soon industrious hands were putting the hall to rights. They swept out the befouled rushes, scattered fresh grass sweet with tansy to cover the stench. Then mended the damaged roof in the north tower, where rain drenched the floor.

Alienore was grateful for the tasks that demanded her attention, though nothing could divert her thoughts from Jervaise. At last she could name the demons that ravaged his soul and carved those lines of bitterness in his face. Guilt, grief, the terrible weight of self-hatred—for events that occurred a lifetime ago.

He said he could never love again. He said he'd renounced God, plunged his immortal soul into peril. But she refused to believe that, not when she sensed his torment. Once Jervaise de Vaux had been her enemy. Now he was the man she loved with all the passion stored in her valiant heart. He was her love, and she would save him.

When the shadows deepened, she glanced up. She was kneeling before the hearth while the potboy shimmied up the chimney to clear bird's nests from the flue.

Brushing off her skirts, she rolled her head against her shoulders to loosen the knots from her labors. Massaging the back of her neck, she hurried to the door.

On the mural stair Raoul stood braced between his crutches. A frown creased his face as he squinted through a curtain of drizzle.

"By my faith, has Jervaise not returned?" Disquiet rippled through her. "'Twill be dark soon—and a storm coming, if I read the wind aright."

"No doubt he found a great deal to discuss with the young earl. Your brother has done little to prepare for war."

"He has been ill, I am told." She made excuses for Benedict from habit. "With an experienced soldier like Jervaise to guide him, my brother shall do well enough."

Raoul cocked her a dubious look.

"Come out of the rain, old friend." She smiled. "No doubt by the time our fish is on the table, Jervaise will return to eat it."

Yet her husband did not return.

After supper she stood again in the doorway, a candle guttering in her hand, and peered into the night. Rain fell steadily from the leaden skies, pounding the bailey into a sea of mud.

An evil night to be abroad, and Jervaise a stranger to these lands. One of the hated Norman conquerors, alone with an infidel squire in a land seething with Saxon loathing, even a hundred years after the Conquest.

"Ooh, milady, come out of this mizzle." Nesta hurried to fling a cloak over her.

"My lord is late returning." Unwilling to abandon her post, she lingered.

"There's a right proper storm blowing up. Maybe he stayed with yer brother?"

"He would never rest willingly beneath the same roof as Sir Bors, of that I am certain. And who could blame him?" She strained to listen for hoofbeats over the rain, while thunder muttered overhead.

"I vow I do not like this, Nesta."

After a worried consultation with Raoul, she sent a pair of guardsmen to meet Jervaise, lest he lose his way on the unfamiliar road. She stood in the pouring rain to instruct them, the rising wind tearing at her skirts. Whining in his throat, Remus milled around her legs.

Absently, she scrubbed his damp ruff as the guardsmen pounded off into the darkness. A flash of lightning bathed the road in its harsh glare. With a yelp, the wolf scurried indoors.

"Come inside, my lady," Raoul called. "This is an evil wind."

And somewhere, my love is lost in it.

In the stark light of morning, the grim-faced guardsmen returned alone, exhausted and mud spattered from a night of fruitless hunting. Grainy eyed after her own white night, Alienore fought back rising panic and forced herself to hear their report.

They had combed the roads between the manor and Lyonstone Keep, but any physical trace of Jervaise's passing had been pounded away by the storm. They'd sought to query the earl, but he would not deign to speak with lowly men-at-arms. The report made her simmer.

Yet Benedict's castellan unbent enough to inform them Ormonde had spent the day at Lyonstone and set forth before sunset. He had not been seen since.

Her stomach sank as she stared into the men's exhausted faces and saw her fears mirrored in their eyes.

"You have done well, my friends," she said. "Take some rest and hot mead to revive you. I will go to Lyonstone myself and speak to my brother."

After a difficult gallop along the storm-churned road, she stared up at her childhood home. It too seemed diminished, somehow less than the shining castle of her memories. Beneath lowering skies, a sinister mist shrouded the heights. Through the gaping mouths of murder-holes and arrow loops, hostile eyes tracked their approach.

"Hail the house!" she cried, rising in her stirrups to glance around warily.

The jagged-toothed battlements chewed at the heavens. A thicket of turrets thrust like spears over the curtain wall to pierce the weeping sky. The moat's brown waters, thick with sludge, lapped the drawbridge as she thundered across with Raoul at her heels.

She had resisted dragging the old knight into the wet, but he refused to let her ride without him. Remus loped along behind, his nose and ears busy with unfamiliar scents and sounds. Unfortunately, he'd smelled nothing on the rain-washed road, though she'd given him Jervaise's scent.

The keep should have stood closed and guarded in these uneasy times. To her outrage, the gates hung ajar and the portcullis was rusted open. When no one answered, dread gnawed at her gut.

In the bailey, a huddle of outbuildings looked sullen with neglect. The smithy stood cold and dark when it should have burned bright, forging swords and armor. The buttery door was smashed to splinters, revealing an overturned table and dusty shelves where once the Lyonstone cheeses were pressed.

A muddy tangle of dogs snapped and quarreled before the donjon. They paused to growl at Remus, who crouched with hackles raised. She called the wolf to her and searched the debris-littered courtyard with dismay.

Why did no sentries prowl the allure, no English long-bows stand guard against the hostile north? Only a trickle of smoke from the kitchens betrayed any sign of habitation. While the countryside bristled with war, Lyonstone Keep stood all but abandoned.

Saint Swithun save me, this is worse than I feared. I should never have stayed away so long.

"This place is little more than a ruin," she murmured. "How long has it been so?"

"I know not, my lady," Raoul said. "My bones ached so with the cold this winter that I barely stirred from the manor. I heard worrisome stories, yet I never dreamed the keep stood in such a dismal state."

"Scots William will find us easy pickings." Alarm sparked within her. "By my faith, I do not know what Benedict can be thinking, but I intend to find out."

Jumping down, she tossed her reins to Raoul. "Wait here for me, old friend."

"Little good would I be unhorsed," he said tightly. "Take the wolf with you. I'll call on my hunting horn if danger threatens."

Mounted and armed with his crossbow, the old knight still made a formidable foe. Standing on his own, braced between his wooden crutches, he could be little help—and knew it.

Determined to show no fear, she whistled Remus to her side and strode toward the donjon. The iron-bound door swung open at her touch, and she walked forward into darkness.

She found her brother alone, huddled in the earl's canopied chair before a struggling scrap of fire, a ratty bearskin clutched about him. His feverish eyes glittered while she asked her questions and held her tongue over sharp observations about the keep's neglect. Explaining the situation curtly, she fought to refrain from shouting accusations that would only rouse her brother's ire.

"I don't know what to tell you," Benedict said. "Aye, your duke was here. Indeed, he made himself tiresome. Insisted on cataloging every sword in the armory, every trained sword arm, my siege provisions, maps and battle plans. Didn't seem to think I knew my own business—me, the Earl of Lyonstone."

No doubt you do not.

But she could not afford to quarrel with Benedict now. "When did he depart?"

"I don't recall." Meeting her glare, he coughed and clutched his bearskin. "Oh, very well. Late afternoon I suppose, with that evil-looking heathen he calls a squire. The storm was rolling in, so I offered him hospitality. But he spurned me— thought he could beat the weather back. Said that his lady awaited him."

His eyes lingered on her mud-spattered boots. Clearly he thought her no lady at all. Fighting for patience, she clenched her fists.

"Brother, he did not return. He is a foreigner in our land—"

"And a Norman, curse them all to hell."

"Our own mother was Norman, Benedict." She struggled to keep her voice level. "This sudden disappearance in the midst of the king's business is most unlike him."

"Send men out to search, then—if the man cannot cross five miles of good road without losing his way."

"I have no men to send." She spoke through her teeth, straining not to heap the blame for that injustice atop his clueless head. "Will you loan me the men to search?"

"You can take them from the levy he insisted we call. I told him he was starting at shadows . . ."

"You call it starting at shadows to defend our borders? He undertakes the measures you should have ordered months ago."

"You seem very fond of Ormonde, sister—a most tender and proper wife." He hunched in his chair like a baleful turtle. "'Tis a pity you were not so dutiful when I arranged this marriage. Would have saved us both a deal of trouble."

"You would have wedded me to a maudlin drunkard! You disregarded our sire's dying wish—" She bit back the furious words that bubbled on her tongue. "But that is past now, Benedict. Jervaise may be injured. He may require our aid—"

"So what if he is? A half-Norman, half-Saracen cutthroat who sells his sword to the highest bidder. All men knew the Raven in the Holy Land. D'you know the story of Damascus, sister?"

In despair she stared at the stranger before her—her cherished little brother, blood of her blood, the golden youth who had ridden so proudly on crusade. Two nights ago he'd seemed almost sane—confused and exhausted, certainly, but hardly the fretful invalid who glared at her now.

"Oh, Benedict." Kneeling, she caught his hand in hers—dry and hot, as if a fever consumed him. "What has happened to you? Was it the horror of war or our father's death?"

"Our father?" His fingers clutched her. "*Our father? Can you still not know?*"

Dread tightened like a fist around her heart. "What do I not know?"

"Nay," he whispered, staring with strange pity. "You truly do not know. Sister—for you are still my sister, no matter what else men call you. I will not disown you."

"Benedict." A spear of pain stabbed through her temple, the first warning stab of a megrim. *Jesus wept, I cannot afford this now!*

"Brother, you are not speaking sense."

"My poor sister." He gripped her hands. "Truly, I believe you knew nothing. Alienore, I must tell you the truth."

"What truth?" she said, hollow. *Blessed Saint Swithun, do not visit this pain upon me now.*

"Theobold of Lyonstone is not your father."

"What?" Agony flared behind her eyes as the vise of pain clamped down.

But she knew—she knew what he would say. Hadn't she glimpsed the monstrous truth the night she fled?

"Sister, you are common born." He squeezed until the wishing-stone ring dug into her flesh. "A bastard, to speak plainly, like the man you married. You are no daughter to the Earl of Lyonstone, though our mother convinced him for a time that you were."

"I will not hear this—this shameful slander. It does you no credit, Benedict, to foul your tongue with that ancient gossip."

"'Tis no lie, and I *will* say it!" Her brother's eyes glittered with fever. "Did he never tell you himself, all the time you spent in his shadow? You are our mother's daughter by a carpet knight, her pauper of a cousin—that old cripple Raoul."

Alienore felt as though she were falling, the world sliding sideways around her. The blinding light of a megrim exploded behind her eyes. She wanted to deny what she heard, but the cold flame of certainty consumed her.

Hadn't she feared this all along? Wasn't that why she and Raoul had quarreled when she demanded the truth and he refused to speak? Wasn't it that awful possibility—not fear of Ponce at all—that sent her fleeing all the way from England to Aquitaine, as if she could outrun the truth?

"'Tis a foul, wretched lie! I do not believe you." A chasm of grief split her heart. "Did our father *tell* you?"

"Not even on his deathbed." Old grief darkened his eyes to lead. "Despite all her sins, he loved our mother too much. He loved *you*, despite everything—loved you enough to pretend to the whole world, even to himself, that you were his."

Desperately she ground fists against her temples, struggled to hold her head together, though it felt like a shattered egg. "God's mercy, if he said nothing and our mother said nothing, then how . . . ?"

"I had it from Sir Bors, and the old man did not deny it. Ask Raoul yourself, if you don't believe me."

Aye, she *would* ask—she would demand the truth from him now, whatever came. She could no longer endure the wrenching doubt. She was an earl's daughter—she *was*, and would believe until she knew otherwise. She possessed strength enough to hear the truth.

"Jervaise," she whispered, her throat aching. Now at her moment of crisis, her heart cried out for him. She ached for the comfort of his embrace, his hands soothing her pounding head, his raspy voice murmuring tender words. Without him, she was truly alone.

If I break into a thousand pieces and shatter on the floor, I cannot help him.

"Clearly some evil has befallen him." As waves of pain crashed through her skull, she dragged herself upright. "Now of all times, scant miles from where the Scots are massing. Brother, I implore you, on your honor as a knight, on the love you once bore me. Help me find him—and for God's sake, raise the levy!"

He met her desperate gaze. "There is no need for a levy, for the Scots are not coming. I have it on the highest authority."

"More of Sir Bors's wisdom? Anyway, where is the silver-tongued adder? Should he not be here, pouring more of his poison into your ears?"

"He is occupied about his business," her brother said

vaguely—when the boy she remembered would have flown back at her. "You may ask my castellan to search, if there are men to spare. Your husband has them all massing in the village. 'Tis a foolish precaution, as I told him, but he would not heed me . . ."

She ran from the hall, left his meanderings behind. Her heart ached for his disintegration, ached with grief and bewilderment. But she had no time to spare for Benedict now. Every instinct screamed that Jervaise stood in peril, and time was short.

And she was an imposter, born out of wedlock, not an earl's daughter after all—if she believed her brother. Everything she was, everything she claimed as hers, every truth she had defended her whole life long had been a wretched lie.

Alienore stumbled through the donjon. Vision blurred, she reeled like a drunkard. Yet she could not outrun the shock of realization bearing down from behind like a tidal wave.

She could not flee Lyonstone as she'd done before, not while her lands crouched, quivering beneath the threat of invasion. Not with Jervaise in mortal danger.

Through the fog of tears, a glimmer of candlelight beckoned from the chapel. Instinct pulled her toward it, seeking the solace of faith. Inside, candles flanked the altar and limned the painted saints and martyrs in halos of gold. Tears spilled down her cheeks as a shuddering sob ripped through her.

Stumbling to the altar, she fell to her knees.

Yet the peace of God eluded her, now of all times, when she needed it most. The serene saints—even her patron Saint Swithun—stood cold and indifferent to her crisis.

Scots William and his howling hordes could bring the walls tumbling down around their ears, and neither the saints nor their uncaring God would lift a finger to prevent it.

Long-buried rage heaved like an earthquake beneath her surface. All her life she'd prayed, fasted, kept the holy days, contained her willful passions and subsumed her desires to a higher cause. She'd striven for virtue and piety—and for what? What manner of god could place her people in jeopardy? What god would see her stripped of the man she loved, with his hidden core of honor—and do nothing to aid her?

"I have no god." Trembling beneath this final injustice, she whispered the blasphemous words. The lightning spear of anger drove her to her feet. Roughly she thrust away from the place where she'd wasted so many hours in futile prayer.

"No god!" She glared at the crucifix with its suffering Christ. "You are a dream, a lie, an illusion."

When even this sacrilege brought no reply, her simmering wrath exploded. A rack of candles stood nearby—wasted tribute to a god who would not help her. She gripped the iron rack in both hands and wrenched it free. Gobbets of hot wax showered down like meteors, spattering her arms and shoulders as she swung the mighty bludgeon.

Her weapon crashed against the gilded rail before the altar. Wood splintered and cracked.

Growling, she struck again, using all the power of her battle-honed body. With a snap, the rail split. Sobs ripped through her as she attacked the rail, the floor, finally the altar itself—all the symbols of her deluded childhood, all a monstrous lie. The mother who'd deceived her, the father who'd kept his silence, the years of futile striving for virtue that could never be hers.

Somewhere, dimly, a horn was blowing, but that meant nothing to her. Through the red fog of rage, she glimpsed the wolf cowering under a pew, but that too meant nothing. When her strength failed, she cried out her grief to the heavens. The wolf flung back his head and howled.

Grasping her lion-hilted knife—the blade she had no right to bear—she fell to her knees, hardly knowing what she meant to do. Turn the blade against herself, perhaps.

Behind her, a shocked voice spoke her name. But she

could not face it, nor the clatter and drag of crutches. Only when a gnarled hand gripped her shoulder did she draw a long, shuddering breath.

Sagging against the altar, she curled around her pain like a wounded animal. Raoul embraced her from behind.

"My dear child. By Saint George's dragon—what has befallen?"

"You knew," she rasped, hoarse as Jervaise after her screaming rage. "You must have always known. Why else look after me all these years?"

For a long time he said nothing, simply held her. At last he heaved a sigh of resignation. "Oh, that these evil tidings should reach you now."

"'Tis true, is it not?" She pressed her throbbing brow to the cool stone—unmarked by all her efforts. "'Tis you, not Theobold, who are my father."

"I cannot say otherwise." His arms tightened around her. "These twenty years and more, Marguerite de Rievaulx has been my one true love."

Seeing the last shred of hope ripped away, she closed her eyes. "Then my entire life has been a lie. Everything I am . . . all that I strove for. Why, I cannot even claim the manor."

She swallowed against the raw scrape of her throat. "Jervaise will wish to annul our marriage."

"Child, do not say so." The old knight sounded near tears himself. "No man can say you are not Lyonstone's daughter— not even the earl himself, and that is God's truth. For we both loved Marguerite, twenty summers ago in Paris—both of us, child. But he could offer her the world, the wealth and title she was born to, while I could offer her nothing but my heart."

Gently she dislodged his grip, and turned to search his careworn face. "And my—Theobold. Did he know?"

A troubled expression shadowed his steel gray eyes, so like her own. "I cannot say what he knew or suspected, child, for we never spoke of it. Yet he offered me a place among his men and loved you as his own. Whatever he may have thought so long ago, he chose to believe the best of us all. Surely he would never have left you the manor if he believed you were not his."

She would have pressed him, but the rattle of mail stopped her. At the door stood a mud-spattered squire in Lyonstone blue, staring in shock at the disarray.

Heat surged into her cheeks. Whatever her parentage, these folk believed her their true lady. She would be selfish indeed to bruise their faith now, when they needed her most.

Sharply conscious of her tearstained face, she rose on shaking legs. Raoul braced his crutches and levered himself up.

She drew a long breath. "What tidings?"

"I come from sentry duty on the border, as the duke ordered yesterday."

"And so?"

"We've spied movement on the road. Milady—the Scots are coming."

Her hand flew to her knife, but the sheath was empty. She spied it on the floor and reclaimed it—badly scratched, but the steel held true. Her instincts screamed for action, but she kept her voice steady.

"How many and how far?"

"A thousand or more." The squire paused as her breath hissed. She swallowed and nodded for him to continue.

"They march with little order, but swiftly. If they don't halt or turn from the road, they will be here by dawn."

She shared an alarmed look with Raoul. "Does my brother know of this?"

"Aye, milady." The squire shifted. "I went to him first, as the duke cannot be found. But the young earl says I'm mistaken."

Even as frustration bubbled through her blood, she knew Benedict would not be moved. His will had been stolen, subverted somehow by Sir Bors. Any attempt to sway her brother would waste precious time—time they did not have.

"What of Sir Bors of Bedingfield? Where is he this day?"

Discomfort flickered in the squire's gaze.

"Well? Do not seek to spare me. Where is the accursed man?"

"We spied him last night, milady, riding for the border . . . with two others." The squire looked unhappy. Clearly he knew the tidings would not please her. "One man was an outlander, a servant of some sort, an old fellow with a turban. The other rode a black charger—and carried a Saracen sword."

"Jervaise." All the blood drained from her body, leaving her cold and shaken. "God's mercy! Bedingfield has tricked him, compelled him—"

"Nay, milady." Again the lad shifted. "I wish it so. But the duke appeared to go freely, of his own accord. He was neither bound nor injured, and he kept his weapons."

Disbelief warred with a surge of relief. At least Jervaise was alive and unharmed as recent as last night. Surely the truth of his situation would be clarified. Never for an instant would she believe he'd betrayed her. Still, the acrimonious words of their last argument echoed through her mind.

He had warned her not to love him, said he would leave her—but surely this was never what he'd meant. Even if he felt no loyalty to her, Lyonstone or England, he would never betray his king.

Seeing Raoul's concerned gaze, knowing priceless minutes were slipping away, Alienore gathered her scattered wits. It would never do to show doubt before her retainers—even the one who was, in all likelihood, her father.

"If Bedingfield is away, that makes our task simpler," she said. "Clearly my brother is not himself, which leaves me no choice but to assume command myself.

"Raoul d'Albini, I appoint you castellan of Lyonstone and charge you with the defense of this keep." Her thoughts raced ahead. "I shall assemble a guard for my own protection and ride at once to Wishing Stone. The manor is not defensible, so all the folk there, our livestock and other valuables must be moved within these walls by nightfall."

"And what of the duke's levy?" Raoul asked. "Some three hundred men with arms, I am told."

"Jervaise meant to lead those men himself. Perhaps he shall still return." Anxiety coiled in her belly. Why had Jervaise not told her his plans? Why could he never trust her?

An impossible notion blossomed in her mind, the only chance her tired brain could conceive. She must think it through. Nor could she voice her thoughts before Raoul, who would surely seek to dissuade her.

"By my faith, our course is clear," she said. "If Ormonde does not return, Lyonstone must lead his men to battle."

Raoul stared, his brow creasing. The squire looked as though she'd gone daft.

"But my lord Benedict refuses—"

"You had best take refreshment and then return to your post," she told the squire. "Rest assured, you may leave the earl to me."

The setting sun slanted red over Wishing Stone Manor as the last cart rumbled off toward Lyonstone. From her chamber, Alienore heard the wolf's howls fade. Though neither Remus nor Nesta had wanted to leave her, they could not aid her on the path she'd chosen.

Grimly, she sharpened her blade against the whetstone. She could not rely upon the lion-hilted long-knife for this. Nay, her broadsword had been made for this duty. At last she sheathed the sword, careful not to mar the edge. Rising, savoring the freedom of her leather chausses, she drew her long-knife. Its rampant lion glared at her.

Imposter, it whispered. *Only a Lyonstone deserves this blade.*

Before the polished plate, she eyed her reflection. Familiar features stared back at her: nose dusted with golden freckles, jaw tight with resolve. Steel gray eyes, cold and assessing, met her gaze.

Her eyes were Theobold's, she'd always thought, like her wheat gold hair. Yet they could also be Raoul's. What point cursing their similar coloring now? Should she open her veins with this blade and empty them forever of the bastard taint?

So she did not deserve to bear the Lyonstone name. So the banner of nobility she'd flown in her pride was naught but a shameful lie. With her lands and people relying on her, she could not afford to let her pedigree define her.

In height, build and coloring she resembled her brother, and that was indeed convenient—but for one small detail. Gripping a hank of her golden hair, she stretched it straight.

Deliberately, Alienore of Lyonstone laid the knife against her tresses and began to cut.

Chapter Twenty-two

Raoul d'Albini felt too old to command a siege. Though he remained mobile on horseback, he could barely crutch along on foot. Yet Alienore had chosen him. No one else could order their defense or make these men obey, and both of them knew it. Before Vespers, even young Benedict had ceased his protests and retired with complaints of a griping belly.

Despite the indignities of age and infirmity, Raoul did what he could. In the end, every man in Lyonstone stood armed and armored, while livestock and terrified peasants crowded—sweating with terror—in the bailey. The gates had been bolted and the portcullis winched down. A double watch patrolled the curtain wall.

Lyonstone's defenses were formidable enough: its moat broad and deep, its murder-holes and arrow loops designed to rain death from all angles. The drawbridge was fashioned for collapse during a siege—but he'd found the mechanism disabled. The village folk had brought what provisions they could, but the castle's stores were sadly depleted. Even worse, he found the well had gone putrid. Now they had to venture to the river for drinking water or else go thirsty.

Someone had made certain the keep could not withstand a siege.

When the last cart from Wishing Stone trundled past without Alienore, his unease deepened. Tearfully, her tiring girl reported that the lady promised to follow later.

Too late, he recalled the cold resolve that had darkened

Alienore's gaze to tempered steel. His gut churned with suspicions he dared not voice.

Saint George guard her from anything rash or reckless. With a groan, he lowered his aching body to a pallet. Knowing he would be useless if he exhausted himself, he managed to drop into a troubled doze.

The long *taroo* of a war horn brought him upright. Cursing, he swung his legs down and gripped his crutches.

Outside, another horn blasted—the deep-throated *bat-bat-bat-hooouuu* that signaled alarm. The lightning charge of danger sizzled through the air to raise gooseflesh down his spine. Shouts and the stamp of running feet echoed along the battlements.

Bracing himself on his crutches, Raoul strapped on his broadsword and swung out to the curtain wall, where torches bloomed against a pallid dawn. Despite the certain knowledge bubbling in his blood, he pitched his voice to calmness.

"Anon now, lads, what's to see?"

"Movement on the road, milord, and our sentry raised the alarm."

Raoul peered out between the crenellations and squinted against the bloody dawn that spilled across the heavens. *Easter morn, God save us—the day Christ rose from the dead.*

Above the anxious voices, he picked out the thud of hooves, the rattle of mail, a horse's nervous nicker.

Then the first sliver of sun pulsed over the horizon. The light streamed across the road, over the black coil of men winding toward the keep.

Swiftly Raoul assessed the invaders: boiled-leather hauberks, crude spears and swords. No siege engines, God be praised for it. But the serpentine line writhed down the road in an endless torrent, hundreds strong, vastly outnumbering the paltry defenders.

Suddenly young Benedict appeared beside him, buckling

a sword over his chausses. Raoul glanced sharply at the lad, saw him whiten to behold the foe.

"Sweet mercy." The boy fisted his eyes. "How can this be? Sir Bors *promised*—"

"Perhaps you will learn to question that blackguard's promises." Despite himself, compassion stirred for the bewildered youth. "These many months he walked free—thus the poisoned well, the disabled drawbridge, the vanished stores. My lord, Sir Bors has betrayed you and betrayed us all."

Overhead, a raven circled. Peering down, Raoul searched the line until he found the man who led the assault— chillingly familiar, a knight on a coal black charger. A pointed Saracen helm concealed his features, but that wicked scimitar of Damascus steel could not be mistaken.

Raoul d'Albini felt a cold chill crawl down his neck.

"Saint George's dragon." He crossed himself, feeling every one of his sixty years. This would kill Alienore. God grant him time to be the one who told her.

In the chaos of men pounding along the wall, the cries of panic below, Raoul paid little heed to the hooded figure who glided up beside him. But the familiar voice sliced through him like an assassin's blade: a distinctive accent, laced with hissing consonants.

"Pray to your patron saint of knights, old man." Sir Bors of Bedingfield smiled. "'Tis the Devil of Damascus, not I, whom the king will behead for betrayal."

"*Traitor!*" Nearby, but not near enough to help, young Benedict cried out. "I trusted you."

The lad fumbled to free his sword—too slow after his illness. Cold realization broke over Raoul like an icy sweat. Flinging a crutch aside, he reached for his blade.

Bedingfield swung a mailed fist. The crushing blow exploded against Raoul's temple. Stars burst across his vision as his crippled legs collapsed. He felt himself falling . . . falling . . . as his world went black.

In the breath before darkness claimed him, Bedingfield shouted the command.

"Our allies arrive. Open the gates!"

Three hundred men made considerable noise, especially when they were trying to be quiet. Alienore's fifty mounted knights were the worst. The rattle of chain mail, laced with curses and hissing pleas for silence, scraped her nerves raw. Her small army mustered in the village square, no more than a mile from Lyonstone.

Silently, she blessed Jervaise for raising the levy before he vanished. Why would he do so if he'd meant to betray her?

She would not listen to the clamoring voice of panic, though she doubted the wisdom of this mad venture. Just moments ago, a breathless sentry had galloped up to confirm the Scots were coming. Since the village stood away from the road, the foe would delay taking it until they seized their main objective—Lyonstone Keep.

But she would not allow the Scots to avoid her.

Tightening her jaw, she spurred Galahad to the square, where all her men could see her. To avoid the betraying spill of light, she gave the torches a wide berth. Nonetheless, a terrible sense of exposure gripped her as she hoisted off her helm. Her shortened hair fluttered in the breeze.

Once the sun rose, this thin disguise would never hold. For now, her chain mail and broadsword made her appear a knight. Her height and coloring were Benedict's, and he'd ventured forth rarely since his return from crusade. Men saw what they expected to see.

A boy scurried to plant her lance in the earth. The Lyonstone banner of blue and gold unfurled above her head.

A woman does what she must when the devil drives.

The wind tossed her cropped hair around her shoulders. The torches flared wildly, casting monstrous shadows. She pitched her voice to carry and addressed them, as Theobold had always done before riding into war.

Imposter. Who is your father now? Grimly she silenced the whisper of doubt.

"Defenders of Lyonstone!" she shouted. "Some of you are soldiers, battle hardened and bold, sworn to King Henry's good service. Many of you are farmers, craftsmen, who march to battle for the first time. You defend your homes, your families, your king—but I will not lie to you. We may all meet our Maker this day."

Around her, men shifted and muttered. Some crossed themselves against her words. She thrust her gauntleted fist into the air.

"Still, we do not falter! We can be naught but who we are. And who are we?

"Defenders of women and children we love, friends we cherish, lands we nurture, like our ancestors before us! Our king summons us to battle. We march with stout hearts, secure in our faith and the rightness of our cause."

She unsheathed her sword and plunged it into the reddening sky. "The Scots have tried us before and they've been repelled. Let's show them, once and for all, what it means to challenge an Englishman.

"Follow me now—to victory."

For a sinking moment, silence met her bold pronouncement. They doubted her—and why shouldn't they, when she doubted herself?

Then, thrusting their swords toward heaven, the knights raised their voices in a thunderous shout. The cry was taken up by the farmers and craftsmen on foot. She let it build to a deafening roar, for courage—not silence—was needed now. The blood sang in her veins as she jammed on her helm.

Couching her lance, she wheeled her charger toward the road. Above the pounding hooves soared the distant *bat-bat-bat-hooouuu* of the war horn.

Streaming from the village, she led her army through a stand of trees. From a tall oak above the road, her sentry saw them coming and waved his white cloth. The signal confirmed that the Scots held their course and bypassed easy pickings in the village to assault the castle. The invaders dared not leave Lyonstone hostile and bristling at their rear as they pierced the tender southern lands.

They would not anticipate an attack from the rear— unless Jervaise had betrayed them all.

Alienore's charger burst from the trees at a canter and surged onto the road. As they crested the rise, the scene opened before them, bathed in crimson from the rising sun.

The Scots marched on the gates in ragged order, behind what had to be a stolen banner—golden lion blazing on Plantagenet crimson. Beneath it, the white wolf of Ormonde leaped against green. Her blood chilled as she perceived the trap.

Surely any man could see this rabble was not the king's army—marching down on Lyonstone from the north? Inside, Raoul must stand fast.

Even as she calmed herself, the long *raaaw* of Lyonstone's horn rolled across the heavens—the peal of welcome. With a clatter, the portcullis ratcheted up. Behind it, the iron-bound gates shuddered and swung open.

Inside her helm, she screamed out a denial. It rang in her ears, deafened her—too faint and far away to halt the disaster playing out before her. Raging, she urged Galahad to a ground-eating gallop. They hurtled toward the gates, her men thundering after. Through the fog of shock, she braced her lance for impact.

Leading the invaders, one man broke from the ranks ahead. Her heart clenched like a fist as the black warhorse swept toward the gate. In the saddle rode a knight in coal black armor with a Saracen helm. His scimitar whirled as he thundered toward the gates, gaping open to reveal the milling chaos beyond.

Alienore overtook the straggling rear guard and shouted her challenge, unable even now to stab a man in the back. Ahead, a brawny soldier pivoted toward her and bellowed as he raised his ax. Her lance bit deep, driving straight through boiled leather into the flesh beneath.

Screaming, the man fell—so young, no more than a lad, God save her. He dragged her lance with him, and she let go before it pulled her from the saddle.

Numb with horror, she unhitched her loaded crossbow, sighted on the gates and the black knight bearing down on them. The ground rolled past beneath her . . . yet the world seemed to slow in its course. Each heartbeat hammered against her eardrums like the knell of doom. She felt each muscle flex, each tendon strain as she raised the crossbow. Squinting, she sighted down the shaft.

Jervaise stood within range, alone and vulnerable, separate from the howling Scottish horde. Bathed in the rising sun, Lucifer hurtled across the drawbridge—why didn't the defenders collapse it?—toward the open gates.

A cleaner shot she could never hope to make. Her hand tightened around the release.

Wait! Her heart convulsed like a dying thing. *He has not betrayed you yet.*

Fire! Her brain roared back as she stared at her love's unguarded back. The gates stood open, the delicate hinges and hasps only a heartbeat from his grasp. If he destroyed them, no force under heaven would close those gates again.

Wait, pleaded heart and soul and blood—all that still hoped within her, the woman who loved him. A sob of frustration tore her throat, but she did not fire. Even if he slaughtered every goodwife in the bailey as he'd allowed his men to do in Damascus, she could not slay him.

In an agony of fear and desperation, she could only watch

as Jervaise galloped undeterred past the murder-holes and into the bailey.

Uncoiling like a panther, he leaped down with Lucifer still galloping. Landed, and rolled neatly to his feet. Now he ran toward the vulnerable gatehouse—but slipped on the loose straw of the bailey. Her heart lodged in her throat.

Exposed for a split second, he scrambled to recover. Suddenly a soldier loomed over him, ax raised for the killing blow.

Without conscious decision, Alienore swung the crossbow toward the soldier and fired. The bolt flew true, punching through mail to the shoulder—only a wounding blow, she hoped. The man staggered back, thank God, and dropped his ax. Jervaise rolled to his feet and dove into the gatehouse.

An eternity passed as she galloped through the Scottish army and wielded her crossbow like a bludgeon to knock swords away. When the weapon was jarred from her grip, she unsheathed her broadsword. Since the ragtag Scottish force was mostly afoot, she surged to the forefront swiftly. Her task was to rally the castle's defenses from within, applying pressure against the invaders from the front, while her own forces advanced from the rear—crushing the Scots between them. For now, her army was holding its own— better armed than the Scots, bolstered and commanded by her mounted knights.

As her charger surged through the opposing army, her gaze never wavered from the open gates. In the bailey beyond, running men and a few panicked sheep fled across her line of sight. She thundered onto the drawbridge.

Before her, the gates trembled—then began to close! A shout exploded from her chest as the realization struck.

Jervaise had not betrayed her. No matter what foul device Sir Bors had used to suborn him, he had bided his time— then broken away to fight for her.

"For Lyonstone!" she screamed as Galahad pounded toward the gates. On the walls, scattered voices took up the cry.

She burst between the gates with only a handspan to spare and exploded into the heaving turmoil of the bailey as the gates boomed shut behind.

Wheeling Galahad in a circle, she took in the scene. Peasants cowered near the walls, mothers clutched screaming children, frightened fathers wielded staffs or harvest sickles, determined to defend their own. Sheep and cattle ran bawling where they would.

Although scattered defenders fired arrows at the foe, the Lyonstone troops seemed curiously disordered, milling without purpose. Though the catapults on the heights were winched back and loaded, no one had released the firing arms.

God save her, where was Raoul?

At least a score of Scots had evidently managed to shove through the gates before they closed. Now the bailey teemed with pockets of struggling men. And there, near the gatehouse, stood Jervaise. As his image seared across her brain, her heart turned over.

Helmless and bleeding from a gash across his brow, teeth bared in a grimace of effort, he strained to heave into place the steel-sheathed timber to bolt the gate. Though the task required six men, Jervaise seemed to pulse with inhuman strength. Sinews stood out along his throat as he drove the timber into its bracket. An instant later, the portcullis clattered down, released by someone in the gatehouse. Crippling relief poured through her.

Without warning, a blow crashed down on her thigh. White-hot pain tore through her leg. Gasping, she stared down into an enemy's snarling face. By instinct alone, leg throbbing, she swung her blade to block his next blow. Warm wetness trickled down her thigh and dripped on the soil, red as her attacker's flaming hair.

As she deflected a rain of vicious blows, more Scots appeared in the bailey, though the gates were secured. Beyond her attacker, a deadly torrent of foes issued from the south tower—through the door to Bedingfield's alchemical laboratory.

Driven by a frenzy of fear, she blocked another blow, then drove her blade sideways with killing force. It bit deep in the hollow between neck and shoulder above her foe's protective armor. With a gurgling cry, he fell.

"All loyal Englishmen—*to me*." The command rang across the courtyard, and briefly the tide of battle wavered. Jervaise was shouting as he ran—away from the gates, toward the tower. A handful of defenders struggled to break away and follow. But the Scots renewed their assault.

Where is Raoul? Desperately she searched for the old knight. A flash of steel at the edge of vision warned her just in time. Signaling Galahad, she sent him pivoting away. Another signal sent his rear hooves lashing out, thudding into her attacker with crushing force. The man flew back without a cry.

At the tower, Jervaise lunged aside as another attacker exploded into the open. The Saracen sword sliced left and right, flashing as it caught the sun.

Standing astride his fallen foe as he commanded the door, Jervaise turned toward her—and froze into utter stillness. Though she'd lost her banner and wore her helm with the faceplate down, she knew with complete certainty that he recognized her. Savagely she drove her charger toward him, battling across the heaving sea of the bailey.

"Hold the gates!" he bellowed at her. "I'll secure the tower."

Objections bubbled to her lips, but she could say nothing before he dove inside and vanished. Over the screams of terrified women and the bawling of panicked livestock, steel clashed in the tower.

Torn between the necessity of holding the gates and helping him, Alienore hesitated. From nowhere, a frightened

cow veered across their path. Galahad reared, striking out
with his forelegs. Cursing the helm's obstructed vision, she
fought to regain control.

Reluctantly she pressed for the gatehouse—a vital strate-
gic asset, where the fighting now seemed fiercest. The invaders would pit their full strength to open the gates. If they did
that, Lyonstone was lost.

Suddenly, a knight sprang down to the bailey from the
curtain wall and landed with a ring of steel before the gatehouse. Tall, broad-shouldered, encased in the Earl of Lyonstone's glittering silver mail, the sight froze her heart. Wheat
gold hair shone like a halo as he hoisted his sword toward
heaven.

"Benedict," she whispered, apprehension closing her throat.
Was it he who'd betrayed them?

"Defenders of Lyonstone!" her brother cried. "Hold the
gates closed. To me! *To me!*"

Sunlight broke through a banner of clouds to illuminate
Benedict of Lyonstone in a blinding light. From the embattled
defenders, a ragged cheer rose. The war horn hailed him with
a long *taroo*, sending shivers cascading down her spine. On
all sides, men in Lyonstone colors fought toward him and
rallied to defend the gates.

Silently she blessed her brother, whose assumption of
command now freed her to help Jervaise. A path opened
before her. Wheeling her horse away, she spurred him to a
thundering canter. The dappled gray leaped over a fallen
man and bore down on the tower. She flung herself from the
saddle as he plunged to a halt.

A searing pain tore through her thigh, announcing the
injury she'd sustained. Half fainting, her head swimming,
she hoisted off her helm and dragged in gulps of blessed air,
swiped an arm across her perspiring brow. A steady runnel
of crimson oozed down her leg, which throbbed when she

put weight on it—but it held her. Holding her broadsword in a two-handed grip, she limped into the tower.

Two invaders sprawled dead before her. Circling them, she crept up the curving stair.

Slices of daylight slid through the arrow loops to pierce the unnatural gloom. Through the walls, the clamor of battle grew muted, as if heard from underwater. Skin prickling, she climbed, cursing the rattle of mail. Dizzying pain speared through her with every step.

There lay another body, clan tartan soaked with blood. She stepped over it—and nearly screamed when a hand clutched her ankle.

"Magician," the soldier croaked. "You promised us . . . you promised . . ."

With a gurgle, he fell back, hand sliding away as his eyes darkened.

Crossing herself, she whispered a prayer for his soul and resumed her painful climb. Twice more she crawled over dead men, sick with relief that these poor unfortunates were not Jervaise. At last, she reached the top.

Before her, a door hung ajar. Murky daylight—and the cool, precise tones of Sir Bors of Bedingfield—leaked through it. Panting quietly, she pressed against the wall.

"Truly, you astonish me." Bedingfield sounded amused, in terrifying control. "First you agree to lead this rabble, then you turn your coat at the first opportunity. Prince Richard would have rewarded you lavishly, but I suppose your loyalty—at this late hour—was too much to expect."

"I swore one oath," Jervaise rasped. "To King Henry. That's the oath I'll keep"

"But all in vain," Sir Bors said gently. "This keep is all but fallen and your cause quite lost."

"All the same, I'll guard these lands to my dying breath."

"So be it."

Steel rang out—once, twice, a flurry of blows. Something crashed to the ground. As in a nightmare, horror riveted her in place, the desperate fear that her appearance would cause a fatal distraction to Jervaise.

"Be reasonable, Raven." Bedingfield chuckled. "All hope is lost. What can you possibly hope to gain?"

"What I value most—honor and my lady's love. For that, I offer you one chance to surrender."

"Oh, very generous, to be certain. But I aim for more than an honorable execution. Though your offer of mercy is touching, I fear I must decline."

Again steel *shinged*, and a man gasped in pain. Able to restrain herself no longer, Alienore eased the door open and peeked inside.

Before her, the poisoner's laboratory spread like a chamber of horrors. From her limited vantage, an inventory of nightmares lurked. On the table, a glass flask held a teeming mass of hairy spiders. Nearby, a coiled heap of serpents writhed in their enclosure. A long-necked beaker held a swarm of rusty insects with barbed tails.

Sir Bors stood behind the table, before an alchemical apparatus—all coils and tubes—and a flask bubbling with viscous green ichor. Though mail encased his powerful body and a sword hung at his belt, the sorcerer's hands were empty. At his back, a door opened on a stair that plunged down to blackness. The scuff of feet and the scrape of metal echoed from its depths.

Around the table stalked a knight in black armor, his curved scimitar streaked with crimson. The bodies of the slain lay heaped at his feet.

A paralyzing relief swept through her to see Jervaise whole and alive—and no traitor. But she'd always known that. She sagged against the wall.

"What are your ambitions?" Jervaise's slitted gaze fixed the alchemist with deadly intent. "What did the king's traitor sons promise you?"

Bors spread his hands, rings glittering green and black. "They promised nothing that is not already mine by birthright—namely, the duchy our brother left to you."

In midstep, Jervaise froze, tension etched in every muscle. "*Our* brother?"

"Our half brother, to be precise. Can it possibly surprise you? Our father abandoned his bastards to fight over his duchy like those scorpions there. Only the strongest will survive."

"You were behind the counterclaim." Jervaise eased forward another step, but the other still stood beyond reach.

"Indeed, and who else?" Bors's hands danced around the apparatus, turning a valve, uncorking a vial. Her eyes hurt as she followed his movements. "For years I had woven my tangled skeins, dispatching or discrediting the rival claimants one by one—even you, Raven. Did you never question the accusations that rained down on you after our father's death?"

Another invader appeared in the open door, and Alienore edged deeper into cover. Bors directed him with a negligent gesture. Raising his claymore, the Scot charged around the table. Jervaise deflected the blow with a whirling parry.

Alienore could no longer remain a passive observer. Flinging the door wide, she strode in with her sword raised.

"You have outwitted yourself, Bedingfield!" Her voice rang out, jerking his pale head toward her. "You reckoned without Ormonde's loyalty to the king—and mine to Ormonde."

Amid the thrust and parry of combat, Jervaise darted her a fulminating look. "Allah's heart, Alienore. You shouldn't be here."

"Fie, Lord Raven!" Sir Bors swept her an ironic bow. "Is that any courteous greeting for your lady? I was expecting her, even if you were not."

"Were you also expecting Benedict to betray you?" She placed Sir Bors between herself and Jervaise. "My brother stands before the gates and orders our defense."

Bors's eyes narrowed as he pivoted to keep her in sight. Behind him, Jervaise ducked another blow.

"You sent those assassins at Le Mans and killed them after." She'd known it, but sought to keep him talking, to deflect his attention from Jervaise.

"Once your brother and your troublesome husband are dead, Prince Richard will grant both Ormonde and Lyonstone to me in reward for my role in overthrowing his father."

"What claim on this shire can you possibly have?"

"My claim devolves from you." Bors gave her a silken smile. "Lady Alienore of Lyonstone—my bride."

Behind him, Jervaise snarled. His scimitar arced forward, carving through the invader's defense. The Scot fell, and Jervaise kicked his claymore aside.

"Perhaps you've forgotten," he rasped. "The lady's wedded to me."

"A trifling complication." Bors tipped a vial over his bubbling flask. "Which, I assure you, shall shortly be remedied."

Fury flared through her. "I would rather be fodder for carrion crows than wedded to a cur like you!"

"If you insist, that too can be arranged." Acrid steam rose from his flask, making her eyes sting and her throat itch. "Perhaps the crows will relish cooked meat."

Still he stood barricaded behind his apparatus, with her crouched on one side, Jervaise advancing on the other. Only the stair behind him offered an escape, where the clatter and tramp of men sounded ever louder. Somehow, God save her, they had to close that door!

Tenderly, Bors cradled the flask. A waft of steam leaked out, fouling the air with a sulfurous reek, and Jervaise froze.

"Alienore," he said, barely audible. *"Don't move."*

"Ah, so you recognize the stench?" Bors smiled. "I warrant

you would, Raven, since it burned away your voice and your honor both."

With a sinking dread, she knew what must be in that flask. Beneath his bronzed skin, Jervaise paled.

"You'd have us think you will use Greek fire?" She drew the alchemist's gaze. "Do not be absurd. You require me alive to legitimize your claim to Lyonstone."

"Aye, your quarrel's with me," Jervaise said. "Let Alienore withdraw."

"I won't leave you," she cried.

Bors barely looked at her, all his attention focused on Jervaise as the greater threat. Stealthily she eased forward.

"Alienore, by the Prophet!" Jervaise scowled. "Do as you're bidden, for once in your life."

"My place is at your side—in life or death."

"How very touching," Bors murmured. "I do believe she loves you, Raven. If you value her, lower your blade *slowly* to the floor."

"Done," Jervaise said. "But let her go first."

"And you, my dear." Bedingfield's eyes flickered toward her. "Lower your sword, and come to me. Pity about your butchered hair, but you shall make me a fine duchess."

"Will you drug me into submission as you did my brother?" Hoping to keep his attention, she lowered her sword slowly to the ground. At his bidding, she nudged the blade with her foot, sliding it out of reach.

Puffing from the climb, another invader appeared in the door, sword gripped before him. Bors addressed him without turning.

"You there—go to the black knight and collect his weapons. Mind that he presents them with his left hand only, hilt first."

Cautious, the Scot advanced. When Bors pivoted to follow the exchange, Alienore palmed the long-knife from her belt.

Inscrutable, Jervaise reversed his sword and offered it.

Not by the flicker of an eyelid did he betray whether he saw her drawing her knife. For a precious second, Bors was fixed on Jervaise, intent as the hooded serpent rearing in its jar.

Her husband was a dead man the moment he disarmed.

"My dear Alienore," Bors said, without looking at her. "Come to me."

"As you wish." She cocked the knife and hurled it.

Her blade flashed through the air. It grazed Bors's ear—missing him entirely, curse her aim—and buried itself in the door beyond.

Leaping aside, Bors swore and dropped the flask. It shattered at his feet and splashed his armored legs. With a blinding flash, a whoosh of flames erupted. The fire crawled eagerly up his legs.

Even then, Bors kept his head. Drawing his sword, he scraped the viscous substance from his legs and boots.

Hearing the clank of armor on the darkened stair, Alienore ran to slam the door in a soldier's bearded face. She rammed the bolt across the frame as a mailed fist hammered against it.

With his invasion blocked, Bors's composure slipped. Standing like a demon in a spreading pool of fire, ablaze from the knees down, he leveled his smoldering blade toward her. "Why, my dear Alienore! I underestimated you."

"And me." Jervaise rose up behind him like the devil climbing from hell. His scimitar screamed crosswise through the air. A shower of crimson exploded as Bedingfield's head tumbled from his shoulders.

Alienore staggered aside as his body toppled. Leaping over the burning corpse, Jervaise charged straight toward her through the flames. His trailing mantle ignited into a sheet of fire, and she screamed his name.

Flinging the burning garment away, he emerged from the sea of fire and dragged her away from the flames.

Despite the sulfurous smoke that burned her eyes and seared her lungs, she clung to him.

"Jervaise." She pressed her face into his singed hauberk. "God be praised . . ."

"Aye," he said roughly. "Allah be praised."

She lifted her head to meet his kiss in a blaze of heat that left her breathless.

"I sent Vulgrin with a message." He crushed her against him. "Tried to warn you. The queen's whelp is here—Prince Richard—allied with Bedingfield. But they captured Vulgrin and left him bound in the wood."

Half carrying her, he strode toward the tower stair. "Pretended to play along, but they never trusted me. I was watched too closely to escape."

"I never doubted you." She knew her heart was in her face as she stared up at him.

"Why the devil not?" His mouth twisted with the old bitterness. "How could you possibly trust me?"

"Because," she choked, coughing as she stumbled alongside. "As I told you days ago, I love you!

"I love you," she repeated, tears stinging her eyes. "And I will always love you, even if you cannot love me in return."

The cool darkness of the stair enveloped them, shelter from the spreading flames. He pivoted toward her, hands closing hard on her shoulders.

"Allah's blood, I was a stubborn fool." Blazing in his soot-streaked face, his golden eyes devoured her. "No use denying it. I've loved you since the first day I saw you and recognized you as the one who rode out in all your glory to challenge me."

She stared up at him, afraid to hope, but longing so desperately to believe. The racket of battle drifted through the walls, but its fervor seemed to be easing, now they'd halted the invasion from within. Flames crackled from the laboratory and consumed the diabolical contents. No one would emerge from that deadly chamber ever again.

Dimly she knew they must extinguish the flames. Sand, she'd heard, was the only way to quench Greek fire. Yet the tower was isolated, and the danger of spreading flames was slight.

Her injured leg throbbed, but she hardly noticed, the pain dwarfed by the magnitude of Jervaise's confession. Aye, she'd dared to hope. Yet she'd feared he might never conquer his demons, never accept her love. The heady knowledge bubbled up, pushing against her chest with the ache of unshed tears.

"Do you know," she murmured, arms slipping around his neck, "I believe I sensed your feelings. No matter what you said, 'twas why I dared to believe in you."

"You took one hell of a risk. I was terrified to admit I loved you. And I'll never know how I managed to deserve you."

His eager mouth met hers halfway. Their kiss blazed through her like a holy light, a declaration of the love that burned bright as faith between them.

Senses swimming, heart surging with triumph, Alienore surfaced from the kiss and laughed. "We must discuss this love of ours when we are at leisure. For now, we have the devil of a mess to mop up."

"Aye." He grinned, teeth flashing against mahogany skin. "A war to win and a kingdom to save."

Epilogue

"I'll be sorry to see you leave us, sister." As retainers bustled around them preparing for the road, the Earl of Lyonstone stepped forward to grasp her hands.

Alienore looked into the gray eyes so like her own and returned the squeeze. Bathed in the golden haze of summer, Benedict—like the keep around him—had recovered from the Scottish assault and Sir Bors's treachery swifter than she'd ever dared hope. The invaders had lost heart and disbanded after Bors's defeat, when their secret access to the castle was sealed against them. As for her brother, he regained weight and vigor daily.

God be praised, the debilitating symptoms caused by the alchemist's potions had vanished completely.

"I shall return next spring," she promised with a smile, "after affairs are set in order at Ormonde. Jervaise and I have agreed to divide our time between his holdings and mine, since both require our attention."

"Wishing Stone Manor will be waiting for you," Benedict said, "under Raoul's good stewardship. The king cannot fail to confirm your inheritance, now that I've supported it."

"We intend to make certain of that." Jervaise pivoted away from the party assembling under his command and strode to her side. "Henry's crossed the Channel to mop up the last dregs of this rebellion and collect his wayward son. We'll pay our respects before sailing."

Leaning into his warm embrace, Alienore looked into his sunlit amber eyes. He'd done a hero's duty, leading the effort to sweep the Scots back across the border where they belonged, while she and Benedict repaired the minor damage to the shire.

Now, three months after the battle of Lyonstone, she realized what a fool she'd been to fear Jervaise would abandon her. They would never know the truth, she supposed, of who had sired her. But it mattered less to her now. She was who she was.

She was Alienore of Lyonstone, Duchesse d'Ormonde, married to a man who loved her.

"We should depart." Jervaise caressed her waist as he released her. Tendrils of warmth spread from his touch, rousing her as he ever did.

As she made her farewells to Lyonstone with Remus frisking at her heels, she felt no sorrow at the prospect of leaving for a time. Together, she and Jervaise had saved her people, restored them to health and vigor. Her future lay with this Saracen knight, with his cunning wit and sinful touch, who'd shown her that love and passion were naught to fear.

Anticipation bubbling in her blood, she spurred Galahad through the gates at his side. Their small procession of guardsmen and retainers, including her faithful Nesta, trotted in their wake. A raven cawed overhead as they set their course eastward, toward the sea.

They'd barely left the castle behind when Jervaise spied travelers approaching on the road. As their defense was hearty and the other party comprised only a handful of riders, Alienore felt little concern at first.

Abruptly, Jervaise flung up an arm to halt their progress. Sudden alertness crackled like flames along his armored body. She followed his narrowed gaze to the lead rider as the party cantered toward them. She noted the big-boned charger—a warhorse fit for a king—his stocky rider clad in a hunter's leather doublet. She marked his tousled red hair and the keen eyes gleaming above his whiskers, and suddenly she knew him.

Flinging a leg over his pommel, Jervaise leaped down and

dropped to one knee. As their retainers scrambled to follow, she dismounted and sank into a curtsy.

"Good my lord," she murmured, falling back on court etiquette. "Bid you good day."

"Well met, my old friends!" Henry Plantagenet flung back his head and laughed. "You need not have ridden out to meet me. I'll not stand on ceremony, after the good turn you did my realm at Easter!"

"We depart for Ormonde," Jervaise said, "now that Lyonstone's in order."

"Then I'm glad to have caught you." Tossing his reins to his squire, Henry swept a burly arm, drawing them away from the dusty road. At his shout, a page ran forward, juggling a wineskin and goblets. Thus, as pleasantries were exchanged, Alienore found herself sharing crisp English cider with her sovereign.

Recalling her responsibilities, she stirred with a sigh. "We are honored to extend the hospitality of Lyonstone, in my brother's name. Our departure for Normandy can wait another day—"

"Your husband would have my head for that, madam!" Henry laughed. "Nay, I'll not keep you from Ormonde another hour, for that would be poor recompense indeed for your good service. I'm lodged well enough at Newcastle while I review the borders. So I shan't remain for long."

Jervaise scrutinized his king. "What other service do you require?"

"Coming straight to the point, as always." Affectionately, the king cuffed his shoulder. "I thought only to deliver this missive here into your lady's hand."

Blinking, she accepted the rolled parchment. Staring down at the red wax stamped with the Plantagenet lion crossed with dangling ribbons and fobs, she felt her heartbeat quicken. Suddenly, she knew why the king had sought them out.

"God's eyes, madam!" Henry's cobalt gaze snapped with

humor. "That parchment will not bite you. It's but the deed of seisin granting Wishing Stone Manor, its attendant lands and revenues into your capable hands."

"You have confirmed my father's bequest?" Though she'd never really doubted it after Benedict threw his support behind her, the achievement of this long-sought dream struck her like a hammer to the chest. Tears filled her eyes, and she struggled to contain them.

The dark scent of musk and sandalwood filled her head as Jervaise supported her, a firm hand beneath her arm. Feeling strength and reassurance resonate from his grip, she sank into her deepest curtsy.

"Your Grace, I cannot thank you enough for your trust. I swear you shall not regret it."

"Nay, now," Henry said gruffly, raising her up. "It's I should thank you, madam—and this rascal you've married—for keeping my borders safe from those impatient sons of mine."

"Aye . . . your sons." A muscle flexed in Jervaise's jaw. "Prince Richard did not appear on the battlefield, and he eluded my efforts to detain him. He's likely returned to France by now."

"Ah, those lads of mine." As he massaged his brow, the king looked every one of his forty-odd years. "I was waging war too at their age—but a bit more successfully. Like father, like sons, hey?"

Jervaise snorted.

"Nonetheless," the king said, "their plan to raise the rebels here has foundered, now that I've captured Scots William. And that spineless cur Philip of Flanders was likewise dissuaded."

"What are your plans now?" Alienore asked.

"Back to Rouen." Vigorously, the king paced. "To break French Louis's feeble excuse for a siege and call my other sons to heel. They'll yield, sure enough, when they find they've no hole to hide in."

And then, after a stern reprimand, Henry would forgive them, of course. She and Jervaise had whispered about it while they lay naked and spent in their bed. The king had no choice but to make peace with his heirs—the heirs to a throne he and his mother before him had fought a lifetime to secure.

As for royal forgiveness, who needed it more than the wife who'd betrayed him?

Glancing up, she found Henry's eyes fixed on her. "And what of Eleanor, you mean to ask me, hey?"

"Aye." She bowed her head. "You will have the grace to forgive your sons when the moment comes. Queen Eleanor is no less in need of your mercy."

"That's her misfortune," Henry grunted. "The woman's been a viper in my bed. I can't allow her to slither free this time."

Her heart ached for her godmother, the woman she'd admired and loved and striven to emulate, for a time. "Surely you cannot mean to divorce her?"

"Nay, that I can't do." Irritably he tossed his goblet to the page, who managed to catch it. "For then Aquitaine would rise. God's eyes, am I to be given no peace this side of the grave?

"But nay. She crossed the Channel with me, and I've installed her—behind walls and under guard—at Old Sarum."

"Imprisoned?" she cried. "God's mercy, Your Grace! The queen must despise that."

"Well, she's earned it." He shrugged. "'Tis a fair castle, and secure. Eleanor will rest there safe enough, though she's forbidden to receive visitors. That includes you, madam. I trust I've made myself clear?"

"Aye," she murmured, accepting the royal decree, even while her heart mourned.

After Henry had taken his leave, their journey toward the coast resumed. After a time, Jervaise cleared his throat.

"Don't take it amiss, what Henry's done to Eleanor. Perhaps, in time, he'll change his mind."

"Perhaps." Unexpectedly, her spirits rose. "Somehow I do not believe Eleanor of Aquitaine will spend all her days behind walls. I daresay there are pages of her history still to be written."

Before twilight, Jervaise called a halt. Their party pitched camp among a grove of shady birch trees near a gurgling brook. Leaving the arrangements in Nesta's competent hands, Alienore strolled along the stream and let the sun-dappled solace of the trees envelop her. Remus bounded before her, following some scent he'd nosed.

Trailing the wolf, she rounded a bend and came upon Jervaise. By instinct, she halted, catching the cheerful hail before it slipped from her tongue. Stripped of his armor, he knelt in his shirt and chausses on a square of colorful carpet. His back to her, he faced east, away from the setting sun.

At first, she could not discern what he did, though the low liquid syllables of Outremer rolled from his lips. Only when he pressed his hands together and bowed, touching his brow to the carpet, did understanding bloom in her mind.

When it did, she clasped her hands, tears of wonder and gratitude spilling beneath her lids. There, firmly planted on fertile English soil, facing the distant Mecca of Outremer, where his heritage lay—like a bridge between past and future—Jervaise de Vaux was praying.